Haverford Twp. Free Library
1601 Darby Road
Havertown, PA 19083
610-446-3082
library@haverfordlibrary.org
www.haverfordlibrary.org

Your receipt lists your materials and due dates

Online renewals at
www.haverfordlibrary.org
or
Telephone renewals at
610-892-3257

Enhance and enrich your life?
Absolutely!

WITHDRAWN

The Oregon Experiment

The Oregon Experiment

KEITH SCRIBNER

ALFRED A. KNOPF NEW YORK 2011

THIS IS A BORZOI BOOK
PUBLISHED BY ALFRED A. KNOPF

Copyright © 2011 by Keith Scribner

All rights reserved.
Published in the United States by Alfred A. Knopf,
a division of Random House, Inc., New York, and in Canada by
Random House of Canada Limited, Toronto.

www.aaknopf.com

Knopf, Borzoi Books, and the colophon are registered
trademarks of Random House, Inc.

Library of Congress Cataloging-in-Publication Data
Scribner, Keith.
The Oregon experiment / by Keith Scribner.
p. cm.
"This is a Borzoi book."
ISBN 978-0-307-59478-5
1. Married people—Fiction. 2. Oregon—Fiction. I. Title.
PS3569 C735074 2011
813'.54—dc22
2011006552

This is a work of fiction. Names, characters, places, and incidents
either are the product of the author's imagination or are used fictitiously.
Any resemblance to actual persons, living or dead, events or locales
is entirely coincidental.

Jacket image: *Kitchen Painting #13, 2008* by Michael Brophy.
Courtesy of the artist and The Laura Russo Gallery.
Jacket design by Barbara de Wilde

Manufactured in the United States of America
First Edition

To Jen, as always

PART ONE

Chapter 1

Naomi awoke to mint. With her cheek still burrowed in the pillow, she opened one eye. Black fields buzzed past, the engine whined. She felt the baby move in her belly, the warmth of her husband's hand on her thigh. She and Scanlon had been driving cross-country for a week, and tonight they'd arrive at their new home in Oregon. Without lifting her head, she cracked her window, and the smell of mint filled the car. Fecund earthy mint carried on moist night air. She used to love mint. Mint tea, mint jelly, mint gum. Like basil, a taste that's mostly smell. Peppermint, apple mint, crinkle-leafed spearmint. She'd never known an entire night to smell of mint.

She'd had these dreamy remembrances before. Like an itch on a phantom limb, her olfactory neurons—understimulated and bored—would register simmering veal, river algae, the powdery aldehyde of Chanel No. 5, sweaty palms on a subway pole. Visual cues often prompted these olfactory apparitions; she'd turn the page of a magazine to a Cheerios ad, and her brain would light up with "dusty grain going soggy in warming milk."

Before she lost her ability to smell—anosmia, the doctors called it, sometimes psychosomatic but in her case not—she'd occasionally wish she could switch her nose off. Eye masks and earplugs were readily available, but nothing for the sleeper awakened by toast burning half a block away or a roommate in the shower before dawn sudsing up with fennel shampoo, nothing from Bose to mask the ammonia on restaurant tables or food scraps sitting in drains, no way to shut out the treacle of mildew, feces, or halitosis.

She was a nose. At least she *had been.* She'd trained at École Givaudan-Roure in Grasse, worked two years for Dior in Paris, a year for Shiseido in Tokyo, then back in New York for Calvin Klein and Manhattan Scents. Her perfume creations were defined by sharp and leathery base notes in the tradition of My Sin, a flapper perfume from the twenties—an era, in her mind, to emulate. (To Naomi the twenties were like the late sixties but with better clothes and some discretion, and without politics to distract from the pure indulgence of the senses.) The quick dry-down from the initial spark of her floral and citrus top notes led to a darker primal place forested with agarwood, lichen, and moss; Naomi's fragrances were a drop of orange-blossom honey sucked from the tip of a lover's finger while sprawled in lusty sheets.

Like many noses, her favorite fragrances were her own. She knew she was creating the same perfumes over and over, trying to chase the scent back through layers of her own memory. Trying too hard: this had been the common complaint through all her years in the industry. Her nose was one in a million for perception and discernment, but her fragrances were too *specifically* evocative and didn't interact fully enough with the skin of the wearer. Or so said her critics.

For bread and butter she'd scented hand creams and hair products, designed three facial scrubs and the rosemary shampoo Scanlon used. She'd been influential in a Calvin Klein project (eventually shelved) to impregnate jewelry and fabric with fragrance. She'd worked on dish soaps (one for Palmolive called Summer Breeze that Scanlon said smelled exactly like camp), pumpkin bread mix, Cap'n Crunch ("preserve its essential smell," they told her, "but tweak it healthier"), shoe polish (to remind us of "all our dads"), a "leather" fragrance for leatherless car interiors, and, for a Japanese fruit importer, an injectible that made their peaches smell peachier.

Then one night her father came into Manhattan to take her out to dinner. Though she could see that something was on his mind, they chatted normally in the restaurant; but his anxiety steadily increased, so much that while driving back to her apartment he rear-ended a taxi. As they waited for a tow truck on the sidewalk in front of Tower Records on Broadway—Natalie Merchant's voice floating down from the awning—he finally divulged what he'd come into the city to tell her.

She shook her head at the news: the wife of her old boyfriend Clair had given birth to twins. "That's what you're so anxious about?" she said, hugging her dad. "Next time tell me at the restaurant, and we'll keep the airbags in the dash."

They had believed no one was injured. But the next morning Naomi woke up with her neck so stiff she could hardly turn her head. She popped ibuprofen and called in sick, and with her first sip of tea she realized she couldn't smell it.

She saw doctors. She had CAT scans, MRIs, and endoscopies. At work she told no one. Sitting with dipsticks at the organ, surrounded by five hundred essences, she created fragrances from memory alone. Surprising, evocative fragrances, she was told by colleagues. She thought about Beethoven composing while deaf, simultaneously flattering and pitying herself, but mostly struggling to even fake it. Finally, after months of anosmia, the work turned depressing, and she quit.

When she met Scanlon she was a consultant, a perfume buyer for New York boutiques. She didn't like it and found herself working only enough to pay the rent. She burned through her savings and too many Dyptique candles, certain that the lavender and rose, anise, sage, green fig, and coffee hanging in the air would heal her. She'd put on Chopin's nocturnes then search the air above the burning candle, knowing there was a smell hovering there that was more physically present than the music she could hear.

She began leaving melon rinds and swordfish scraps in her garbage pail for days. She left un-rinsed yogurt cups, tuna cans, and tubs of cottage cheese out on the kitchen counter, sure that the next time she stepped inside, she'd get knocked flat by the rotting stench. She never did. But the first time she brought Scanlon back to her apartment for tea, she saw his face pucker. She lit a stick of incense; he sat by an open window. She knew it was time to give up.

And now she was leaving both New York and the industry behind, her departure freighted with the fact that in her twelve years as a nose—through the hundreds of candies, cleansers, Pop-Tarts, and ointments for athlete's foot she'd worked on—not one of her perfumes ever made it to the bottle.

Through a half-open eye, the lights of Douglas, Oregon, came into view. She imagined mint still hung in the car. And stronger smells: gravel dust, macadam, and soda-pop sugar infusing their floor mats and the soles of their shoes from ten days of rest areas and fast-food parking lots, all of it now cooked up with the heater on their feet.

She sat up straight. She really thought she was smelling. Was it possible? Since her pregnancy there'd been hints—a whiff as she passed an Indian restaurant, a cloud of diesel smoke blasting from a city bus—but they never lasted more than a moment. As she drew air slowly through her nose, Scanlon switched off the blower and the smells were lost.

They rose up the east side of the bridge crossing the Willamette River, then dropped down the west. Scanlon eased to a stop at a red light on the edge of downtown. An alarm was ringing from the Wells Fargo bank on the corner—an actual bell, like the fire drills at school when she was a girl. Apparently, somebody had thrown a brick through the bank's front window. Two other cars waited at the intersection, their drivers and a few pedestrians glancing without much curiosity at the broken glass. No flashing lights were racing to the scene. Squeezing her thigh, Scanlon spoke softly: "We're gonna like it here."

They passed a Blockbuster and a church, motels and a Mexican drive-thru. She gazed out the window at a row of used cars with bright yellow prices in their windshields, parked around a concrete island where gas pumps had once stood.

After several blocks of old Craftsman bungalows, they bumped over a railroad crossing and the houses turned newer—tiny cottages, then tracts of ranch-style houses. Naomi remembered how dispirited she'd been sitting at the computer in their New York apartment searching through Douglas real estate websites: page after page of identical low-slung ranches pictured against a gray sky, each with a wet pickup parked in a wet driveway. They'd looked for weeks, made countless calls, then Scanlon had flown out and bought one in a weekend. She couldn't even remember what it looked like.

Their headlights glared off the white door of their detached single-car garage. In ten days of driving Scanlon had shut down the engine fifty or sixty times, but this time was different: a silent finality.

"We made it," he said.

He opened the front door of the house with a sweeping gesture. "You'll hurt yourself," she warned, but he insisted on carrying her (and thirty extra pounds of pregnancy) over the threshold onto a rectangle of green and gold linoleum. She stepped out of her shoes and walked across their living room, curling her toes into the beige wall-to-wall carpet. Scanlon kissed her—"Welcome, my love"—then flipped on a bright ceiling light. The walls glared white. The skimpy baseboard and trim were glossy white. The house was a box, divided into smaller boxes. Their furniture would help, some color on the walls, her kilims to break up all that beige carpet, but mostly the house felt like an overlit basement. If she'd expected colors from apricot to aubergine, the previous owners must have coveted the white urbanity she'd grown tired of after all those years in New York.

"Not as much character as an older place," he said, "but totally solid. They were still using old-growth fir for two-by-fours out here in the sixties."

She was exhausted. "That's good," she said.

They dropped the shades, inflated the Aerobed, and tucked in fresh sheets and both comforters. They curled up on their sides, foreheads touching, and even before she was warm, he slid his hand up under her nightgown and kissed the tops of her breasts. She couldn't shake the sense that this was a camping trip to a remote patch of the world from which they'd soon return home.

And then she smelled it—crushed dandelions and sweet pickle brine. His scalp.

"What's wrong?" he asked.

She'd never smelled his scalp before. Dried figs or dates. "I'm just so tired," she said, and his hand on her thigh stopped moving, then after a few minutes he rolled away and she could hear the heavy breath of his sleep.

But Naomi was wide awake, her heart racing. She stretched her neck toward him and sniffed his scalp again. She got up from the air mattress and walked around the empty house, smelling old grease mixed with Ajax under the stove's burners, the woody smell of closets, scorched carbon and ash at the fireplace. She opened the back door onto the night: the new smells a particular combination of laurel leaves, mulch, salty dew pushing in from the ocean (*Pacific* salt), and dozens of ferns and mosses and rotting stalks. These couldn't be files from her olfactory memory bank.

Her nose was back.

A train whistled in the distance as she pushed the door closed, looking across the room at her husband asleep on the Aerobed. The smell of his scalp was a surprise—not what she'd imagined—and she wasn't sure she liked it.

. . .

In the morning, while Naomi slept, Scanlon opened the front door to a small older man, his thick gray hair neatly combed.

"Mr. Pratt," the man said, waggling his clipboard. "I'm Edmund."

But Scanlon was gazing over his head at the green Mayflower tractor-trailer barely visible through the fog; there was a long screech as someone pulled out the ramp.

"Marvelous Monday," Edmund said.

Scanlon looked down at him. "What time is it?" he asked.

"We're early birds. But it'll take us a minute to get connoitered."

The back doors of the truck swung open. Edmund turned and scurried down Scanlon's new front walk, nearly disappearing into the mist.

In the living room Scanlon searched for his watch in the heap of clothes. Almost seven. He opened a shade. Naomi was snoring, curled up fetally. The snoring was new since she'd been pregnant. He touched her hip, and she raised her eyelids.

"I'm freezing," she said, hugging her shoulders.

"It's the movers."

She rubbed her eyes, squinting at the window. "Why's it so gray out? You said it didn't rain in the summer."

"I don't think it's raining," he said.

"Four full months of sun. Rain the rest of the time."

"That's what they told me." He watched fog creeping into the house through the front door as he'd only ever seen in black-and-white movies set in London. Dickensian fog.

Naomi pulled on yesterday's clothes and went to the picture window as big as a garage door. As a boy, Scanlon had envied his best friend for having a picture window, and now, in the twenty-first century, thirty years too late, he finally had his own. Driving around Douglas with the realtor, he'd wanted one of the Craftsman bungalows closer to campus—roof timbers exposed at the eaves, deep overhangs supported by chunky columns over a solid front porch—but those were either too expensive or student rentals. He'd been enraged by the blocks of beautiful old houses split up into apartments, couches out front, beer kegs on the lawn, shiny 4x4s parked in the street with doors flung open and stereos pounding for the kids drinking beer on the porch.

"The air's opaque," Naomi said, staring out the window.

Who were these Oregon kids—these kids who'd be his students—with better stereos in their pickups than their living rooms? "I'll go for coffee," Scanlon said. "You want a decaf?"

"I can't take eight months of rain and four months of fog. I can't do it, Scanlon."

Three quick raps rattled the screen door, then Edmund popped in. "Morning, missus," he said. "It's a wonderful day to be alive!"

"This fog," Naomi said to him. "Is it unusual?"

He looked out the door, combing his fingers back through his pelt of hair. "Like this now?"

"The fog," she said.

"Oftentimes it's a little more soupier."

Naomi's shoulders fell.

"Coffee!" Scanlon said. "What do you take in yours, Edmund?"

"Not for me." He was jouncy with extra energy, his bones loose in their joints. "One cup at breakfast primes my pump."

"How about your partner out there?"

"Clay's got his pop."

Naomi passed across the beige carpet as Edmund hooked the screen door open. Once she was in the bathroom, Scanlon asked, "It's really foggy all summer?"

"Most mornings," Edmund said. "But it burns off by nine or ten."

"Then it's sunny?"

"No sun like Oregon sun, Mr. Pratt. Warm honey in a deep blue sky."

Scanlon cracked the bathroom door, then pushed it open just enough to step inside and give Naomi the good news.

She was sitting on the toilet, one hand flat on her belly, the other holding a clean puff of toilet paper to her nose. "That's good," she said, sounding distracted. She was, he feared, feeling unmoored and uncertain, waking up in a house she never thought she'd live in, in a place she thought she'd never see. "It's going to be fine." She rose up like coming out of a squat—a pregnant woman—and splashed water on her face. "Everything's really fine."

But it wasn't fine. The history of their relationship was this: Scanlon was her caretaker; he kept her afloat. When they met, seven years ago, she'd been without her sense of smell for fifteen months and on Paxil for six, yet she was still depressed. The rush of their love drew her into the daylight, but the presence of the drug, and the possibility that it was an essential lubricant in their day-to-day relationship, even an elixir for their love, always weighed on his mind and, he felt certain, on hers. When she got pregnant, a surprise to them both, she quit the drug, and—another welcome surprise—her spirits didn't sink. Still, the dynamic established early on remained an unspoken arrangement between them: Scanlon protected her from industry friends when dinner conversation turned to the nose, navigating her through a world in which she felt lost, deprived of the pleasures she most loved, like living in a foreign country whose language she'd known intimately then forgotten entirely.

Scanlon had become her guide—her surrogate nose. She taught him to distinguish between a dozen different lilies, breeds of dog, the smells of the city at seven a.m., noon, and midnight. When they were pretending to peruse a menu inside the front door of a new restaurant, he'd describe the smell of the place; if it wasn't delicious, they didn't sit down. She taught him to identify the vegetative barnyard odor of bad cabernets, and each spice in an Italian sausage. She asked him to describe the smell of his past lovers (he had no idea) and herself (crisp apple, buttered toast and, when she hadn't showered in a few days, molasses and capers). After a month with Naomi, Scanlon realized he'd never known what peanut butter actually tasted like. Or ginger ale. Or the smell of an elevator, a museum, or freezing rain melting from an ice-encrusted branch in the morning sun. He sometimes disappointed her with his average olfactory pipes, but then he'd describe an aroma so exquisitely she was elevated, as if by music. Naomi had taught him to experience the world more fully—which was as good a definition of love as he knew.

"Why don't you drive downtown to Starbucks," he suggested as Naomi washed her hands. "I'll stay here and deal with the movers." If he could get their couch in place before she got home, hang some art on the walls, unpack the Takashima lamp she'd brought from Tokyo, she might see how the house—how this life—could work.

From the front stoop, he again offered the movers some coffee.

"You could walk to the edge of campus," Edmund said. "*Nice* walk in the morning. Any number of coffee shops."

"Perfect," Scanlon said, and they followed him to the sidewalk.

After giving Naomi directions, Edmund tipped a wardrobe box from the deck of the truck to his back and humped it into the house.

Scanlon spread his arms and leaned over Naomi's belly to hug her, holding her head to his chest. "It's gonna be great," he said.

"I know."

"Just as soon as we see our stuff in the place." Their voices sounded close, like the fog was a blanket they were talking under.

"Anyway," she said, craning her head away from his chest, "it won't be for long. Only until you get your book out."

"Right," he said. This had been the promise.

Naomi set off, covered up in sweats and a baggy fleece. He loved how every day she grew fuller. Her skin tightened over the swell of her belly, her breasts grew heavy, her face softened—she was filled up, brimming. He loved how pregnancy stretched the thin fabric of the tank tops she'd been wearing since summer began, and in the last weeks, after her belly button popped, that private nub of flesh was sexier than a swollen nipple. Her fertility, her womanness, rose to the surface of her body like a reminder of their lovemaking.

A dozen steps away, her figure disappeared, enveloped by the fog.

At the ramp of the truck, Edmund's helper was sucking on a straw sticking from a quart-sized Pepsi cup. Scanlon extended a hand to shake, but the kid turned away, pretending not to notice, and dropped his cup, ice cubes rattling, on a stack of boxes. He reached to the top of the load and tugged on the corner of a furniture pad until it spilled open, and an end table, the one from Naomi's grandmother, tipped into his hands. Ignoring Scanlon, he banged down the ramp.

Scanlon put a foot up on the moving van's bumper and gazed at the outline of his house through the fog: a perfect rectangle except for the chimney—which the home inspector said needed repointing—and the TV antenna banded to it.

Their bikes were leaning against the side of the truck, so Scanlon rolled them down the driveway into the garage, where rough wood shelves jutted from the studs, bare except for gallon- and quart-sized rings of paint: the colors of the siding, the trim, the kitchen walls. Rusted spikes angled up, waiting for the rake, hedge trimmer, loppers, extension cords, and brooms that Scanlon didn't yet own. He would organize nails and washers in jars; he'd screw in hooks for their bikes; he'd build a workbench beneath the window where he'd assemble the strollers, baby swings, and exersaucers that were about to come into their lives.

Fatherhood would change him in ways as obvious and pronounced as the changes to Naomi's body. He, too, would become bigger and fuller, carrying his love and their family within him. He was counting on it. He was aware that he often became too obsessed with his work, and looked forward to the baby refocusing and deepening him, just as paying attention to Naomi's well-being, especially in the early years, had made him a better man.

He'd start his first project tomorrow: an Adirondack chair and footstool for Naomi. Along with the rest of her body, her ankles had swelled, and after the first week in the car they were throbbing. In a South Dakota Days Inn lobby, while Naomi slept, he'd printed out a plan he found online that required only a jigsaw and a drill. He'd pick out some clear cedar one-by-six, and by midweek Naomi could recline in the chair with her legs and feet elevated on the scroll-shaped stool.

Back at the truck, Edmund was lugging an old Fender amp that Scanlon had barely plugged in since college, when he'd played guitar and sung backup for Imelda's Shoes, a dance band with a rowdy and loyal campus following. "Last time we moved," he said to Edmund, a little embarrassed by the sheer quantity of *stuff*, "we did it all with a U-Haul mini mover and a car."

Edmund stopped. "Couple of young people making it," he said.

Scanlon started to say what he'd really meant, but Edmund continued: "The wife and I, first time I moved her, it couldn't of been no more than three thousand pounds into a one-bedroom. Then, in seventy-six, I moved fifty-two hundred pounds into a three-bedroom. Eighty-four, just shy of seven thousand pounds into our first house, and ninety-seven, eight thousand nine hundred pounds into the new house down in Silver Lake. And now we're empty nesters." He shook his head, grinning, baffled and pleased as hell at this pound-for-pound recap of his life.

"Goes to show you," Scanlon said, looking down the street and trying to gauge if the fog had begun to clear. The apple tree in the neighbor's yard had been invisible twenty minutes ago, hadn't it? He peered into the gray for a glimpse of Naomi.

"Now, *this* one," Edmund said as the kid pounded up the ramp. "He's a sort of monk. Real ascetic. Doesn't have a bed or a TV. Just a room. Four walls." He wore black jeans, a black sweatshirt, and combat boots—not really Scanlon's vision of a monk. "Tell him, Clay. Tell him how you sleep on the floor and eat all your meals at the bus station."

Clay yanked on a strap holding back the load, releasing it. "Who's had more hot-dog burritos this week?" he said, more soft-spoken than Scanlon had anticipated. Like the jingling loops of steel chain dangling from his back pockets, his voice was light and musical.

"Point taken," Edmund said. "Point taken." He turned to Scanlon. "Have you tried them, Mr. Pratt? Hot-dog burritos?"

Scanlon shook his head.

"They taste just like it."

"A real blending of cultures," Scanlon said.

Edmund watched him, seeming to wait for Scanlon to finish his thought.

Dew drew out the essences of lavender and sage, tomato and zucchini leaves, roses and jasmine. Moisture in the air, the fog's weight, kept the scents from dispersing. It was real. She drew in the smells. Creaky olfactory receptors sparked from her nostrils to her brain. She was lightheaded, absurdly happy. These gardens were tremendous: herbs, vegetables, perennials, and annuals filling front yards, spilling onto the sidewalk and filling the narrow strip along the curb. Many were populated with Buddhas, teak benches, broken teapots, hunks of quartz, or colorful blown glass. Then she passed a house with four cars and three ATVs parked in the yard; another with busted bikes and toys strewn in unmowed grass, a fence gate hanging by one hinge, and a sheet tacked up for shade in the picture window; a third house had a white sign nailed to the front offering $CASH$ FOR YOUR HOUSE with a phone number.

According to the mover, campus was two blocks ahead, but she could walk like this forever, endowed again with her capacity to experience the world. And then came another garden, and this time . . . basil, rosemary, and—yes, woolly apple mint. She bent down, pinched off a leaf, and flicked it beneath her nose as she walked, remembering the mint fields last night. The whole night smelling of mint.

The first café she saw was an old yellow bungalow with sage trim, SKCUBRATS hand-painted in peacock blue over the porch. The place was funky—wooden tables and wobbly mismatched chairs, the blackboard menu covered with swirls and flowers in colored chalk—but smelled wonderfully of coffee, cinnamon, butter, the warm cream of steaming milk. Her hunger stirred. She ordered a decaf latte and a carrot muffin from the girl at the counter and sat at a table in the window.

She rested her cup on the hard rise of her belly. Out the window, through the fog, an old pickup rolled by; the granddad behind the wheel wore a sharp clean cowboy hat, as did his wife across the seat, and between them their hound dog sat up proud.

Then a woman coasted up on an old cruiser bicycle. She was around thirty with dirty-blond hair pulled back in a ponytail, wearing Thai fisherman's pants, a batik top, and the high-tech sandals of this new generation of hippies. A red gas can pocked with rust was bolted to the rack behind her seat, its spout curving back like a civet cat's tail. *The Revolution Will Not Be Motorized* was painted in purple on its side.

The woman chained her bike to a pole and came into the café, her lovely, big-mouthed smile moving from Naomi's face to her belly. "Hey," she said in a voice mellower than any voice anywhere in the Northeast. "Welcome." She passed by. Her blond ponytail reached to the small of her back; the bottom few inches, as if the tips had been dipped in dye, were chestnut. She stepped behind the counter and disappeared.

Naomi brushed muffin crumbs off her belly, then picked up a flier from a stack on the window seat. The Pacific Northwest Secessionist Movement. She drank back her last milky sip of latte and was about to get up when the woman appeared at her table.

"Come check us out," she said.

Naomi waved the flier. "This?"

"Next Thursday." The woman slipped into the chair opposite her. "I'm Sequoia."

Naomi had expected patchouli, but the sandalwood and jasmine—probably solid perfumes—were a surprise and a good straightforward combination for her. She was overheated from biking, and the scents rose off her skin with the walnut shell, milk, and oat grain smells of her body. She was an earthy beauty—busty and generous in the hips, green eyes, and a tiny green stone piercing the side of her nose.

"Naomi," she said as they shook hands. "It's for my husband. He's a professor at the university. This is his sort of deal. His research."

"No way." A small pink scar—thin as a pencil line—stretched up her lip when she smiled. "What's his name?"

Riding a tricycle out from the kitchen, a little girl, three or four years old, steered toward them. She climbed up onto Sequoia's lap, then eyed Naomi across the table. "I'm Trinity," she said.

"I'm Naomi." She touched her belly where her baby's head sat. "He's just starting this fall. Scanlon Pratt."

The little girl unbuttoned the top of Sequoia's shirt. She removed a breast with two chubby hands.

"And he studies secessionism?" Sequoia asked.

The girl lifted Sequoia's breast to her mouth and started to suckle, her eyes darting between Naomi and her mother as she listened to the conversation, her lips and jaw pumping at high speed.

Naomi wasn't a prude. She believed in nursing at the workplace, in restaurants, government buildings, even Wal-Mart. And she believed in nursing for a long time, giving the baby a fair shot at various antibodies and an intimate mother-child bond. "Secessionism," she heard herself saying. "Mass movements, radical action." But this seemed really bizarre. The girl dropped the breast and reached across the table to pluck a napkin from a basket. Maybe it was the girl's Converse high-tops. Or the skull tattoo—it *had* to be temporary—on her arm. Or maybe that the girl nursing across the table was wearing a watch.

"Urge him to come," Sequoia said. "I'd be grateful."

The girl licked her lips and wiped them with the napkin, then said, "That was tasty."

It had been nearly an hour, and Naomi still wasn't back. Through a dull caffeine-withdrawal headache pushing at his temples, Scanlon watched his new neighbors back out the driveway, their brake lights glowing red through the fog. The movers were jimmying the couch through the front door.

Following them inside, he showed them where to set the couch, and then fell back onto the cushions. The fireplace with its raised hearth and jagged bricks set a retro tone for the whole house. Frank Lloyd Wright meets Dick Van Dyke. Ceiling lights were frosted glass, spraying out gold stars and zeniths. In the kitchen, curving white steel with chrome pulls formed the '59 Eldorado of cabinets. But the prize here was an orange Formica built-in table shaped like a teardrop with matching swivel chairs of molded white plastic and orange vinyl padding. Buying a house from old people who'd preserved their last remodel so long had endowed them with a museum piece.

The old folks had planted fruit years ago, too, and now he and Naomi would be harvesting from mature trees and bushes, each one identified on a hand-drawn map passed along by the realtor. Scanlon had immediately set himself on an internet crash course so he could productively prune and cultivate their little city lot of apples, pears, and blueberries. He'd learned about soil amendments for the marionberries and figs, and planned to build a new trellis to encourage pollination between the male and female kiwi vines.

He opened the back door and dropped down the steps to the concrete patio, covered carport-style with green corrugated fiberglass. They'd get a table and chairs, and have grad students over to drink wine from short tumblers. Kids would ride trikes in circles while Scanlon grilled kebobs on the barbecue, another item to add to the list.

He kicked through the long wet grass—he needed a mower, too—and at the edge of the yard he came to the apple trees: overgrown and wild, they hadn't been pruned in years. He touched an apple, small and tight, no bigger than an apricot. In another couple months they'd have bushels of juicy crisp Galas.

Feeling as if he were in a dream, he took a few steps through the fog and the next bunch of leaves and fruit came into resolve: marionberries, the prickly vines heaped up over a sagging trellis. Standing there, eating plump berries, he wondered what else they'd need to buy. He'd heard that lots of baby stuff simply materialized either as gifts from relatives or from a network of mothers—their instinct smelling a coming birth—who delivered well-worn but clean bundles of receiving blankets, PJs, and onesies. They'd been getting a little supplementary money from Naomi's parents over the last few years, though mostly Scanlon had tried not to spend it, trying to squirrel it away for times like this. Her parents had put up most of the down payment for the house, too. But now that Scanlon was on a regular salary and they wouldn't be moving every year, all those extra expenses would settle out. Edmund was right: a couple of young people making it. Well, thirty-six and thirty-nine, but making it.

Scanlon had ended up here by accident—by luck, really. The Pacific Northwest was the true front line of radicalism in America—environmental demonstrators, anarchists, survivalists, anti-globalists. Seattle erupted when the WTO came to town, not Boston or New York or D.C. Scanlon had traveled across the country to Seattle—partly for research and partly to show his solidarity—and he'd felt an excitement in the streets like nothing he'd known from the tweedy, Volvo radicals back east. In Oregon his research could be more hands-on, in touch with the players, inside their heads. That's what was missing from radical and mass movement studies in the East—an understanding of what was happening on the ground. Many of his colleagues at Binghamton and Brandeis wrote exclusively about the sixties, or the forties, or the thirties. They did research in response to other research. Scanlon knew an anthropologist who was a leading scholar on Quechua Indians but didn't speak Quechua. From a hot-springs resort in Ecuador, on a Fulbright, she did her research by interviewing tourists and watching the TV news from Quito. Scanlon had lost a Georgetown appointment to a man who'd written a highly regarded book about American and French farmers' attempts to shape national policy. Every few years, over crop subsidies or tariffs, all the farmers in France drove tractors to Paris and parked the length of the Champs-Élysées, holding the street hostage until they got what they wanted. The thought of it made Scanlon's heart race, but this guy—now two years from tenure at Georgetown—had never bothered even to go to France.

Scanlon, on the other hand, was jumping right into the chaos. Primary material would fuel everything he did. Spending eight years working in five departments, learning the various methods of all the scholars in his field, he'd now landed in the middle of every source he'd need. Their baby was a month away, his job was tenure-track, and he'd bought his first house. His life was beginning. A new life.

With a handful of berries he wandered along the back side of the yard toward the blueberry bushes, drawn by an earthy smell like mulch or woodchips but sweeter, more like compost or, he realized with another step, pot. He stopped and, peering ahead through the fog, made out the shapes of two bushes and a standing figure. Suddenly, an ember glowed bright red and Scanlon froze. After a moment, he heard a hissing release of air. The mover.

Clay held out the joint.

"No thanks," Scanlon said. "Want a berry?"

"I hate fruit." As Clay put the joint to his lips, Scanlon spotted, on the underside of his forearm, a tattooed Circle-A—an A for anarchy inside an O for order, meaning anarchy *is* order. This was exactly what he'd expected of the Pacific Northwest: the second person he meets is an anarchist. A primary source smoking dope right in his backyard.

"How do you like living around here?" Scanlon asked.

The mover rolled his eyes, then took another hit and held it in his lungs.

Scanlon ate a berry. "I mean, what do you do for kicks?"

"You a professor?"

"Yeah," Scanlon said, apologetically.

"You have a PhD or something?"

Scanlon nodded.

"Where'd you go to college for that?"

"NYU."

"New York?"

"That's right."

"You know what pisses me off?" the mover said. He leaned forward and released a long watery stream of spit onto the grass. "People who come here to lecture Oregon kids on what's what according to New York."

Slowly chewing a berry, Scanlon kept his eyes on Clay, who'd be more intimidating if not for the tender voice. Scanlon's mentor, Sam Belknap, would pounce on this moment. He'd told Scanlon the only way he'd nailed the book on César Chávez, the *definitive* Chávez book, was to challenge and befriend him until eventually (and with an egomaniac like Chávez it didn't take long) he started showing off; that's when the rhetoric fell away and he revealed himself unintentionally. "How about if you come talk to one of my classes this fall?" Scanlon said. "I do a unit on anarchy."

The kid snorted, a high-pitched, stalling-engine laugh. "You teach *anarchy* at the *university*?"

"Or we could do an interview."

This, apparently, struck the kid as even more absurd.

"For my book."

The mover laughed again. He brought the joint to his lips, and his head twitched—some sort of tic—but he held his hand steady until he got a hit.

The smell of pot smoke in the dense fog carried Scanlon back to Sam's porch in Bronxville in the weeks after his wife had died. The spring Sam retired, Maxine was diagnosed with cervical cancer, and lasted only until November. At the funeral, Sam looked to have aged a decade, and when Scanlon checked in on him after his family had left, he was distracted and forgetful, so Scanlon canceled his classes and stayed in the spare room for a week. He cooked for Sam and got him out to movies, and they spent hours every day talking radical action and mass movements, talking about books Sam wished he'd written and Eastern European cities he'd planned to visit in the coming years with Maxine. Scanlon cleaned out closets and repaired an old gate-leg table in the basement shop—Sam had taught him woodworking over the years. He made drinks for guests and ushered them out when Sam grew tired. And when out of the blue Sam said, "I haven't toked up in twenty-five years," he went down to NYU and inquired with some former students until he scored, then he and Sam passed a pipe in an icy fog, and stories of the seventies quickly turned to the sixties before settling into the beatnik years in the Village early in Sam's marriage. For two days he described Maxine with awe, still mystified by her a half-century later—snaking her hips and shoulders when she danced, playing the flute to Coltrane, dabbing a fleck of tobacco off her tongue with a pinkie and flicking it with a long painted nail, starting *Lolita* one night in the soft chair by the radiator and staying up until breakfast to finish, then doing the same a week later with *The Ugly American.* Without knowing he was doing it, Sam showed Scanlon what it meant to fall in love, then fall deeper, to keep falling.

Clay blew a plume of smoke into the fog, and Scanlon reached forward until the joint was placed in his fingers. He sucked in a couple quick hits and the smoke expanded in his lungs. Holding back a cough he said, "I just thought I'd give you the opportunity. Express your views. I don't give a shit."

He reached back with the roach, but Clay said, "All yours," and brushed by him, heading back to the house. Watching him pass between the patio and the garage, Scanlon took another hit, then rolled the roach between his thumb and fingers until it scattered at his feet. Clay paused at the garage window. Paused, or was time getting sluggish? The birds were slurring, the fog seemed thicker, more soupier. And just as Scanlon thought, Shit, I'm very stoned, the kid lifted his elbow like a wing and popped it through the glass.

Scanlon sprang toward him—"What the fuck!" he shouted—but Clay had vanished through the fog. The gate latch clunked, and he heard feet whisking in the grass. He looked down. He was walking, his shoes were wet. When he looked up, half his face was reflected in the garage window, a line of broken glass running between his eyes, over the bridge of his nose, and across a cheek. He reached through the hole where the other side of his face should have been. It really *had* happened. Shards lay on the sill and inside on the floor—the tinkling strangely continued to sound in his head. How stoned was he?

He could complain to Edmund, probably get Clay fired on the spot. But he wouldn't. He wouldn't do anything. And the punk knew it. A lesson in anarchy.

And Scanlon needed a few lessons. His last paper, in last winter's issue of *Domestic Policy,* had left hiring committees around the country underwhelmed. Other than Douglas, only one department—Arizona State—had invited him for an interview, and they never made an offer. He'd played up the publication so much—it *was* a big deal, *Domestic Policy* was tops—that Naomi panicked when interviews didn't come through with Stony Brook, Rutgers, Cornell, Binghamton, or the other six universities with openings. She'd asked him point-blank: "When do we explore other options?"

"We don't!" he blurted, and the ensuing argument made clear that with their baby in her belly, with midlife waiting in their next cracked-linoleum college-town apartment, any romantic illusions Naomi had harbored about academia—the life of the mind, the noble pursuit of teaching—had swirled down the drain of low-paying one-year stints, the irrelevancy of academic work to the rest of the world, the incomprehensibility that a shot at tenure in Douglas, Oregon, was an offer too good to pass up.

He assured Naomi they'd get back to the Northeast. He didn't want to spend his life in the sticks any more than she did. But this job put him on the tenure track, he'd explained, even pleaded. He would immerse himself in northwestern radicalism, get his book out, come up early for tenure, and leverage a job back east—in Binghamton, where they liked him, maybe even Princeton, Columbia, NYU. He'd do it before the baby enrolled in pre-K. Any doubts he had about the plan's viability he kept to himself, and often, he had to admit, *from* himself.

He wove between end tables and stacks of boxes through the living room to the kitchen. Naomi wasn't there, but he found a white paper cup standing on the orange table. He sat down, spun around in the chair, and took a sip of the coffee—lukewarm and too creamy—looking out the front window as Edmund and Clay carried Naomi's bureau down the ramp. Her T-shirts and jerseys stretching tighter as her belly grew, short black skirts and perfumed sweaters, the blouses she wore for work. And sometimes no blouse. Just a fitted blazer buttoned up to her cleavage, with nothing but a black bra . . .

"Sort of bizarre," Naomi said.

He swiveled again and was face-to-face with her belly. "Cheers," he said, raising the cup.

"The woman who runs the café—"

"They're bringing in your clothes," he told her. He loved the pucker of her lips when she spoke.

"Her daughter was like three or four—and still nursing. What surprised me is that it made me so uncomfortable."

The fullness had come to her face in the first few days. She'd known immediately. They spent Thanksgiving weekend in a barely heated cottage on Cape Cod, so chilly they ate their turkey and mashed potatoes under the quilt on a bed made of driftwood. She had forgotten to pack her diaphragm, and before they went back to New York on Monday, her cheeks and breasts had begun to swell.

"What's wrong with you?" Naomi said.

He tipped back his head and sucked the last drops of coffee through the hole in the lid. "Is there more?"

"Your eyes," she said.

He loved her dark eyes. "Did they bring in the bed yet?" He lowered his voice and reached for her leg. "Wanna go to the races?"

"Are you high?" She, too, lowered her voice. "You're high."

"Research," he whispered. "That mover's an anarchist. And his weed. Holy shit, Naomi. I've heard of this Oregon homegrown. Communes and cults in the hills. Free love, organic lettuce, killer dope, and they don't pay taxes. Welcome to my fieldwork. We're living on the fringes."

"Couldn't you drop out of society *after* we unpack the nursery?"

"We'll name our baby boy 'Free' and dress him in black onesies."

"Let's just start with the kitchen."

"I'm starving," he said.

"There's grain bars in the car. And get the cleaning supplies from the trunk."

"I could go for a doughnut. A glazed doughnut. I can't remember the last time I had a doughnut. Or chocolate glazed. With steak and eggs, and—"

Suddenly she was crying, her hands in fists by her cheeks. "I'm freaking out in this place, and you promised you'd help me make it work, but instead you're acting like this is high school."

He reached his arms around her, but she pulled away.

"For God's sake, we're having a baby," she said. "In Oregon."

"It's gonna be okay. Let's just take a breath and—"

"I don't want to breathe. I want to get the kitchen unpacked."

He needed to settle her down. It's what she relied on him for. His reassurance. But he was too stoned and couldn't trust his judgment to not say the wrong thing. She turned back to the sink, and he said, "I'll get the 409."

From the driveway he could see the anarchist at the top of the ramp, sipping on his soda. Scanlon grabbed a grain bar from the car and tore the wrapper with his teeth as he lifted the box of cleaning supplies onto his hip, the whole time watching Clay. The asshole had busted the window right in front of him! Performing, Sam would say. Scanlon would stay close to him, see him again soon, and he'd let him act up, then discover whether there were any real principles behind the antics.

He wouldn't even try to explain to Naomi that getting stoned with him today was the first step in building trust that could lead to primary source material for his book and get them back to the East Coast. Much of the criticism of his *Domestic Policy* article had been unfair, though some of it—especially that his critical perceptions had been compromised by his sympathy for the movements he wrote about—probably had some merit. But it wouldn't happen again, because his analyses would now be unassailable. He'd no longer have to guess what, for example, Pacific Northwest anarchists believed. He had a live one. And he would never again endure the humiliation of last spring's issue of *Domestic Policy,* in which the first seventeen pages were devoted to five scholars in the field brutally slaying his article from the previous issue. To remain a player and not let the beating force him into the hall of shame from which scholars often didn't emerge, he needed a quick, impressive publication, and the kid stomping down the metal ramp in black combat boots, shouldering the mini bureau containing silky puffs of Naomi's bras and panties, lacy nightgowns and slips, was just the sort of source that could make it happen.

In the kitchen he slid the cleaning supplies onto the counter and swallowed the rest of the grain bar.

Naomi tore open a Mayflower box. "Utensils," she said, pointing to the end of the counter with a spatula. "Start with that drawer."

Scanlon sprayed. He smelled the 409 fragrance that said *clean,* and could almost taste the antibacterial solvents. He scrubbed the drawer, digging at years of crud in the corners and wiping it all away.

After a time Naomi was standing beside him with fistfuls of knives and forks. "That one's probably done," she informed him.

Edmund pounded across the living-room floor and set a dish box down in front of the fridge. As he walked off, Scanlon turned to Naomi and whispered, "We should smoke pot more often."

"For Christ's sake." She arranged cutlery in the plastic organizer.

"I mean *after* the baby. After you're done nursing. You know. In life."

"Good plan," she said, popping the band of packing tape on another box.

When he finished all the drawers and cabinets, as Naomi stacked plates and nested bowls, he drifted into the living room. Touching the mantel, he thought about having a corner for kids' stuff—a toy sink and stove set, a Playskool tool bench—and where to hang his oversized photo of the Yucca Mountains, golden under a glorious sun, a thin line of protesters blocking the road, himself among them.

Hefting one end of their mattress, the anarchist wobbled backward through the front door. *A quick publication,* Scanlon thought, falling to the couch. Out the window he could see the blueberry bushes at the far end of the yard. The fog was lifting. He closed his eyes.

In the kitchen Naomi set steel canisters of flour and brown sugar at one end of the counter, then pulled the toaster from a box and plugged it in beside them. She chose a cabinet for spices, and one to keep empty for now—reserved for bottles, nipples, sippy cups, and tiny plastic dishes with bunny ears. As she clanked dinner plates and cookie sheets, the movers lumbered from room to room—smells of cardboard, coffee, and sweat. With each trip they anchored the house a little more solidly, weighing it down with books and bureaus, Scanlon's boxes of research, her leather chair. Each trip into the house made moving out more difficult.

Suddenly exhausted, she filled a glass with tap water and sat back in a kitchen chair, a hand on her belly. She fished in her pocket for the snip of woolly apple mint, then dropped the leaves in her glass, closing her eyes and breathing in the smell as she took a long drink, and when she opened her eyes, the young one was standing in the doorway, his arms around a box marked COOKBOOKS, staring at her. She slowly sipped her drink, sucking at the mint, then rested the glass on her belly, watching him slide the box on the counter and leave the room without looking back.

Mint. As a girl, she made long summer trips to her grandparents' in Vermont, where she and her summer boyfriend Clair, a French Canadian, would slip easily back into their heated romance. When she was nineteen—one of the last times she saw him—as the morning's first truck of raw milk arrived, she'd left her grandparents' house, passing through their small creamery, the routine she'd been repeating most summers of her life. The cement floor and three stainless steel pasteurizing drums were hosed down and shiny, but the smell of sour milk stayed with her as she walked the half-mile toward town, crossed the tracks (creosote and biting rust), cut behind a home-heating-oil depot, then caught the first whiffs of auto-body putty wafting from the body shop Clair's father owned.

She'd intended to give Clair a muffin and continue on to the drugstore for her grandmother's prescriptions, but he was on his coffee break, his coveralls unzipped and peeled down to his waist, and within minutes they snuck up the back stairs to the vacant apartment over the shop, crashing onto the bare mattress and making love to the whirr of grinding wheels and the rumble of compressors.

Afterward, downstairs in the office, she lifted the lid from the cut-glass candy dish and clicked a sugary Canadian mint against her teeth with her tongue.

Smells were all that remained of that day: strong sharp base notes married with tender top notes. This is what she seemed bound to re-create over and over, the combination of smells that revived that moment. It was the fragrance the industry had pegged her for.

She should tell Scanlon she had her nose back. Not yet, though. It was still too close. This new olfactory life took her into herself, not out to the world. She wouldn't even be able to say it.

When he opened his eyes, the house was quiet. Sun flooded through the picture window. The living room was a maze of cardboard towers. How could they have so much stuff? In the kitchen he opened drawers and cupboards. Except for a stack of cookbooks on the table, Naomi had done it all—Cheerios and raisins, salad tongs and olive pitter, the cups and saucers from Grasse had all found their place.

And next to the cookbooks, weighted down with Naomi's keys and cell phone, was a yellow sheet of paper: the Pacific Northwest Secessionist Movement. Meeting next Thursday. He stared at the paper. He read it again, laughed out loud, then snatched the phone and dialed Sam Belknap's number.

"Pratt, my lad." Sam's voice sounded strong and clear.

"How's the hip?"

"Better than ever." He was lying.

"What did the doc say?"

"The man doesn't know a hip from a jawbone. Did I tell you he's British? Couldn't get rich enough under socialized medicine, so he sets up shop at New York–Presbyterian."

"But did he say the hip needs to be replaced?"

"The good doctor had read a piece I wrote for *Food and Wine* about British naval traditions around the drinking of port." Scanlon knew Sam had become an authority on port wine twenty years ago while writing his book on the Basques and Andorrans. "I'm wearing a paper nightgown, and he's pumping me for recommendations on decent bottles in the *fifty-dollar range.* Brags that he did his medical training in the British navy. 'Naval man,' I say to him. 'So you know on a ship the port bottle is always passed to the left, typically preceding a jolly round of buggery.'"

"And then he said your hip was fine?"

"Precisely. Doesn't want to see me again. But what about *you*? How's Oregon?"

Scanlon told him about Clay and the flier he was holding in his hand. "I can do good work here. Solid, *important* work."

"I'm glad to hear the fire in you," Sam said. "It's always been there, even when it sputtered." He was referring to when Scanlon, mid-dissertation, declared he was quitting. He'd laid it all out in Sam's NYU office, tracing his passion for radical action and mass movements to a recurring childhood dream in which he was in danger, a threat lurking around every corner or chasing him at a sprint, until he spotted a cop, or a man in a suit and tie, a nun, a soldier, a mother—night after night he runs to the authorities to be saved, but when they turn and show their faces, they're the menace he's desperate to escape.

The dream wasn't hard to interpret: his father and mother were narcissists whose parenting philosophy blended strict moralism with hypocrisy and neglect. Like the parents of every other kid he knew, they eventually divorced. He was forced to go to Catholic school and church on Sunday, where he couldn't drag himself up from the boredom long enough to even consider its foolishness. They moved frequently when he was a kid; his father blamed the weak job market on OPEC, his mother on feminism and Japan. Born into a world of assassinations and race riots, weaned on the lies of Vietnam and Watergate, he grew up in recession and oil crunch, then watched Americans swallow trickle-down economics and secret CIA wars as the cure. By the time he was watching the Iran-Contra hearings in college, having lost all faith in government, religion, and family, he was bound for grad school. But once there, studying historical challenges to institutional powers, he concluded they were so entrenched that the only logical reaction was despair. "I'm done," he'd told Sam years ago, snow falling outside his office window and melting when it hit the street. "I'm going to Nova Scotia to raise sheep."

"There's no sheep in Nova Scotia," Sam had told him (actually there were), "but more to the point, you're right. It's all hopeless. I'll speak for myself here. I discovered long ago that if I wanted to be an academic with any sort of heart and soul, I needed to admit that ideals, hopelessness, and cynicism all exist in me at once."

Now, as Scanlon watched Edmund sitting in the cab of the truck and flipping through pink and yellow inventories of their possessions, Sam recounted his trip to Wounded Knee in the seventies. "I'd always wished the Native Americans could've organized a viable secession. By now they've missed their moment."

Sam's voice was losing its strength. They'd talked too long. "Maybe see somebody else about that hip," Scanlon said.

Sam turned the phone away to cough, then came back on the line. "Listen, Scanlon," his voice full of gravel. "Don't get too giddy about the anarchist next door. You know your tendencies."

"You take care of that hip, Sam. No need to worry about me." Then he signed off, wishing as he always did with Sam that he could have done more to breathe life back into this man he owed so much.

At the back of the truck, the ramp was still down. Scanlon set the flier on top of the cookbooks and looked in his wallet: forty-three bucks. He took the two twenties out to the street. At the top of the ramp, Clay was folding the quilted pads and stacking them neatly. Scanlon walked halfway up the ramp. "Short day," he said.

Clay didn't respond.

"Maybe I'll see you around town."

Clay yanked a strap tight on a tower of pads, then started another stack. On the floor of the van he'd swept up torn bits of cardboard and twists of tape.

"I don't teach till September," Scanlon said. "I could buy you a beer."

"Must be nice—" Clay's head twitched "—jerking off all summer."

Scanlon looked at the sky—a deeper blue than he'd ever seen. Matisse blue. The fog had completely lifted. Sun-heated steam rose from the grass and leaves and the black roof of his house. He stepped to the top of the ramp and lowered his voice. "Could you get me a little of that pot?"

Clay snapped dust from a pad.

"Just a small amount." Scanlon reached toward him with the cash.

He folded the pad and set it on the stack. Scanlon took one step closer, and Clay's head twitched again. Then he snatched the bills and thumbed them into the front pocket of his jeans.

"As much as you can get me for forty bucks," Scanlon said, then pounded down the ramp to the sidewalk.

"Yo, bitch," Clay called. "You're supposed to tip us."

Scanlon turned back. "That was the windowpane."

In the bedroom, sunlight swathed Naomi as she lay curled on her side in her great-grandmother's four-poster bed, beams so bright she seemed to Scanlon to be floating. Her maternity shirt was unbuttoned up to her breasts, and her bare round belly seemed to buoy her. Long kinky hair spilled out in a tangle over the white sheet. Her heavenly rump and back waited to be spooned. He pinched off his shoes and slid in behind her. She started awake and scooched back into him, both of them making minute adjustments until they found the familiar fit. "Sorry about before," she said. "I'm just anxious. I . . ." He waited for more, but she'd fallen back asleep.

Though not wanting to wake her, he buried his face in Naomi's hair and laid his hand on the warm skin of her belly. He imagined slipping down between her legs, where she'd changed not only to the touch but also to the tongue and nose. "Describe it for me," she'd said in the first weeks of her pregnancy. But he'd failed her. Less girl, more woman, was the best he could do. Less French kissing and bikinis, more toast crumbs and coffee in a rumpled bed.

He spread his fingers. From inside his wife's belly a tiny foot, or an elbow or knee, pressed into his palm.

At least he was trying. In the last few weeks he'd flushed sponges down toilets at Burger King, squeezed superglue into locks at Blockbuster, poured rice in the oil fills of bulldozers clearing Wakonda Hill for another swath of McMansions. Doing his part.

His back was sore. After offloading the professor and his pregnant wife this morning, he loaded a two-story to La Grande and didn't clock out until six. Now, just after dark, he hoofed it past Staples, T.G.I. Friday's, KFC, Bed, Bath and Beyond. A long walk—a mile up the strip, then back downtown—but he'd seen the heap of bricks where three old bungalows were leveled to expand the SUV inventory of Timber Ford-Lincoln-Mercury, and a brick from back in the day, encrusted with mortar mixed by the hands of the early Douglas settlers—a brick like that seemed right.

Headlights glared from the Burger King drive-thru. Only two blocks away was the Uptown Cafe, owned and operated for fifty years by old man Jorgen. Famous omelets, burgers, biscuits and gravy. But they poisoned themselves with Burger King instead.

Not everyone, though. Clay had to give some credit. A percentage of people in Douglas had an awareness. They bought local, kept the money in the community. They understood there was no point in sending your cash to corporations back east or down in California or, worse yet, Texas. He sneered at the line of vehicles idling at the drive-thru, oblivious inside their climate-controlled biospheres of genetically altered meat fumes.

Downtown at the Green & Black, he set his bag with the brick on the floor between his feet. 13½ was hunched over the counter by the coffee urns, giving away cheese sandwiches on white bread, leftovers from Food Not Bombs. Clay swallowed a couple triangles and poured himself a cup of water.

"That kid Panama's in town again," 13½ said. "From Seattle."

Clay slipped another sandwich into his mouth.

"I told him maybe you'd be around." He poured a coffee and pushed it toward Clay.

"I'm around," Clay said, then took the coffee to the window table where Flak was teaching a couple kids. He shook Flak's hand and sat down.

"You live in a system," Flak went on, "where people literally fucking die when their blow dryers and Cuisinarts don't work. You remember that whole power-grid thing that summer?" The kids nodded dutifully, high schoolers, hair spiked up with gel, new black clothes, freshly tattered. "The best thing we can do is prepare for the day the system collapses. No air conditioning, people freaking out that they have to sleep on the sidewalk. They're dying. What we do is get ready. When the power goes down across this country for good, when the oil and gas spigots run dry, which *will happen,* my friends, *we'll* be eating fresh fruits and vegetables. *We'll* know how to make our own beer and shoes. *We'll* be organized locally. When the U.S. Treasury collapses, when Visa and American Express and greenback dollars are worthless, *we'll* be flush in *Douglus* dollars."

Panama came in and caught Clay's eye. Flak noticed him too, but kept on talking. "Makes you understand that destruction isn't enough. Yeah, the order has to crash, but we're gonna want the water system and the fire stations and the bridges when it does. We'll take them over locally, but we'll *need* them. I'd rather teach my son how to make shoes and bread than teach him how to blow up a dam. Still, I know boys will be boys, so when the cops bring him home and say he was busting out store windows, I'll say, 'Thank you, occiffer, I'll take it from here.' And then I'll ask him, 'Son, what was the store?' and if he says, 'Office Depot,' I'll say, 'Don't get caught next time,' and if he says, 'Ma and Pa's Stationery Shop,' I'll beat his ass."

Clay respected Flak, but he was wrong about many things. Clay, for example, would never hit a child.

At the counter, 13½ backed off to the kitchen when Clay shouldered up next to Panama, who said, "I've got stuff to do in Arcata, but I'm coming back through next month." Panama was an upbeat kid, always involved. He'd done some treesitting. He'd burned a Weyerhaeuser mill. He'd freed four hundred wild horses and burros on BLM land in Redmond. He'd been to Hamburg and Amsterdam. Like Flak, he was a lot smarter than most of the anarchists you came across.

Clay passed him his coffee cup. "That sounds good," he said. "I'll get it ready."

Panama drank some coffee, then handed the cup back, and they both listened to Flak for a minute.

"That other thing," Clay said. "How about it? I've done some preparation. Real simple detonators."

"That's your own deal," Panama said.

"I could use a partner," Clay told him.

Panama took a step toward the door, shaking his head. "That one's suicide."

An hour later Clay moved through the shadows beneath the bridge, his black bag pulling heavy on his shoulder, nervy glints of moonlight off the river. A whistle blew as the train rolled into Southtown. His boots crushed through woodchips and mulch, then he squatted low, watching a yellow light go red, watching for cars coming over the bridge and the occasional pedestrian in downtown Douglas after ten p.m. on a Monday.

The whistle blew closer. Crossing gates dropped, lights flashed, bells rang.

Crouching down beside the Bank of America, he could see that the Wells Fargo across the street had already replaced their glass. Tonight was risky, just one night later, but as his plans became more sophisticated, he needed to ratchet up the risk and test his abilities. These local actions, even the operation with Panama, were honing Clay's skills for devising plans and carrying through under pressure—training for the big one.

After he threw the brick tonight, he could probably just walk the four blocks back to his room, but he would stick with his plan. *Make a plan, stick to it.* First priority, *always:* no one gets injured. Second priority: don't get caught. Third priority: achieve the objective of destroying property owned by religious bigots, corporations, and the U.S. government. Disrupt the system to hasten its downfall.

He ran through the plan in his mind. In seconds he'd be across the tracks, and a minute later the train would pass by at walking speed. Three engines, a dozen flatbeds stacked with lumber and plywood, then raw logs with mangled bark oozing sap, then open-topped cars heaped with pulp for the cardboard plant downriver—the screech and clank of hundreds of tons of slow rumbling steel—and with an easy hop he'd be sitting in an empty boxcar, his legs hanging out the door.

On the river side of the train, Clay would be invisible. They'd roll past his buddy's auto-body shop and Crazy Eights, where Randall would no longer run Clay a tab. Behind the bar the tracks hooked left through the old switching yard, a desolate space cut off by the highway. It was one of the oldest parts of Douglas, but over the decades brainless development had left it orphaned. A tiny old church, abandoned for half a century, was all that remained under a sick orange halo from the Home Depot across the highway.

He'd ride the twenty minutes to Fullerton and spend the night at a friend's place a block from the tracks. In the morning he'd hop the five-o'clock back to Douglas and get to work an hour later.

The train was two blocks away. The ground shook. Clay rose from his crouch, and for a long moment the world paused to provide him his chance: he tossed the brick back and forth between his hands, the earthy red dust dry in his nose; he cocked his arm as the train whistle blew, and heaved the brick like a catapult, not a quarterback, savoring the heartbeats from action to result. The plate glass buckled, then dropped, along with everything reflected in it. The glowing Bank of America sign, the seven-story riverfront luxury condos, the courthouse, and the Church of the Savior—all of it crashed straight down, and in the seconds before the alarm, the last falling shards tinkled like a baby's music box.

Chapter 2

Thursday morning, a week after arriving in Douglas, Scanlon took his bowl of Cheerios into the backyard. Plump blueberries came off by the handful, and he kept dropping more in the bowl as he ate. Barefoot, in boxers and a T-shirt, he stood there looking at his house, mostly settled, although a dozen boxes sat unopened in the nursery; they still needed a crib and a changing table, a glider and a mobile. The afternoon before, Naomi had taped paint swatches up on most of the walls. The coffee table was covered with catalogs dog-eared for bassinets, Baby Bjorns, diaper bags, and bureaus.

She was deep in the forest of primal motherhood. She'd said almost nothing to Scanlon during these preparations, and when he'd tried to sneak into that forest yesterday, patting her butt and saying, "Scratching a nest, building up the twig mound," she emerged slowly, stepping over gullies and branches, pushing aside ferns. A long moment passed as she chewed a mouthful of peach, then reluctantly lowered the fruit from her face, wiped juice off her chin with her free hand, and said, "This may be the best peach I've ever tasted."

Naomi had ventured deep into that forest, he knew, because she secretly hoped their baby would ease the distress she'd carried with her since she was nineteen; she'd had a baby all those years ago, a baby boy she never held or so much as glimpsed. He was swept from the delivery room too fast for her even to smell him. Hours into their first date, Scanlon felt the weight of her anguish over losing her nose, but it wasn't until weeks later, when she told him about the baby, that he understood how fully she defined herself by loss. *Their* baby, growing in her belly, embodied her chance of recovery—a risky bargain, and he felt sure she wasn't aware of its likelihood of failure.

With his cereal and blueberries he moved over to the new chair and sat down. It had turned out well—the angles so key in an Adirondack chair—and Naomi loved it. He'd routed ogees into the edges of the arms and corbels, and sanded the wood as smooth and soft as her skin. He just wished she could smell the cedar.

His bowl empty, he went back to the kitchen, poured a cup of coffee, and unrolled the *Douglas Union-Gazette.* The lead story was about the war: a surge of troops. Below the fold was a photo of a local collector of Pepsi memorabilia standing proudly before his artifacts, an article about the endangered habitat of the snowy plover, and another about how the state prison medical budget was being sapped by meth mouth. At the back of section C, in "News About Grangers and Grange," he learned that dogs were doing a great job managing cougars; that the red, white, and blue tennis shoe insurance banquet was a success; that the motivational speaker scheduled for the Elks Club "Sunday Best" pork-loin barbecue didn't show up. On the op-ed page he skimmed "Dawg Declares," a column from the point of view of a dog, then on the back of the section he saw a full-page ad for Douglas's sesquicentennial celebration in October.

"Listen to this," he said when Naomi came into the kitchen in her robe. "Craft fairs, face painting, solar- and wind-power exhibitions, hemp spinning, music, drumming, African boot dancers. And there's a lumberjack contest. Splitting, bucksaw, ax throwing, chainsaw, log rolling on the river. What's 'slow-chop,' do you suppose?"

But she wasn't listening. She was dunking a tea bag in a mug held close to her face, breathing the steam. He could tell she was thinking about motherhood, about doing everything exactly right.

"How's our little man today?" he asked.

She looked to be considering this, but then said, "I'm going to take this back to bed," and brushed past him with her tea.

According to Naomi, most people relied primarily on sight to orient themselves, but for her it had always been smell. Once she lost that sense, she felt constantly dislocated, and their cross-country move would only have compounded her unease. He was fascinated by who she once was, by her dormant genius (for which his own nose was a hack stand-in), and he found himself wondering, should it ever come back, if she'd be more resilient, happier, if she'd need him less.

Gazing back at the towering, page-high photo of last year's Mr. Douglas, bearded and rugged, an ax over his shoulder, he rubbed the stubble already on his chin. There were two divisions, amateur and semipro, the ad said. Contestants were encouraged to sport Oregon Trail beards, plaid shirts, and logging boots. He had the wrong glasses, the wrong hair, completely the wrong look. But like his anthropologist friend who lived in a Bolivian village in a dirt-floor hut, eating guinea pigs and learning the local dialect, Scanlon was going native.

That night, just before eight, he climbed a flight of stairs that rose steeply from the sidewalk between the Rainy Day Café and the Birkenstock store. The polished wood floor of the Odd Fellows Hall tilted toward the front of the building, where red and yellow yoga mats were stacked in the corner. Pushed back against them were an electric guitar, a drum kit, and a cardboard cutout of Jeff Bridges as the Big Lebowski, Scotch-taped where it had been torn. In the opposite corner, a pair of desert combat boots stood at the base of a waist-high cross, an army helmet placed on top, dog tags dangling below. Floor-to-ceiling palladian windows with green fluted columns looked out over the street. A lot had gone on in this room—an old building for Douglas, built in 1898, according to the facade. Like a frontier hotel or a vaudeville hall, the scrappy elegance had been maintained through the century with glossy paint and floor wax and smears of spackle on the plaster cracks.

By 8:10 the room was getting crowded. Scanlon sat toward the back in a folding chair. He'd anticipated the pot-bellied hippies with wiry gray hair and their twenty-something counterparts—tie-dyed, dreadlocked, slung with infants—but not the waitresses, plumbers, and mechanics of the uniformed working class. He hadn't expected the blazers and ties either, on men with neatly trimmed hair and starched collars. When two loggers from central casting walked in, he felt ashamed of his three-days' worth of whiskers. A dozen healthy tan faces chomped green apples and handfuls of trail mix. There were a few Native Americans and several large bunches of Hispanics, two or three different groups of Asians speaking their own languages—Chinese, Korean, Hmong, he guessed. A black couple with a young son playing his Game Boy. Two headscarves and a turban.

At twenty after—still no urgency about starting the eight-o'clock meeting—conversations around him showed no sign of flagging: kayaking, fly fishing, homeschooling, doulas, the end rot on everyone's tomatoes, a good chimney man, a phone number for organic mint mulch composted for at least two years, another number for grass-fed beefalo. He decided this was a complete waste of time and was heading for the door when a stocky, bearded man thrust his bear paw in front of him. "Hank Trueblood."

"Good to meet you." He shook his hand. "Scanlon Pratt."

"Haven't seen you at the meetings before." Trueblood was in his fifties, drinking black coffee, rocking on the balls of his feet. "New in town?"

"About a week."

"Where you from?"

"East Coast."

"What brings you to Douglas?"

"The university." It was starting to feel like an interrogation. "How about you? Are you from here originally?"

"Born and raised."

"What do *you* do?"

"Douglas Fire Department. I'm the chief."

A public-employee secessionist: was this a potential angle for an article?

"Let's do it, people!" came calling over the din.

"Hey," Scanlon said. "I'd love to talk more. Let's grab a beer."

"Any time, professor."

Scanlon returned to his chair. Professor? He was sure he hadn't mentioned that. The chief was now up front, holding the elbow of a statuesque woman and whispering in her ear. She'd draped a hand over his shoulder and, still listening, slowly turned her head until she was looking directly across the room at Scanlon. She was beautiful. Green eyes, plump lips, a dazzling smile.

Once the room quieted down, she announced, "My name's Sequoia, for any new people here tonight." Which got a big laugh. Obviously nobody else was new. "It's José's turn to run the meeting again."

The remaining coffee-klatch energy drained from the room with audible sighs and groans.

"I've done a lot of work on the tax question." José was around Scanlon's age, wearing a dark suit, a briefcase propped open on his knees. "I've composed a set of proposals for discussion involving sales, income, and property tax, import-export duties, casino tax," and he rambled on in a monotone about percentages and credits and revenues, all of it punishingly boring, without any context, and apparently of no interest to anyone in the room, most people staring at him blankly, fidgeting, knitting, reading, balancing checkbooks.

"So I propose a system whereby—"

"We don't need a *system,*" someone shouted out. "Systems are the problem!"

"*Eliminate* tariffs. Don't devise new ones!" A general ruckus was building.

"Eco-regions," another voice insisted. "Until watersheds determine the political boundaries and—"

"Deirdre, you snake. Everyone in this room knows you just want to log those redwoods!"

"Without Canadian and Pacific Rim trade—"

Complete pandemonium broke out—shouts, accusations, and pleas for calm—until finally an ear-splitting whistle pierced the room. It was the fire chief, two thick fingers in his mouth, cheeks puffed up and red.

Sequoia let the silence resonate, taking a long breath. "We're caught in an eddy, people. We can't just keep disagreeing. We have to *do* something." She held her arms out to her sides.

She was soothing, mesmerizing, but Scanlon still knew the PNSM was hopeless. The man in front of him got up for a fresh cup of coffee, then someone joined him and started crunching on a cookie.

"I want to introduce you to a guest tonight," Sequoia said, and Scanlon saw his chance to escape before the next sermon.

"He'll give us a broader overview and ideas for how to proceed."

He'd stood up and was sidestepping between chairs toward the exit when she said, "He's a professor of mass movements and radical studies at the university. Scanlon Pratt."

Sixty people shifted their bodies, chairs squeaking, necks craning.

He cleared his throat.

"What are your thoughts?" she said. "About how we might proceed."

He was pinned between the knees of Chuck from Chuck's Plumbing and the back of a chair. Chairs scraped the floor, opening up space around him.

"Well, it seems like you're on the right path," he lied, and Sequoia's smile grew wide and radiant, her eyes on him alone. "It seems like you're getting things done. I wouldn't presume to offer advice."

Heads nodded. Enough said. A self-satisfied bunch. But as the chatter resumed, Sequoia looked away, radiance draining from her as if he'd poked a hole through her skin. He'd disappointed her.

"However," Scanlon said. He lifted his hand and said it again more loudly, riding over the voices with the opening lecture for his unit on mass movements. "Any mass movement needs to first establish common principles, and those need to be based in a real understanding of social theory." He paused as Sequoia turned to him. "If you don't know how things work, you can't know how to change them. You need to develop a common vision for your new state. Is it a state? Or a nation? How is it governed, et cetera? You need strategies for implementing that vision. And you also need to understand that if you're serious, if this isn't just a discussion group with no real intention of actually *doing* anything, then profoundly radical action is required. Unshakable broad coalitions must be forged, and an unflinching commitment to the principles, vision, and strategies is imperative." He spoke over the heads of everyone in the room, directly to Sequoia, and the more forcefully he spoke, the more her face sparkled.

And he started feeling his genuine belief that a more just system in which humanity could flourish more fully really was possible, and that it began with groups of people like these before him tonight. Yes, the system had us by the throats. Yes, if it wasn't good for oil companies and the NRA, it would never happen. But he'd learned from Sam Belknap that life was about embracing contradictions, then working toward something that smelled like truth. For Naomi and their baby, for Sam, for himself, he had to try.

"Even with all of that," he continued, "your chances of achieving even the most token sort of secession from the state of Oregon or the United States of America is beyond remote. And I'd add," he said, "that if you researched successful secessionist groups, you'd know you don't have much working for you. First you need lots of money. You also need a leader. I don't see how you can possibly do anything by the consensus of whichever sixty people happen to show up on a given night. You need to elect a leader and a council, give them real authority and then respect and support it. A successful movement will have a coalition of at least eighty percent of the population in the secessionist region. You're no coalition at all, just sixty individuals. You need to broaden your appeal with good leadership and, again, clearly defined principles and all the rest. But most importantly, at this stage you need publicity and public relations, starting with a decent name. The best ones evoke a martyr or some event that arouses passion. At any rate, a name with a little jing. PNSM, I don't know, it sounds like a regional association of podiatrists."

The beams overhead were massive, milled in an age when Oregon Douglas firs grew to the size of redwoods. Filbert's occupied an old warehouse—the loft constructed around a two-story stainless steel tank where they brewed the beer Scanlon was drinking.

"There's dozens of groups working for secession in the Pacific Northwest," Hank Trueblood was saying. "Every scenario—separate nation, fifty-first state, aligning with BC. It makes so much goddamn sense, is the thing." He took a long draft on his IPA. They were on their second beer, having sought each other out after the meeting. Scanlon wished that Naomi could have heard Hank extolling the rain that keeps everything green, the pals he floats the Rogue River with each summer, another bunch who camp together in the Wallowas, friends who smoke salmon, distill gin, and produce biodiesel in their backyards. Last March he skied in powder to his knees at nine thousand feet, mountain biked the next day through old-growth forest on the edge of town and, a day later, in sixty-five degrees and full sun, was eating oysters on the coast.

Scanlon liked him and felt he possessed secret knowledge about keeping life in balance. Full of energy and drive but low-key about it. He was all to the point—no bullshit. "Is that *really* your first name?" he'd asked right off the bat. Scanlon laughed, then explained it was a family name and that his friends called him Pratt. Hank was as surprised as Clay that the university would have anybody teaching anarchy, and Scanlon told him that his research was on radical action and mass movements, but his bread and butter were the American politics core classes for majors. He then quickly steered the conversation back to tonight's meeting.

"Secession can only make us better off," Hank said. "And I mean *our* bread and butter."

Sipping the golden ale, aged in a pinot noir barrel, Scanlon tasted the wine suffusing the beer but could barely pick out the fragrance. He'd try to describe it for Naomi when he got home.

"Year after year," Hank said, "Oregon ranks near the top of the hunger stats, and there's just no excuse. The taxes that Nike alone sends to Washington could feed them all. Never mind our other resources—the water we'd control, the agriculture and fishing, not to mention green technology."

"Why don't you work with one of the more established groups?" Scanlon asked. "Some of them have been going for decades, right?"

"More than a century for the State of Liberty folks down south of here. I *did* work with them for a while. It was a distance, but I'd drive down for meetings and help out however I could."

"And they've had some real success," Scanlon said. "Declared independence. Elected a governor."

"But that was 1941, and only a handful of counties on either side of the Oregon California border. In Yreka, their capital, bears on leashes led a torchlight parade to the inauguration. Men with hunting rifles set up roadblocks on the highway, handing out copies of their declaration along with State of Liberty windshield stickers. The roads were dotted with State of Liberty signs. It was a national spectacle—the *whole world* took notice—with all the events captured on newsreels and scheduled to play in theaters around the globe on December eighth. But then December seventh came, and the only story was Pearl Harbor, so they abandoned their secession for the sake of national unity."

"But aren't they still active?"

He shook his head. "They're living in the past. It's all about the *mythic* State of Liberty now. The independent state of mind. There's a State of Liberty National Scenic Byway. The Feds named it, for God's sake, and put up the road signs. They've become a quaint bit of Old West history."

"But I've read they're doing stuff. Like the Klamath water war?"

Hank's face darkened. "That didn't get them any closer. To my mind it *lost* them ground." He stared into his beer for a long moment before continuing. "There's so much at stake with water. The Upper Klamath Lake irrigates thousands of acres of farming and ranching. After the dry winter of 2001, the Feds closed the headgate at the top of the irrigation canal so that all the water would flow into the Klamath River for endangered coho salmon and suckerfish. A bunch of farmers busted the headgate open with blowtorches, the Feds closed it up again, and this went back and forth until federal marshals arrived. You had environmentalists out there supporting the Feds, and farmers coming in to protest from all over the West. A couple nights they got the gates busted open again, and for a month or so I was sure somebody was going to pull a trigger. A few of the local boys were the sons, grandsons, and great-grandsons of the men who blocked the highway in 1941, so their sense of mission ran deep. And the Klamath Indians have water rights around Chiloquin, too, so they had their own stake in the standoff. Don't get me wrong—I don't think Indian rights trump everybody else's or that environmentalists have a better case than farmers and ranchers. The point is that the wilderness trail you want to hike on with your children runs through trees that are gonna get cut if your neighbor's gonna feed *his* kids. And it's neighbors who've got to work these matters out. Not a suit in some air-conditioned high-rise in Washington, D.C."

"What about that?" Scanlon said, seeing his opening. "You're a government employee. Isn't there a conflict with you working for secession?"

"So I'm a hypocrite?"

Scanlon let the question hang.

"We're in a situation where it's impossible to live a day without making implicit or explicit moral compromises. Period. Still, there may come a time when the PNSM gains some ground, and I'd have to drop out. I won't be that cop at the water war."

Scanlon shook his head, unsure of what he was referring to.

"As the summer heated up and the fields dried out, a lieutenant on the local police force—a rancher himself—drove out to the headgate with a bunch of deputies to deliver beef to our encampment. At dusk, lit up with spotlights from the police cars, he read a prepared statement over his patrol car's loudspeaker. I was sitting on my tailgate looking across the dry canal at the Indians and environmentalists on the other side, and the armed marshals posted on top of the headgate. I don't remember the details, but the speech was provocative, to say the least. Clear threats of violence to anyone who opposed opening the gates.

"That's when I came home. In 1941 the secessionists took up their rifles because the Feds refused to build roads to promote logging and mining. Although most of the ranchers and farmers encamped at the headgate in

2001 had no connection to the State of Liberty, there were enough of our flags flying that anyone could see who we supported. Whether it's water or property rights, opposition to hunting and fishing licenses or *any* federal regulations, they've gotten too single-minded. The majority aren't serious about forming a new state anyway—they want no government at all. So libertarian they're really anarchists. And then there's their pot-growing wing. The Statue of Liberty reggae band tours the West raising money to legalize marijuana. Talk about a weak coalition—Oregon rastas at one extreme, bear poachers at the other.

"Even if they could get their act together, their ambitions are too small. I want Portland and Seattle and Vancouver. I want all of Cascadia—from Mendocino to Prince William Sound to the Continental Divide. Those watersheds create a region that's logical, manageable, and sustainable."

Scanlon could tell that Hank had said this last part enough times he was completely convinced by it. "I can see why a lot of the people in the Odd Fellows Hall tonight are eager to go along with you," Scanlon said, "but I wasn't expecting the middle-class types."

"They've all got different reasons, which as you've noticed makes consensus impossible. A lot of them are just there for a good debate over coffee, not to say their ideals aren't noble. In fact, it's some of the same faces you see protesting the wars every Friday evening in front of the courthouse. They believe in what they're doing without much regard for the efficacy of their methods."

"The world needs those people," Scanlon said, meaning it.

Hank nodded. "Nobody in that room has it too bad, unlike the State of Liberty folks, who really do have valid gripes. But in both groups, ideals of equity and fairness and local control are on everybody's mind.

"And I'll tell you, Sequoia's on top of all this. She's very solid. She's the heart and soul of the PNSM, and we couldn't ask for better. But we need an intellectual focus, too. The sorts of scholarly and theoretical things you discussed tonight. That's where you could be a big help. That's where we need you."

Scanlon held his tongue. The only honest thing to say was that they didn't have a chance. Instead, he gave Hank his phone number and grabbed the check. "Let's do this again." There was a lot to learn about Douglas through Hank's eyes.

"Good talking to you, Pratt."

. . .

Naomi missed New York. She called her old friends too much. She read the *Times* Arts section too closely. She found herself waiting on street corners in downtown Douglas for a blast of hot fumes from a city bus. A jackhammer, a car horn, even the briefest snarl of traffic soothed her like a smell from childhood.

She'd always assumed that if things didn't work out in New York, she'd end up back in Paris. She didn't romanticize it, just knew the city excelled in the things she loved the most. The beauty of Paris was that of humanity's best efforts. Art and architecture, food, fashion, and fragrance. She had come to understand after her daily walks around their neighborhood that Douglas's beauty had less to do with humanity than with wild, uncivilized nature.

And it was stunning: old-growth forests wet with moss, mushrooms, sword ferns, and rotting wood, even during the rainless summer. Wild grasses, firs as tall as skyscrapers. She'd quickly come to love the moist embrace of the fog. The gardens around town—front yards of wildflowers and unruly Russian sage—were meant to imitate wilderness, not tame it into regimented rows of flowers and manicured hedges. The striking beauty of the place was the breeze that came up over the coastal range from the Pacific, carrying with it traces of sea salt and fertile, decaying forest.

Every day she took a different route, discovering more gardens and smells. The days were getting too hot for her to be walking at eight months, and this afternoon she planned on swimming at the university. But she wasn't about to give up the daily intoxication in her nose; in the last two weeks she'd refreshed olfactory memories and added hundreds of new ones.

Stepping slowly around a corner, lightheaded, only a few blocks from their house, she saw a green moving van, a fridge wrapped in a quilted pad standing in the street, and the mover, Edmund, wiping sweat from his forehead with a washcloth.

"Mrs. Pratt," he called. "Am I right? I never forget a shipper."

She stopped in the shade beside the truck. "Lovely day."

"Well put, Mrs. Pratt. I appreciate the sentiment." He hung the wet cloth over the side mirror, then called over her shoulder. "Hey, Clay. Guess who pops out of the woodwork?"

She turned. He was coming down the front steps holding up an exersaucer and rocking horse like a hunter with fresh kills. She stepped out of his path, but he stopped. "Miss New York," he said, all taut skin and ropy muscles, scars and smeary tattoos. His head twitched. Sweat collected in the dip above his collarbone. He smelled boyish and feral. He smelled like heat. Then, on a breeze, she smelled Pacific salt and damp forest floor, morels, moss, rotting cedar—or was it Clay?

"Scorcher," one of them said as her legs went watery and the sky flashed, sparking with white light, her eyes rolling back, then her neck . . .

Coming to, she was slumped on the rocking horse in the shade of the truck, Edmund fanning her with a clipboard. Clay's arm, hot as a pelt, was propping up her back, and with his other hand he was holding a Pepsi cup in front of her chin. Cool drops fell from the cup to her arm, and she lipped the straw and sucked in the sweet drink. The first swallow, icy through her chest, revived her.

"More," Clay instructed, his face close to hers.

And she did as he said, tasting his warm saliva along with the sugar and fizz. She looked into the cave of his mouth.

"Swimming's better toward the end," he seemed to be saying. "Especially in this heat."

"Any number of fine pools in town," Edmund added.

She took one last drink and pushed off the head of the rocking horse to stand up, seeing that it wasn't a horse at all. It was a wolf.

For an hour she'd been back and forth between the bedroom and the toilet. Edmund, who'd insisted on walking her home, had made too much of her lightheadedness to Scanlon, who'd made her drink too much lemonade when he wasn't insisting she lie down to rest. She suspected he liked her in this weakened state. Seven years ago he'd genuinely saved her from an increasingly desperate depression, cared for her through the lows, been patient and tender as she adjusted the Paxil. But when she gained strength and rediscovered her place in the world, he still wanted to be her caretaker.

She sat on the toilet looking at changing tables in a Target circular while Scanlon stood at the mirror combing through his patchy beard, which reminded her of photos she'd seen of him onstage, mid–guitar solo in his old college band—scraggly, hip, self-assured.

"Looks good enough," he said, "except for a thin spot here." His department chair, whom he hadn't seen since his interview last February, had asked him to come in for a meeting.

She could smell the lemonade in her urine. How would she tell him her nose was back? Olfactory pleasure had been their shared experience: he perceived and described; she summoned a memory, tricking her brain into sensation. She and Scanlon had been one. Now that she was wandering the world without him, drunk with lusty stimulation, she'd need to break the news in a way that didn't make him feel that some old lover was encroaching on their marriage, a lover with whom she'd had a passionate connection that Scanlon himself was neurologically incapable of matching. To make matters worse, that old lover was standing between them, even as they kissed, and didn't much like what he perceived of the husband.

"I don't want to make a scruffy impression," Scanlon said.

"You could shave it and forget the whole thing." The oils collecting in his new facial hair had, in fact, amplified his scent.

"Screw that." He combed over a bald patch on his jaw. "I can't do my research if everyone suspects I'm from Connecticut."

"But you *are* from Connecticut."

"That's a low blow," he said, poking her with the comb.

Her wish that his scent was what she'd imagined for him—or else a pleasing surprise—weighed on her like regret. "But you still want to get back east as soon as we can, right?"

"We haven't even been here a month. What's your hurry?"

"I've had . . ." She was on the verge of telling him about her nose, but not now, not when there was tension between them. She took a breath and said calmly, "I just want to make sure the plan hasn't changed. That your first priority's getting the book out—not just entering lumberjack contests."

"This is just for fun," he said. "And who knows? Maybe it'll lead to something that gets me going on a chapter."

"So you haven't started writing yet?"

"Let's just focus on settling in for now. There's a baby to birth, a nursery to paint." He set the comb on the counter, inches from her nose. "Maybe you should rest today," he murmured, patting her head, "and try the pool tomorrow."

She took hold of his wrist and moved his hand away.

. . .

That afternoon, he cut through the quad to the simple brick building that housed the Political Science and Sociology departments. FORESTRY was chiseled into a slab of granite above the front door. Inside, the building was quiet—a desolate, tumbleweed silence that only summer and Christmas break can bring to a campus. The polished floorboards squeaked with each step.

Although it had been thirty years since the Forestry Department left Blodgett Hall and moved to its sprawling new quad, a floor-to-ceiling painting still wrapped around the walls of the two-story lobby rotunda. On Scanlon's left, young men depicted in clothes circa 1950 planted seedlings while others inspected their needles, making notes on clipboards. Beyond them, in a forest thick with ferns and moss, lumberjacks (two of them bearded) were felling trees beside a logging truck. Next to them, a saw mill and a pulp mill floated along the horizon like the Land of Oz, then a nuclear family stood arm in arm, their eyes cast up at carpenters nailing rafters atop the framing of their new home. Finally, curving over the building's front door, stacks of newspapers rolled off a conveyer belt and led back to the beginning—a young man digging a hole for a seedling. The cycle of life, as clear as in grammar-school filmstrips.

The staircase was wide, chunky wooden steps with worn edges. The banister belonged in the mansion of a Victorian lumber baron. Deep turnings in the spindles, ornate moldings, relief carvings of trees and axes on the massive newel post. Repairs through the years—split moldings and a medallion that didn't match—were all coated in thick layers of varnish. He squeaked to the top, then walked through the door marked POLITICAL SCIENCE.

The outer office was empty, the assistant's computer blank, her desk tidy. He peeked around the corner to the inner office and saw a man standing at a table and hunched over a book, his back toward him.

"Hello?" Scanlon said, and the man turned. It was, as he'd suspected, the chair, and to his delight, Cebert Fenton, who'd been clean-shaven in February, now sported a fledgling beard, even splotchier than his own. Thin and mangy, a sorry-ass beard.

He was holding what looked to be a dictionary open in front of him, running his index finger down the page. "There it is," he said. "Hah!" Then he looked up. "Do you know what the German word for 'pretzel' is?" He clapped the book shut. Bright-eyed and very pleased, he announced: "*Brezel.*"

Fenton's research concerned reunification, and his latest book was on Germany. Scanlon knew all through the interview process that his own interest in mass movements was helping him with the chair, and probably hurting him with the other members of the department.

"Are pretzels what got the two sides back together?" Scanlon asked, regretting his flippancy even as he said it.

"Exactly the opposite. The pretzel developed differently on the two sides of the wall, and now they can't stand each other's versions. You've got East Germans living in the West who travel back to their old neighborhoods to stock up. So, will they ever fully reunite?"

"Keep your eye on the pretzel," Scanlon said.

"Bingo."

They looked at each other for an awkward moment; Scanlon was unsure whether they were joking. Then Fenton offered his hand and they shook. He was deeply tanned, especially over the top of his shiny bald head, which, since Fenton was a small man, Scanlon viewed from above. What hair he had was dark, flecked with white, and buzzed short. His scraggly beard was completely at odds with the rest of his presentation—neatly pressed khakis and a fussy yachting belt, boy-sized tasseled loafers, a peach-colored polo shirt clinging to the lithe, compact body of a man who'd done fifty sit-ups and toe touches every night before bed for the last thirty years.

"Getting settled in?" he said. "How's the house?"

Scanlon remembered that even in February, during his campus interview, Fenton had been tan. "It's all great. We're just trying to get ready for the semester. And the baby."

"Of course. I'd forgotten. What's your wife's name?"

Svelte. Could a man be *svelte*? "Naomi."

"You don't know how lucky you are. There's no place like Douglas to raise a child. The parks, the mountains, the ocean. You have no idea of your fortune."

"How about the mass movements out here? Have you done any work on them?" Scanlon knew he hadn't published anything on the Pacific Northwest.

"There's nothing to reunite. We've got secessionists, though. Survivalists, polygamists, anarchists. Take your pick."

"What about the secessionists? Anything there?" Scanlon asked, pretending this was the first he'd heard of them.

"PNSM? Pretty ragtag, from what I know." Fenton kept looking, back and forth, from Scanlon's beard to his eyes. "I doubt there's any real political theory worth speaking of. Certainly no successful action. Might as well be Thursday-night discussions on recycling Styrofoam, or how to make yogurt from goat's milk."

Of course Scanlon already knew this was the case, but part of him had hoped that just maybe the group had a drop of credibility—if not a movement then an inclination, a shambling drift.

"No," Fenton continued. "Nothing local. Not for me, anyway." His fingertips crawled through his beard like a blind man reading a face, apparently feeling out the thin spots. "The Dakotas might unify," he said wistfully. "Mostly, though, I look across the ocean." He gazed out the window as if trying to spot reunifiers in Korea or Cyprus.

They were both silent for a moment until Fenton blurted, "To discuss!" still looking outside. "The spring issue of *Domestic Policy* ended up on the dean's desk and he—Well, with funding cuts in recent years, we haven't had many hires. So there's lots of 'what ifs' and twenty-twenty hindsight and egg on the face. I went out on a limb for you, Dr. Pratt, so I want you to front-load your research and pull the trigger. An article or three, rat-a-tat-tat, a monograph A-SAP." Then he stopped as abruptly as he'd started.

Scanlon's heart sank. *Shit!* A warning. A threat!

"Your office," Fenton said brightly, and Scanlon followed him down the hallway to a tight dogleg and a door with a plaque that read, PROFESSOR PRATT. Fenton worked a key in the lock and opened the door partway, and when Scanlon took a step forward, Fenton stopped and turned back so they nearly bumped into each other. They stood inches apart.

"I notice you're growing a beard," Fenton said.

Scanlon smiled. "It's sort of silly. I read about the Mr. Douglas competition—"

"So that's it." Fenton cut him off, pulling on his own whiskers. "How long since you shaved?"

"A couple weeks."

"See this?" Fenton slapped at his own chin. "Six days. Five, really. Today'll be the sixth." Then he forced another laugh, stepping around Scanlon and down the hall. "Good luck," he said, chuckling.

Scanlon pushed the door open. An oak desk, heavily shellacked, was dappled with sunlight coming through two tall windows. A new computer sat on the desk, a dusty IBM Selectric next to it on a typewriter table, a file cabinet was stuck in one corner, and empty bookshelves lined the walls. He leaned back in his chair and put his feet up on the desk. "What the fuck was that?" he said, hearing the quaver in his voice. Fenton had rattled him. Goddamnit, why did his job have to start off like this? A quick article or three was already the plan. Now he'd have to get them out even quicker. He felt confident the writing would come easily. Sequoia had pleaded with him to become involved right after the PNSM meeting, and Hank had worked on him over beers. Well, he would. And he'd one-up the bastards who ripped his work apart for being rosy-eyed about mass movements. Scanlon had studied every secessionist movement on the planet. He knew why they failed, and he knew the blueprint for success. He'd nudge the PNSM along—maybe a token secession, merely symbolic, but a little taste was better than nothing—and he'd study every detail of the process and turn it into a book. There was no reason he couldn't become the leading scholar on American secessionism, with the street-cred to back it up.

He picked up the office phone—no dial tone—and then he pulled out his cell and called Sam Belknap. "I'm tearing the protective plastic off the padded arms of my brand-new desk chair," he said.

"Getting right to work?" Sam said, delighted.

"I'm gonna make my mark from this office, Sam. Radical change and mass movement flow through the air and water out here. Distrust of government, anger, fear—they're all juiced up, and I'm in the spot to make sense of them. Kosovo is old news. Quebec'll never happen. The Basques and Tamils will always be considered terrorists. But a tiny secession from history's greatest empire by the Pacific Northwest Secessionist Movement could shake the world."

"I never heard of them."

"They're small but fierce, and with a little help from me—"

"You're joking."

"Not at all. Plus there's these extreme right-wing Christians north of here and hippies living off the grid—"

"Stop!" Sam barked, then fell into a fit of coughing. Scanlon heard him take a drink and clear his throat. "Look, you've got a first-rate mind, but you need to publish some solid work. Enough of smoking pot with anarchists. You'll be sending your CV to East Jesus State if you don't buckle down."

Except for Sam's breathing, the line was quiet, and Scanlon gazed out the window at a tree with the biggest leaves he'd ever seen. Beyond it, students played soccer and Frisbee and jogged around a track. Beside the field, a fenced patio was connected by sliding glass doors to the swimming pool. It was so far off that when he saw Naomi in her black one-piece—gently padding across the white concrete—at first he didn't recognize her.

He'd never told Naomi or Sam about the strange e-mail he got in the spring—"just checking in," Fenton had said, confirming that Scanlon still wanted to move "all the way across the country," reminding him of the "onerous teaching load, the dearth of research funds, the high expectations for publishing." And he wouldn't tell them about the threat Fenton made today, either.

Scanlon gazed at his wife in the distance. He knew he'd presented her—and Sam, too—with an optimistic scenario, full of bravado for instant success and a prestigious offer back east. He couldn't bear the thought of disappointing either one of them.

When he finally said "I know," his voice cracked. "Of course you're right, Sam. Take care of yourself, and I'll call soon."

He raised the window and leaned out on his elbows. Standing beside a chaise longue, Naomi was stretching her back and rolling her neck. She bent down for a towel and pressed it to her face, turning toward the sun. And there was the shape of her: long tan legs, her huge round belly and full breasts. How was it possible she still had a month to go? How could her belly grow any bigger? Although Scanlon was excited for the baby, part of him wanted to keep Naomi exactly like this forever.

She dropped the towel and lowered herself onto the chaise. She drank from her water bottle and screwed on the cap. He hoped he told her often enough how beautiful her hands were, how they moved like music, and how much he loved to follow the ridge of her collarbone from her shoulder to her throat, to breathe in the cinnamon-pepper smell of her ears.

She'd settle in soon enough. She'd be herself again, and it was about time; since they'd arrived in Douglas, not once had she wanted to make love. He turned from the window, smoothed his hand over the top of his oak desk, and switched on his computer.

Ideals, hopelessness, and cynicism, he would have reminded Sam if he hadn't been struck dumb by the scolding. Yes, it was naive to think that secession of any scale would be granted without a struggle, but it was equally naive to believe that restoring morality to the U.S. government—its treatment of the poor, its support of dictators, its focus on profit over humanity—was any more plausible. Equally idealistic, equally hopeless.

When he heard the Microsoft chimes and his computer screen popped on, he looked back toward the pool, but Naomi was gone.

As she lowered herself down the ladder, her wedding band clanked on the stainless steel and the baby tugged hard against her spine; her hips ached, and she tried not to consider the mechanics of her bones literally being pried apart. She let go and bobbed in the chest-deep water. Graceful. Light.

She pushed off the pool wall, gliding for a moment, then doing the breaststroke down the slow lane. She frog-kicked and pulled her fingers through the warm water, imagining her baby doing the same thing inside her. Last night, Scanlon had read aloud from the *Pregnancy Journal. Day 219: If your baby is born today, it might have a callous on its thumb from sucking in the womb.* A hardworking baby, he'd said, his hand on the southern slope of her belly, a place she no longer could see.

Naomi would revel in the baby, skin to skin, day and night, lapping up every flutter of his eyelids, every flail of his chubby arms and legs, and with her nose back she'd be able to smush her face into his rolls of fat and take in his smell as he, with a newborn's olfactory keenness, would know his mother from oils in her skin and hair, from her breath and the smell of her milk. Mother and baby would become one, inseparable—an experience her industry friends warned her against putting her career on hold for. "Professionally, intellectually, emotionally," one of them, Liz, had said, "it's not good for a woman." But none of them understood what this baby meant to her.

After some months—eight, ten—whenever she felt ready—she'd planned to take the baby with her to boutiques in the Pearl and Portland's other trendy neighborhoods to see if they had any competent buyers. But now, with her nose back, she could work to create her own Pacific Northwest perfume, maybe even a breakthrough fragrance—seaweed, piñon, cedar sap, lichen, lavender, wild grasses—with the refinement of the new

San Francisco and Seattle cuisine, a Pacific Rim sophistication, silky hints of Japan and Hong Kong. She could finally work with ambergris, with which she'd had only a passing acquaintance.

There were ways to make it work. Eventually, for her career, she had to be back in New York, but Scanlon needed time and she owed him the chance. She'd been unfair to suggest this morning that he wasn't working fast enough. He was very smart, her husband, and she believed he knew as much as anyone in his field, though he always got antsy with projects. He had trouble focusing—reaching in other directions that complicated his argument to the point where it wriggled out of his grasp. There was also the issue of analytical distance: when he went out— no, *came* out—west to write on the Yucca Mountain protests, he ended up living with protesters in a tent city, where his notes and laptop were stolen, and getting himself arrested. In the end he produced a short piece for *Mother Jones*; the academic article never coalesced.

After a couple laps, muscles fired in her chest and glutes that had been dormant for years. While long walks in the heat had become too strenuous, she'd never felt more powerful. She'd been off Paxil for eight months, she could smell again, and soon she'd be holding her baby, and she'd never let him go. For years the shadow of loss and depression were always just two steps behind her, waiting for the chance to throw a heavy, sour cloak over her head. Those days were now gone.

With blood surging through her limbs and belly, she reached for the pool ledge but instead gripped a foot—ten toes curled over the blue tile. "Excuse me," she said, tipping water from her goggles.

"No worries," the woman replied. She was sitting on the edge, hugging her knees, water dripping from her arms. She was about fifty, Naomi figured, a racer's bathing cap and a Speedo suit stuck tight to her lean body, a dark splotchy tan. "You're doing a good job in there," she said. "Nice efficient strokes. Despite the ballast."

In this age of political correctness, pregnant women seemed to be the last unprotected, objectifiable subclass. She took a deep breath of chlorine fumes.

"How much . . ." the woman began. "I mean, just how pregnant are you?"

"Thirty-four weeks," Naomi said.

"You're big."

Basta! Naomi thought. "Do you work at the university?" she asked.

"Animal sciences."

"You teach?"

"I do research," the woman said. "I teach a little. What's *your* connection?"

"My husband starts this fall in political science."

"So you're a trailing spouse?" When Naomi's eyes narrowed, she quickly added, "It's just a university term. A designation."

My career, Naomi wanted to protest, *beats the hell out of yours,* but instead she looked down the length of the pool, adjusting her goggles. "Take care," she said, then bobbed under the lane marker to the ladder and hoisted herself up. Her swimsuit was still baggy in spots, anticipating an even bigger belly, and as she climbed step by step up the ladder—feeling the woman's eyes on her back—water drained off her as if she were a Volkswagen Bug pulled by a crane from the bottom of a lake.

Heading for the sunny patio, she glanced back over her shoulder as the woman launched herself off the block, her body smacking the water's surface like a plank, her arms and legs immediately propelling her down the lane with barely a splash.

Naomi lay back on her chaise and closed her eyes against the bright sun. Not a stir in her belly. Swimming had put the baby to sleep. Afloat in a floating world.

She still felt contained by her own parents—wrapped up in their embrace—and she'd do the same for her baby. As a kid, when Naomi decided she wanted a bat mitzvah, her father sent her to Hebrew school and bought her a tallis, and her mother spent two years converting and learning to read the *siddur,* and as a family they lived the calendar with a wholehearted commitment that reminded her now of the enthusiasm with which Scanlon immersed himself in projects and with which he would no doubt take up fatherhood.

"Sweetheart," she heard, taking a moment to realize it was him. She squinted against the sun. He was on the other side of the tall fence, his hands clutching long iron bars on either side of his face. "My office is right up there," he said, pointing far off at the back of a brick building. "I could see you from my window." He looked handsome, excited. He was floating in this new world of possibility. "Are you done?" he asked.

She took a deep breath—mint mulch and cut grass. She could sleep right here, but the sun was already too hot on her skin. "In a minute. Yeah."

"There's a wonderful cedar smell blowing over from that grove," he said. "Melted brown sugar. Sticky."

"Nice," she said, knowing it was actually Douglas fir. The needles, not the cones or bark. Greener, she thought, than he'd described.

"I'm gonna check out the climbing wall. Meet me by the front door?"

"Twenty minutes," she said. She really did have to tell him about her nose; this wasn't fair.

She lay there for three deep breaths, then carried her towel to the locker room, where she nearly ran into the woman from the pool.

"After *you,*" the woman said, then followed her down the row of lockers. "My name's Blaine. Blaine Maxwell."

"Naomi Greenburg."

Blaine pulled off her bathing cap and shook out thick silver hair. Naomi peeled her bathing suit around her belly, let it plop to the floor, and stepped out of it. She took her towel to the shower. Warm water shot out like needles on her skin, and she closed her eyes.

"Your body's compensating really well." At the next showerhead: Blaine. "Do you feel it? You're swinging your legs from the hip. Very smooth. People think of hippos as awkward striders, but they run with tremendous speed and grace. That same sort of straight-legged, high-stepping waddle that you've developed."

Naomi could accept the objectifiability of pregnancy, and she didn't mind sharing the experience. But comparisons to hippos?

"People are surprised," Blaine went on, slapping suds from her shoulders and underarms, "that of all the mammals—"

"Do you have children?" Naomi twisted off her shower.

Blaine stopped. She rinsed her face, trying to keep her hair out of the spray, then she turned, her hair appearing grayer now, wet and matted where it edged her face, and she looked at Naomi. Shutting off her shower, she said, "We didn't"—too loud in the sudden quiet, reverberating off the tile, and she dropped her voice—"we didn't have any luck in that area."

Oh, Christ, Naomi thought. Now she'd hurt her feelings. She snagged her towel off the hook. "What's your area of research?"

"Leaping, primarily. But running and jumping too. Any ground mobility." If fazed, she'd recovered quickly.

"Kangaroos? Rabbits?"

"They're actually jumpers. Or, more commonly, hoppers. I'm studying the Pacific leaping frog. A true leaper."

At their lockers, Naomi began what was becoming more and more of an ordeal: drying her body from the belly down. Blaine made no effort to conceal her study of every undignified reach and grope.

"From what we know about muscle and mechanics," she continued, "this frog shouldn't be able to leap nearly as far as it does."

Naomi lifted a foot to the bench.

"And really remarkable acceleration, even for a leaper." Blaine stretched and yanked a sports bra into place, then buttoned up the kind of squared-off shirt they sell in backpacking stores. She stepped into a pair of walking shorts, then Tevas, fastening Velcro at her feet, waist, and wristwatch—all before Naomi had adequately dried her inner thighs.

"I actually just started in on a new grant for acceleration. Got my dog Franklin on the payroll. He's at full speed in three strides. Outstanding for a dog. A goose, by comparison, is up around six or seven strides."

Naomi was exhausted. All this talk of striding and leaping was wearing her out. Talk, period. She lowered herself to the bench and dried her calves and feet.

"If you're curious," Blaine said, "we could put you on the treadmill and videotape your stride as it adapts."

"Not really my sort of thing," Naomi said.

"My grad students would be relieved. They have a hell of a time keeping the geese focused. Someone's got to kneel down at the back of the treadmill to catch them when they suddenly quit running and get shot off the belt. Franklin's better about it, takes it very seriously. And he should. He's on the payroll. NSF pays for his food and vet bills."

She'd been letting Scanlon take pictures of her every few weeks—nude pictures of her belly. It made her feel sexy that he so loved her pregnant. She wished there'd been pregnant photos of herself at age nineteen.

"I read an article on Sherpas recently. The incline and decline, the loads. It doesn't just affect muscle development but bone density too. And talk about adapting strides. Your load's a cakewalk by comparison. Your pelvis, I notice—"

"Great meeting you," Naomi said.

Blaine took the hint. She gathered her things and finally was gone.

Naomi took another fifteen minutes getting dressed, stopping to rest before putting on her socks and running shoes. No question: pregnancy was more exhausting this time around.

Out front, she passed her wet towel and suit to Scanlon, the smell of a dog's coat on his hands. She *had* to tell him.

"Do you want me to bring the car around?" he asked.

"Let's just go slow."

She hooked her arm around his and they walked across the grass, the cuttings already drying in the sun, grainier and bitter. "I was petting this Deutscher boxer," he said, "and he belonged to the most fascinating woman. She researches how he runs."

Naomi cocked her head, feeling a water bubble in her ear. She tried to wiggle it away with her fingertip, but that made it worse, plugging her ear up tight.

"Tomorrow for lunch." Scanlon's voice sounded miles away, but his smell—the sweet brine and dusty skin she'd only known for a month—was on top of her. "You're gonna really enjoy this woman."

Naomi rushed with guilt for disliking how he smelled, and for keeping her nose a secret. Guilt and sadness for all of it.

Clay tongued the tender bump on the inside of his lip; it hadn't bled, but if he nibbled at it, the taste of blood would seep through the flesh. He dropped a buck and change in the tip jar as the young one—the girl with the cross dangling in her cleavage—no hair net today—slid the foil bag and the icy waxed cup across the counter. The Greyhound had just come in from the coast, and he watched the line of passengers slump through the station. No one he knew. Heading out the door, he snagged a newspaper from a garbage can and read the front page as he went around to the alley and up the stairs to his room.

Chewing his hot-dog burrito, he looked for an article he knew he'd find—if not today, then tomorrow—reporting that in a week or two they'd resume blasting Siuslaw Butte between Douglas and the coast. Soil had been unstable, with unexpected erosion and slides, streams and watersheds compromised—so the roadwork had been suspended. But now the proper officials had pocketed their payoffs, the relevant regulations had been rewritten, and for at least the next year they'd get back to the business of blasting.

Mountain roads that took generations to complete seemed to belong to another era, but this stretch of the Douglas–Yaquina highway was less than three miles from the section Clay's father had been blasting ten years ago. The state couldn't stop themselves—they leveled, widened, straightened. It was their nature.

He sucked Mountain Dew through the straw, twirled the ice, and sucked again, surveying his afternoon's work: spread out on the floor beside his mattress he had two spools of 24-gauge wire, two 6-volt lantern batteries, PVC pipe, end caps, cement, ten mini flashlights, a cordless drill, wire cutters and pliers, five old-fashioned blasting caps of the type his father used when Clay was a boy. The caps had come from a grisly Portland anarchist, hard core, originally from New Jersey was all Clay knew. And time in prison. Definitely a different edge, these East Coast anarchists. The caps were spendy and just about ran Clay dry, but the rest came from Habitat for Humanity and pawnshops. The drill was nearly gunnybag but would last the job.

He'd been working on this plan for a year, and last night when 13½ told him the grisly dude would be through town today with the caps, he felt the rush of forward motion, of possibility. But the truth was, when Naomi swayed this afternoon and dropped into his arms, bashing him in the mouth with the top of her skull, and he maneuvered her onto the rocking horse, his lip swelling, his hands supporting her back and her hard full belly—*that* rush was altogether different.

When the sun finally shone through the white curtain on their bedroom's western wall, Scanlon slowly awoke. The curtain filled with honey light, billowing with the easy breeze, as full and round as Naomi's belly.

Her deep peaceful breathing beside him sounded like the sway of leaves and tall grasses in the summer wind. He smelled the swimming pool. She lay facing him on her side, naked, the white sheet pulled up to her waist. Her belly and breasts rested on the mattress; her small hands were pressed together under her cheek. Soon they'd be three.

Although he still awoke at night panicked about supporting a family, they'd come a long way in a year. Last summer, looking ahead to their second year as dorm parents in a girls' boarding school outside Boston, he was half-time at BU and had picked up a survey class at Northeastern. Naomi did the dorm-parent duties in exchange for their rent, cafeteria food, and a small stipend. Still, with grad-school loans to pay, health insurance that the school required but didn't cover, a car payment, and a new computer, the girls had more pocket money for Saturdays in Boston than Scanlon and Naomi did.

They were mostly run-of-the-mill rich girls from New England and New York, but there was also a pair of sisters from Qatar. Actual princesses. They shared a room outfitted with an absurd stereo that was delivered and installed by technicians, a silver samovar, and a freestanding wardrobe for overflow from the closets. Twice each term they invited Scanlon and Naomi into their room for tea. With their legs folded under them, the princesses sat like jade statues on the zebra pelt covering one bed. Scanlon and Naomi slumped on the other—cheetah, he thought they'd told him—and stirred sugar cubes into the delicate cups with spoons that seemed to be solid gold.

At Christmas the princesses presented them with two Rolexes. They thanked the girls profusely and wore the watches in the dorm for a few weeks, and Scanlon came to like having all that money strapped to his wrist. It surprised him, violating all his politics, but he felt successful wearing that watch. He felt powerful. It was glitzy—diamonds in the face and lots of gold—and the few times he wore it to Blockbuster and 7-Eleven, he liked that people noticed. He was given better service. He could be more demanding, then look straight ahead while eyes followed him, everyone anticipating his next move. When Naomi wore hers, he could easily imagine her as rich and rarefied; she had the exotic Jewish features he associated with biblical beauties in the movies, or Cleopatra, or Nefertiti, or . . . whatever it was, she was reminiscent of the foundations of our cultural ideals of beauty. And the watch was like draping her in jewels, laying her back on silk pillows, and dismissing the slaves. She became in his imagination a princess herself—one he had full access to.

For a few weeks these fantasies idled around in his head, but finally he and Naomi did the only sensible thing: they put the watches up on eBay. Days later they were holding a check for nine thousand dollars, their heads spinning with the thrill of it, their stomachs hollowed out with guilt—or fear they'd be found out. They set most of it aside for making payments—and somehow it was gobbled up in months—but they spent a thousand or so on good dinners, shoes and a necklace for Naomi, a DVD player, books that Scanlon could get from libraries but enjoyed the luxury of owning. And as *toro* and *ikura* slid chocolaty over their tongues at a wildly expensive sushi bar in Back Bay, Naomi's sexy feet strapped into shoes she'd rarely have the occasion to wear, they weren't royal and powerful, but giddy with the almost sleazy excitement of getting away with something so sweet.

He rolled quietly out of bed and went naked to the kitchen, where he filled two tall glasses with ice and lemonade. There was mint on the counter—stalks that Naomi had brought home—and he pinched off a sprig for each glass. After five o'clock, it was still a beautiful afternoon outside. When he slipped back into bed, Naomi's rhythmic breathing paused, then she took a long deep breath, and lifted her head. "Hi, lover," he said, then twirled a glass, clinking the ice.

"Mmm," she said into the pillow, curling an arm around his knee. "I have to pee so bad."

He took a big sip of lemonade and clinked the ice again. She winced, reaching up to still the glass. "That's not helping."

"Well, then go," he said, "and come back," which she did, and they sat facing each other cross-legged, kissing between sips.

"I have some news," she said.

"You're pregnant?"

"My nose is back."

"What?"

"My nose." She was beaming.

"But how?"

"I think it's related to this." She pressed her palms into her belly. "I've had hints of smells since Cape Cod."

"You didn't say anything."

"I didn't trust it. Couldn't believe it."

"So that's when it started?"

"No. Just since we got to Douglas it's really back."

"Oh my God." He hugged her and wiped the tears from her cheeks. "I want to celebrate," he said. "Dinner. Wine."

"You're drinking for two now," she said. She touched his hand, steadying it. "You're shaking."

"I'm stunned. This is so wonderful." For the first time since he'd known her, she fully possessed her peculiar genius. There was suddenly more of her, like when she got pregnant: a deeper, more complicated woman to love.

"Pizza," she said. "I've been craving it." She kissed him. "With smelly things. Kalamata olives, garlic, basil."

"We'll go to that place," he said, cupping his hand between her legs.

"Yes."

"The one by campus. You love that place, right?" He felt a sort of give beneath his fingers—softening, opening. Smells would be a new connection between them. "And for pie, that other place," he said. "By the river with the beautiful view."

"Marionberry pie with ginger ice cream," she said. "And a decaf latte."

She scrambled to her knees and plucked the mint from her glass, took it between her lips, pushed him on his back, and settled over him—a plunge that left them both short of breath.

"I want to experiment," she murmured, her hands planted on his chest. They rocked together, her weight rolling from her hips up and over her hard belly to the points of her palms, like she was rolling over a yoga ball, then she pushed into his chest and rolled back down to straddle him. "With our lovemaking, with smells," she said, and bit through a stem and pressed two leaves of mint between his lips. "Hold it there." She sucked at the mint, her wonderful belly rolling into his, gasping inhalations through her nose. "All these new smells out here to experiment with."

"The sexy smells of Oregon."

"The Oregon experiment," she said, throwing back her head and closing her eyes. "The two of us."

Scanlon's own eyes were wide open. He wanted to look, to run his gaze over her contours, to get lost in the beautiful landscape of her body. Her breasts had already been lovely, and now they were bursting. He brushed his fingertips over her nipples, bigger and darker in these last months, then laid his hands on her belly—full of their baby, their love. He studied the long scoop of her throat, her lips pursed as her breathing sharpened, her fingertips digging into the skin of his chest, her heavy eyelids, her nose and cheeks, her kinky hair—like snakes or flames—growing in more fully, like everything else in his wife, this beautiful woman who men had been carving into stone for two thousand years.

The next day, on their backyard patio, Naomi tried to focus on Blaine's husband but was distracted by the broken windowpane in the garage. Cool must, grass clippings, gasoline in a plastic jug, and the tinder of old lumber poured through the sharp-edged hole. "Of course, when we arrived in Douglas," Roger was saying, "autumn of eighty-four, there was no Chez Paul's, no Grotto, no brew pub, not even a decent pizza to be had in town."

"My only point," Naomi said, "is should a twenty-four-dollar entrée be served by someone who calls you 'guys'?"

Roger took a slow sip of his drink, then stared at the wedge of lime. Blaine looked at Naomi quizzically, as she might stare at a hopper who'd just leaped.

"Oysters," Scanlon said, easing the silence. "We had Kumamotos and Yaquinas last weekend. East Coast oysters are nubs of rubber by comparison."

He asked Roger and Blaine how they prepared their oysters, and they talked of flavored oils, oyster kebobs, bacon-wrapped, and pepper pan-roasted. A bird swooped down on the marionberries, tugged at the vine, and lighted on a branch above their heads, a berry pinched in its beak.

Roger sipped his drink and set the glass back down on the concrete slab by his feet. "Steller's jay," he said. "As you probably know."

Naomi's mouth was full of chicken salad. The bird was much brighter blue than any jay she'd ever seen, with a striking black head and mohawk. "I've noticed them but didn't know what they were called."

"Sometime," Roger said, "I'll take you down to the wetlands. Some of the best birding in my life is ten miles from here." Naomi's face must have betrayed her because he quickly added, "If you have an interest."

He was a nice man, more reserved than his wife, and older too, maybe sixty, but no less athletic. He had large strong hands and strappy muscles tensing beneath the weather-roughened skin of his arms. His airy white dress shirt, pressed by the cleaners, hung above khaki pants full of pockets and zippers.

"Of course we never thought we'd stay here more than a few years," Blaine said.

"It'll be a wonderful place to raise your children," Roger said.

God, what if they were here that long? What if he got tenure but couldn't land an offer back east? She and Scanlon would come to appreciate the restaurants; they'd imagine growing old here, grateful they lived in Douglas and not down the road in Tangent or Burnt Woods, Boring, Shedd, or Drain. Their kids would grow up boastful, "born and raised" Oregonians. There'd be 4-H. Her daughter would go on dates in proud pickups. A son in vo-ag and the high-school pistol club. Or they'd move to a commune in the hills—her son's life spent juggling and sewing bells to his floppy velour jester's hat, her daughter worshipping the moon and making art with her menstrual blood. Would her daughter have a baby of her own at nineteen?

Naomi had already surrendered one baby to a life that was out of her control; she would raise the rest of her children as *she* chose.

The Adirondack chair tipped too much weight onto her lower spine, so she shimmied forward and sipped her lemonade, tuning back to the conversation as Scanlon touched her arm and said, "We love it here."

Blaine and Roger gazed at him, open and engaged. They were comfortable.

She flashed on the first time she'd ever seen Scanlon—at a party in New York thrown by an industry friend whose husband worked for the mayor. Scanlon was telling a joke to six or eight people, and she watched, thinking he was handsome, then charming. Dark curly hair, broad shoulders, a habit of touching two fingers to his chin when he paused for timing. His audience leaned in, eagerly waiting for what came next. He sipped his wine, as if he'd never let the punch line go, then delivered it—irreverent and crude—and everyone broke into laughter, including one woman who wasn't apt to find much humor in "bitch." But he'd won them over—Naomi too—and she decided she'd meet him before the night ended. When she did, she was surprised to find he didn't work at city hall, having met plenty of men who used their bright eyes and quick smiles to win sympathy and votes. He'd be a good leader, though, she thought. And she'd been seduced, even aroused, to learn he was an academic, using his charm not for money or power but to engage students, and for jokes at parties, and to unknowingly attract her.

She'd had no sense of smell for over a year when she agreed to go to the party, only because her friend, a nose, promised her it was her *husband's* party, *his* friends. Most of Naomi's were noses, a few were chefs, one tasted for a wine importer and wrote off and on for *Wine Spectator*. By this time, she could barely taste food. Good wine, except for the numbing effect, was wasted on her. Hoppy porters she could taste, and she appreciated the fizz. "The kale's yummy," Naomi had said, mostly to herself, one night at dinner, and the conversation immediately shifted. "Can you really taste it?" one friend asked. "For me the smell of the sesame's a big part of the flavor," another observed. "What *does* it taste like? To *you*?" asked another. They intended no malice. To them, Naomi was a curiosity. A subject to explore. And, she felt as months passed, an oddity. Pitiable. She couldn't bear to be around them and made more frequent excuses until she was seeing no one except her father, who drove into the city once a week to take her out. She was drowning in loss.

That year her baby's birthday was harder than ever—a ten-year-old boy—and with the loss of her nose, the one frayed connection she had to him had been severed. She'd heeded the advice of doctors and adoption counselors that she not hold him after he was born but now knew that had been a mistake. She hadn't realized how quickly they'd snatch him away, or how empty that would leave her. She'd also agreed to a closed adoption—no names, no contact—choosing file 372-NY because "mother" was a middle-school art teacher and "father" was a journalist. They enjoyed cross-country skiing and European travel, and had three long-haired Dachshunds; they'd built an oven from clay in their backyard for baking bread; they lived in the state of New York.

Naomi had not seen her baby. She hadn't smelled him. She possessed only a tear-hazed memory of a lump in a blanket passed between hands, the sound of a confused cry, and the odor of her amniotic fluid and blood. Because this was all she had to know and remember him by, the bodily smell of his birth came to represent her baby. Each month her menses conjured a visit, bringing not only a sense of loss and regret but also a comfort and even joy that she'd come to rely on. Losing her nose felt like losing her baby all over again.

When she thought back to those first weeks with Scanlon, she mostly remembered him from a distance, as she'd first seen him—across the living room engaging strangers with a joke, across a busy café delightedly penning questions in the margins of student essays, or through the doorway of his kitchen on a Sunday morning competently scrambling eggs in the nude with a quick wrist and a dash of salt as she lay curled up in his bed, warm, cared for, ravished.

He'd saved her, and she fell in love with him for it. But throughout those years she'd remained disconnected from her sensuous life. Scanlon remained fine to look at—from a distance or up close—but the spark of newness faded quickly, which she attributed to her useless nose, marooned career, and the futile longing she felt for her baby. Of course, she reasoned, the rush of falling in love was bound to lose its surge, just as the rush of her entire life had diminished to a trickle. But Scanlon was the best thing in it. Naturally their lovemaking became less exciting to her, even as he revealed that it became better and better for him; if she couldn't smell him, she couldn't know him, couldn't fully connect with him. When she got her nose back, she'd convinced herself, their love and passion would roar back to envelop her.

"The Pacific leaping frog," Blaine was saying. "That's a misnomer. He inhabits only a tiny region, a few hundred square miles in the Oregon coast range. A true leaper. The males are especially powerful. No one understands how they can leap as far as they do." She hesitated, then leaned in conspiratorially. "I'm on to something, though. Between the base of the leg muscle and the testicles there's a tiny gland that produces a hormone that seems to supercharge the muscle the instant before it springs. And the hormone . . . what a smell it has. Incredibly powerful. It makes us all a little loopy in the lab."

"What's it smell like?" Naomi asked, suddenly fascinated.

"I can't say. I've never smelled anything like it."

"But if you had to. If I held a gun to your head."

"A gun?" Unzipping a pant leg, Roger paused. On his left leg he was now wearing shorts; on his right, long pants.

"It's unpleasant," Blaine said. "*Very* strong."

Naomi's hands were in fists. "But what does it make you think of?"

Blaine didn't shrink in the face of this challenge from a trailing spouse but rose to it with greedy pleasure. "Like a chemical that could make five grams of muscle propel a ninety-gram reptile nearly three meters. Like exertion. Adrenaline. Drive and desire and hunger coiled up in the groin."

"Language, dear," Roger quietly scolded, though Blaine was obviously pleased with herself.

"I'd like to take you up on your offer," Naomi told her. "I'll drop by your lab."

Their plates were empty. Scanlon returned from inside the house with fresh drinks, setting a cold glass in Naomi's hand and sitting beside her with his arm over the back of her chair. He was perspiring.

Over the years, much as she created fragrances from memory, she'd invented smells for Scanlon. The few times he'd picked up someone's guitar and played, he'd smelled of spruce and oak. When he shoved a man in a subway car who'd had his hand in Naomi's purse, pinning him to the door with a fistful of his shirt and throwing him onto the platform at the next stop, she'd smelled powerful base notes of cloves, creosote, body putty, and mineral oil. Kissing her in the park was dried maple leaves and honey. In bed, his mouth on her neck, nudging, nuzzling, then his first thrust inside her—rich sweet tobacco and musk. As he gathered up the pieces of a woman morose and purposeless in her sour apartment, he was a steady onshore breeze, low tide, on a hot night. She'd invented things so real they became his smell; they became *him.*

The passion would blossom, she'd convinced herself. When she got her nose back. But her nose *was* back. His scalp and skin were in the dusty family: canvas stored in the basement, pages of a book pulled from a garage-sale box, a stranger's wool sweater. From his crotch: steamy rain on a hot sidewalk. None of it was bad, or offensive, or even unpleasant. But all of it belied the dashing visuals of the man whose self-possession could command a room. The man who'd saved her. It was like he was a different person. As if she'd lost him.

She knew it would sound petty to anyone else, but it was literally chemistry—the percentage of certain hormones in his sweat, the levels of bacteria in his mouth. She'd known of marriages gone sour for lesser reasons: a friend who couldn't bear to be in the same room with her husband while he brushed his teeth; another who divorced hers for the flair with which he shined his shoes.

She closed her eyes tight.

"What is it, sweetheart?" Scanlon said.

Tears spilled from under her eyelids.

"Hormones," Blaine declared.

"Allergies," Roger offered. "Welcome to the grass-seed capital of the world."

Scanlon kissed her cheek.

She covered her ears and held her breath. They had no idea.

Chapter 3

As Sequoia circled her finger around the rim of a cup, it caught on the chip, surprising and rough, like a lick from a friendly cat. In the weeks before opening the café she'd thrown plates, bowls, and mugs on the wheel, most of them wobbly or pouty-lipped, the glazes runny, but all of them warm and skookum. Through the years they broke one by one, and this afternoon County Health ordered her to junk anything chipped, amounting to most of what was left. So now, at closing time, done with payroll and next week's schedule, finishing up her orders—eighty pounds of white flour, forty pounds of wheat, seven gallons of plain yogurt, dried oats, tofu, vegetable oil, walnuts, and raisins—she scrolled past linens and cutlery and clicked on four cases of dishes from AA Restaurant Supply. Microwavable. Made in Cambodia. Mugs without Sequoia's thumbprint pinching down the handle, plates without the concentric grooves of her fingertips. A compromise to her vision of Skcubrats.

"So *that's* who you are," she heard from the front. "Hey, Sequoia, do you know who this is?"

She submitted her order and logged off. Her landlord, Ron Dexter, still hadn't left. She'd sent Keiko home half an hour ago, cut the music, and cashed out, but Ron sat scouring the *Union-Gazette* and smacking his lips whenever he caught sight of her, hinting that he'd take a muffin or cookie not worth saving for day-olds. But tonight she'd packed everything from the bakery case in a canvas bag; all was spoken for.

"This is America Sanchez," Ron announced, looking at the only other customer, her latte and lemon square long gone, working on her laptop. "You *are* America Sanchez, aren't you?" He was gushing.

The woman snapped her laptop shut, turning her face toward him and forcing a nod.

Ron tugged his gray beard, then clapped his knees. "Can you believe it?"

Sequoia believed it. Or she didn't. She didn't care. Ten o'clock on a Tuesday, and she wanted to go home. She had no idea who America Sanchez was.

"The crack reporter," Ron said. "Channel nine. Portland's power source for news."

She did look exactly like a TV reporter—pumps, pantyhose, bony legs, her hair cut razor straight at her shoulders, rich skin that would look lush in any light. She was heading out.

Ron hobbled after her. "A picture. One picture." And the woman stopped by the door, then waited as Ron dug in his pocket for his cell phone.

Sequoia locked the windows and flicked off the light in the juice case. Ron had an arm around the woman's shoulders, working the cell phone with his other hand. "I'll give you a copy, Sequoia. To hang in the café."

As if. A photo of a TV reporter named America and her soon-to-have-his-knees-replaced landlord who'd made a career of leering at Sequoia and the girls she hired?

Sequoia tried to let go of her resentment for Ron—it was uncharitable, unloving, and disrespectful—but there was a fucking limit. A, he was fighting to keep the new neighborhood center from going in beside his house for fear it would lower his property value; B, he'd been dicking Sequoia around for over a year about selling her the Skcubrats building. Not that she was surprised. Any day of the week, she'd take a Republican over a baby-boomer hippie when it came to business. The Republican will lie, cheat, and screw you the best he can, but then he'll close the deal and move on to the next one. Ron, however, felt dirtied by the entire experience, an arena in which he'd always been powerless. Entitlement rushed through him with the knowledge that to settle for anything less than every last penny and drop of blood was to cave once again to a corrupt society. This was his chance to demonstrate that he wasn't bending over for capitalism. If, in selling to Sequoia, he could outdo a Rotary Club developer, he felt he'd beat capitalism at its own game, compensating him for dirtying his hands and for failing—through years of Che berets and twenty-dollar checks to the ACLU—to topple the system.

And now, against her nature, Sequoia's own mercenary mind began working. "Could I ask you something?" she said after turning off the bathroom lights. "Have you ever heard of the PNSM?"

The reporter looked at her blankly.

"The Pacific Northwest Secessionist Movement," Sequoia said hopefully.

"What are they? Like survivalists?" Her clear, steady voice sounded exactly like TV.

"No, no. We're a diverse group of Oregonians who think the region can do better economically, environmentally, and morally than the federal government —"

Ron's cell phone finally flashed, and the reporter dislodged herself from him and leaned back into the door.

"If I send you a picture," he was quick to ask, "would you sign it?"

"Sure," America said.

She was already on the porch when Sequoia called to her. "Would you consider covering a PNSM meeting?"

"What's the group done? What's it doing now?"

"Interestingly," Sequoia said, "we're formulating some proposals that promise to—"

America cut her off. "You have to *do* something to be on the news. It has to be *news.*" And the door slapped shut behind her.

It was another ten minutes before Sequoia got rid of Ron, took the last of the trash out to the dumpster, and turned off the lights. She knew the TV gal was right. She turned off the lights. The professor—Scanlon Pratt—had inspired everyone at the meeting last month, but they needed more than a pep talk. They needed *him.*

The babysitter, Chezzi Trueblood, was in bed with Trinity, both of them asleep, when Sequoia slipped out at midnight with her thick gardening gloves and the canvas bag bulging with muffins, cookies, and scones. As she moved down the sidewalk, Ruth's motion light blinked on. Sharky barked. But mostly the houses of her friends and neighbors were darkened and, she knew, empty.

Tonight, in this corner of the universe, a hushed excitement and urgency juddered through the air. She went left at the end of the block, spotting John and Alice coming down their front steps, tipping their heads at her, moonlight shining off their white hair. With oversized canvas gloves John made a muffled clap. Alice hugged a stockpot to her belly. They joined her wordlessly, heading toward the railroad tracks. Ahead Sequoia could see Jenna—her broad back and long frizzy hair—stomping across the park with her sturdy legs and heavy boots. She played *djembe* in an African drumming group, and her body always carried that earthy, soulful beat.

Dark silhouettes emerged from shadows at a hundred yards—Karen, Todd, and the other John, all of them instantly recognizable to Sequoia from a high-stepped stride, a favorite poncho or hat, a bounce in the shoulders. Jasmine, Paul and Sue, Deana and Kenny, then Cocoa, Amy, Kathy, and Phil. They carried buckets of tools, coils of rope, thermoses, and baskets of food with a big-hearted sense of purpose. Tonight they were *doing* something—*news*—as she'd wanted to tell the TV reporter; she'd wanted to throw it in her face. But this wasn't for the PNSM and had to remain a secret until they were done. As Sequoia stepped over the tracks, she heard the bulldozer fire up in the darkness.

"It's loud," Alice said. They could barely hear their boots scraping on the gravel and stone of the old switching yard.

"Then we'll be quick," Cocoa said. "No worries."

Sequoia could now see the bulldozer in the moonlight. Across the barren ground—nothing but rusty train parts and beer cans—Jim Furdy was positioning the machine in front of the long-abandoned church. In Douglas you always knew somebody (or knew somebody who knew somebody) who had access on short notice to an acetylene torch, a cider press, a marimba band willing to travel, a portable sawmill, a chakra healer, a bulldozer. As it happened, Jim Furdy lived in the neighborhood, and his business—wells and excavations—backed up to the railroad yard.

Jim shut the engine down, and they gathered around as the hot, diesely metal creaked itself cool and he stood on the dozer's tracks. Alice offered Sequoia a cup of her three-bean stew. "It takes ten or twelve people to lift a phone pole," Jim said.

"Out of curiosity, how many to lift an elephant?" Hank Trueblood asked.

"The question," Carly said, "is how many Republicans does it take to *screw* an elephant?"

"Laugh it up, pranksters," Jim said, "but no hernias tonight. Especially you graybeards." He hopped down to the ground. "Somebody help me hook up the cables."

Alice organized the food on one side of the church. Sequoia and Hank and the first ten people who ambled over rolled a phone pole away from the weeds that had grown up around it.

Months ago they'd jacked the church off its stone foundation and slipped timbers underneath. The windows had been removed. The few pews that hadn't been looted through the years were stowed under a tarp on Jim's lot. Sections of the roof—where moss had led to rot—were cut away. By spring the old church, purchased from the city by the neighborhood association for one dollar, was ready to travel the three hundred yards across the tracks and be transformed into their new community center. The city agreed to a dollar-a-year lease for a corner of the park; the association signed a contract promising to maintain the church for a century. They'd had two months to move it, at which point the chunk of barren land it occupied would be transferred from the city to Northern Pacific Railroad, who planned to tear the church down. The paperwork had all been very easy. But then, to everyone's surprise, nobody knew a house mover.

The first bid, from an outfit in Eugene, came in at $38,000. Carly announced this at the next meeting, admitting that while she wasn't really a numbers person, it was a big increase over the $2 they'd already budgeted. A company in Portland was willing to do it for fifty-one-five.

That was when Jim Furdy suggested they move it themselves: his bulldozer could pull, his backhoe could push, and a score of neighborhood minions could carry phone poles from back to front to use as rollers. He had a reliable source for decommissioned phone poles.

He applied for all the necessary permits and permissions. Six weeks, two public hearings, and countless written proposals later, replies started coming back. Northern Pacific refused to let the church cross its tracks (even though this was a public right of way) because of likely "damage to rails, ties, connections, bed, etc.; risk to engines, cars, cargo, etc.; risk of accident, incident, slow down, stoppage, etc.; risk to railroad personnel (and non-personnel) of bodily injury, death, etc." Northwest Power—whose motto was "Your local electric company" but who acted less neighborly since they'd been ingested, digested, and spit out by Enron—would pull aside the power line for $6,381. The city refused to allow a vehicle with non-pneumatic tires along this half block of their precious pavement. Furthermore, a neighbor who lived next to the park opposed the community center, arguing it would harm his property value. He was vocal at the hearings and even threatened to sue. This was Ron Dexter, Sequoia's landlord at the café.

A week later, Jim called a clandestine meeting of the association, inviting select members by word of mouth instead of the listserv. "I took some measurements," he said. "If we cut the roof off, we can sneak it under the power lines."

"But what about driving the bulldozer on the pavement?" Sequoia asked. "What about Ron?"

"We can keep trying to do this by the book," Jim said, "and watch Northern Pacific tear the church down in a week, or we can just take it. Quietly. At night."

The tingle of delight and mischief was immediate. Plans were made, secrecy was sworn. And if not for that secrecy America Sanchez and a camera crew would have been here right now with Sequoia making a plug for secession.

It was after one o'clock before she heard another big engine come to life in the distance. The backhoe, piloted by Jim's son, Pete, came at them out of the darkness. Jim started the bulldozer, the first four phone poles were rolled into place, and as the engines revved, everyone stepped back, fearful that the church might explode into splinters.

But it didn't. It slipped off the timbers and started to roll. Quiet cheers went up, Hank hugged Sequoia, Carly ate a scone. And then the real work began. Jim wanted rollers every six feet. Under the rumble of the machines, they whispered instructions to one another, dragged, lifted, lugged. The whispering was absurd, given the diesel engines, and as they labored, Sequoia kept an eye on a particular spot at the backs of the houses. Sure enough, before long a light went on. Ron's house. Five minutes later, with blue lights rolling lazily, a police cruiser crept through the oil drums and rusted train parts in the yard. The plan was to keep working, which everyone did, while Sequoia showed the cops their title to the church and explained that for another three days this was public land, and that until they crossed the tracks they weren't in violation of anything.

"Noise ordinance," Ron shouted. He'd followed the police out with his flashlight, and was now snapping photos with his cell phone.

The police put in a call to Northern Pacific, and in the hour and a half it took for two of their inspectors to arrive they'd shined their headlights out in front of the bulldozer, written $90 noise violations to the Furdys, and were on their second mug of three-bean stew. They'd also ordered, after the first hour, a hysterical Ron Dexter to keep back at least thirty feet. The railroad inspectors examined the plank ramp that Jim had fabricated and laid over the tracks to protect them, then consulted with the police, then gestured for Jim to shut her down. But at a few feet per minute, Jim's bulldozer pulling, Pete's backhoe pushing, the rest of them hauling phone poles even faster now with their adrenaline surging, the old church kept bumping ahead with an unstoppable combination of physical and moral momentum.

Thirty feet from the tracks, the inspectors told the cops to arrest them all. After preparing another ticket for an unauthorized railroad crossing, the cops radioed the station to find out how much the fine should be. Jim reached down for the ticket and tucked it in his pocket with the other one.

Twenty feet from the tracks, the inspectors told Sequoia they could cross, but not until they posted a $20,000 bond for damages. "Unlikely," she said.

Ten feet from the tracks, the lead inspector stood in their path in his white jumper, reflector vest, and white hard hat, seeming to fancy himself the tank-stopping student in Tiananmen Square. But when the bulldozer's headlights glared in his eyes, he reevaluated his commitment, took several quick measurements and flash photos to augment a lawsuit, and slunk aside.

The church rolled over the tracks and down the alley. Kenny climbed the walls, serving as lookout as they passed easily under the power lines. He and Jim and five or six others had removed the roof in sections that afternoon. It would increase refurbishing costs, but free labor was abundant and Jim had a solid lead on a barn coming down in Tangent with good straight rafters.

Jim pulled the bulldozer onto the street, then stopped for a moment to collect his $120 "non-pneumatic tires on the roadway" ticket. Everyone had agreed to put up twenty-five bucks apiece for the expected fines, and they hadn't come close to that yet. The police flipped on their blue lights. An official escort.

They were deep in the middle of the night. The fog had begun to roll in with wisps of ocean air. Houses lit up. Curtains parted. Sequoia would have loved to trade places with one of these people submerged in sleep, awakening from a dream, and going to the window to see the old church gliding down the street. It was magical. And they'd done it. Even Ron had surrendered.

Or so they thought. At the end of the block, on the street in front of the plot of city park where the church would come to rest, a car was parked: a twenty-year-old Volvo station wagon plastered with bumper stickers for Dennis Kucinich, divestment in South Africa, whales, and impeachment. Ron's. He leaned against it, arms crossed.

They sounded like an invading army. The phone poles rolled, the bulldozer tracks clattered, the engines rumbled. More lights popped on in houses. Jim stopped his dozer blade a foot from Ron's bumper and stood up. "Move the goddamn car, Ron!" he shouted.

Ron cupped a hand behind his ear as if he didn't hear.

"I'm tired!" Jim shouted. "We're all tired."

Ron ignored him.

"Three strikes, Ron!"

Ron's arms tightened across his chest. The machinery and the phone poles, the twenty dear friends and neighbors, the church, and even the blue police lights were perfectly still, all awaiting Ron's next move.

With a little rev in the engine, Jim lowered the blade, eased forward into the rear end of Ron's Volvo, and added the car to the caravan, pushing it to the end of the block while its owner stood back helplessly.

Some tricky maneuvering was required to swing into the park, but in another half hour they had the church in position. Pete set up the jacks, and shortly before dawn, working through the fog, the new community center—although propped on temporary timbers—sat on the land where it would remain.

Cheers and hugs, hoots and sighs. Sequoia was wildly happy and gushingly grateful, especially to Jim Furdy, whom she gave a long and special hug.

At home, she kissed Trinity and Chezzi, still sleeping, and out back, with the morning's first light whitening the fog, lowered herself into the hot tub. "Bite me, America Sanchez," she said out loud, letting her arms float. They'd done it.

And now for the PNSM. The professor would get them to stop *formulating* and start *doing*. Sure, at the meeting he couldn't hide his reluctance. He had his own reasons for being there—they all did. But she could sense his passion. And she saw how he responded to hers. He was the one, she was sure. She'd just have to bring him along.

Naomi was getting close—two more weeks. In bed beside Scanlon, she lay curled on her side, deep in sleep, as she had been for over an hour. Tonight, like most nights these last few weeks, they watched a video after dinner, Naomi dozed off halfway through, and, with the sink full of dishes, they stumbled into bed.

But as soon as he switched off the light, Scanlon felt like he'd downed a pot of coffee, his anxiety like the frenzied clacking of a thousand cockroaches. Anxiety about money, the baby, his marriage, the semester, his research. Pull the trigger, Fenton had said. A quick publication or three. Scanlon hadn't spoken with Sam Belknap since the scolding.

He'd been exploring micro-secession, arguments against "bigness," the feasibility of functional independence. Last week he'd reread Sam's book on the Basques and Liam Peterson's study of East Timor. He didn't believe that the PNSM's plans for secession of the entire Pacific Northwest had legs, but something no bigger than the county and no smaller than a Douglas neighborhood would at least be a rich academic exercise worthy of a quick publication. This afternoon when Hank phoned Scanlon to suggest a strategy chat, the obvious subtext was to get him on board. And they were set to meet in the morning at nine.

Not too far off, sirens wailed across the night—unusual for Douglas on a Wednesday—and he thought of the firemen relaxing in their rows of corduroy Barcaloungers until the call came in, then rushing for the pole. He raised his head to see the clock over Naomi's shoulder: 12:45. He pulled the covers up tight to their chins, still amazed at how in Oregon, even now with days approaching ninety, most nights dropped below fifty.

But the sirens didn't let up, and dogs down the street had started howling. Hank would cancel if they had to fight a fire all night; by morning they'd all be sleeping or spraying down trucks and drying out hoses.

He tried listening to his breath to relax. Naomi got pregnant at

Thanksgiving, and for those first couple months—until the job offer in February—he often woke up in a panic. Down in the deep sea of sleep, pressure worked into his dreams, pumping him full of worry and fear, his heart pounding, surreal pictures surging by with flashes of those old dreams where the grandfatherly doctor becomes the torturer he's fleeing, until he broke through the surface, awake, gasping for air. How would he pay for a changing table, car seat, jogging stroller, violin lessons, braces? It was already adding up—prenatal vitamins, home pregnancy tests, a Pea in the Pod maternity dress. Luckily this past year they'd had health insurance, but plenty of years they'd let it lapse. Naomi had never turned her business as a perfume buyer into much money. Not that he blamed her, it was just a fact. She'd done well in New York as a fragrance designer, but that was before they met. Scanlon knew he lifted her spirits, that she admired the apparent ease with which he found everyday happiness. He'd sprung her from a moldering life, waiting in her apartment for her nose to return, paralyzed with fear that it wouldn't. The night they met he told her he'd taken a one-year position at Union College in Schenectady, and it wasn't until they'd moved there together that he understood he'd provided her with an escape from New York. Her reluctance to leave the city was only a show. Without her nose, unable to work at what she loved, New York had become an oppressive, day-and-night reminder of illness, failure, and loss, her sensual life hacked out of her. She was dying to get out, and have a place to go.

Moving to Oregon was no different. Although she would never admit it, she'd wanted to come, to put even more distance between herself and the gaping stare of her former life. But now that the genius within her had awakened, she could have that life and career again. He'd lost his role as her surrogate nose, and he missed that intimacy, missed being the intermediary between Naomi and her sensuality.

And it didn't help that in the last month she'd completely lost interest in sex. He'd never felt more distant from her.

A car raced down the street. His eyes shot open, and he thought he saw a blue light—police lights—slice around the edge of the blinds and across their bedroom wall. A branch from the honey locust tree tapped on the window with a gust of wind.

Naomi slept through just about anything, so he tried listening to *her* breathing, to be soothed by *her* rhythms of sleep, letting his eyes settle closed, and it seemed that despite the sirens in the distance and the dogs up and down the street, he was tired enough to drift slowly off, the tension slowly dropping from his body and mind . . .

Three sharp knocks spun him around in bed. He looked at the clock—1:07—and sat bolt upright, silently holding his breath as three more knocks came faster, more urgent. He slid from under the covers and into his robe, then tiptoed through darkness down the hall to the living room and peeked around the corner. Squinting, he sneaked back to the bedroom for his glasses. Five quick raps this time, harder and louder, and in the moonlight he could now see a figure through the glass in the back door, and he froze: one o'clock in the morning, a police car flying down the street, an intruder in their backyard banging on the door. Naomi's bathing suit was hanging over the Adirondack chair, and she'd left a baby-clothes catalog on the seat. Scanlon's blood rushed with the full force of his role as man of the house.

The phone was at the other end of the couch. It would only take a moment to call 911, and maybe the room was dark enough to conceal him. As he made a dash, one eye on the back door, the intruder waved furiously, pressing his nose and forehead to the window. Scanlon took a slow step toward the door, then another, peering cautiously through the glass . . .

It was Clay, the anarchist. He felt a ripple of relief but held on to the phone, still considering making the call.

Then Clay reached into his pocket and produced a fat joint. Scanlon was in a tight spot. Maybe he didn't need the police chatting with Clay in his living room. He set down the phone, put his hand on the knob, and retracted the deadbolt.

It occurred to him that Clay could be freaking out on crystal meth or whatever drug anarchists favored. (He should know that, and made a mental note to find out.) He cracked the door. "What do you want?"

"Sorry it took so long," Clay told him.

Scanlon said nothing.

"The shit I owe you. The pot." He waved the joint in Scanlon's face.

"What are you doing here in the middle of the night?"

Blue lights flashed by the side of the house, darting across the marionberry vines. Clay crowded in closer to the door. "Could I have a glass of water?"

Scanlon stood firm.

"I'm very thirsty," he said. "I'd really owe you."

Against all good sense, Scanlon stepped back, letting the door swing open, and Clay hurried past, reeking of gasoline. He looked around the room, apparently taking note of windows and exits, then sat on the floor in a shadow beside the fireplace and the overstuffed chair.

Scanlon reached to switch on the lights, then sensed he shouldn't and left them off. He dragged the ottoman over and sat down with his elbows leaning on his knees. "What's going on, Clay?"

"Nothing. I was in the neighborhood and wanted to deliver your pot."

"Gimme a break."

He stuck the joint in his lips. "You want to burn one?"

"No, I don't." Scanlon's robe had fallen open, and he pulled it closed. "I want you to tell me what you're doing here, then leave. Or just leave. My wife's sleeping and I should be too."

Clay's fingertips fidgeted with the laces of his black boots. "What about"—his head jerked twice—"that glass of water?"

Scanlon sighed, then went to the kitchen and ran the tap. When he got back with the glass, an orange ember glowed bright in the dark room until Clay released a plume of smoke.

"Asshole!" Scanlon said, so loudly that he was afraid he might've wakened Naomi. But only two nights ago they'd read in the *Pregnancy Journal* that secondhand smoke in month nine can damage the baby's fine-motor skills. He lowered his voice. "Not in the house. My wife's pregnant."

"Just one more hit," and Clay sucked on the joint again.

"Get out of here!" Scanlon demanded. "I'm not screwing around."

Clay moved to get up, then leaned forward and squinted at Scanlon's midsection, gesturing like ET with a bent finger. "Bummer," he said, holding his lungs full of smoke. "I hope my cock doesn't get all meek-looking when I get old."

Scanlon glanced down at his penis bobbing out of his robe, then wrapped the robe tight and cinched the belt. He'd had enough of his anarchist. "Move it, asshole! Get out!" He'd been so high when Clay smashed the garage window that he didn't fully compute that this stranger had vandalized his new house right in front of him. He should've reported him to Edmund or thrown the little shit against the side of the garage and hit him, but instead he'd let this menace into his home in the name of scholarly research. Sam Belknap was right to be disappointed.

Clay swiped the ember on the side of his boot.

Scanlon raised a fist. "Get the fuck out of my house."

And then a flashlight beam slashed across the side windows. Scanlon looked around, confused. Two cops were searching his backyard. He thought first of the cloud of pot smoke hovering in the room, then of the general guilt that always seized him around cops, and then of the fact that the lights were out—a couple chums getting high in the dark. If he turned the kid over to them now, how would he explain?

But then he thought, This is *my* house. Cops have barged into *my* backyard. "You stay there," he said to Clay, who'd scooched farther back into the shadow of the chair.

The cops were taking short, quick steps, bending forward with their heads lowered like bloodhounds. When Scanlon flipped on the patio light, their faces turned toward the house. He opened the back door and stepped onto the concrete stoop, about to speak, but the cops beat him to it.

"Have you seen anyone suspicious?" one said.

"Male. Five-ten," the other one clarified. "Black clothes with anarchist insignia."

"Nobody like that," Scanlon said, stepping down to the patio and pulling the door closed behind him.

One cop shined his light into the marionberry vine, then around the back of the garage, and his partner said, "If you see anybody, give us a call. Sorry to disturb you, sir."

The other one pointed toward the garage. "Mind if I look inside?"

Scanlon shrugged. The cop pushed open the side door and shined his light in the corners and up in the rafters, then let the beam linger for a moment on the broken pane, still not replaced after these two months.

They latched the gate, and Scanlon stood there watching their lights dart around the next yard. His bare feet were cold from the concrete, the chilly night air creeping up his robe. His heart thumped powerfully in his chest.

He went back inside to the sharp smell of pot and gasoline, and standing over Clay he reached down for the roach and the Bic. He torched it up, drew in a lungful, and let it go. "What did you do, Clay?"

The kid's head twitched. "Thanks for getting rid of them."

"You owe me." Scanlon took another hit. "Lots." His pounding heart rushed the THC straight to his brain, and he was immediately high. He fell back into the overstuffed chair and enjoyed the joint, the luxury of letting it burn in his fingers between drags without a thought of passing it to Clay, the sweet smoke flashing a slide show of high-school memories through his mind. He was getting much too stoned, he knew, but it didn't really matter. It was the middle of the night. It was still summer. He'd lied to the cops, harbored a suspect. They'd called him "sir." Homeowner. *His* backyard. Cops dressed as commandos—pants tucked into high black boots, uniforms with military doo-dads. That was a problem: they give the impression they're waging a war, making the rest of us the enemy. Did they notice how nervous Scanlon was? He knew that cops were trained to expect a little anxiety in the innocent. In fact, the icy-cool ones were probably guilty. Scanlon had bought (and tried to buy) booze so many times before he was twenty-one that his heart, to this day, beat faster in liquor stores.

He'd forgotten this part. When the whole room is your heart and you're inside it and the ceiling and walls squeeze in and out with each of your heartbeats. He heard his name and thought about Cindy Feagan back in the third grade, all pigtails and crooked teeth. They'd eaten sundaes together at Dairy Queen, and where was she now with that cute smile and those perfect drawings of horses and castles like they were right out of a book? He could totally go for a sundae right now as he heard his name again, and in high school he and Jane Swallows got stoned once and ate sundaes at Friendly's. He remembered telling Naomi early on about this girl he'd been hot for his senior year, and he knew he liked Naomi when he said, "What a name. Jane Swallows," and Naomi quipped, "To her credit."

Through the syrupy memory and the palpitating room he heard it again: "Scanlon." And this time he realized it was Naomi. "Pratt!"

Clay smacked him on the arm and plucked the roach, long dead, from his fingers.

Scanlon sat up, but he was . . . this was. . . . oh, this was gross-motor skills completely whacked. He was standing. Upright, he believed. And he could see Naomi doing the sumo walk toward him down the hall, her hands reaching out to the walls on either side.

"Sorry," he said. "We were just . . ." Words eluded him.

"This is it," she said, and groaned.

"Have you noticed," he asked, "that you groan a lot more since you're pregnant?"

"It's time," she said.

Time for bed, he thought, time to wake up, time for Clay to hit the road. Then he realized. "No way," he said.

"Get my slippers and my bag," she told him, then she flipped on the light and screeched.

He covered his eyes against the brightness.

"What the hell?" she said.

"Not now." Scanlon peeked out from behind his arm. "It's not for two weeks."

She held a towel under her belly, staring at the two of them, trying to understand. "Party's over," she said calmly, nodding at Clay. "You need to go home." It must be that no one moved because she said, more assertively: "Anarchist. Go!"

Scanlon made a move toward her, his eyes slowly adjusting to the light, his mind slowly processing the towel and the water puddling around her feet.

"You've been smoking pot? Oh my God. Perfect. Just fucking aces."

"But it's *two weeks*!"

She doubled over, grabbing the doorframe. "Owww," she moaned, and Clay was at her side, taking hold of her arm.

"Hee-hee-hee-hoo," he said, which definitely rang a bell for Scanlon, but at the moment he wasn't able to summon all he'd learned in Lamaze class. "Even though your water broke," Clay said, "we should time the contractions."

"I need a—" but another stab cut her off, tears running down her cheeks. "Dry pants. My coat."

The bag was packed. Slippers, okay. A coat. Which one? And he'd intended to fix a few bagels with cream cheese. Some juices. Fruit. A thermos of coffee. "Your water broke," he said, senselessly. He felt paralyzed by the seriousness of the situation. Was there time to do it all? "I'm supposed to have snacks," he said, as he and Clay helped her sit down on the coffee table. "Coach's snacks."

"They should be five minutes apart," Clay offered, almost whispering.

She ripped her arm away from Scanlon and cocked it to elbow him in the jaw. "Do it!" she shouted, then jerked her other arm free and thrust her face inches from his. "Please, what's this guy doing in our house?"

"You might not need to go to the hospital yet." Clay's shoulders dropped apologetically. "I'm just saying."

"Shut up!" Scanlon snapped. "You need to leave." But Clay didn't move. "You've fucked this up enough already," he shouted. "Get the hell out of here."

Water trickled down her leg. The towel was soaked. She took a deep breath. "He's right," she said. "The timer's on the stove," she told Clay. "And stay in the kitchen until I get changed. And you!" She backhanded Scanlon's chest. "Sweatpants. Coat. Bag. Snacks."

Naomi smelled gasoline and thought this might be one of those weird olfactory experiences that comes with labor; she'd smelled pot from the bedroom but mistook it for a combination of the warm amniotic fluid soaking her and the rotting hosta leaves outside their window. She'd been confused by memories of her water breaking seventeen years ago, as bloodhounds can be confused by an unexpected scent slashed across the trail. Scanlon had helped her dry off and get dressed, and now the anarchist propped pillows under her shoulders and back and under her knees, then sat cross-legged on the floor beside her with his thumb on the cooking timer's red button, ready for the next contraction. Up close she saw the dark holes pierced by tight silver loops in his eyebrow and lip. The tattoos of a hovering gull on one side of his neck and "Billy" on the other looked splotchy and crude. Jailhouse tattoos. His skull had a five-o'clock shadow; his lips were chapped, his small teeth square and gray. His black clothes were torn, covered with drawings and silver spray paint. What if her baby boy grew up like this? How do you mother an anarchist?

Scanlon was banging dishes in the kitchen. Still no sign of her suitcase or slippers. "Do you work in a gas station?" she asked Clay.

"Nah." His head twitched. "But sometimes I huff gasoline."

"Oh my fucking Christ. Scanlon!"

"I'm just joking." Clay smiled, exposing a black hole where he was missing a tooth. "Trying to relax you."

Steel fingers gripped her lower back, then a crushing weight dropped on her uterus and pelvis. She groaned and heard the beep as Clay popped on the timer. Scanlon rushed in from the kitchen and kneeled at her side, patting her hair cloyingly.

"Hee-hee-hee-hoo," Clay breathed.

And seeing Scanlon's penis hanging out of his robe—as the contraction tightened around her like a rope—heightened his blame for all of this.

"Hee-hee-hee-hoo."

She tried to follow Clay's coaching and breathe. "Hee—" she eked out, and as both men panted in her face, she recalled that when a boar breathes in a female's face, she reacts to a chemical in his saliva by arching her back, steeling her haunches, and flicking up her tail—a "fixed-action response," no free will involved. She'd once smelled the boar's-breath concoction that's sprayed up the snouts of domestic sows to make them more receptive to artificial insemination.

She smacked Scanlon's hand away. "Get—hee-hoo—dressed!" Closing her eyes, she breathed through the contraction, sweat running down her face.

When it was finally over, Clay said, "Level-two breathing. Deep and steady until the next one, then we'll check the timer. And relax your neck and shoulders."

She was squeezing his hand in a death grip. He had tiny ears, she noticed, tender-looking rosy ears.

Scanlon came through the living room, dressed, and he set her bag by the door.

"You've done this before," she managed to say.

"Just once." Clay looked at his boots. Did his cheeks flush?

She heard running water and dishes clattering in the sink. "What the hell is he doing?"

Clay got up, peered into the kitchen, then came back. "Washing the dishes."

"Leave the goddamned dishes!" she shouted.

"I've got everything ready," he called back. "You just do the timing and let me handle this. You don't bring a baby home to a kitchen full of dirty dishes."

Clay smiled—a sort of sweet smile, somehow. Boyish despite the metal piercing his face. "Nesting," he said.

"How long has it been?"

He looked at the timer. "Four minutes."

She took a deep breath. "Do you have a baby?" The possibility horrified her, but she also felt a warm wave of hope and good faith: We're all in this together, raising the next generation to be better than we are.

"I do," he said, "but listen." He sat back down on the floor. "Your husband out there, he's sort of a lightweight. Pretty wasted. Normally I'd say let him wrap his middle-class car around a tree. Nature wins. There's sort of a . . ." It seemed Clay couldn't find the words for all of society's contradictions and injustices sinking into his gut. "It's this whole dichotomy . . ."

Naomi stared at him, struggling to maintain the generous impulse: Parenting brings out everyone's best, she made herself think. It takes a village.

"But it's not the baby's fault. Yuppie parents and whatnot."

Finally she had to shake her head. "I'm not really following."

"He shouldn't be taking you to the hospital," Clay said. "I think I'd better drive."

For God's sake, he was right. "We'll—" Two daggers stabbed her in the back. "Ahhh!" she howled. "Time?" Her hand clamped down on Clay's. "The time?"

"Four minutes, fifty-six seconds."

Again, the crushing weight. Again, Scanlon at her side saying, "Breathe."

"Hee-hee-hee-hoo," Clay chanted in her other ear.

Scanlon pulled on her arm. "After this one we'll go."

Brutal, punishing pressure. She wanted an epidural, right now.

"I'm driving," Clay said.

Scanlon looked at him like he was crazy. "The hell you are."

"You're too wasted," Clay said. "Hee-hee-hee-hoo."

"I'll handle it from here." Scanlon stood. "Ho-he-he."

"Ahh!" Her uterus clenched up tighter. She touched Scanlon's arm, nodding. "Safer," she said, more air than sound through all the pain.

Scanlon gave her a puzzled look.

"She said it's safer if I drive," Clay said, using hand gestures now to coach her breathing.

"Safe?" Scanlon protested. "A fugitive anarchist?"

She clenched her eyes shut, trying to bear the peak of the contraction, squeezing Clay's hand to the bone and submerging into a painful sea of purple. Far off she heard the men competing as coaches. And then a howl rose toward her, rising faster, gaining strength toward the surface, louder, until she was shaking her head as it surrounded her: a guttural roar from the center of the earth.

After a silent moment she opened her eyes. Her husband and the anarchist were both staring at her, their jaws dropped, their faces white, frightened, and helpless. The contraction had passed. "We should go," she whispered.

They each took an arm and brought her to her feet, then lowered her to the edge of the coffee table. Scanlon draped her coat over her shoulders, saying, "See you later, Clay."

"Okay," Clay said. "One thing. Just gimme a second." He took Scanlon by the wrist and stood him in front of the overstuffed chair. "Then I'll leave." He pointed two fingers and a thumb at Scanlon, reached toward his eyes and drew back, then again, back and forth, like Crocodile Dundee subduing a wild beast. Then he thrust both palms toward his chest, stopping well short of touching him, and Scanlon fell back helplessly into the chair.

"Please," Naomi said, "give him your keys."

Scanlon reached in his pocket, and she believed he knew in his heart that this was the right thing, that only stubborn masculinity and an admirable proprietary impulse had made him resist.

"Hey," Clay said brightly, taking the keys, "could I borrow some clothes? These are kind of dirty for a hospital."

"Forget it," Naomi ordered. "C'mon."

Scanlon sat up on the edge of the chair—"No, he's right"—and exchanged a knowing nod with Clay. "It'll just take a second." They disappeared into the bedroom, leaving Naomi waiting, slumped over on the table, a raincoat draped on her shoulders, completely at their mercy. If the actions of these men endangered her baby, she would cut out their hearts with a bread knife.

When they finally emerged from the bedroom, Clay said, "I look like such an asshole. There's a limit."

Scanlon was pushing him down the hall. "We've gotta go," he barked.

Clay appeared in the living room dressed in Scanlon's clothes—a white turtleneck that covered the tattoos, nearly white khakis, old white tennis shoes, and a red Gap baseball cap that Scanlon's mother had given him and he'd never worn. White supposedly made someone look fatter—and black, more gaunt—but it had the opposite effect on Clay. He looked like a skinny, moping Haverford boy who'd just been cut from JV tennis. The cap brought out the pink in his ears and cheeks. There were still the piercings, but those seemed inconspicuous given the rest of the makeover. "If anyone sees me," he said, "I'll get stomped."

"No anarchists are likely to show up in the maternity ward in the middle of the night," Scanlon said, taking Naomi's arm.

"You said emergency room."

"That's the entrance we use."

"It's not uncommon for a fair number of my friends to visit the ER in the early-morning hours."

Naomi laughed before she realized he wasn't joking. "I appreciate your helping out," she said to Clay, "but we better go. Remember the baby." This was all practice for dealing with toddlers.

Scanlon eased her into the car, helped her with the seat belt, then slid into the backseat with her bag. Clay got behind the wheel, small compared to Scanlon in the driver's seat. As he backed out, Scanlon said, "Careful."

In the street Clay shifted the Honda into drive and hit the gas. "A mean machine," he muttered, smirking into the rearview mirror.

"Eyes on the road," Scanlon said. "And watch out for cops." Sure enough, just then a police car with lights flashing shot down the cross street.

Clay turned at the Stop sign. "I truly was kidding about huffing gas," he said to Naomi. "Anyways, gasoline sucks for huffing."

She gripped her shoulder strap. "That's a comfort," she said, and although she really wasn't worried—it was only a five-minute drive, and Clay seemed perfectly competent—she felt herself suppressing a mother-wolf instinct that fed hormones to her brain compelling her to rip these men apart if anything went wrong. Not knowing whether her first baby was living a life of love and joy and fulfillment was the greatest burden Naomi carried; what she *did* know, the promise she'd made to the baby she was about to meet, was that *he* would be mothered lovingly, exquisitely, and given every chance to flourish.

On the four-lane strip they passed the birdseed store, Goodwill, the credit union, McDonald's, and Starbucks. She looked over at Clay: both hands on the wheel, his gaze fixed on the road. As impossible as it seemed, his gentle voice, his confidence, and even his nervy intensity put her at ease.

Then his face lit up. Ahead, in a snarl of police and fire truck lights, black smoke rose under the lampposts shining down on Timber Ford-Lincoln-Mercury. Clay slowed as they passed, and they all three looked: water spilled over the curb and foam collected on the blacktop around the charred smoking skeletons of three SUVs.

. . .

Scanlon no longer felt stoned; the excitement of the birthing room and the reality of their coming baby cleared away any residual fog. Monitors were attached to Naomi's belly and a fingertip while Clay helped her through a contraction; she finally got an epidural and everything settled down a notch. Many notches. Her face relaxed. Clay sank back in a vinyl La-Z-Boy, and Naomi called Scanlon over, pulled his head down, and kissed him on the lips. "Thank you, sweetheart," she said, scratching his beard.

The nurse came in and checked the monitors. "It could be a while," she said. "You should all get some rest." Then she pointed at Clay, reclined; he knew the drill, knew it was time to relax. "This one's good," she said.

Scanlon sat on the edge of the bed and held Naomi's hand; both he and Clay had visitor's badges stuck to their shirts. His resentment toward Clay for creating a near disaster—husband and wife would have been peacefully resting when her water broke if not for the intruding anarchist—was diminished by his overwhelming relief that it had all turned out okay. *Partially* diminished. "So, Clay," he said, "you're an anarchist furniture mover *and* a Lamaze instructor?"

"He has a baby," Naomi said.

Scanlon looked at her. How did she know? What had he missed?

"I have a little girl. Ruby Christine. She's thirteen months." The room felt suddenly quieter. Tranquil.

Scanlon was about to ask if he saw his daughter much, but he was pretty sure he knew the answer. He squeezed Naomi's hand again, knowing she was thinking about her teenage son, wondering if he had a girlfriend, if he laughed easily, if he had a good nose, if he was loved.

For a time they sat silently in the dimly lit room. Clay and Naomi let their eyes close. Scanlon slouched on the edge of the bed, listening to the monitors. When he laid his hand on Naomi's belly, she opened her eyes a crack, smiled, then closed them again. She'd thanked him. Unbelievable. What an idiot he'd been. He'd known the baby could come two weeks early, and he shouldn't have been smoking in the house anyway. Well, he was done with that. From now on he was a parent, always on call, ready to take charge. His devotion to Naomi and the baby would be complete, tending to their family's every need.

Clay touched his knee. "You can have the chair. I'll hit the lounge till the buses start up."

"Don't let your friends see you looking like a Gap model."

"I'll stop at your house for my clothes."

Scanlon smiled. "I appreciate all your help tonight, but I'm not giving you a key to my house."

"Don't worry," Clay said. "I unlocked the back door before we left."

Super. The baby would come home to a clean kitchen, only there'd be a meth lab in the nursery. "Don't fuck anything up, okay?"

Clay leaned into the bed, looking silently at Naomi, then touching her belly. He'd stepped in as surrogate, as intermediary—the role that Scanlon had cherished. But given the intimacy of the last few hours—the fact that Clay's hands smelled of Naomi's amniotic fluid—Scanlon let the touch pass. He understood he'd been unmanned by Clay this evening, and it wouldn't happen again. He would rise up to meet fatherhood. Just as Naomi hoped the baby would lift her from the loss of her first child, Scanlon would take their baby in his arms and rise above ambition, self-involvement, and ego. Fatherhood would make him a better man.

At the door, Clay turned back. "Lose the beard," he said over his shoulder. And he was gone.

He was the real thing, for sure. A bad attitude and a hooligan. Christ, he'd torched those SUVs. But he was also a father. Although Scanlon didn't yet know the specifics, he'd learned tonight that Clay lived by a code. He'd learned that Clay cared. Scanlon would maintain a critical distance from him, observing, studying, and when he found the right argument, Clay would be his proof.

And then he remembered the fire chief. "Damn," he said. "I'll have to call and cancel."

Naomi raised her eyelids. "What are you talking about? Anyway, it's so late."

"But someone'll answer. It's a fire station. I'll leave a message." And to his surprise, the chief was there. "Our first baby," Scanlon told him, his eyes filling with tears. He remembered the first times he'd heard himself saying, "My wife." The thrill of it.

"Congratulations!" the chief said. "How close is she?"

"I think it'll be a while."

The chief told Scanlon that several of the men who were training to be EMTs hadn't yet observed a birth. Would his wife consider it?

Scanlon held the phone to his chest as he asked.

"Observe?" Naomi said.

"Just some paramedics, I think. It's part of their training. Seems like it'd really help them out."

He almost never slept. Not since he was seventeen. It was one of the things Clay never told anyone, even Daria. He'd lie with her in the dark, anticipating the airy whistle in her nose, off-key and wavery, like everything about her. Watching her sleep night after night, he fell in love because it was then, when she was at peace, that he could see through her skin: fearless principles fueled by anger and sublime vision. All night, while she slept, he talked to her, just as he sang to Ruby Christine when she was still in Daria's womb. If he could talk to Daria like that again, she and their baby would come back to him.

On a couch beside an aquarium, he stared at a muted hospital television—a smoldering Humvee lay on its roof in a roadside ditch near Baghdad—and he drifted off, like a soldier sleeping on his feet, finger on the trigger, and with a gasp he surfaced in an explosion of glass and a rush of air.

Since the night Clay took care of the anarchist from Sacramento, he and Daria were tight. He was living in the park in Portland—he'd kicked around with Daria and her friend Giselle for a few days—and one night he found them in the men's bathroom at Firestone. Giselle was beat up bad. J.J. had done this to other girls—everybody knew he'd put a suburban girl, a weekend anarchist, in the hospital where they wired her jaw shut—so Clay took off and found him with the crowd that hung out by Chinatown. "Bitch should think about who she tells no," was what J.J. said, "or she'll get it again. Her loudmouth friend, too."

Clay went down the alley and saw a porcelain sink next to a dumpster. He grabbed it by the corroded galvanized trap still snaking from the drain, and when he got back to the corner, he broke the sink in two over J.J.'s back. Later, he realized he must have hit him in the neck, because from what he heard, J.J. was living with his parents in Sacramento and shitting into a plastic bag.

On the TV, Iraqi children scavenged sunglasses and a CD from the wreckage.

Naomi and Scanlon. Middle-aged people having their first kid. Twenty years to prepare and they still weren't ready. Clay had gotten Daria off drugs, everything, as soon as the pee stick turned pink, and *he'd* quit, too. And he'd gotten the mover job, selling out for the baby's sake, but what had that accomplished? Ruby Christine was being raised by the same Christian fanatics Daria had fled at age fourteen.

Watching Daria sleep had given him a focus in the dark hours of the night. Her breathing, her pursed lips, her body changing through pregnancy—for Clay, they were like mantras.

A world that would tear Daria and Ruby Christine from him was a world that was wrong. Tonight he and Panama had done a little bit toward making the world right, a world where he could have them back. But tonight was only a start—preparation for the big show.

The morning fog had lifted when Sequoia pedaled by the church, perched on temporary timbers. Yellow caution tape wrapped the building, which was papered with DANGER, KEEP OUT, and PER ORDER signs from every self-important agency in the county. Dilapidated and uninhabitable, it was a genuine eyesore. She glanced at Ron's house. For the moment, until the building had its roof, doors and windows, and a coat of paint, his paramount property value had tanked. She smiled, meanly.

And it would stay in the tank until the caution tape and stop-work orders were torn away and they could begin restoration. Before the rain started, the center would be buzzing with papier-mâché classes for kids, yoga, art shows, poetry nights.

With her staple hammer she pounded a flier to the phone pole at the end of the narrow street leading down to Crazy Eights, then headed back toward the café. The last few months she'd worried the fliers were nothing but a waste of paper. It was always the same sixty people at the meetings, always on the first Thursday of every other month, always the same disagreements. But Scanlon Pratt had made her understand that a good sales job didn't compromise ideals but instead spread the word. And America Sanchez made her realize he was right. There was plenty for everyone to agree on: our forests were clear-cut to benefit other regions of the country; the tax structure was skewed for the rich; religious and corporate interests controlled politics and the press; the military served corporate and religious imperialists; our water and air quality, schools and public services were all in decline. For five years the PNSM, while unanimous on what was wrong, had been deadlocked on what to do about it. But the movement's own new roof and restoration were underway: this morning Hank Trueblood was wrangling in the professor.

When she got back to Skcubrats, Ron Dexter was planted on the front porch reading the paper. Sequoia stapled a flier to the phone pole in front, then went up the steps. Her building—Ron's, that is, the one she wanted to buy—was a tiny one-story bungalow with a covered porch and an eyelid window in the low-slung roof. It had battered fir floors, a stone mantel, dark chunky woodwork, six tables inside and two on the porch.

Ron, too, was a professor. When he moved up to Douglas from LA in the sixties, he'd bought the house for twelve thousand dollars. Around fifteen years ago the street went commercial. Ron initially rented to a hair salon, then to a burrito joint, and finally, seven years ago, to Sequoia. He raised her rent annually, twice backing off a few bucks when she threatened to leave.

And that was another thing about Ron. His wife made soap and sold it at the farmers' market, where she accepted Douglas Dollars, the local currency exchanged for goods and services. Sequoia took them as well at the café, and spent them on massages, her handyman, daycare for Trinity, and the organic farms that supplied her produce. Ron spent his wife's in Skcubrats, *always*, but months when Sequoia came up long on Douglas Dollars and short on U.S. tender, Ron refused them for even a portion of her rent.

From behind his newspaper, as Sequoia slipped past, he said, "This ain't over."

The screen door slapped behind her. Inside, nothing looked right: the tables were pushed too close to the walls, Keiko and Journey hadn't restocked the cookies or juices, bus bins were full, a child's sweater was abandoned under a table. Trinity sat cross-legged in the window seat drawing with crayons, and when Sequoia bent down to kiss her, she covered the drawing with her hands. "Hi, Momma," she said.

Sequoia dropped the fliers beside her daughter and neatened a stack of the *Organic Thymes*. "What're you working on?" she asked.

"Some stuff."

"What kind of stuff?"

Trinity held both hands flat over the drawing. "Art stuff."

Sequoia's heart was racing. Her skin felt brittle, as it did when things were wrong, as brittle as the fog frozen in spiderwebs outside her kitchen window on the coldest winter mornings. She looked toward the counter where Journey was steaming milk, the steamer sputtering, O-rings going bad again. Out the window, in the street, a police car came to a stop and double parked. She was pulling Trinity's hand away from the drawing.

"No, Mommy," Trinity said, fighting her. "I'm not drawing him. I'm *not.*"

Sequoia pried her thin wrists apart—yanking too hard—"I told you to stop!" and then, frightened by the onslaught of her own voice, she looked from the drawing to her daughter, who was staring wide-eyed at the door.

"Uh-oh," Trinity said.

Sequoia looked over her shoulder as Ron fell through the screen door and hit the floor with a thud. Journey yelped. Sequoia rushed over to him—a heap on the floor—and dropped to her knees in the clay shards of a broken bowl, touching his grimacing face. "You're crying," Ron said, his breathing strained, and she wiped her nose, then tasted blood: the shards had cut her palms.

"Damn knees," Ron explained. "Second time they gave out this week. Gotta do the surgery."

And as Sequoia helped him to his feet, his heavy arm across her shoulder, and led him hobbling to a chair, a cop clomped across the porch and came through the door.

Ron cringed, rubbing his elbow.

"Some water?" Sequoia offered.

He winced. "Latte."

"Sequoia Green?" the cop asked.

She'd stained the sleeve of Ron's shirt with her blood.

"A summons," the cop said, then read a litany of her crimes as Trinity drifted within inches of him, enchanted by the weapons and Velcro cases strapped to his belt. When it sounded like he'd exhausted the list, Trinity asked him, "Do you have any stickers?"

The cop slipped a sticker of a gold badge and one of McGruff the Crime Dog from his breast pocket and handed them down to her.

"That latte," Ron said.

The cop flipped through the summons. "Oh, here's one more," he said. "Accessory to a hit-and-run."

Sequoia glanced out the front window at Ron's Volvo, parked at the curb. Its owner straightened and bent his knee like he was ratcheting a rusty lever to make a tennis net taut. "Make it a double, will ya?" he said, wincing.

Trinity patted the police badge to her chest, then held up her drawing—a heart with M-O-M written inside. "See, Momma. It wasn't him," she pleaded. Red marks from Sequoia's grip still burned on her wrists. "I wasn't drawing the broken boy. I wasn't." It was Sequoia's greatest fear: that she was passing her own trauma to her daughter.

Slammed into the purple. Blinding purple pain. "More drugs!" she screamed, and the nurse said, "Not long now," and Scanlon's face hovered above her cooing, "Hee-hee-hee-hoo."

And here finally was her doctor saying, "Good job." Everyone praising Naomi for such a good job. *How about doing yours?* And the wrong thing about her doctor was she wore a fleece jacket that was purple! Maybe plum, they might call it plum, but by any name it was fucking excruciating. "We're pushing now," someone was saying. *Impossible!* she thought. *It won't go. This baby is deformed.* A head like a toaster. Naomi was pushing a four-slice toaster out of her vagina. And there was a disturbance in the back, under the TV. They were filing in. Tall men, broad-shouldered, dark-blue fireman uniforms, identical badges and patches. Then a second row, and she was ignoring her husband and the doctor, their obsequious coaching and praise. *Tongs,* she hoped she screamed. *Use the fucking tongs!* She smelled watery scrambled eggs being wheeled down the hall, Chinese food on her doctor's breath, and, coming off the firemen, chrome polish.

As the hard plastic toaster handles tore her open, she peered through the purple and counted the firemen. One, two, three, four, five, six, seven, eight, nine. Nine bearded firemen, their hands folded in front of their crotches. Cringing. Slumping. Trying to get smaller. *Nine Bearded Firemen.* Every mother Naomi knew was writing a children's book—this could be hers. She looked at her husband. *And one more makes ten.* Then the firemen's faces all changed. One, two, three, four, five, six, seven, eight, nine bearded faces. Four with grins. Five with horror. Pain rushed out. A bump, a slip, then the purple faded and she heard the tiny cry, and she panicked: *Get the baby!* she was trying to say. *Don't let them take the baby!* But Scanlon was gazing at her, his eyes beaming, tears running down his cheeks. Frantic, she reached her arms toward the cry, a wail rising from her throat, then Scanlon stepped aside: her baby in the doctor's hands, now delivered to her. She held his hot body to her chest and put her nose to his shoulder and ear, both of them burrowing. She smelled afterbirth and blood, and searched beneath those smells for his own skin, grown and nourished inside her for these nine months and finally beside her forever. She smelled the beginnings of his whole life, the essence of her boy: the scent of almonds.

Scanlon's hand covered their baby's back. His face pressed close to Naomi's. His beard seemed fuller, transforming him into a very kind lumberjack. Mr. Douglas.

"I love you," he mouthed, pushing slick hair off her face, then kissing her forehead.

She grabbed a pinch of his beard—a fatherly beard—and said, "You're going to win."

Staring into the fridge. Not much in there, when you thought about a married couple, a household. Leftover ziplocked pizza. Jam, dark bread, skim milk, and spicy mustard. Yogurt, eggs, and a jar—he read the label—of wheat germ. Nothing you'd eat. A bowl of leftover spaghetti with green sauce and chunks. Two bottles of beer. Not even beer—ale! No Mountain Dew.

But in the rack on the door there was a carton of Tropicana with extra pulp, the orange pictured on its side sliced down the middle, oozing juice. Clay pulled out the OJ and looked for a little cup but found only a tall glass. He poured out a splash, stopped, then screwed the cap back on the carton and shook it up. Then he poured a quarter glass, bright thick juice rushing through the round mouth. He tipped in a little more, then more, and kept going until the juice was brimming over the lip.

The biggest glass of orange juice he'd ever held. He gulped some down, then raised the glass to feel the excess of it and wandered over to the silver-framed photo on the hallway wall: Naomi in her wedding dress, laughing so hard there were little wrinkles in her nose. He gulped greedily, and a trickle of juice dripped off his chin and ran down his hairless chest. He was completely naked.

There were laugh wrinkles at the corners of her eyes, too. He used to make Daria laugh like that. He wiped the juice off his chest, then wiped his hand on his thigh, listening to the chug and swish of the washing machine. He'd neatly folded the borrowed clothes and placed the stack on top of the hamper. But when he'd grabbed his own clothes from the heap on the bedroom floor, the gasoline stench was too much. So he put everything in the washer with his socks and underwear and extra suds. Goddamn bourgeois comforts.

In the bedroom, on the bureau, there was a photo of Naomi pregnant at the beach, a black bathing suit stretched tight over her belly—seven months at least—and ocean water icy at her ankles, wind blowing those wild kinky curls, Italian-looking sunglasses. She could be a movie star in California, or down in Rio.

He took another big gulp, sucking at the tiny plump sacks of nectar until they popped. So damn sweet and cold. A whole meal. Rich. Staring at the picture, he fingered the bumps of his ribs, his hip bone, and then noticed, propped between a jewelry box and a picture of the two of them, a yellow Kodak envelope. He slipped out the pictures, and when he saw the one on top, his head jerked so sharply that juice splattered on the bureau and down his leg to the floor. Naomi, nude, her hands flat on her belly, posing right here on this spot in front of the bureau. He rattled down his glass. His fingers had gone twitchy. She stared straight into the camera. Clay couldn't stop blinking as he flipped from one picture to the next. Jumbled coils of her hair tickled the bare skin of her shoulders, the tops of her breasts. Her hands lay protectively on her belly, possessively. Through the roll of film her belly grew, casting a darker shadow over the tangle of nearly black hair and her funny, kind of crooked legs.

The washer had long stopped when he chose the most recent, most pregnant, photo. She was turned to the side with one knee forward, hiding what lay between her legs, her arms crossed over her breasts, her long fingers hooked over her shoulders, tangled up in her hair. The other photos, anything more revealing—his heart lagging before each thud—would have been too much.

He slid open a top drawer and pulled out a pair of Scanlon's socks and used them to wipe the juice from his thigh and the floor and the bureau. Then he stuffed the socks back in the drawer and pushed it shut.

PART TWO

Chapter 4

The baby squealed, but Scanlon was already awake. It was six a.m., the first day of classes. He rolled out from under the covers and scooped their swaddled boy from the bassinet, then passed him to Naomi in bed. He was a good eater, every two hours all night. Scanlon opened the shades a few inches and cracked the window, letting in fresh morning air, still cool and smelling of night fog, then he crawled back beside his wife and baby in warm milky sheets.

They called him Sammy. Samuel Gilbert Pratt. They also called him Little Man and Mr. Jiggles. Weirdly, he was born with lots of body hair, lanugo, which Scanlon learned wasn't very unusual, especially for babies who come early. Sammy even had lanugo on his face, and in the delivery room no one had minded the obvious jokes batted around by the firemen about the baby winning the Mr. Douglas contest because they were all so thrilled to be in that place, in that moment, together. For an hour the firemen were their extended family.

Naomi's hair spiraled down the pillows. Scanlon kissed her nose. For most of the last two weeks, she'd left her cotton pajama top unbuttoned, open, available, offering up her astonishing swollen breasts, her plump nipples oozing milk. Sammy's feast. Scanlon had never felt more in love with her—she'd created the gift of their baby—or found her so sexy. "No intercourse for six weeks," the doctor had said, then added, "*At least,*" with a whip-cracking glare at Scanlon, the sort of authoritarianism that made him resent female doctors.

Sammy's head looked tiny compared to her breast. His mouth opened enormously, his spread lips covering half of his face. Bred for sucking, like an aquarium creature suctioned onto the glass. After a few minutes Sammy's face pinkened, the pump in his jaw slowed, then stopped, and Naomi finally popped him off. Head bobbing, milk-drunk, creamy lipped, he collapsed on her shoulder for a belch and a snooze.

By seven, Naomi and the baby were back asleep, and Scanlon had showered and dressed and was sitting at the kitchen table with a mug of coffee and an empty glass of juice, brushing toast crumbs off an article in the *Union-Gazette* about the torched SUVs.

They'd caught one of the perpetrators, an anarchist from Seattle named Panama, who told the police he'd come down to Douglas "to f— with corporate America's stranglehold on the people and the planet." Fair enough, Scanlon thought. The police had chased an accomplice, but Panama wasn't talking. He'd been arraigned and was awaiting trial while the police harassed local anarchists, skateboarders, and Courthouse Square drummers for a lead on the arsonist who got away. Was Scanlon the only person who knew?

He'd been thinking through an article about the futility of certain radical acts. Blowing up airliners put a crimp in an economy—the desired effect—but torching SUVs was little more than an adolescent prank. He wanted to understand if Clay really believed that stuff could change the world, but there'd been no word from him for two weeks, not since taking his parting shot at Scanlon's beard as he left the birthing room.

With Naomi and Sammy still zonked, Scanlon slipped out of the house with his leather satchel—empty except for his newspaper, a tunafish sandwich, and a single page of speaking notes for his first class—and walked the fifteen blocks to campus. Although it was still early, Douglas had undergone an overnight transformation, the lazy summer streets suddenly coming alive with bikes, cars, pickups, and pedestrians, all heading in the same direction as Scanlon.

On Lewis and Clark Boulevard, which ran along the edge of campus, Scanlon passed a funky row of shops selling pizza, smoothies, ice cream, tarot readings, travel, and tattoos. Skcubrats was bustling so he waited in line, peering back toward the ovens, but he didn't see Sequoia. He and Hank hadn't yet rescheduled their meeting, nor had Scanlon's article on micro-secession advanced beyond the initial conception. His entire academic production this summer amounted to ideas floating around his head about a secessionist movement in name only and an anarchist on the lam. Time was slipping away.

The woman behind the counter—a familiar surge of midlife panic pumped up his blood pressure when he realized she was half his age—wore a tapestry skirt tied low around her full hips, revealing a tattoo of a goddess whose wings were spread across the small of her back. He'd heard it said that you knew you were getting old when cops were younger than you. But counter service girls—ice cream, coffee, sandwiches—came first. It had seemed like forever to Scanlon that the girls scooping his ice cream were always a few years older—sixteen or seventeen, with the bodies and secrets of women. When asking for a double scoop he'd try to deepen his voice, and then hand over a crumpled single knowing that to these girls he was a mere child. But after what felt like a century of summers, he rose to their age, flirted over the counter, lingered there, made dates. The girls were as intrigued and shy and playful as he was. And did that period last even a summer? Could he have held court across that glass case of brightly lit ice-cream tubs for more than a season? Half a dozen cones later he was already older than the girls, who looked through him—their eyes flitting to someone just over his shoulder—just as they had when he was a boy. In an instant they grouped him in with their teachers, their fathers, strangers on the bus. Naomi had kindly informed Scanlon that around his fortieth birthday sweat glands throughout his body, inactive until that age, would power up—she swore this was true—and begin producing "old-man smell."

He ordered a coffee and a scone. The tables were full, but he found a spot to stand and sip the strong coffee, still glancing into the kitchen for Sequoia. He filled his mouth with the buttery scone studded with chocolate chips, macadamia nuts, and white raisins. He wasn't sure he'd ever had a real Scottish scone, though he felt certain they were a more sober experience, more austere, something closer to Civil War hardtack, something you might have to bust apart with the stock of your musket before eating. Finally, with no sign of Sequoia, he left.

At the corner, waiting to cross the street, he looked at the tattered and sun-bleached announcements stapled to a phone pole. Bands and drum circles, used mountain bikes, textbooks. A lost chameleon, *8 inches long, green if he's mellow, black if he's freaking. Baby boa constrictors, $60, cute! Join—The Pacific Northwest Secessionist Movement.*

The logging mural in Blodgett Hall looked smaller this morning. The rotunda was full of students, and Scanlon felt that surge of excitement that came with teaching. He climbed the stairs and was turning down the corridor when he heard his name, and through a wave of students he spotted one of his new colleagues, Chuck Patterson, whom he'd met on his campus interview. "You've been up early these mornings," Chuck said with a knowing smile. "The chair mentioned you'd be very prolific this fall."

What the fuck? Scanlon wanted to say. Could they let him teach a class before tightening the thumbscrews?

"I deliver your newspaper. Six a.m."

Scanlon laughed.

"You're on my route."

Scanlon feared this was not a joke. He flashed to what he remembered of Chuck Patterson from the website. Tenured years ago. No book. Doctorate from . . . He couldn't come up with it. "Gets you up and out," he said.

"*Carpe diem* indeed. Christmas break and summer it's fantastic. I'm up at five, and by seven my workday's done."

Definitely not a joke. "Well, thanks," he said, clapping Chuck's arm. "The paper's always right there on the driveway. Smack in the middle. Every morning." His senior colleague, a man who would sit in judgment of him for tenure, promotion, and pay raises, was a paperboy.

The office door beside his was open, and the man at the desk jumped up and shuffled to the doorway, limping. "Ron Dexter," he said.

"Scanlon Pratt."

They shook hands.

"Radical studies?" Ron said.

"And mass movements. You?"

"Good question. I sort of did McCarthyism, then a little red-baiting in the eighties. But mostly now I plow through the surveys, which—not sure they mentioned funding cuts and class size in your interview—have become *completely* unmanageable." He'd added this last bit with perverse delight.

He then shadowed Scanlon into his own office next door. "I always liked this office," he said, limping in. "Those bookcases with the glass doors, savor them. There aren't a lot of niceties here. Nothing like you're used to back east." With his forefinger and thumb, he delicately pinched the tarnished brass knob on a glass door, opened it a crack, and clicked it shut. Then he leaned his elbows on the windowsill. "And this office has the best view in the department." He waved Scanlon over. "You see that?"

He was pointing toward the pool.

"From my office, that tree blocks the line of sight. But from here you've got a clear shot of the pool patio." Ron took a moment to formulate his thought: "I like a woman who looks good wet." He tugged at his wiry gray beard and plopped down in the chair facing the desk. "As you'll discover, Oregon women have bigger breasts. It must have something to do with Oregon corn," he said thoughtfully, "which I'm told is genetically altered."

Scanlon looked at his open door, and Ron read his mind.

"Don't worry," he said. "Nobody cares what I say. They've all written me off." Then he added, "Have a seat."

"Actually," Scanlon said, "I've got some prep to do for my ten o'clock."

"It's the first day," Ron countered. "Hand out the syllabus and let 'em go early." He twisted around in his chair and played with the glass door again. "I tried to move into this office, but Fenton wouldn't let me. What do you think of him?"

"He seems great," Scanlon said.

"He's a cocksucker."

Scanlon's eyes again darted to his open door.

"But sure," Ron went on, "you've got to say that. You *should* say that. You should believe it. Only way to get off on the right foot. But you'll see soon enough."

How did Scanlon always start off with the wrong crowd? As a kid, every time they moved, on the first day of school he somehow attracted the delinquents, the vandals, the bad attitudes, veered toward firecrackers, spit, and the crash of breaking bottles. This pattern dawned on him around junior high, but he seemed unable to do anything about it. On a school trip to Sturbridge Village he'd wanted to join the kids learning to play the fife on the village green, or pouring silver spoons and grooming horses, but soon found himself with a set of twins from New Jersey smoking cigarettes in the Colonial Inn and shoving ketchup and mayonnaise packets into a butter churn and ramming down on them.

"Well," Scanlon said, standing. "It's good meeting you."

Ron tapped a fingernail on the glass in the bookcase, rattling the pane in its delicate wood mullions. "You get used to the meager provisions," he said. "Scrubbing your hands raw with powdered Boraxo under the cold tap. There's no hot water in the whole building. It's like *The Grapes of Wrath*—you just keep going, find a little pleasure where you can. After a few years in this department, the forty-eight hours it takes to send a fax won't seem strange at all."

"I guess I'd better get to work," Scanlon said.

"Okay, I get it." Ron stood up and straightened his trousers, but instead of stepping toward the door he moved to the window. "What you'll notice," he said, "something we can both enjoy is . . ." He waved Scanlon over. "Have a look."

Scanlon didn't move. "No, I really—"

"Scanlon," Ron coaxed. "I just want to show you this one thing."

So again, against his better judgment, he went to the window.

"That red car," Ron said. "A classic. Nineteen fifty-seven Porsche Speedster. Belongs to our devoted chair, Fenton."

"Nice," Scanlon said, in the tone of a conversational closer, pushing back from the window.

Ron took his elbow. "That big tree—"

"You told me. It blocks your view."

"But what do you think of that branch?"

Twenty feet up, the lowest branch on the tree hung out over the parking lot, leafless and covered with moss. "It looks dead," Scanlon offered.

"I figure that's two-thousand dead pounds. And Fenton always parks in that spot on the end. But when that branch comes crashing down . . ." His face, bright and joyful, was lost in fantasy. Finally, he turned away from the window and left. But only a second later, he stuck his head back in. "Maybe I shouldn't have said all that."

"Oh, it's fine," Scanlon said, wondering how this man could have ever survived all the hyperawareness of sexual harassment and student grievances.

"Well, just don't say anything to anybody. If Fenton noticed the dead branch and started parking somewhere else . . ." He shook his head. "Christ. I've been waiting fifteen years for that fucker to fall."

. . .

"I'm a new father," Scanlon told his first class, "so if you see spit-up on my shirt, rest assured it's not my own." The students laughed politely. "We'll study radical action and mass movements in this senior seminar—" his voice caught on "seminar" as he stood at the lectern overlooking thirty mismatched desks, every one occupied "—with a particular focus on secessionism, my current research area."

He put up his first PowerPoint slide: *Whenever any Form of Government becomes destructive . . . it is the Right of the People to alter or to abolish it, and to institute new Government.* Scratching and clicking—pencils, pens, and keyboards. They looked earnest and fresh-faced, healthier than students back east. "Whose quote is this?" he asked.

"Thomas Jefferson?" came tentatively from a woman in the front row. Beside the notebook on her desk, she had a pear, a beautiful, perfect pear with two green leaves curling from the stem.

"And the source?"

"Declaration of Independence."

"Excellent," Scanlon said. "From the founding document of our nation right up to the U.S. support of Kosovo, the United States has demonstrated support in principle for secession." It felt great to be back in the classroom. His first day on tenure track. He didn't care about waiting two days to send a fax. What was the hurry? Fenton was right: they were lucky to be here. The students were eager and handsome. They looked comfortable, like this morning they'd jogged in the old-growth forest and this afternoon they'd paddle the Deschutes. They'd arrived at the classroom door on longboards and roller blades. The engineering students electrified their Razors and parked them outside Blodgett Hall with the mountain bikes and cruisers. No one raced for trains in Douglas, sat in traffic, or burned up their days commuting.

"What are some reasons for which secession might be justified?" he asked, and at that moment he smelled the sweet meat of pear: she'd taken a bite. As students called out answers—"Economic discrimination," "Racial," "Religious," "Moral impasse"—Scanlon stepped around the lectern, the rugged floorboards squeaking, and stood closer to the woman with the pear. She took another bite, and as she made a note she held up the pear as a waiter holds up a tray, as if she were offering it to him. For two months now they'd been eating fruit from their yard—first the berries and figs, then pears, and just this week the early apples. All of it juicy and sweet, all of it in abundance. A warm breeze blew in the wide-open classroom windows, carrying the fragrance of the hemlock tree outside. The woman bit again and sucked at the juice. If it ended up taking them a while to get back to New York, well, this could be a good life.

Naomi taped Sammy's dirty diaper into a ball, shoved it down in the Diaper Genie, and could barely smell the whoosh of extra-sweet baby powder. She'd developed a sinus infection; her nose was stuffed up, and she was taking antibiotics.

And Joey was coming. Scanlon's mother. "To help." Naomi's heart sputtered at the thought. She'd wanted to come for the birth, but Naomi put her foot down. "Come when the baby's a month old," she insisted. They'd called to tell Joey she was pregnant, and the birth, still six months away, seemed far off. "Why don't you stay four or five days?" Naomi offered.

"That's not enough time to bond," Joey protested. "And they're hardly newborns anymore by then."

"They're still plenty new," Naomi noted.

"How about when it's a week old I'll come for three weeks?"

"Four weeks old for a week and a half," Naomi countered.

"Two for two."

Naomi ground her teeth. "Three weeks old, you come for one. Final offer."

"Okay," Joey said with forlorn resignation. "If that's how it has to be. Practically a toddler before I set eyes on it."

Six months later, they made their calls from the delivery room: Naomi's parents, Sam Belknap, Scanlon's father, and, finally, Joey. When she called back an hour later, after making a plane reservation, she said, "I have to stay ten days. It's all they could do. Nonrefundable. And not cheap."

In the hospital bed, with Sammy at her breast and only a few hours old, Naomi had counted out on her fingers the days until her mother-in-law arrived.

And now, nineteen days later, Sammy sleeping on her shoulder, Naomi dusted. She'd done heaps of laundry. She'd taken Sammy to the supermarket to stock up on the cookies and coffee cake that Joey lived on. She ate like an adolescent fantasy. Naomi had surely seen her eat a bite of salmon, maybe even a leaf of lettuce, but her sustenance came from Starbucks muffins, Pepperidge Farm cookies by the bag, her homemade garbage bread (apparently famous among her circle in East Hartford), all washed down with white Russians and mudslides. Joey weighed a hundred pounds, had never exercised in her life, had permanently tanned skin, and was either heroically healthy—a heart that at sixty-eight was just getting started, a body that would scare off cancer with threats of starvation and hostility—or she was one danish away from a massive coronary.

Scanlon's father, Geoff, was a lawyer who'd spent most of his career helping companies evade responsibility for their defective products. "It should've been lucrative," Scanlon told Naomi not long after they met, "but my sense is he wasn't very good at it. Or he was lazy. I'm not sure which. But he'd be at a company for a few years and then he'd tell my mother and me over dinner that we'd be moving on." Scanlon was never sure, even to this day, if his father got fired all those times or just quit.

They lived in one middle-class suburb after another, all pretty much the same. "Doesn't really matter if you're outside Baltimore, Hartford, or Albany. In fact," he told her, "I sometimes get memories mixed up between the houses, the schools, the groups of friends." Naomi believed this occurred more often than he realized. He swore that all on the same day, his parents forgot he had a final championship Little League game and weren't home to drive him so he called neighbors for a ride, but no one stepped up and he had to bike ten miles in blistering heat to the game, arriving in the second inning; that his coach shoved a boy from the other team after a rough collision at home plate, the other coaches running across the field and beating him to a pulp while kids and parents looked on horrified; that the mayor of East Hartford was convicted of embezzlement and their parish priest for flashing old women in the Kmart parking lot; and that a black man, in a case of mistaken identity, was pulled from his car by police on Scanlon's street and clubbed. Naomi had suffered her own memory confusion with anosmia since she seemed to shelve all memories, even those unrelated to smell, in her olfactory library. Third grade was the smell of chalk dust and Twinkies; fourth grade was Mrs. Hubler's thick stockings and her snot on the tissues she tucked under her sleeves; seventh grade was the butter and apricot smell of her own blossoming sexuality; Vermont was mint, creosote, body putty; her lost baby was amniotic fluid and blood. With Scanlon's well-intentioned but average nose, she understood how files might end up scattered on the floor.

During his freshman year of college, his father was working for Virtual-Kombat, a videogame company in Hartford. Their heavily advertised Beirut Blast had some software defects that became apparent only after 800,000 units had been sold. Geoff helped hammer out a deal in which new units were mailed to every customer.

But then Geoff quit his job to handle the class-action suit against Virtual-Kombat for user time lost before the units were replaced. It was never clear to Scanlon whether his father had swiped mailing lists of customers from the company or what other shenanigans might have gone on, but several countersuits were filed. In the end, the class action demanded twelve bucks for each of the 800,000 customers—a total of nearly ten million dollars. The company settled out of court for six million. The army of litigants got checks for three dollars each while Geoff took the customary thirty-three percent. He then told Joey he was divorcing her immediately, and her own lawyer got her a million-dollar settlement. Scanlon's father bought a Winnebago and had been traveling the country ever since. His mother redecorated their East Hartford split-level in a Pottery-Barn-meets-Danish-castle motif. They each had a cool million: the American Dream come true. Scanlon remembered Geoff raising his hands at the wonder of it all. "Everyone wins," he proclaimed without a trace of irony.

Scanlon's relationship with Sam Belknap, Sammy's namesake, provided him with the antidote to his parents. Sam could be crotchety and irreverent, even a scold, but Scanlon was always good to him and he was grateful and showed goodness in return. Naomi had actually wept when she realized it had never occurred to Scanlon to expect any such thing from his parents.

As Scanlon was getting ready to drive to the airport in Portland, Sammy wouldn't stop crying. They'd paced him back and forth in the living room, taken him out to the yard to distract him with leaves and berries, forced a pacifier into his mouth (producing the deafeningly opposite effect), nursed, patted, played Mozart, bounced. "Why don't you two come with me?" Scanlon finally suggested. "The car ride might settle him down."

He called the airline, hoping Joey's plane might be late, and discovered it was running half an hour early. So with dishes she'd planned to wash piled in the sink, a full Diaper Genie she'd planned to empty standing by the door, Naomi buckled her screaming baby into the carrier and snapped the carrier into the hot car—unshowered, hungry, exhausted.

Five minutes out of town, Sammy was snoozing. Naomi was in the backseat, behind Scanlon, and she looked over his shoulder into the rearview mirror, raking her fingers through her hair, wishing she'd thought to grab a brush. Or lipstick. And a shirt. Anything besides her flip-flops, sweatpants, and baggy, faded pink T-shirt with cakey yellowish splatters on both shoulders.

"The teaching was good," Scanlon whispered over the car noise. "Really sharp comments. Very eager. Nice kids, I thought. Polite and deferential."

She rested her head back. Sammy was completely at peace, a tiny nut strapped into the seat. No sign of the hour-long crying fit. She could imagine what he'd look like as a young man—or a boy, anyway. Handsome and bright eyed, a gentle, surprised face. Like his father's. Sammy had the same fierce appetites for food, comfort, sleep. An immediacy to his living, an urgency to his needs. And she loved the tiny birthmark dabbed at the corner of his mouth like a downy pink feather on the face of an exceedingly innocent-looking cat.

"After my second class, Intro to World Politics, a huge lecture class, this eastern Oregon girl, a freshman, tells me she felt lost. *Literally* lost, it turns out: there's more people in the class than her hometown." But he was confident he could make the class work, and his enthusiasm reminded her of those first months with him, how she'd admired his belief in teaching, exposing students to radically new ideas, teaching them to think, making them better—all of this at a time when Naomi felt she'd never accomplish anything again.

"One of the seniors—he's double majoring in poli sci and viticulture—makes pinot noir in his garage. He's going to bring me a few bottles. And not to be outdone, this other guy pipes up, says he's bringing me smoked Chinook." The hum of the road worked into Naomi like a massage. "I didn't think anyone would make the connection to Hume," Scanlon was saying, "but sure enough a hand goes up in the back . . ."

With a jolt, the freeway momentum of her sleep stopped short. The engine was off, creaking as it cooled, and Scanlon's face was close to hers in the parking garage. Sammy snoozed beside her. She'd slept for over an hour. Wiping drool from her chin, she focused her eyes on her husband, then down her shirt where a dark saliva trail wormed around Sammy's creamy spit-up stains. "Do you want to wait here?" Scanlon was saying.

She did. She wanted to sink back to sleep beside her baby. But her bladder was stretched so full she could only take shallow breaths. She peered out the door past Scanlon, wondering if she could relieve herself in the garage. At times like these the clichéd war metaphor for parenting was spot-on: just as spit-polished soldiers train for precisely executed campaigns but end up hungry and stubbly faced, sticking scraps of torn underwear in their ears to keep out the blowing desert sand, mothers dream of walks with the stroller and naps in the sun but find themselves squatting between cars to piss on the grimy cement floor of a parking garage.

She couldn't do it.

"We'll come," she said. "Grab the sling." And with hovercraft smoothness, Scanlon unclipped the baby carrier and hoisted it up without disturbing Sammy's hard-fought slumber. He draped the empty sling around his neck and set off across the pedestrian bridge for the terminal, and Naomi followed, a plastic Safeway bag containing four Huggies and a canister of wet wipes crackling against her face as she picked sleep from her eyes.

Naomi was coming out of the bathroom when she heard Sammy's cry from across the terminal. In a rush her milk let down, two dark, heavy eyes opening wide on the front of her light-pink chest. A statuesque woman—wearing Vera Wang Look and a charcoal-gray suit, a sleek leather bag strapped over one shoulder and colorful bangles chiming as she snapped her cell phone closed—took Naomi's measure then screwed up her cheeks in a sort of smile that Naomi took to mean, *How sweet. Somebody's got to do it. Thank God it's not me.*

Naomi hurried across the expanse of carpet toward Sammy's cry, her flip-flops snapping and her body jiggling under the loose T-shirt and sweats. When would she have her body back? Her head was stuffed up, her boobs were ready to explode, her nipples were chapped. There were whole regions of her body, geographies of flesh, that she'd been piggybacking for some time but had been too exhausted to explore. She could ignore them until they jostled her, like a sweaty fat man with a good punch line slapping her on the back. When had she last showered?

Scanlon handed off the baby—hysterical, a national emergency—and she sat cross-legged at the base of a column and hiked up her shirt, so Sammy could latch on, his cosmic screams collapsing in on themselves, sucked up into a black hole. He nursed in peace, on the bank of the steady stream of arriving passengers, occasionally tugging on her nipple as he craned toward a tinkling silver-belled anklet, a squeaky-wheeled rolly, twin girls shouting, "Daddy!" Scanlon slid the carrier next to her with his foot and leaned back against the column, the quilted sling drooping across his torso.

She wished her own parents were coming down the concourse, but they wouldn't be able to meet Sammy until spring. They were living on an island near Fiji, and getting in and out was a major ordeal involving outrigger canoes, seaplanes, and top-heavy lorries. Her mother, a nurse, helped run a clinic in the village—a two-year job through an NGO, and with rising seas devouring the island, two years might be all the coastal villages had left.

Then she saw Joey, a walking advertisement for outlet malls. Chanel purse, Gucci bag, Yves Saint Laurent scarf—all of it, Naomi was sure, a steal. She thought Joey looked frailer than usual. Thinner, less nimble on her three-inch heels, a dusty cast to her face. But when she saw Scanlon, she brightened and her jeweled hands snapped up to clamp his face. He kissed her on the cheek and she tugged on his beard. "Who can believe the foliage?" she said, meaning the beard, already inspecting Naomi, nursing on the floor with the plastic grocery bag beside her. "Good God," she said to Scanlon. "You look like immigrants."

That frailty, Naomi quickly realized, was only wishful thinking.

"I hope Oregon's not like Israel," Joey said.

Naomi had already heard enough, but Scanlon endured this stuff, practically expected it.

"You're Jewish, Naomi. You've seen this, I'm sure. Tastefully dressed, college-grad-type Americans who happen to be Jewish go off to live in Israel and sail back to their own country looking like babushkas."

There was an announcement for a flight to New York. Had Joey stayed long enough?

"Anyhow, hand over my little boy," Joey said, reaching toward Naomi with both hands, snapping her fingers against her palms like a toddler who wants to be picked up. Or like a crab.

"Even by this age," Joey said, still resentful she wasn't seeing Sammy until he'd aged to a grizzled three and a half weeks, "they're so precious." She was watching a silver-haired man in a business suit straddling a briefcase and thumbing the *Wall Street Journal.* Her hands kept snapping. "Give," she said.

"He's eating," Naomi said.

The man folded up his newspaper and headed off toward the food court.

"You all must be starving," Joey announced.

"Not really," Scanlon said. "Are you, Naomi?"

"No. We should get home."

"Don't worry about me," Joey said. "I'm in no rush. Have a little bite. How far is it?"

"Nearly two hours."

"Good Lord. *I'll* say. Timbuktu."

Sammy was done. Naomi pulled him off and laid him over her shoulder for a burp, and Joey took a few steps back to disassociate herself from the peasants. "The steakhouse," Joey said. "That'll do. Come on, Scanlon. We'll get a table." And she walked off.

"Is that all right with you?" Scanlon asked.

Naomi nodded.

"You want a smoothie?"

"Not hungry."

"Yeah. Me neither."

Down the terminal, they watched Joey veer into the steakhouse. Sammy released a long burp. Naomi wasn't sure why, but both she and Scanlon laughed.

Joey waved to them from a table by the bar. She reached for the baby and Naomi laid him in her arms as the waitress appeared with a White Russian. Shifting Sammy to one side, she received the drink, took a generous taste, and said, "Who wants what?" holding the waitress at the table.

Scanlon shook his head.

"Nothing for me either," Naomi said.

"For God's sake," Joey said to the waitress. "An order of french fries for the table." She took another swallow, then gave her attention to Sammy. "You big bad boy," she said, waving a finger in front of his face. "Oh yes, I saw this in the pictures." She flicked a glued-on nail at the birthmark at the corner of Sammy's mouth. "Well," she said in a tone of remaining positive despite adversity, "it'll fade."

When the fries came, she ordered another drink and pushed the plate across the table. Scanlon ate a few, and after a while, as Joey worked on her drink, Sammy asleep in the crook of his grandmother's arm, Naomi poured ketchup on her bread plate and twirled a french fry in it. "So," Joey said as Naomi took a bite, "how's the weight coming off?"

. . .

For almost three weeks he'd been keeping clear of Douglas, staying in a squat house in Portland with a guy named Speed, another named X, one chick who didn't talk, and another from Duluth who never shut up. "I mean you should've seen it," she repeated for days. "A Winnebago with California plates takes a turn right in front of the streetcar, the old-fashioned kind, vintage, all wood. And it rips that Winnebago open like a sardine can. Like opening up a dollhouse. Their precious fucking Winnebago exposed. I mean, is that the perfect metaphor? These old fucks from California burning petroleum and polluting the air and crashing into a vintage street car, a symbol of some glorious past that's nothing but a myth? I mean, is it fucking perfect?"

Clay nodded, then ate some more tuna out of the dented can.

"There was Miracle Whip, too," she said. "A huge jar on the pavement. Splat."

Clay scooped up tuna with a broken Lorna Doone.

Speed didn't come back to the house for a few nights, and on the third night the girl from Duluth came into the room off the kitchen where Clay was laid out, not sleeping, on the floor between boxes of stolen wire and pipe that turned out not to be copper, old clothes that smelled like the furniture pads stacked at the back of the truck, and a brand-new game of Monopoly. She stood over him with one hand on a coil of the worthless wire, not talking for the first time ever, and pretty soon they were fucking. She had a hard, solid body, and lying on her back she pulled her knees up to her shoulders. Calves and hips with real girth, tits that stayed put, muscular tits, like she spent her life before Portland slinging hay bales onto flatbeds. Afterward, she started to cry. Or maybe she grew up in a city and was just born strong, genetically. He realized he didn't know where Duluth was. Which state.

The next day Speed reappeared, and Clay thought it best to clear out. He had major shit to take care of. He needed a vehicle to get out to Siuslaw Butte. He needed a better plan. So an hour later he was sitting on the backseat of the Greyhound, his head on the window, a curtain of chilled air moving up the glass. He counted his money—down to nothing. He'd go by Mayflower this afternoon and tell them he wanted to work tomorrow. The dispatcher would be pissed off. *Three jobs I was light a guy. You want work, you make yourself available.* But more than likely they'd have something for him. Nobody wanted Saturdays, and there was always a truck rolling in Friday night that got held up at Grant's Pass or Shasta or in traffic through San Francisco or a breakdown. Better tips on a Saturday. They'd give him shit, but they'd hardly mean it. Or they'd mean it and it wouldn't matter. Clay knew he was one of their better movers. They hired the worst sorts of derelicts and drifters. Old guys, hair slicked back with oil that doesn't cover the smell of booze. Shoes with no socks, rattling into the lot on sorry bicycles, late, sweating. They don't eat a thing, just wait to get paid and start sucking down beer. Edmund refused to work with them. Had too many bureaus let go on him halfway up the stairs. Edmund preferred the college kids, hard bodies in Nike T-shirts. But second to them, he usually grabbed Clay.

So this was what he was going home for. No, not home. He never really thought of it as home. Or Yaquina either. The house he'd grown up in was torn down, the whole neighborhood—bungalows full of fishermen's families and boatbuilders, engine mechanics like his dad could've been—was now a golf club, right down to the beach, a private course reserved for Californians living in the new condos surrounding the harbor. Talk about a fucking metaphor. He should have told that one to the girl from Duluth.

A busload of problem kidneys. A constant parade in and out of the toilet and the whole back of the bus reeked of blue chemicals. Living with the crap we make. You swallow your spit all day, Flak liked to say, but spit in a cup and the idea of swallowing it becomes revolting. He thought he should switch seats, but instead turned his face to the window to breathe the circulating air. He doubted he knew anybody in Yaquina anymore. The only reason to go would be to check on Billy. But Clay didn't drive. Driving Naomi to the hospital had been the only time he'd driven in nine years. Cars were part of the problem. And Californians.

No, Douglas wasn't home, but he'd been living there nearly five years. Paid rent. Knew people. Had a crew. Hooked into the network from Arcata on up to Seattle. Nothing you'd call home about his apartment—his room, actually. A single mattress on the floor. Never bought any sheets, so every couple weeks he'd flip the mattress over. No pillowcase either, so he'd put a clean T-shirt over the pillow each night and wear that one the next day. He had a blanket he'd lie under, awake in the dark.

The worst time was when the sounds stopped. He appreciated a frat party that went late, drunks hooting and hollering at two and three and four a.m. Without them, after the midnight Greyhound came in and the 7-

Eleven closed and the bars shut down, besides a few late-night sirens, the hard quiet got inside his head and squeezed. As well as he knew anything, he knew silence: the oppressive weight of all that was not.

There was a friend of Flak's who'd done two tours in Iraq, said he needed noise to sleep. Said quiet was when bad shit happened. Back in Douglas quiet stalked him in his sleep, turning him into a madman. Went to bed with a loaded AR-14 under the blankets, which scared off his girlfriend. He had to reenlist, get back to the chopper base in Baghdad for a decent night's rest.

When Clay drifted off to sleep just before dawn, he'd dream of smashing glass and crunching steel, and he'd wake with a jolt and carry that torment through his day. His mind was pulled down so hard it hurt his neck.

Memories reached toward him like fingers of smoke in the darkness: Ruby Christine in his arms, the warmth of her wound up tight in clean blankets, black eyes rolling like marbles, her magnificent strength, even the nurses said so. And later, with the baby asleep on Daria's chest, Clay was curled in beside them on the hospital bed, crinkly when he moved, and he realized that all the shit of his life—his father going off the deep end, Billy dying, his mother losing it—had led to this moment. If any one thing had been different, he wouldn't be drifting off intoxicated by the warm room and Daria's warm skin, her peaceful face, their baby's randomly flopping arms. Heaven. And he rested his head on Daria's shoulder, closed his eyes, and slept deeply for hours, slept like he hadn't since Billy was killed.

Two days later, Daria and Ruby Christine were gone. Still gone.

The silence wormed in, and not long after it the sound of Ruby Christine's cry inside the house in Idaho. Clay had taken the Greyhound, then walked to Daria's parents' house, a white ranch on a street of white ranches, the dry wind blowing up dust. A big man opened the door. Clay recognized him from a picture and knew he was Daria's father, but hadn't expected the other resemblance—Ruby Christine. "Wait here," he said, and closed the door. On the front steps, Clay leaned on a wrought-iron rail, picking at chips of black paint and blotches of rust with his fingernail. And then he heard the baby cry. A sweet, hungry, healthy demand. That day she was one week old. He closed his eyes, half sat on the rail, and let his daughter's spirit flood him. And he didn't sense anything else until a large hand clamped his upper arm. A cop. Two cops. They put him in a cruiser and then on the Greyhound and waited until the bus pulled out. Clay got off at Walla Walla and went right back. This time he didn't hear his baby, and the cops threw him in jail for the night before shoving him on the bus at dawn.

If hatred and violent yearnings and blinding anger got hold of him at four a.m., they didn't let go for days. He became them. In those times Clay believed in demons, in possession, and hoped he believed in exorcism.

And then he remembered the picture. The photograph of Naomi. Her pregnancy, her arm covering her breasts, embarrassment in her grin. The picture was next to his mattress, propped up against a Mountain Dew bottle. He remembered the dark tan on her legs and arms and how the sunlight coming in their bedroom window wrapped around the white skin of her belly, her eyes looking straight at him.

Through the tinted bus window, across miles of pasture, Mount Hood was out. Llamas grazed beside sheep. Grass-seed fields shimmered electric green under the sun. A few more miles of interstate. He was suddenly excited to get back to his room, to look at the picture. He hadn't felt anything like this in a long time. Anticipation. Urgency.

At dawn, she slipped out of bed and pulled the covers over Trinity. She put her hand to her daughter's forehead. What did Trinity know, and how could she know it? She was born four years after the boy fell, and Sequoia had told her nothing of the details; her daughter had absorbed Sequoia's horror through her skin.

But it would pass. The *Bleigiessen* had been a good omen. Sequoia had done it every year as a girl—a German tradition, her father's, to foretell the coming year—and this past New Year's Eve she'd clacked the hunks of lead into a huge spoon and helped Trinity hold it over a candle flame. As it melted, smoke twisted from the searing murky liquid, and when they tipped the spoon over a bowl the molten lead hit the cold water with an explosive crack, hissing bursts of steam, and Trinity dunked in her hand to retrieve her prophecy. "A sun," she declared. Rays of lead beamed out from the center. "A bright sun that lights up the deep dark and scary."

Sequoia turned the heavy *Bleigiessen* on the nightstand to face Trinity so her sun, glowing under the scarf-draped lamp, would be the first thing she saw when she awoke. Then she closed the door to let her sleep.

At the kitchen table with the water heating, she opened the morning paper straight to the op-ed page. Without even reading the column, she felt a rush of relief: Dawg Declares had weighed in on the church moving.

The police chief, Baxter Hazelton, had come down hard; he'd reprimanded the two cops who'd done nothing but issue tickets at the scene of the crime, he'd accepted all of Ron's complaints, and through statements to the *Union-Gazette* he'd scorned "this group of vigilantes who defied the law and stole a church under the cover of darkness when the good people of Douglas were innocently sleeping."

Hazelton had been elected by mistake. He was the conservative law-and-order candidate running against Stemp Godwin, who'd been chief of police for eighteen years. Every six years a right-winger would be pushed forward to run against him, and every six years he won in a landslide.

But five years ago, Stemp had a stroke two weeks before the election. Even in a coma, he almost won, but after a hand recount Hazelton was declared the winner by fewer than a hundred votes.

Five years later almost no one would admit to having voted for Hazelton, whose incompetence matched his arrogance. He handed out jobs to hunting buddies. He'd been involved in accounting scandals. There'd been talk of a recall, but mostly people were holding their noses and waiting for his term to expire, figuring he couldn't do too much harm.

But now Hazelton pledged to destroy the "hazardous building." He'd heaped on thousands in fines. He said Ron had been "terrorized." He threatened Jim and Pete with prison. He charged everyone in the group with throwing a brick through the Bank of America window.

Dawg Declares was penned twice a month by a woman in her seventies who lived in a converted school bus up among the heavy firs and mossy live oaks of the coast range. Except for right-wing Christians and Humvee drivers—the proud Hazelton supporters—no one questioned her moral authority. Mountain-dweller asceticism, simple unqualified opinions, old age, and good-heartedness earned her enormous respect in the community. Mother Teresa mixed with the Dalai Lama and Yoda. City counselors and citizens alike accepted her evenhanded judgments.

So as Sequoia read the column she was comforted. Dawg declared that this local effort to save a historic church and create a new community center should be "shampooed, brushed, belly-scratched, and given a treat" by one and all. The column ended, "Dawg scolds YOU, Chief Baxter Hazelton: Bad cop. No doughnut." Sequoia believed that the police chief, the railroad and building inspectors, and even Ron Dexter would be shamed into acquiescence.

She was reaching for the phone to call Jim Furdy when she spotted his letter to the editor:

> When we couldn't do it their way,
> we did it the American way.
> Which is to say,
> We did it anyway.
>
> —Jim Furdy, Douglas

Sammy latched on—5:57 a.m.—and while he nursed Naomi drifted toward sleep but was yanked back by Scanlon's heavy breath catching in his throat. She'd had trouble falling asleep last night, partly because Joey was watching Leno on the other side of the wall—though she couldn't make out the words, she'd heard the quick rhythm of Leno's cracks and the audience laughter—but also because she couldn't stop thinking of Sammy's big brother. He'd been "baby" to her until his first birthday, when she named him Joshua. She told no one about the name (all these years later she'd never even told Scanlon), but it had helped transform him from a hospital receiving blanket squirming with lumps of guilt and fearful loss into a child, separate from her.

That separateness felt more defined when she went to France, even more so in Tokyo. Although she felt hollowed out watching Parisian three-year-olds in smart wool coats by the river, then four-year-olds with brothers and sisters climbing up slides in Japanese playgrounds, she was increasingly sure she'd done the right thing.

But when she came back to New York, Joshua's nearness clutched at her like heat. The fear that she'd made an irrevocable mistake returned. Weeks after her father told her the news about Clair and his wife having twins—weeks into her anosmia—anger and a desperate sense of loss took hold of her: Clair had two babies now, and she had none. Night after night she'd come to the conclusion that she wouldn't forgive herself, couldn't *regain* herself, until she held her own child.

When she fell in love with Scanlon, he wanted to wait for the stability of tenure track before contemplating pregnancy; and although it was difficult, she waited. Finally, though, last winter, when it looked like a job would come through, she couldn't wait any longer and intentionally left her diaphragm at home (Scanlon still didn't know she'd left it on purpose) when they went to Cape Cod for Thanksgiving.

Last night, long after Leno had ended, she fell asleep crying. Sammy's birth was supposed to redeem her, supposed to relieve the burden of her loss. But as she nursed him these three weeks, bathed him and changed his diapers, blew between his toes and fished his limbs into onesies, she could summon no forgiveness for herself. Staring eye to eye at Sammy, she was appalled that she'd surrendered Joshua to strangers. How could she have done it? What kind of woman turns away from her baby?

She cried through the two o'clock feeding, then the four. And now, at 6:10, she switched Sammy to the other side, and a pinch in her nipple clawed into her breast. "Christ!" she shouted.

Scanlon shot up. "What is it?"

Sammy started crying.

She tried to get him back on her nipple, but the pain was too intense. "Goddamnit," she said. "This breast infection, whatever the hell it is, it's worse." She was panting from the pain as she tried again to bring Sammy to her, his wailing mouth sucking at the air.

"Just relax," Scanlon said. "Take it easy."

She got Sammy on and he sucked hard, frustrated, and after a moment the pain pulled back. Bearable.

Scanlon was patting her head.

"Fuck," she said. "Something's very wrong." As her milk flowed easier, she let herself relax. She kissed the top of Sammy's head.

"Let's get you into the doctor this morning."

"It's Saturday. I'm not going to urgent care. Those bozos."

"Well, let's just think this through." That tone of his. Would he always be the caretaker?

She kissed Sammy's head again—and gasped. She sniffed his scalp. She sniffed behind his ears for the scent of almonds. Her heart thumped. He reared back howling from her breast. Her neck and shoulders clenched as if claws were ripping at her flesh. She blew her nose into the sheet and lurched at Scanlon, trying to smell his breath: blank.

Scanlon felt her spiraling down. He'd seen it before. She sat sobbing at the kitchen table, clutching the phone while he rubbed her shoulders. His mother rocked Sammy in the living room, but he was crying, hungry, and Scanlon knew Naomi couldn't handle him right now. She'd called her ENT in New York, and her New York allergist and OB/GYN, but got their weekend services, and no one had called back. Sammy wailed.

"Bring me the baby," she said.

"Let my mother bounce him a little," Scanlon suggested. "Just to settle him down."

"Joey!" Naomi called, then blew her nose and took Sammy into her arms.

When his gaping mouth found the nipple, he was silenced, like a soundproof door had whooshed shut. Naomi winced, and Scanlon saw it all: she was crashing. Anxiety had gotten on top of her again. Exhaustion had allowed the demon to tighten his grip, and now it was riding her to the ground. The best thing he could do was to not let her surrender. To keep her moving. In those early days, before they'd zeroed in on the right antidepressant, the right dose, he'd bring her coffee in bed, then pull her to her feet and button her shirt and get her out for the farmers' market or a weekday matinee.

He held out a tissue and tried to sound cheerful. "See if you can blow a little more."

Sammy jerked away from her breast with a howl. "Damnit," Naomi muttered. She moved him to the other side and he screamed louder in between dry, aggravated smacks.

"Let's go outside," Scanlon said over his cries. "Come on," he insisted, taking Sammy from her arms. "Get dressed. Now. We'll take the cell." And after half an hour of pandemonium—the baby inconsolable, Naomi spiraling downward even as Scanlon helped her dress, Joey chasing her around the house with cayenne pepper saying, "Just one snort, they've done studies"—he was lifting a sleeping Sammy, who'd conked out on the short drive downtown, from his car seat into the stroller, and they were walking in the sunshine down Lewis and Clark Boulevard to the sesquicentennial celebration.

"I think the registration for Mr. Douglas is by the library," he murmured. Still not a peep from inside the covered stroller. "Do you want to come with me?"

"I'll wait," Naomi said, pointing to the benches surrounding the fountain in the park.

"How about a coffee?" Scanlon asked. "A little caffeine to jumpstart your nose."

She was watching two teenage boys on stilts, videoing each other with their phones.

"It'll come back," he said, with no idea if he believed it.

"Sinus surgery cured Jill's vertigo," Joey said. "That plus the hysterectomy. And daily doses of cayenne."

"It's just a freak thing," Scanlon said, his hand at the small of Naomi's back.

She squeezed the bridge of her nose. "It's the sinus infection. And maybe the antibiotics. Has to be."

"It'll pass," Scanlon said. "And in the meantime . . ." He started to say he'd be her nose again, but thought better of it. "How about that coffee?"

"Black," Naomi said glumly.

"Five minutes," he told her.

"Thanks," she said, and kissed his cheek and pushed the stroller into the park.

Joey gripped his arm, dramatically. "Do you have a halfway decent day spa in this town?" She gave him a conspiratorial nod. "That girl's a stress ball."

She was probably right, although Scanlon would never admit that to his mother. For Naomi, getting her nose back in this new place full of new smells was every bit as disorienting as losing it had been: for nine years a drought-stricken swath had cut through her world, and suddenly it was flooded. Plus a baby. She didn't have the resilience.

They passed the beer garden and food stalls, enchiladas and pad Thai, elephant ears from the Women's Service Organization, Lions Club hot dogs, wine tastings, Give Pizza Chance. All summer Douglas had been lousy with festivals. Every other weekend the streets were closed and the park filled up with booths selling black walnut cutting boards, tie-dyed onesies, pottery, hand-blown glass, redwood-burl yoga stands and gun racks, rusty old saw blades with messages stamped out in the metal: *Welcome, God Bless USA, Old Fart.* Bandstands were erected, drum circles formed. Today, an artist was sculpting a beaver from a truckload of wet sand dumped in the middle of the street, kids with flowers and flags painted on their cheeks were watching Waldorf School puppet shows, City Skippers jumping rope to "Crocodile Rock," and Uni-dykes, a lesbian unicycle club, trick pedaling in formation. When Joey set her eyes on the acre of loot, she peeled off with barely a nod.

At the registration table he wrote his thirty-dollar check and was given in return a two-page list of tomorrow's events, *Amateur Division* printed at the top. He hadn't said amateur; she'd simply known. A blunt verdict on his attempt at going native.

Reading the list as he wandered back toward the food stalls, still unsure what "slow-chop" was, he looked up and saw the Skcubrats booth and, behind the counter with sun in her hair, Sequoia. It had been nearly two months since the PNSM meeting, and with all the excitement of the baby and the new term, despite a few visits to the café, he hadn't seen her since.

Under her Skcubrats banner hung a dozen signs, hand painted with rainbows and clouds, offering coffee, tempeh burgers, and tofu pancakes. Also, "Two sugars & hold the human suffering," "The official brew of PNSM," "Dine with dignity," "Douglas Dollars Accepted," "Donate here for Franklin Park Neighborhood Center," "We Apologize to You & Mother Earth: the county health department requires that we use high-detergent, antibacterial soaps."

Next to the hot griddle, Sequoia mixed batter with a long wooden spoon while her helper took orders and money at the counter. A little girl with dreadlocks was finger-painting at a child-sized table in back.

Long strands of dirty-blond hair hung in Sequoia's eyes. She seemed a little dirty all over; not unappealingly, not at all, but like she'd rolled out of bed and skipped a shower. As she dipped a ladle into the huge bowl and tipped out circles of batter, their edges sizzling on the griddle, Scanlon called her name. She lifted her face to him, pushing aside her hair and leaving a smear of batter on her cheek. She stared at him for a moment—inquisitive, confused, stoned looking—before her face brightened and her radiant smile lit up.

"Scanlon Pratt," she almost sang. "I've been hoping I'd see you around. How's the baby? How's tricks?"

She was wearing a short, tie-dyed T-shirt showing lots of belly, a long hempy-looking skirt, and sandals. She had big feet, dirty toes. She flipped a row of pancakes, then slapped two on a paper plate and moved toward him. Her long limbs easy and loose, she seemed disjointed yet somehow graceful: everything ended up in exactly the right place, though he couldn't follow how it all got there.

"Amazing," he said. "Beautiful. Three weeks old."

"Hank was sorry you guys couldn't connect." She handed him the plate.

"Me too."

"You're coming to the meeting, right? Next week."

He hadn't noticed the thin, feline scar on her lip. "Of course I'll be there."

"Maybe you'll have some good ideas for us," she said. "Strategies."

"I hope so."

"Like a new name. I was talking about that with Hank. You're so right about PNSM." In a long silence she took a deep breath, her astounding breasts rising, floating, then settling back. She smiled. "How's your wife?"

"Great. She's loving every minute."

"Really? I had the sense . . . I don't know . . ." And as her green eyes softened, he found himself telling her about Naomi's newly recovered sense of smell abruptly abandoning her this morning. He spilled out the whole story—antidepressants, erratic moods, painful nipples—and as he spoke, her warm griddle cakes heavy in his hand, Sequoia's face was vibrant, her body strong. She was effervescently healthy.

"Give her this," she said, and poured a cup of tea. "And she needs to call my friend Angel for acupuncture." She wrote a phone number on a paper napkin and handed it to him.

He looked over his shoulder at the line of customers and reached for his wallet.

"No, no," she insisted. "What's mine is yours." And then she turned back to the griddle—her blond hair gathered into a messy ponytail, the tip at the small of her back dyed dark brown.

Sequoia. Built like a tree: sturdy, lush, limby. He imagined a sticky sap smell in her hair and skin. He imagined her swaying in a powerful wind. He imagined hiding in her branches, the tickle of her aromatic needles.

Approaching the bench by the fountain he saw Naomi sitting with her legs crossed sharply away from Joey, who was lecturing the back of her shoulder. Spotting him, she raised her hands in exasperation. He'd been gone a long time.

"Tofu pancakes." He smiled, hefting the plate. "I've never even heard of them, but they're very substantial. Sort of malty. Like bark, or potting soil."

He shook his head. "Not bad, though. Just earthy. Like a staple for the Aztecs."

"I need to find a bathroom," Naomi told him.

He handed her the cup of tea and the napkin with the phone number.

She took a sip. "This isn't coffee."

"Remember Sequoia? I hope you don't mind I told her about your—" he glanced at the pancakes, then back at Naomi "—situation. She was very sympathetic. Acupuncture and this tea, she said." He twirled a piece of pancake in a puddle of thick honey.

Naomi reached toward a garbage can with the tea, but then stopped and took another sip.

"So I'm telling you," Joey cut in, taking hold of her wrist, "a mother should—"

"Sammy's going to wake up any minute," Naomi said. "Rock him, okay? And I'll feed him when I get back."

Scanlon offered a bite of pancake on his plastic fork. "Taste?"

Naomi shook off Joey's grip. "All yours," she told him, and walked off.

"I was trying to tell her," Joey said, "you should let the baby have some space. A little breathing room. She shouldn't be carrying him around like that all the time. He'll get dependent."

He peeked under the hood of the stroller: Sammy looked tiny in his blue skullcap. "Tofu pancake?" he said, offering his mother the fork.

She turned away. "Good God, Scanlon."

He ate a sweet mouthful dripping with too much honey; he hadn't realized how hungry he was until Sequoia laid the plate in his hands. He hadn't eaten all day—from six to ten this morning had been all Naomi. He'd let himself believe over the last couple of months that these crises were winding down, that a perfect baby and a nose back on line would be enough to let her just live for a while. Maybe still, he hoped. Maybe he could lead her back.

He and Joey looked over to the edge of the park, where with a long screech of brakes a vehicle creaked and teetered to a stop. It was either an old school bus that had been converted into a camper—a silver Airstream bubble at the back, RV fiberglass clapboards on one side—or an RV that had been patched up with pieces of a school bus. A crooked stovepipe stuck out of a window and elbowed above the blue tarp stretched and tied down on the roof. Some parts were painted purple, others yellow. Plastic toys were rubber-cemented to the hood. It looked like the home of a mad Australian living on dingo meat and lizards in the outback. Was the Northwest where all the nation's derelict buses ended up?

"So, Oregon," Joey said, still pronouncing it wrong. Scanlon had corrected her several times but was giving up. "It's like—" she looked out over the crowded park, scrunching up her face "—like they're stuck in the sixties. Hippie-dippy." Not quite satisfied, she added, "But also ticky-tacky. A certain refinement, the sophistication we take for granted in New England, is sort of—" her voice rose up in the teenage affectation she'd recently adopted "—lacking."

"Well," Scanlon began. He was about to explain the radical tradition in the Pacific Northwest; the competing interests of loggers, fishermen, and environmentalists; the direct line between pioneer spirit and libertarian politics. He wanted to celebrate a truly middle-class town, where there were more people *in* the July Fourth parade than watching because every kid was riding his bike down Lewis and Clark Boulevard to the cheers of his grandparents and aunts and uncles. True populism. He thought he could explain the pleasures of a college town, like the retired poli sci professor who'd taken up furniture making: the home of every faculty member Scanlon had visited was graced with tables and bookshelves that the emeritus professor had crafted from local black walnut, alder, and oak; all across town, over his Nakashima-style dining tables daughters were telling their professor parents they were getting engaged, at his hand-planed desks essays and monographs were being written, in his Mission beds babies were being conceived (and affairs conducted). But instead, tired of his mother and resenting her for heaping stress onto Naomi's plate, he said, "Not everyone wants to stay in East Hartford keeping track of how many invitations they get to Charter Oak Country Club for the leg-of-lamb buffet."

"Don't get snide with me," she said. "Your father and I *lived* through the sixties. The *first* time. I did yoga when *that* first started. You kids have this romantic image, but let me tell you—*everyone* was on drugs. It's a wonder the country pulled through. Lots of our friends moved to Berkeley. One lovely couple—he had a very good accounting job—moved to Tangiers, for God's sake."

She held up her hands to examine her rings in the sunlight. "We knew three couples who moved out to Berkeley," she said, "and they all got divorced. One man overdosed. One came back to New York and joined Bank of America's corporate-training program. He was the *only* one who didn't get arrested at some point or another, and I'll have you know he's presently executive vice president of the Charter Oak Country Club. Two rapes, three abortions, and the only one still living in Berkeley either works undercover for the FBI or he actually *is* a poet."

The plastic door slammed shut, and Naomi stood outside the Porta-Potties on the edge of the park taking deep breaths. Nothing had ever smelled so good: sun-heated plastic, blue chemicals, and human waste. She stuck her nose in the cup and sniffed Sequoia's tea, discerning cloves, cardamom, cinnamon bark, anise, ginger, and lemongrass. There was more. Orange peel? Pepper? She laughed. It was cayenne. Maybe Joey was right.

Her nose had begun to come back even before Scanlon gave her the tea. She'd smelled her own skin, her body, as she warmed in the sun on the bench, and when Joey sat down there was the scent of dry-cleaning fluid on her blouse. But when she stuck her nose in the tea—a blend she didn't know—she let herself believe it was really happening. Thank God.

Beside the Porta-Potties in a grove of huge trees, college-age women were buckling on harnesses and hoisting themselves on colorful lines up into the branches. *Free Skool—Treesitting 101* was spray-painted on a bedsheet strung between two trees. The women swung overhead, weightless, burdenless. Nothing to Naomi had ever seemed so free.

When she returned to the bench, she reached into the diaper bag for her wallet but pulled out the camera instead. She dug deeper, whispering to Scanlon, "I'm getting a drink," and as soon as Sammy heard her voice, his tiny cry proclaimed famine. She dropped both wallet and camera back in the bag and wiggled him out of the carrier, Sammy squeezing his eyes shut against the sun and stretching his mouth wide as a bullhorn. Cooing, Naomi slid onto the bench and hiked up her shirt, the sudden pinch of pain eased by the scent of almonds and her milk.

"Of course in my day, nursing was a radical act," Joey declared. "I nursed Scanlon despite the doctor telling me I was probably doing more harm than good. And he was a *ferocious* eater." Joey eyed her son, smiling with a creepy flirtatiousness. "Insatiable."

"Why don't you and Scanlon stroll around the festival for a while?"

Naomi said. All she wanted right now was to be alone with her baby, to smell and to nurse.

Joey shifted closer to her. "Lemme tell you a few things about nursing."

"Let's go, Ma," Scanlon said. "We'll buy you some pottery. No sales tax out here."

Now she leaned her shoulder into Naomi's. She toyed with the cloisonné pendant at her throat, pretending to whisper but speaking loud enough for Scanlon to hear. "Apropos of nursing, I've observed that Scanlon has always been drawn to women with a bosom."

"Cut it, Ma," he called.

It was a fact, Naomi knew, that women were more sexually inclined when they were ovulating, and that men were aroused by ovulating women; lap dancers' tips increased by ninety-two percent during ovulation. It was also a fact that women were aroused by the smell of another woman nursing. Joey always made sexually inappropriate remarks to Scanlon. *Always.* When they danced together at the wedding, his mother cocked back her head and stared into his face with the freaky grin of a virgin bursting with desire. The possibility that Naomi's nursing was stoking any of this in Joey made her squirm.

"I'd like to buy you a negligee," Joey said. "This can be an exciting time in a marriage, despite the —"

"C'mon," Scanlon said, pulling her off the bench. "Let's go."

"We'll have a spa day, then we'll each get something," Joey persisted. "I noticed JP's PJs downtown."

"Now," Scanlon ordered, "or I'll sell you to the hippies on that bus to keep as a pet." He pulled his mother to her feet. "We'll give you fifteen minutes or so," he told Naomi.

"Make it half an hour." Naomi smiled, and they walked off.

It would be worth taking Joey to that store, if only to confirm her suspicions about Douglas. JP Lutz was the young bride of Harold Minor, a senior member of Scanlon's department. She'd been his grad student at UCLA, where he did not land tenure but landed a wife. She followed him up to Douglas, where she spent a decade failing to finish her dissertation on Taiwan. Since then she'd played at being a travel agent, a sourdough-bread maker, and a landscape designer, and for the last five years she'd owned and operated JP's PJs. Despite her academic career coming to a screeching halt, she talked the talk, managing to work phrases like "a rubric that repurposes ambivalent tropes" into a discussion with Naomi about the quality of Lands' End bath towels while they nibbled Trader Joe's mini quiches piping hot from the microwave in Cebert Fenton's living room.

Joey would find no negligees at JP's PJs. Only flannel pajamas, bathrobes, fleece slippers. The anti–Victoria's Secret. Or, as Naomi had said one day when she and Scanlon walked by the store: "The latest in nighttime fashion from Manitoba."

JP Lutz was a trailing spouse.

She switched Sammy to her other breast, gritting her teeth when his mouth took hold. For his sake, she'd begin taking better care of herself. Anosmia was no longer an option. Use it or lose it, people in the industry said, referring to acuity, but for Naomi the implications were more dire. Her nose, the breast infections, her career, and her spirits were intertwined, and she had to give herself over to all of them in order to be the most vibrant, healthy, fulfilled, and loving mother possible.

The sidewalks and pathways between craft stalls were getting more crowded. Foot traffic bottlenecked. Balloons, pinwheels, Cat in the Hat hats. From across the park she heard a marimba band poink out the first notes of a song. A woman at least ten years younger than Naomi, lugging a crying toddler on her right hip while her sobbing preschooler hung on her left arm, pushed a double stroller in which a black lab was curled up asleep.

More marimba players joined in, the music louder and more frenetic as Sammy opened his eyes and turned his head to look up at her, tugging on her nipple. She smiled and touched his head, then pried the lid off the tea cup, twirled the cool dregs, and sniffed. Orange peel, yes, and behind the cayenne was roasted chicory. Burnt. Her nose was as good as ever. She was ecstatic. Then, looking up over the heads of the fairgoers, over blue and white and green tents, she saw a figure dressed in black rise up into the air on a red nylon rope. He tugged the rope and rose higher, his feet dangling, his buttocks and groin riding in the black harness. He pulled again, and she followed his ropes up to the quivering branch of a black walnut tree towering over the park. The marimba music swelled—a happy, frenzied sound of heat and sweat and brightly colored robes—a tug-tug at her nipple. And suspended far above the fair, after another tug on the ropes, was Clay.

. . .

"That's good. That's very good," Sequoia said as Trinity held up the picture she'd drawn: the view over the food stalls and the bandstand to the Cascades, where fresh snow covered the Sisters, brightening the perfect rectangles of clear-cuts patching the foothills.

By mid-afternoon, Trinity was getting antsy and Sequoia, bone tired, still had to run by the café to do receipts. In a few minutes Journey would show up, and she and Keiko would handle the booth until it closed at eight.

"Can we get my face painted now?" Trinity asked.

"Just a few minutes, sweetheart. You've been very patient." And as soon as she said it, Journey appeared, tying on her apron.

On the grass behind the booth, she gave Trinity some milk and Journey brought her a tempeh burger and a cup of honey lemonade. She lay back, sipping the drink and smoothing her daughter's hair, then heard his voice: Scanlon was at the counter, taking change from Keiko and pouring cream in his coffee.

"I didn't see you there," Sequoia said, coming around front. "All day at the fair?" She liked the nappy beard. He was handsome, in a professorish, normal-haircut, pleated-khaki-shorts way. She'd always liked a man in glasses. If she'd been his student, she would've had a crush on him. Not the sort of thing she'd ever act on, but sitting in his class she would have allowed the power of his intellect, sexuality, and authority to slip through her skin.

"The baby's been sleeping," he said. "I think it's good for him to be out in the air."

He'll be a wonderful father, she thought. The right balance of idealism and practicality, of providing shelter and caring for his child's heart, nurturing both the mind and body. Her own parents loved her, but when it mattered most, in their all-out rally to protect her, they'd lost sight of what she truly needed. A day after she confessed and the boy's father split open her lip, she was on a plane for Zurich and then installed on the eighth floor of the St. Sebastian Hotel, consumed with grief for the boy who'd been entrusted to her care and now, in critical condition, lay in a hospital bed. It was completely her fault. From the hotel window she couldn't even see down to the street—just hundreds of rooftops as jutted and steep as the Alps behind them—and by the time her father's lawyer called to say a return ticket was waiting for her at the front desk—that the situation had been handled—this might as well have been an asylum. She'd entered a dark period from which she didn't emerge until she failed to graduate from the private school she loved in Portland, until she changed her name from Marcia Beckmann to Sequoia Green, until she left her parents' home and discovered that we heal not through the mind but through the body. She joined the secessionists the month Trinity was born, and the two brought meaning back to her life. She'd still been waiting for the last piece, but now it had appeared—Scanlon Pratt, who would bring the movement to fruition.

"A little better," he was saying about his wife. "I think your tea might've helped."

"I know every doula and midwife and nursing coach in town," she said. "Let her know. I'll hook her up."

"Sometimes I think she just needs to relax." He looked away when he said it, down at the ground.

"How about you?" she asked. "This has to be stressful."

"Somebody's gotta stay strong." He laughed nervously, and Sequoia saw his face and shoulders tighten—his body revealing what his words withheld.

"I can hook you up too," she said, then hugged him and pressed a warm tempeh burger into his hands.

Scanlon headed back to the patch of shade where he'd left Naomi and Sammy, his heart beating a little faster from the hug. The tempeh burger tasted pretty good.

Sammy's head was bobbing with the rhythm of his sucking, his eyes closed. Naomi gave a tired smile. "Joey?" she asked.

"Couldn't find her." At the sound of his voice, Sammy's eyes opened and he twisted his pink head away from Naomi's breast for a blurry look at his father.

"You want a bite?" Scanlon asked.

Naomi inspected the half-eaten burger, the green tempeh bleeding into the brown bun. "Didn't you hear?" she whispered, deadpan. "Soylent green is made from people."

"You've cheered up." He leaned over Sammy and kissed her cheek. "Your nose is back."

She smiled, nodding.

"For good this time," he said.

"I need to make sure of it. Plenty of sleep. No more colds. And these pollens—I've got to figure that out. There's gonna be some changes." The last bit sounded like a threat, which seemed ungracious given his round-the-clock nursing.

"Sequoia offered her extensive connections to the Douglas alternative-medicine scene."

"You've been seeing a lot of that girl." Naomi rested Sammy on her shoulder and patted his back.

"She wants to help. She's got a big heart. Her little girl was there."

Naomi's mind had wandered, and they were silent for a minute. Then Sammy burped. "Hey," she said. "I saw your anarchist."

"Clay?"

"The one and only."

"What did he say?"

"He didn't see me. He was on the other side of the park, climbing trees with the Free Skool people."

"Let's go look," he said, feeling the return of his excitement—a rev that Naomi had dragged down with her threatening tone and, even worse, her unwillingness to share the relief and glee that her nose was back. An emotional stinginess.

He dodged fairgoers with the stroller and cut a path for Naomi, who followed with Sammy in the sling. He led her by several strides as he passed a candle maker, then spotted the Free Skool banner and ropes hanging from the trees. He scanned the area, rattling the stroller over the grass. Finally, deep in the grove, he saw Clay and another guy sitting on the back of a park bench, their four black boots lined up on the seat. Clay caught sight of him, and Scanlon held up, waiting for Naomi, then they both walked into the shade. The two anarchists stood up and turned their backs, practically whispering. But these were the conversations Scanlon needed to hear. What motivated these guys? Did they know anything about the *history* of anarchy? Where did they feel they fit into the tradition? Or did they think about stuff like that at all? Were they just hooligans?

The other one walked off and Clay turned, standing on a root as Naomi and Scanlon approached. "Make any purchases?" Clay asked. "A unique little something to brighten the home?"

"Hi, Clay," Naomi said sweetly, and Clay's pose fell away as fast as a dagger dropped from his hand. "You want to meet Sammy?" She lifted the swaddling blanket.

Their baby was beautiful, Scanlon thought, looking at his old-man face with his pushed-in chin, Naomi's dark complexion, his blistered upper lip, eager eyes, and bushy wild hair.

Clay leaned in. "Hey, Sammy," he said, apparently as riveted by the sight of their baby as Scanlon was.

There was a long, intimate silence, and Scanlon flashed on Clay's hand touching Naomi's belly in the hospital. "We're gonna have two more," he blurted. "Davis and Junior."

"Thanks again for all your help that night," Naomi said.

Clay nodded, forcing his hands in his pockets. His head twitched. Then he turned to the side and spit. "Good to see you," he said, and backed away.

"Hey," Scanlon called. "We've got the barbecue fired up if you want to come by sometime."

Clay threw back his head, and they watched him scuff off through the trees.

It began with Scanlon's stomach making a quarter turn, like the barrel tumblers his neighbors used for compost, and by eight o'clock that night he was doubled over on the toilet. While his wife gave their son a bath, fed him, sang lullabies, put him to sleep, he was remembering Sequoia's squinty green eyes and stunning smile, the feeling of her body against his, her breasts like pillows beneath her thin cotton shirt, the smell of sesame oil and tempeh in her hair—and to be clutching his gut while tofu and tempeh cramps reduced him to a degrading hour of stink and waste was clearly his just deserts.

After an hour of misery, the god who still reigned over lapsed Catholics decided Scanlon had paid his penance for lust in his heart. Naomi showered, then he did too. Joey had gone out. She'd met a man at the festival, both of them admiring handcrafted glass bowls, Joey pulling a line Scanlon had heard countless times. Pointing at the price tag, she made a show of biting her lip and said, "Your taste is exquisite." And this stranger, a widower, a retired professor from the school of pharmacy, invited her for a drink at the Grotto, where a jazz combo was playing in the wine bar.

In bed, while Sammy nursed, Scanlon read with a mini light clipped to Leavitt's study of secessionist movements, a book he'd cited in his dissertation but hadn't looked at since. Once, after a conference panel, he tried to talk to Leavitt, a Yale prima donna, who promptly blew him off. Later, he looked up the Tillman argument Leavitt had referenced in his talk and confirmed that he had in fact, as Scanlon had been trying to tell him, been wrong.

Draped over Naomi's shoulder, Sammy burped. Scanlon put down his book, swaddled him tight, and laid him in the bassinet. They adjusted pillows and blankets, then Naomi opened a window and went into the bathroom. When she came back, she re-tucked Sammy's fleece blankets and lay on her side next to Scanlon, pulling the comforter up to their ears, their foreheads and knees touching. He felt like it had been a day of heavy lifting. "How could a nine-pounder completely pummel two healthy adults?" he whispered.

"The ninety-pounder isn't helping any," Naomi said.

Joey had put on a blue cocktail dress and too much jewelry for Douglas. Scanlon had told her she didn't need to bring anything so fancy, that jeans, a few shirts, and fleece for the evening would serve her well, but she'd gone out with glass beads clicking on the fringe of her shawl, wafting perfume she'd nicked from Naomi.

"She'll be surprised," Naomi had said, "when the jazz combo turns out to be a couple of hillbillies playing the spoons and a saw."

Scanlon couldn't help thinking that Naomi herself was missing the point of Douglas, missing the real character of the town. With her nose back—the thing she'd wanted so desperately for nine years—it bewildered him that she could still be so negative.

"Rachel called while you were in the shower," she said now. "They were in a cab heading down to the Blue Note for Jimmy Scott." Her lips were inches from Scanlon's, but her voice was faint. "A midnight set in New York seems about as far from our lives as a can-can show in Paris with F. Scott and Zelda."

They'd only been here two months. She was sabotaging their lives; she wouldn't give the place a chance.

He spoke to the ceiling. "I wish you hadn't told my mother about getting the down payment money from your parents." Joey had expressed her profound shock at Douglas real estate values, confounded that anyone would shell out East Hartford prices *here,* and that's when Naomi had mentioned the money. "I really didn't want anyone to know," Scanlon said. "No one needs to know." It was a point of pride, and hearing Naomi toss it off so casually felt like a betrayal.

"Fine," she said. "Sorry."

They lay in silence for a few minutes, then Scanlon asked, "How're the boobs?"

"Oh, man. Thank God. They feel better."

"That's good," he said.

"I'll still call the docs again on Monday. And your girlfriend, too."

"Which girlfriend?"

"The one with the big—" she raised an eyebrow "—heart. I might try acupuncture."

"Let 'em give it a stab?"

"Well, I can see their point."

"They can be very sharp."

"Anyhow," Naomi said, "I'll see what else Sequoia suggests. Obviously she's a veteran nursemaid." She smirked. "I hear she's been suckling soldiers since the *first* Gulf War."

Scanlon saw nothing wrong with Sequoia still nursing Trinity. "I bet she'll help. She's so . . . well, she's really generous."

"So you said."

Sammy was already snoring, and Scanlon rolled onto his side. He touched his nose to Naomi's, then he kissed her. He kissed her neck, her ear. As the air between them warmed, the smell of her milk—now *her* smell—became heady, intoxicating, and he unbuttoned her pajamas and kissed her breasts. He drew her nipple into his mouth, lolling it with his tongue. When he sucked, she flinched, and he backed off. Slowly he reached with his lips again, closed his mouth around her nipple, and tasted a drop of her milk.

But she put her hand to his cheek and gently pushed him back. "They're kind of sore."

"You said you were okay."

"The sharp pain's gone, but they're sore from nursing. Normal sore."

He kissed the swell of her breast. "I'll go easy," he promised. "I want to try—"

"But—" she shifted away, back into herself "—that's for Sammy."

Neither of them moved for a time, then she buttoned her pajama top and he rolled onto his back.

"With my nose today," she said, "it's my canary in the coal mine. I need to start taking better care of myself. For Sammy's sake."

"What more—" he began, then changed course. "What would help you take better care of yourself?"

"More sleep, less stress. Your mother isn't helping."

"I know she's not."

"I need to find the right balance—to be a great mother *and* to be creative. Those are my two priorities. All the books say you can't do one without the other."

Scanlon waited to hear how *he* fit into the balance.

"It's taken me a lot of years to let go of my first." Her voice had dropped to the damaged and contrite monotone reserved for the baby she gave up. "I'd thought that when I had another baby, I'd be able to step away from the decision I made. But when I look at Sammy—so innocent and tiny and perfect—when I hold him and nurse him, I'm . . . horrified." She spoke now through tears. "I don't know that person who gave her baby away. I'm scared of her. That she could *do* something like that."

"No," he said. "You did what was best for him."

"How can you say that? We have no idea what his life is like."

"It was best for him, even if it wasn't what was best for you."

"Goddamnit," she said, her voice rising. "You think this is about me? I'm going to give everything I have to mothering Sammy. I'm sorry if that means there's not a lot left over for—"

"You don't like the way I smell, do you?" he blurted. "My breath or something."

She became very still. Scanlon smelled her milk in the sheets, the warmth from her body, their sandalwood soap, pillowcases damp from their hair.

In a small, disembodied voice, as if through a tiny speaker across the room, she finally replied: "What a thing to say about someone."

Long after she'd fallen asleep, Scanlon was staring at the ceiling. He heard his mother come in, listening as she watched TV, then used the sink and toilet. He heard her settle into the spare room.

Sometime later, he stood naked at the picture window in the dark living room staring out at the street. The sourness had returned to his stomach.

He opened the front closet and pulled on the stiff Carhartts and logging boots he'd bought for the contest. Then he clomped to the garage, where his brand-new ax was leaning in the corner. Out back by the blueberry bushes he went at the mossy firewood left behind by the sellers, swinging the ax down hard, splitting every knotty, knock-kneed log in the pile, dripping with sweat for an hour, pounding again and again, eyes and hands stinging, until the entire stack was reduced to kindling.

There was this guy Clay was meeting about detonating cord, a guy who claimed he could supply Chandler G-99 presplit. Clay could fabricate his own from wire and blasting caps—easy—but genuine Chandler hexamine-nitrate slurry, which this guy said he could acquire in quantity, would be more reliable, and safer. The professional route. 13½ indicated he'd kick in the cash. Bricks and superglue and molotov cocktails were essential messages in the struggle, but a soldier finally dials it up a notch. Shit, with real det cord and a good hit on the explosives at Siuslaw Butte, Clay could bring down Mount Rushmore.

The series ran back and forth across his room, starting with the lantern batteries in the corner by the heater, then fifteen-foot lengths of wire zigzagging over his mattress and across the floor—*bam!* in the corner by his box of clothes, *bam!* under the light switch, *bam!* beside the fridge, *bam!* under the window. Last night he wired it into the alarm clock he'd set for five minutes as a test, knowing he could prove to millions that the corporate-federal slavemaster was vulnerable; he'd provide the boost they needed to cut the master down. He waited. The alarm chirped, and the ten mini flashlights he'd used in place of blasting caps lit up the perimeter of his room like a carnival.

The dry run had revealed some problems. When he cut up the PVC pipe, he discovered it was cracked—about what you'd expect for ninety-nine cents from Habitat. The wire cutters would do, but the strippers were so rusted they compromised the precision and speed so essential for last-minute adaptations. And without batteries, he had nothing. He realized he'd have to carry backups.

He propped a boot on the windowsill and laced it tight. Out the window, the clock on the courthouse read ten past eleven. He pissed and ate the rest of a cold and dry hot-dog burrito. Spongy. Sometimes he wished he had a microwave. The guy with the Chandler G-99s said he'd be at the Green & Black around eleven. Afterward, Clay planned to hit the all-night laundry, where college girls in sweats and T-shirts would be marking up textbooks with squeaky yellow pens. Stepping over the wires, he stuffed his duffel with dirty socks and underwear, his other jeans, his towel. Under the pile of dirty shirts was the professor's red Gap hat, and he put it on and looked in the bathroom mirror: Citizen Clay. He looked like any asshole in a Range Rover.

The baby was a little jaundiced, he'd noticed this afternoon in the park, and he wondered if Naomi was having trouble nursing. His friend Royce had struggled for weeks, and Maria, too. She'd had infections the whole first year. Daria might still be nursing. Ruby Christine was fourteen and a half months now. She could weigh as much as twenty-five pounds. Walking. Running! At that age Bumblebee, Royce's girl, loved flowers—"nahnee," she called them—and dogs and cement trucks.

Ruby Christine. What did she love?

Naomi looked weak today. Like the day she'd fainted. No light in her face. But Clay hadn't missed how she'd glowed when the professor invited him to their house. At first he'd thought *no way* because he didn't trust Scanlon or what he wanted—it was obvious he wanted something—but Naomi was different, and there was the baby, too. He sat down on the mattress, moved a wire, and laid his head on the pillow, fixing his eyes on the photograph of Naomi, replaying every moment of her labor until he heard the courthouse bell strike midnight. He'd missed the dude with the G-99s.

Through the soundless stretch of night he stared at the photo, dipping into sleep and letting his dreams do the work of confusing Naomi with Daria, swirling them into one.

In the morning, on the riverbank downtown, Scanlon stood in a line before the judges with blistered hands and a tweaked muscle in his neck. While Naomi slept, he'd added suspenders to his Carhartts, pulled on a Pendleton shirt, and relaced the logging boots, pondering their incongruously delicate, tapered heel. Down the line he saw a few firemen who'd been at the hospital and, standing between two giants, the very short Fenton wearing a black bowler hat.

The scores came in. Scanlon got a respectable 8.5 on appearance, and he went on, despite the burning blisters, to split his log in one chop. As he shouldered his ax and turned proudly to face the small crowd, Fenton stood there frowning, his arms crossed.

"I could've split that with my nine-iron," Fenton said.

"In my years as a tree feller," Scanlon began, "I developed—"

"Nobody likes a smart aleck. Did you see the log they gave me?"

Scanlon had—he'd needed four chops—but he shook his head.

"Six knots. Two of them major. What did you score on that ridiculous get-up?"

"Eight-five."

"That's BS. Frickin' BS."

Away from the department, standing tall in his boots and gripping an ax, Scanlon felt a surge of power, as he had flaunting the Rolex. "Do you think that hat might've hurt you? With the salt-and-pepper beard, you sorta look like a riverboat gambler."

"Damnit," Fenton spat. "Unlike the rest of you jerk-offs all gussied up for some bogus Disney movie, I'm sesquicentennially accurate. Read your goddamn history." He spun away, but after a few steps turned back. "And Pratt," he said. "Don't get your fingers burnt." Then he stormed off for real.

Any hubris Scanlon might have felt was quickly squashed. In the slow-chop, two-foot logs were clamped upright on heavy metal stands. He was expected not to split the log but to cut across it, to essentially chop it down in as few strikes as possible. He watched the other so-called amateurs draw chopping templates on the bark-stripped logs with magic markers; they looked like golf pros rehearsing the angles of their swings, their stance, their contact points. Then they polished their blades, as shiny as chrome, cartoonishly oversized, like something a knight would use to hack through armor. Finally, they sprayed the blades with silicone and beheaded their logs in seventeen chops, twenty, twelve. The judges gave Scanlon the hook at forty, and thank God. His hands were bleeding, his forearms quivering. The ax might have slipped from his fingers and shot into the huddle of spectators.

He took a cup of apple cider and a doughnut from the McCulloch trailer. After each slow-chop kill, a few timber fellers from the semipro category surrounded the log. "These chops up here?" they'd say, pointing to clefts in the wood. "All wasted." There was a lot to learn.

The final event for amateurs was speed-chop—counting seconds instead of chops—and then the semipros moved on to chain saws, ax throwing, pole climbing and, finally, log rolling on the river. Chain saws scared Scanlon, the pole climbing seemed impossible, the log rolling—not a chance. Hard core, was all he could think.

The muscles in his forearms were still quivering as he brought the shaky Dixie cup of cider to his lips and read a poster on the trailer celebrating the westward expansion: "The cowards never started, the weak died along the way, only the strong survived." According to McCulloch, he was the descendant of a long line of cowards. In the past Naomi had accused him of being a "classic academic," in effect a bourgeois dilettante who got his jollies flirting with radicals and mass movements but ultimately retreated to the safety of the middle class. The thumping he suffered in *Domestic Policy* accused him of much the same.

He watched the competition to the end. One of the firefighters at Sammy's birth won the amateur category. The winning lumberjill was the captain of the university's logging-sports team, and the man crowned Mr. Douglas in the semipros was officially sponsored by McCulloch. Scanlon shouldered his ax and headed for the car.

He'd left a note for Naomi this morning saying he'd be home around noon, but approaching the car he felt a reluctance, even a mild dread: she'd be exhausted or depleted, or the pain would've taken hold again; or Joey would be making her crazy, and he'd be expected to soothe the whole situation. He never imagined himself the sort who stops for a scotch and soda after leaving the office, not for the drink but to postpone getting home. He believed such men existed only in movies from the fifties, but he suddenly realized, as he recognized the impulse in himself, that his father had been one of them.

He walked past the bike shops and the longboard shop and Filbert's, which according to Hank had the best salmon burger in town. He crossed the street in front of the bus station, and across the parking lot he noticed a group of Native Americans frying dough in kettles over a propane stove—a heavenly smell. Behind them, a Quonset hut nearly hidden in the alley was identified by a small sign as the university's Native American longhouse; he supposed this was a fund-raiser.

In his book on Wounded Knee, Sam argued there was tremendous justification for secession in indigenous rights—the moral imperative of a conquered people. This would be a cynical argument—there were no more than a half-dozen Indians in the PNSM—but one that could buttress a larger case involving past and present economic injustices. The longhouse itself would be on sacred ground. It might be a start.

"A real lumberjack," Scanlon heard, and he looked across the sidewalk where a little boy was pointing at him, pulling on his mother's sleeve. Scanlon tugged on his beard and squared his shoulders, stomping his heels a little harder, flapping the ax blade like a fighter pilot wagging his wings. He didn't even balk as he passed by his car. He crossed the tracks, wound through the boot dancers and the bandstand, the bamboo flutes and chimes, until he was standing in a short line at the Skcubrats booth.

Under the tent she was laughing with one of her helpers—something about a mojito and blueberry pie. Sequoia, the Queen of Mellow. At the griddle, dipping her capacious ladle into an immense bowl, hugging the bowl to her swayed hip, she laughed again, throwing back her head. While the pancakes sizzled, she flicked each one with a pinch of cinnamon, then flipped them onto a plate with a sprig of mint. She was an earth goddess preparing for a ritual involving warm pools surrounded by ferns, fragrant oils, and sacred pleasure.

Naomi had mentioned experimenting with smells in their lovemaking. The Oregon experiment—all the new smells that had rushed back into her life. But that afternoon had been the last time they'd made love—lemonade on their tongues, mint in their lips, her wonderful belly, full of their baby, rolling into his own. And he realized now, with the slap of betrayal, that she'd held mint in her lips to mask the smell of *him*.

After a moment he caught Sequoia's eye, and as she smiled and waved the ladle at him, a drop of batter splatting her bare shoulder, the customers between them craned back to see who deserved such a friendly greeting. She was sexy and voluptuous and beautiful, obviously. But what excited him most was her vigor, her strength. She was healthy, burstingly *un*depleted, overflowing with more than she could ever give away. Which was why it felt so good to give something back to her. From that first night, when he perceived her disappointment in his blow-off of the PNSM, he'd wanted to please her.

"Mr. Douglas," she said when he reached the counter.

He dropped the ax head to the pavement between his boots and rested his hands on the knob of the handle. "I didn't win," he said.

"Because you were in the wrong competition."

"And what should I—"

"The Village People meet the Chippendales. Sing some disco, then strip."

"I look like a *stripper*?"

"No," she admitted. "You look like a cute professor dressed up for Halloween."

He felt himself blush, and was glad she missed it as she stepped back to the griddle to work her cakes.

"You come up with any winning strategies in the night? For secession?"

"My main thought," he said, unhappily shifting away from flirting, "is that the group's too focused on the minutiae of policy. How you'll run the schools and clean the streets can be worked out *after* you've got a groundswell of public support. At this point, it's salesmanship. People need to know that for every dollar the Pacific Northwest sends the Feds, only eighty-seven cents comes back. They need to know what the region's contribution to the war could've bought at home. They need to know the Pacific Northwest's economy is larger than most countries', and that energy independence is actually feasible here. The immediate strategy needs to be winning people over to the *idea* of secession. That's why the name's important."

"How do you like the Northwest Alliance for a Better Way?" she asked.

"Terrible."

"I know."

"The point is," he said, "the name's gotta have some jing."

She pushed her hips against the counter and handed him a plate of pancakes. "These are special," she said.

"You added extra love?" he asked.

She leaned over the counter, putting her lips to his ear. "Something like that." Wafts of sandalwood, coffee, cooking oil, and the syrupy citrus aromas of her body rose up from her hair, her mouth, her cleavage. Her lips brushed his ear as she whispered, "A couple drops of jing." She drew away with a playful grin.

"The Oregon Experiment," he blurted.

Suddenly she was beaming.

"That's it," he said. "Our new name."

He dropped his ax in the trunk, and driving home past car dealers on the strip, he could still feel the brush of her cheek on his own and her body pressing into his right through the heavy Carhartts. She'd loved the name. She'd been wild about it. She'd come running around the counter and hugged him, a hug wriggling and prodding toward full-body massage.

His sexuality had been deadened, and now it was electric. His heart still thudded, her gaze still mesmerized him. But shit. He swerved into the Famous Footwear parking lot and turned off the motor. He couldn't do this. He loved his wife. And Sammy. He *worshipped* Naomi, for God's sake. And her emotional and physical depletion was understandable. He had to understand what she was going through and be patient. With her nose back—her olfactory world gone haywire yet again—she was overwhelmed. Did she even know what smells she liked and disliked? Right now Naomi was unavailable, and obviously Sequoia was wide open. But he wouldn't cheat on Naomi. He couldn't. He would not repeat the selfishness of his parents; he would live life right. And he had to focus on why he was involved with the secessionists in the first place: to get their family back east. Their *family.* A few quick articles, then a book charting the successes and failures of a tenable micro-secession, his "soft ideals" redeemed, the *Domestic Policy* blip forgotten, Sam Belknap made proud, at which point he'd move Naomi and Sammy to Cambridge or New York, where they'd inhabit the ultimate ideal: the transcendent marriage, the loving family, the enviable career. He wanted Sequoia, no doubt. His body screamed for her. A cabin in the forest by a stream for a week. But giving in to temptation would be corrosive, the ideal forever stained.

He started the engine and steadfastly drove the eight or ten blocks to their house. "I'm home," he called in the kitchen, but no response came. And through the living-room window, he saw them in the backyard: Naomi and Clay on a blanket in the shade, folding a heap of laundry, Sammy conked out beside them in his bouncy seat. No sign of Joey. Naomi laughed, then covered her mouth and looked at Sammy to make sure she hadn't woken him. Scanlon stood inside the screen door, listening.

"You had a *great* labor," Clay said. "I love labor."

Naomi laughed again. "Easy for a man to say."

"Labor's the first and last great confrontation. You're telling him, 'Get out!' and Sammy's saying, 'Make me!' From the moment of conception the baby's power increases every day. In labor, the mother and baby are equals—a fair match. But then birth squeezes us into submission. For the rest of life, whenever you feel the power coming back, a cop smacks you down."

Naomi folded what looked to be a pair of Clay's underpants.

"Daria's labor was epic," Clay said. "Ruby Christine was an anarchist before she was born. Kicking and fighting all thirty-seven hours. Daria's teeth were chattering most of the second day. She got these spasms in her uterus that rippled right up to her jaw."

"Oh, man," Naomi said. "Toward the end I had spasms in my vagina—"

What the hell? He punched the screen door open, and they fell silent, watching him descend the concrete steps and stride toward them in his logging boots.

"Hey," Naomi said.

"Lumberman," Clay said. "How many board feet would you guesstimate are in that blueberry bush?"

Naomi suppressed a smile, looking away and folding a black T-shirt painted with a Circle-A; she was stacking his clothes on the Adirondack chair.

Clay reclined on an elbow, extending his legs and stocking feet toward Scanlon. His boots stood unlaced at the trunk of the tree. "Your hands look wasted," he said, and Scanlon shoved them in his pockets.

"Clay cut down that branch," Naomi said. "The one that was banging on our bedroom window."

Scanlon peered at the shoulder-high stump on the tree. "I was gonna do that this afternoon."

"He says both trees need some pruning."

"And the laurels," Clay added.

"He says he could do it."

"For a price," Clay said.

"If you're looking for odd jobs," Scanlon told him, "you can fix the garage window."

"Never been much of a window glazier. I focus more on the breaking."

"I'm willing to hire you," Scanlon said.

"I ain't cheap."

"I'll pay what you're worth." He turned to Naomi. "Take the baby inside. Clay can fold his own laundry." His tone was resolute: she picked up Sammy and stood without a word. Scanlon didn't doubt his wife's fidelity, but he wouldn't sit back while she talked about her vagina with a punk who was bent on unmanning him.

If Scanlon had to compromise scholarly distance to pick Clay's brain, it wouldn't be by giving him access to his wife. He'd get to Clay himself. Like Blaine Maxwell and her Deutscher boxer, he'd have his research subject on the payroll.

. . .

When Scanlon finished taking measurements for the broken pane, Clay was stuffing the last of his clean laundry back in the bag. "You can come with me to the hardware store," Scanlon said. "We'll get what you need to replace this glass next time."

"Like I said—"

"If you want work, you'll do it."

"Like I said," Clay repeated, and stopped there, still fucking with him.

Backing out of the driveway, he looked over his shoulder and Clay glanced back too, their faces nearly touching, and Scanlon flashed to Naomi's labor—the two of them coaching her, all three faces huddled close. Was it possible the kid imagined she would even be tempted?

"What do I owe you for the pruning today?" A security beam dinged as they entered the hardware store.

"I need some stuff," Clay said. "Okay if you just cover it?"

"Depends on what it adds up to."

Clay veered off at the first aisle, and while the woman behind the counter cut the glass, Scanlon found the glazier's points and putty. He also needed primer, and to get the paint matched. He'd pay Clay for the yard work, but he could do the window on his own time.

As the woman wrapped the pane in brown paper, Clay stood an eight-foot length of PVC pipe against a rack of safety goggles, rolled end caps on the counter like oversized dice, set down two big batteries, pulled wire cutters from his back pocket, and as he squeezed the red handles, apparently inspecting their precision, the anarchy tattoo on his forearm rippled with stringy tendons.

"What's all that for?" Scanlon asked.

"Pipe bombs."

"Nothing to joke about," Scanlon said, he and Clay and the woman price-scanning the batteries all looking at one another nervously, like birds. He handed over his credit card. "Seriously," he said, and it wasn't until Clay said, "My fish tanks. Filtration. Temperature control," that Scanlon realized he might not have been joking at all.

PART THREE

Chapter 5

By Halloween night, Joey had been gone for three days and the rain began in earnest. Drenched bunnies and Pooh Bears stood at the front door as Scanlon dropped bite-sized chocolate bars into their waterproof bags. Tiny princesses and ballerinas wore tiaras over rain hoods, their shiny jackets floating up on cushions of tulle, and shivering superheroes sprinted from house to house. The firemen fared best: plastic helmets and face masks shed the rain from their heads and down their ankle-length red plastic coats to their rubber boots. All evening long the rain kept pounding on the roof and the kids kept pounding on the door, the youngest ones with parents standing back under umbrellas, the older ones driven by the greedy frenzy Scanlon recalled from his own boyhood. He couldn't remember the last time he'd lived in a place where kids still trick-or-treated.

By nine o'clock the doorbell stopped ringing and he reluctantly closed up shop, wishing Sammy were old enough to join in, wishing Naomi had felt up to it.

He opened the bedroom door and saw she was done nursing. The light was turned off, Sammy was sleeping in his bassinet, and she'd withdrawn behind her eye mask and earplugs, now curled on her side on the far edge of the bed facing the baby, her new white-noise machine shushing away.

In the last two weeks she'd started acupuncture with Sequoia's friend Angel, who'd sent her to an herbalist, who then sent her to a reiki lady who in turn sent her to a therapist who'd begun unlocking her fascia. Naomi's practitioners all agreed that antibiotics could cripple her nose. For yeast infections, she painted a purple root called gentian violet on her nipples; for blocked ducts, she'd started in with cabbage. She'd drawn into herself and her health care regimen so completely that Scanlon feared it would lead to a major crash. Nightly, she told him she wasn't in the right space for intimacy. His sexual hunger had reached the point that watching her every evening at the stove blanching cabbage leaves and cupping them over her breasts left him with a hard-on.

He closed the bedroom door and decided to go out for coffee. To Skcubrats. But as he swung the car into a spot out front, he noticed that Sequoia's bike with the gas can bolted to the rear wasn't chained to the rack, so he sat in the idling Civic for several minutes as the wipers made intermittent passes, staring through the café's big front windows. He didn't see her inside.

He'd been to her house before. Last Thursday, he'd dropped her at the curb after the meeting where she'd taken a vote on the new name. Though there was some objection, and nearly an hour of discussion, in the end "The Oregon Experiment" was adopted. Sequoia had sent a press release to the *Union-Gazette* announcing the change, but the paper hadn't run it.

For the rest of the meeting Scanlon had held the floor, laying out the basic arguments for secession with a clarity and simplicity that left many in the room suspicious. Groups loved to complicate, whereas action required streamlining. He organized a committee for polling, another for PR, and a third to raise money. In under an hour he'd whipped them into shape.

Passing Franklin Park, he slowed. Streetlights shone off the wet blue tarps stretched over the roof of the old church that Sequoia and her neighborhood guerrillas had hijacked. Wound with yellow police tape and papered with official warnings and orders, on the verge of collapsing under its own weight, it seemed to him an apt metaphor for the United States government.

Lights were burning in her bungalow, so he came up on the porch and tapped the knocker.

The door cracked, and Sequoia smiled, buttoning her shirt, her hair mussed. "I was just laying with Trinity," she whispered.

"Oh, I'll go."

"No, no. She's asleep. I was about to get up and do some work."

The walls were bright yellow. Dark, Craftsman-style woodwork surrounded the windows and the fireplace, and propped in a corner among a collection of musical instruments he spotted a Gibson acoustic guitar. He sat on a low and squishy loveseat draped with an Indian tapestry and piled with pillows, and she went to the kitchen. A pedestal table in a nook was stacked with papers, a printer, and a glowing laptop. Trinity's artwork was framed and hanging on the walls, along with several brightly colored amateur paintings, a Matisse cutout, and an anti-draft poster he hadn't seen in years: Joan Baez and her two sisters sitting primly on a parlor couch wearing miniskirts, knees together, with the caption *Girls Say Yes to Boys Who Say No.*

Sequoia returned with two mugs of tea and a bowl of cherries. "Welcome," she said.

"I drove by the church," he decided to tell her.

"I have to go to court tomorrow. To face charges. I'm so pissed."

"This chief of police, Hazelton, seems like a prick."

"Even worse is Ron Dexter. If not for him, all this would've passed."

"Ron Dexter?"

"From your department."

"I can't stand that guy. He wastes my time. He stands in my office doorway telling jokes about snake charmers and virgins. I have to sneak in and out when he's not there."

"Same in my own café. He's a worm." Then she recited his various offenses, from opposing the neighborhood center to jerking her around on the Skcubrats sale and refusing Douglas Dollars.

"God, I'm sorry," Scanlon said. "I wish I could fire him or something. Or kick his ass."

They were silent for a moment. Sequoia sipped her tea and stretched out her legs, her bare feet crossed at her ankles on the coffee table. Her little toes were pinched, he noticed, as if they'd spent some time crammed into fancy shoes.

He sipped his tea. "This is a great mug. The handle's right, balance is good, the lip's comfortable. Perfect."

"Take it," she said without a thought. "It's yours."

"No, but thanks."

"I'd like you to have something I made with my hands."

He sipped again and the tea, steeped from roots and barks, flowed over the rim of a mug that seemed form-fitted to his lips.

"For all you've done," she said, "you deserve more than a *cup*. You've energized the whole movement."

"I haven't really—"

"You don't know how much you've done," she insisted. "There's a new excitement. Mo*men*tum."

"All I did—"

"The name's huge. You've gotten us on track in a way we'd never have done on our own. But the biggest thing is your sense of credibility. It makes everybody feel like they'd better take the movement seriously. They take *you* seriously."

"I'm flattered, but—"

"Things would *really* take off if you were elected director."

He shook his head. "I couldn't," he said, though she gazed into his face with her imploring green eyes. "I really can't. I'm so busy with the university. My teaching. Research."

"But isn't secessionism your research? Couldn't you study us better from the inside?"

"A critical eye requires distance."

"So you're going to be critical?"

"I just mean objective analysis."

"There's no such thing," she said, with such certainty and finality that he couldn't respond. She put her hand over her heart. "Your passion is genuine. I feel it." She touched his knee. "Don't say anything now. Let's not even discuss it. It's too much happening at once. Your semester just started. You're just getting to know the group. Don't even think about it." Then she raised her foot over the bowl on the table, and with her toes picked up two cherries by their stems. With yogic flexibility she brought her foot to her fingers, broke the stems apart, passed one cherry to him and popped the other between her lips.

"Nice guitar," he said.

She chewed the cherry, pushing the pit around her mouth with her tongue. "Do you play?"

"Not in a long time," he said, then Sequoia jumped up and brought him the Gibson.

He strummed a few chords and tuned it up—it hadn't been played in a while—then held the pick between his lips and began plucking out "Blackbird," his fingers squeaking on the heavy strings. He was so rusty that the chirping notes thumped out like a dirge, so he changed course, took the pick and hit the power chords of "Sweet Jane," looking up from the neck to see Sequoia smile, thinking of Jane Swallows and a sunny patch of grass in front of his high school where a bunch of them would sit around in the afternoons of his senior year, and when the refrain came back around he sang. His gritty, sometimes off-key voice was suited to Lou Reed, and this was one of the few songs in the Imelda's Shoes list on which Scanlon sang lead. On the next chorus, Sequoia sang with him, a little tentatively—the first time he'd seen her do anything without unrestrained vigor.

"Holy cow!" she said when he put the guitar down. "You're amazing. Play some more. Start a band. Why aren't you a rock star?"

He laughed it off.

"Why aren't you out there performing? Get a record contract. I'm serious."

Of course she *wasn't* serious. "It's just something I left behind. Another life, I guess."

This caught Sequoia, like a pinprick to her skin. They were quiet for a time, and he watched her mood deflate.

"Can you really leave a life behind?" she finally said.

"Probably not." He hadn't meant it so literally.

"I'd like to believe somebody could. But look at you. The music's *in there.* I watched you sort of become that other person while you were playing. I could tell it was another life, another you stepping up from your past." She paused, looking away from him then back. "In *my* past, I devastated a boy's life, his whole family's, and when I tried to make amends, they wouldn't let me. They've never forgiven me, and maybe they shouldn't. If my father's pal hadn't been the state deputy attorney general, who knows where I'd be now? I've tried to leave all that behind—that other me—but like you and the music, it keeps showing up. Even Trinity can see through me. From the time she was a baby, she's had a strange sixth sense for damaged people. I can tell she senses it in your wife. She knows Naomi has suffered."

She ate another cherry, spit the pit into her hand, and squeezed his knee. Naomi had suffered through anosmia, but his bigger fear at the moment was the haunting intrusion of her first baby and the nineteen-year-old girl who'd given him up.

"Thanks for playing," Sequoia said. She smiled and rose up on the couch, and with a deep breath she shook off the funk that had seized her. "I should get to sleep."

He reached for the coffee table with the mug.

"That's for you," she said.

He held it as he stood.

"I was jonesing for a soak before bed." She yawned. "You want to come with?"

He clasped both hands around the cup, not sure what she was offering.

"Hot tub," she said. She took the mug from him and set it down, then took his hand and led him out into a cool, misting rain.

Under the awning, she released his hand and turned her back to him. In a few smooth motions her shirt fell from her shoulders and her fleece pants dropped down her hips. She flipped up the hot tub cover, releasing a plume of steam, and slipped into the water to her chin with a moan.

Scanlon was not as quick or graceful about undressing. He unbuttoned his shirt cuffs, unbuckled his belt, and pulled his legs out of his pants one at a time, careful not to spill his change or keys between the boards of the deck, then hung his clothes on pegs. Sequoia's eyes were closed as he submerged tentatively into the scalding tub. "That's good," he said.

She opened her eyes and smiled at him across the black water and the length of her naked body, then closed them again. They listened to the night: the sudden rap on the deck when a breeze flicked drops off the ends of thousands of redwood needles over their heads, a car engine gunning toward campus, a train whistle downriver. Every few minutes she took a long breath, as if preparing to speak, then slowly and deliberately let it go.

After a time, she stirred the dark water with her arms and legs and in a single heart-stopping motion she rose up to sit on the edge of the tub. It was Ingres, Scanlon was pretty sure, the Frenchman, who'd painted the Turkish bath scene he knew; Sequoia could have been his model. Her long hips sloped like the arc of dolphins. Her tummy looked pliable, like a place you'd want to lay your head for a better look at her plump, weighty breasts, pouring off steam. One was tattooed with a hummingbird, its slender bill probing her rosebud nipple for nectar.

"The thing is," she said, almost in a whisper, "if you were director, you'd have access to every piece of the movement." She reached up and squeezed the clip from her hair, then rewound her mane and clipped it in place again. Her skin glistened. Water beaded at her chin, at her elbows, at the tips of her nipples.

Twenty-seven of her neighbors crowded in front of Judge Browning's bench for the nearly thirty-minute reading of their alleged violations of the law. At least two of them had been out of town that night, but feeling they'd helped move the church in spirit they came to face their judgment.

Browning had a reputation as a fair and thoughtful judge. Although Sequoia had never met him, she knew his story. Standing beside the court stenographer, she could see framed snapshots on the wall above a cluttered desk behind his bench. One looked to be him on the reservation—he was Nez Perce—and another was a black-and-white of soldiers in front of a grass shack. Browning had served in Vietnam, and in the late seventies, as a lawyer here in Douglas, he'd put himself on trial for war crimes. Finding himself guilty, he called on federal marshals to arrest him, but they never came and a decade later he was elected to the county bench.

Halfway through the clerk's reading of their crimes, Browning got up, refilled his coffee, and shuffled through papers, stopping to examine each one, then setting it aside. No doubt these included Ron's complaint, but she hoped he also knew that despite the railroad inspectors' minute measurements with calipers and lasers, their X-raying for stress cracks, they could demonstrate no damage. Zero.

The final five minutes of charges seemed painful, Browning slumping lower in his seat with each new violation, his face dropping morosely. When the last and smallest was read—$65 for a dog being off leash in a playground—he asked to see the sale agreement and title to the church, which Jim presented. He then asked for any and all documentation regarding permits to move the church, and one by one the papers were handed to him via the clerk. Finally, he asked if anyone present had thrown a brick, or was an accessory to anyone who had, through the windows of the Bank of America or Wells Fargo.

They all shook their heads.

"Speak," he ordered.

"No, your honor," they said in motley unison.

The judge looked more depressed by the minute, and Sequoia was getting worried. The clerk had announced the tally—$41,510, plus the cost of tearing down the church, with criminal charges pending.

"The citations," Browning bellowed, "will stand."

Sequoia's spirit sank to the floor, along with everyone else's.

"The fine for each citation will be reduced to one dollar."

And just as quickly they were elated.

"In addition, each of you is ordered to complete forty hours of community service, which will be performed in the rehabilitation of the former church slated to become the Franklin Park Neighborhood Center. You'll need to coordinate this with a parole officer whom the clerk will appoint."

"Your honor?" Jim asked.

Browning stared at him.

"Could we pay the fine with Douglas Dollars?"

A relieved chuckle spread among them, except for Browning, who dropped his gavel one time on the block and disappeared into his chambers.

They hugged and rejoiced, made prison jokes, and decided to go en masse to the parole officer—"the foreman," Jim called him. And when the jubilation waned, some went off with Jim for beers at Filbert's, a few went back to work, the rest went home.

Sequoia unlocked her bike from the rack, hugged Paul and Susan once more, and pedaled to the daycare to pick up Trinity. Today was one of those rare November days when a line of blue sky peeks over the coast range and the cloud cover parts for the sun—a bonus day to be celebrated—so they stopped off at the park.

"Higher!" Trinity shouted, and she pushed the swing hard. As well as the court business went today, the whole scene—metal detectors, lawyers, police, accusations, men in dark suits—had put Sequoia on edge. Still feeling queasy, she took a deep breath and gazed at Trinity's hair riding on the wind.

"Higher!" she demanded, and Sequoia pushed harder, trying to piggyback on her daughter's joy. A wisp of cloud blew across the sky. Trinity held her red shoes straight out in front of her, the gold sparkles glittering in the sun as she clicked the heels together. Two chipmunks—scratchy on the bark of an elm tree—chased each other around the trunk, then a sudden crash and rumble sent them shooting up into the branches. Four anarchist kids, one of them a girl on a longboard, were coming down the walk. Another carried a wooden highway stake, striking bench backs, garbage cans, and the chain that draped between low posts around the flowerbeds. Another—medium height, thin, and all in black—was staring at Sequoia and Trinity.

"Higher!" Trinity called, and Sequoia gave a good shove. His stare was unnerving, without a shred of self-consciousness, and she flashed back to the bailiff who'd stared at them like they were guilty, like their recklessness had—

A kick! The sharp heel of Trinity's shoe caught her flush on the mouth. She yelled in shock, doubling over, reaching out to steady the swing that was angling off-kilter.

"What happened, Mommy?"

Tasting blood, down on her knees, she sucked on her lip. The same spot where the scar was.

Trinity was standing in front of her, alarmed, patting her hair. "Mommy?"

"I'm okay," she said. "It just surprised me. I wasn't paying attention."

A shadow covered them, and Trinity looked up.

"You all right?"

Holding her mouth, she stood up and turned. "It's nothing." Then she forced a laugh. It was the kid who'd been staring at them.

"There's a drinking fountain by the—" he pointed "—over there."

She nodded.

"Your mom's okay," he said to Trinity, his voice kindly, gentle. "Just a little bash in the mouth."

Trinity scrutinized him. Wordless.

The kid's head twitched—two times—uncontrollable, it seemed—and then he scuffed off in his combat boots to catch up with his pals, Trinity pointing after him.

Later, standing in front of a mirror at home, Sequoia curled back her lip. It wasn't so bad: a tooth-sized patch of mangled flesh, already healing. She swished with salt water. The contusion had inflamed the thin scar on her lip. She watched herself pucker, smile, exhale. Then she filled two bowls with rice and stir-fry, and she and Trinity sat cross-legged at opposite ends of the loveseat for dinner.

"What if pigs had trunks?" Trinity asked.

"Then they'd search for peanuts in the mud." Sequoia speared a zucchini triangle with her chopsticks. "What if trains had wings?" she asked.

Trinity looked at the ceiling. "Then clouds would look like railroad tracks," she said. "What if we had hammers instead of hands?"

"Then we'd fix everything as soon as it broke," Sequoia said. "What if—"

"What if I saw the broken boy again?"

"You wouldn't!" she snapped, then said more calmly, "Because he's not real." And she thought of him now: seventeen years old. Quadriplegic. The family had moved away to be near his rehab. Minneapolis would already be snowy. Trinity was gnawing at the cuticle on her thumb, and Sequoia pushed her hand away from her mouth.

At the courthouse and afterward, that horrible day had elbowed into her consciousness, and this evening, instead of backing off, it was stalking her. "What if—" she began, but Trinity bit down on her thumb. "Stop it!" Sequoia shouted, and took her daughter in her arms.

Muffled against her chest, Trinity said, "I see him all the time."

"No!" Sequoia yanked open her shirt. She believed in the body's power to heal, in the power of touch. Through the body all relations and experiences were imbibed; by touch and feel we perceive the world. So if Trinity's hallucinations flared, she held her tight and nursed her to sleep. But now, as her daughter suckled, she was haunted by a recurring doubt: that her fear of repeating her parents' mistakes had created its own neuroses in Trinity, which was precisely what her psychiatrist father would smugly insist. But as quickly as that doubt gripped her, she denied it: No—through the body we reach the spirit, heart, and mind, not the other way around.

"Have you ever worked?" he asked.

The professor gave him a look. "I teach at two o'clock today."

"I mean actual work," he said. "Like *work*." He'd cleaned out their gutters—a nasty job in the wet, up to his elbows in leaves rotted to slime—and was now hosing off his arms.

"When I was a kid—" Scanlon began, but Naomi interrupted, opening the back door and calling, "Come wash up inside, Clay. With warm water." He'd seen her at the picture window, glancing out every few minutes with Sammy on her shoulder. During the morning she'd offered him apple cider, which he'd declined, then coffee or tea, and he'd told her straight-faced, "My religion prevents it."

"Oh," she said, "Mormon?"—a cute-as-hell combination of surprise and knee-jerk respect.

"Dewdism," he said.

Her head cocked. "I'm not familiar with—"

"I'm the Dewdha," he said. "The Mountain Dewdha."

"Ah," she said, a smile brightening her puzzled face. "Not one of the major religions. Although I've seen your ads."

"It's a feel-good religion. No crusades or slaughter. Less gore, more lemon-lime."

And her face was still sparking when she returned from Dari-Mart with a 32-ounce cup of Mountain Dew.

Following Scanlon inside, he wiped his boots on the mat. Naomi led him to the kitchen sink and turned on the tap, flicking her finger under the water until it ran hot. As he washed his arms, she plucked a fresh towel from a drawer and held it there, waiting for him to rinse away the suds. She was making soup. Chopped celery and red onion were heaped on the cutting board. A bunch of shiny wet carrots with greens shooting off their tops. A head of garlic. Steam rose from a simmering pot, smelling of chicken fat, pepper, and spices.

"Anyway," Scanlon said, his arms folded across his chest, leaning on the door of the fridge, "when I was a kid, my dad made me rototill this huge garden every year. Like half our backyard. Trust me. Connecticut humidity? You have no idea."

Clay took the soft towel from Naomi and dried his arms right up to his biceps. "*Rototiller,*" he scoffed. "The machine does all the work. You just follow it around and make sure it doesn't run over the cat."

"The shit you think you know," Scanlon said, but Clay had made Naomi laugh.

"Stay for lunch?" she said, taking back the towel and folding it. Which made no sense with a wet towel. "Soup'll be ready soon."

"Panama's trial starts today. I gotta go. Skulls to crack." But the soup smelled damn good.

Scanlon reached into his back pocket for his wallet and slipped out a couple twenties. "Next time you do the window."

He snatched the cash, and when he dropped down the stoop Naomi said, "Crack a skull for us."

Rain held off as he hoofed it down to Courthouse Square. There was a drum circle. Some cops. The scrape and rumble of skateboarders doing ollie grabs, tailslides, nosegrinds, and nollies. A heelflip thwacked too close to Clay so he threw an elbow—Back off. The cops seemed cool enough, keeping everybody on the side of the square by the county courthouse. A tall stone building more than a hundred years old, it was painted white and had a clock tower, and over the door were bronze sculptures of pioneers trailing an ox cart. The federal courthouse next to it, built on the site of the old Egyptian Theater, was gray cement, cubic, with small tinted windows. It looked Soviet, like a prison or bunker.

Clay said hey to some girls who lived at the Random House and looked up to see Flak approaching the cops with a box of doughnuts. Food Not Bombs was supposed to serve sandwiches at lunchtime, but who knew where he'd got three pink cardboard flats of doughnuts. Flak was an older guy, maybe thirty-five. He wasn't tall, but he was strong. Quick and strong. The cops all knew him. Everybody did. But the cops ignored him and his doughnuts, chattering away even as they straightened up their line and rested their palms on their clubs.

"I *know* you guys like doughnuts," Flak was saying. A real performer, he was holding up the box on one hand and reaching out with the other like a singer. The drums got real hushed, everybody watching. "I seen you guys eating doughnuts before." A couple cops finally cracked a smile. "See?" he said. "We're all brothers." And Flak believed it, even though none of them took a doughnut.

"Where ya been?" Entropy said, tugging on Clay's pant leg, and he wondered if she or any of the other girls knew. He could tell Flak at least suspected. He'd seen Clay splitting a beer with Panama down by the river the night before they torched the SUVs.

"We've been here since morning," Entropy said.

If people at the Random House knew, then lots more had heard. Clay had told no one, and he was pretty sure Panama hadn't either, so no one really knew. Except for the professor, and maybe Naomi. And for a minute, as the drums beat louder, and he moved through the kids in the square, it was just Clay and the photo of Naomi, her picture coming to life with one sunny hand sliding down her eggshell belly.

"Clay!" Flak shouted, clamping an arm around his neck and throwing solid, easy punches against his chest.

Clay spun around and tried to flip him over his hip, but there was no getting Flak off balance, so they struggled until Flak let go.

"Long time no see," Flak said, even though they'd shared a Mountain Dew right here yesterday.

"How goes it?" Clay said.

"Beautiful, man. Free doughnuts for the people. But the occiffers ain't partakin'. Hey, we gotta get somebody to teach doughnut making for the Free Skool." He turned toward the kids who were watching him. There were always kids watching Flak. "Who knows how to make doughnuts?" he shouted.

"Stand back," a voice ripped through a bullhorn. Everybody up front dashed away from the cops, then turned to watch an Asian kid called Fugu taunt them with "Panama's a martyr, motherfuckers," and making like he was about to nail them with his Big Gulp full of pop.

"Your sort of thing," Flak said. "Go back him up."

Clay ignored him. There was a time this was exactly his sort of thing, but not today.

Fugu shouted, "Die, you fucking pigs!" Then, like pulling the pin from a hand grenade, he yanked the straw through the lid with his teeth and heaved the cup at the cops. Before it hit the ground, they'd slammed him onto his belly, given him three Taser zaps, a knee in his back, and crunched his face into the cement.

"Fugu's supposed to teach harmonica at the Free Skool," Flak said.

"He's not that good anyway," Clay said.

"Maybe he'll bone up in County. Come home a virtuoso."

"He'll be lucky to get County," Clay said. "Attacking cops and terrorism, with alert-level yellow and whatnot."

"They'll search his place for sure," Flak said. "Better be clean."

The crowd cheered for Fugu as the cops dragged him cuffed and bloody behind their lines. Rain started to fall, and a smell came off Clay's wet jacket that he'd noticed earlier but couldn't place: chicken, onion, spices—Naomi's soup. Then, watching a police car spin around the corner with Fugu in back, he thought, Search his place.

That night, after dark, Clay stripped his apartment of the wire and blasting caps, the tools, flashlights, and dissected alarm clock. He put it all in a garbage bag that he stuffed in his duffel and hoofed down to a spot on the riverbank where he used to get high. Behind the footing of a train trestle there was a tiny cave, hollowed out by erosion. Transients and kids knew about it, but he'd take a chance. He tied the garbage bag up tight and shoved it in the back of the hole. Nothing that couldn't be replaced.

He sat on the footing and looked out over the river. He stuck his nose into his sleeve and sniffed deep, the smell of Naomi's soup arousing a tug of hunger.

Naomi needed a break. She needed a shower. She needed to shave her legs and take a nap. She needed to put cabbage leaves and ice packs on her breast. This was her third infection in three months, but she refused antibiotics. She ran to two or even three appointments a day—acupuncture, reiki, lactation work. They'd also suggested yoga, meditation, and a weekend at Breitenbush Hot Springs, but she didn't want to take time away from Sammy. Her nipples were permanently painted with gentian violet, staining his lips and mouth like he'd been feeding himself fistfuls of berry pie. She packed her infected breast in ice between feedings but couldn't numb the hard, painful lumps: ten pounds of potatoes forced into a five-pound sack. And all day long—every minute—she obsessively sniffed almond in the folds of fat under his chin, carbon encrusted on the fireplace brick, Summer Breeze Palmolive in the kitchen, jars of mustard and pickles, afraid that if she didn't keep her nose firing, she'd lose it again. As she walked through the living room with a basket of laundry, she realized she could still smell Clay in the house.

The only real relief came from Sammy. If she could bear the initial pain and the first few seconds of suckling, the flow of milk and release of pressure were comforting. She tried expressing milk in the shower, but the self-flagellation of wringing out her inflamed breast was beyond her.

Scanlon wanted to help, but she told him over and over that short of mastectomy there was nothing he could do. Could he give her a back rub? She didn't want to be mauled. Could he run her a bath? The shower felt better. Make slow, gentle love to her? Again, the mauling. Slow and gentle, he promised. No needless jostling, she insisted. Could he pleasure her with his tongue? She really wasn't in the mood right now. A glass of water? Another ice pack? Yes, she said. Fine. Thank you.

It made her anxious that he'd do anything that took him away from writing, but he claimed he'd roughed out an article that would work as a book chapter. As long as the secessionist movement fed his writing and didn't distract him and made him less demanding of her, maybe it was a good thing that after meeting with Sequoia last week he'd agreed to be its director. "Only as a figurehead," he assured her.

With Sammy asleep and the monitor on the vanity, she stepped into the shower. The water pressure was pummeling, so she tapped the faucet handle down to weaken the spray, then with both hands held her swollen breast under the water like it wasn't part of her body—like holding up a feverish raccoon, its claws tearing into her chest. But under the warm spray the claws began to retract. The relief would be temporary, allowing her to breathe, to loosen up and navigate back to herself.

Despite the recurring infections, she was reclaiming her body. She and Sammy were in sync. She made as much milk as he needed, and he kept coming back. When he was on the healthy breast, she'd gaze down at his tiny head, at the metronome rhythm of his jaw, and feel more connected to him than she ever would've expected. *My own flesh and blood.* She felt it. Understood it. She would look down at her son and know a sort of love that was far more profound than anything she'd experienced before. Closing her eyes, wrapping her arms around him, releasing herself to the tug-tug-tug of his desire, she felt a physical intimacy that moved her to tears. Tears because his suckling pulled on a thread of passion deep inside her body, and because for all of Scanlon's good intentions—offers of foot rubs in front of a fire, genuine expressions of his desire to make love to her—compared to what she and Sammy were experiencing, any physical intimacy with her husband seemed crass, a hump and a grunt on the floor.

Sequoia worked on the movement during lulls at the café and at home late into the night. The *Douglas Union-Gazette* ran her press release (albeit trimmed down to only a few lines) announcing Scanlon as their new director, and included the new name. This won them some publicity but lost them Hank. The mayor had objected to his fire chief, a public employee, leading a secessionist group, so Hank took a step back, but Scanlon had picked up the slack. There'd be no more mulling, processing, whining. He had everyone focused on a specific task. José handled polling. Natalie looked into investors. There were questions about boundaries, about Native American land and their casinos, about property rights. Scanlon took a conference call with a Mormon splinter group who'd inquired about openly practicing polygamy. Taylor was building a website.

Scanlon set up groups to study the holdings of timber companies and the concerns of fishermen and environmentalists, and to find common ground. They looked toward the Pacific Rim. They discussed the irrelevancy of Washington, D.C. José asked four hundred random Oregonians whether they'd support a hypothetical secession if their overall tax bill were reduced by a quarter; twenty percent said yes. Cut their taxes in half? Forty-three percent. They were on the way toward Scanlon's benchmark of eighty percent support.

"We need something that defines us," he had said. "Typically, ninety percent of a seceding populace will share religion or ethnicity, and we don't have anything like that." She took notes on her laptop, bookmarked websites, created spreadsheets. Scanlon had no idea how much he knew. It was almost too much—in too many directions. He talked, she took it all in.

"More tea?" she whispered. Trinity was asleep in the bedroom.

He nodded.

As she poured, he said, "Another nice cup."

"It's yours," she said.

"I can't keep taking your mugs."

But she told him about the health department, that all her café mugs were now restaurant supply and her cupboards here at home were overflowing. She sat down beside him on the couch and they sipped in silence. "That's the least of it," she said, and explained that County Health was demanding new exhaust hoods, drains, and food-prep surfaces. She couldn't invest that sort of money in a rental. "I made Ron Dexter another offer yesterday. More than it's worth. I'm paying a realtor, for God's sake."

"And what did Ron say?"

"Same as always—he'll 'sleep on it.' And he winks."

Scanlon clenched a fist and punched his knee. His outrage was genuine, which made her trust his principles all the more. She believed he would fire Ron if he could. Or kick his ass. She'd been so distraught about the café that she'd even considered calling her father for help, for money. But she'd resisted; she wouldn't succumb. Scanlon would know what to do.

Then she told him about the church. Despite Judge Browning's ruling, the building inspector, a hunting buddy of Hazelton's, had cited Ron's many complaints to justify denying permits allowing work to begin. There was still no roof. The tarps blew off in the last storm, and rain had damaged the floors.

"Let me talk to Dexter," Scanlon said. "See what he wants to back off."

She tipped her cup to her lips, held it there even after it was empty, then put it on the table beside his and refilled them both from the yellow teapot she'd painted with a hummingbird, its bill reaching up the spout. "I know what he wants," she said.

Scanlon understood, and his eyes went wide.

"I'm tempted," she said, "just to hold my nose and give it to him."

"No." His face turned red. "No fucking way. I'll think of something."

He hadn't seen Fenton since the Mr. Douglas contest, but when he finally did, the chair pulled him into his office to look at a tattered old black-and-white photo framed on the wall: eight loggers standing across a huge stump with their two-man saw, come-alongs, and axes displayed like elephant guns atop their trophy game. Three of them wore bowler hats.

"You're right," Scanlon offered, and couldn't help grinning when he added, "You were robbed." Fenton's eyes hardened as Scanlon backed toward the door saying, "Well, there's always next—"

But Fenton interrupted him, rattling off that Scanlon would sit on two more committees, he'd judge the department essay contests, and he'd cover Dexter's classes while Ron was out for knee surgery.

"You're joking," Scanlon said with a hopeful smile.

"And don't forget: the first year of any appointment is officially probationary."

Back in his office—shocked, nauseated, irate—he phoned Naomi at home, then on her cell, and left messages for her to call as gusts of wind pelted rain against the windowpanes. He stared out at the bouncing branch suspended over Fenton's Porsche.

Then he knocked on Ron's door, trying to calm himself before going in. Dexter was standing at the window with one eye on a newspaper and the other on each sway and twitch of the branch. "I've thought about getting up there one night and sawing partway through. But what about the blade marks? Wouldn't somebody notice?"

"Let me ask you this," Scanlon said. "I seem to be getting punished by the chair."

"You mean over the Mr. Douglas thing?"

Scanlon was astonished.

"Everybody knows," Ron said. "Some of us thought it was pretty ballsy of you to go up against him."

"I wasn't going up against him," he protested. "I just thought it would be a kick."

A crack sounded outside. They both jerked their heads and gawked at the tree like two men, bored by their own desultory chat at a baseball game, suddenly riveted by the smack of a bat. But the branch disappointingly hung on.

"Ten years back," Ron said, "we hired a guy from Duke. Top-notch. Nineteenth-century Europe. Turns out his wife was a big gardener, and in their second year they placed number six in the June garden walk. Fenton and his wife are gardeners too, and they *didn't* place. The next year the guy taught five days a week at eight a.m. Word is Fenton blocked his tenure. Poor sot teaches in North Dakota, last I heard. These days it's harder for him to get away with that sort of shit, what with every color-blind, transgender gimp suing over the height of urinals. Which is lucky for you, my friend. You wouldn't be here if the dean had let Fenton withdraw your offer."

Scanlon's face betrayed his shock.

"This is news to you? Sorry, pal. When you got publicly ass-fucked in *Domestic Policy,* Fenton looked like such a moron for giving you the offer that he tried everything to rescind it. But the dean was afraid you'd sue."

Scanlon stared at the dead limb doing its little dance in the wind, a flirtation, a tease above Fenton's red car, gleaming in the rain like a candy apple, good enough to lick.

"Cocksucker," Ron said. "Am I right?"

It had happened again: Scanlon falling in with the wrong crowd. "Let's talk about that branch, Ron."

Skirting the campus, Naomi walked through blocks of old bungalows with couches out front soaking up rain, kegs on the roof, towels and centerfolds and busted shades in the windows, the trashiest houses marked by the orange front doors and $CASH$ FOR YOUR HOUSE signs that a local landlord littered the town with. A jacked-up pickup rolled past, giant tires humming, then turned onto a muddy front yard, and two college kids, their caps turned backward, pounded up on the porch and kicked the orange door. Standing there, they looked too big, as if this were a playhouse. Then the door opened and they went inside.

Scanlon had come back from campus in a rage about his department chair, and Sammy, too, had been in a bit of a rage. She'd considered canceling with Clay, but she didn't know how to contact him and needed to get out of the house. Angel was right: she needed short breaks to sustain her vibrancy and energy as a mother. So she handed her baby off to Scanlon, said she was going out for a while, and left the two of them to deal with their troubles together. She missed Sammy already.

She took a left at the copy shop and crossed over the Northern Pacific tracks that ran down the middle of Mill Street. A beater car splashed through a puddle; its bumper sticker read, *VISUALIZE moving your yuppie ass back to California.* Two blocks down, the street turned into a gravel road that looked like a driveway for Heeber Auto Glass. In any other city she'd call this an area in transition, but sketchiness here seemed enduring. The gravel continued along the tracks past Douglas Radiator Repair *(A great place to take a leak),* J. B. Welding, and Little Tim's Transmissions. The oil-blackened cinderblock garages were open to the road. Grimy men swung oversized hammers, clanking and thudding amid torches, sparks, the whine of air tools, rusted heaps of contorted metal, sawed-off oil drums, suspiciously murky puddles. Not a half mile from campus, she was walking through the Middle Ages.

Then she saw the Independent Auto Body sign and the breeze shifted and she smelled it: the acrid, toxic, wonderful smell of body putty. A grinding wheel whirred up dust around a figure in coveralls, goggles, and a mask. She stopped, inhaling, remembering. That morning with Clair was like a hundred others, except it was the day she got pregnant, and while the smell of blood and amniotic fluid was her most direct connection to Joshua, she could also conjure him through the smells infusing his conception—sour milk from her grandparents' creamery, heating oil, body putty, creosote, mint.

But her heart now belonged to Sammy, and she took one more long smell of the body putty and decided to go home to him. Clay would have to understand. She turned back, then a voice startled her. Clay was rising over the tracks. As their eyes met, his toe caught on the rail and he lunged toward her, nearly falling to the ground.

"Hey," he said.

"Nice neighborhood."

"You think so?"

"No."

His head twitched. "It's there," he said, pointing at a cube of cinderblock that had once been a garage, its sign depicting the eight of hearts, diamonds, clubs, and spades. "Or we could go someplace else."

"I don't have a whole lot of time." She checked her watch—Sammy would still be sleeping.

Looking toward the body shop, Clay lifted his chin, and a figure coated with dust tipped his grinding wheel in response.

She suddenly feared she might be putting herself in danger. "Friend of yours?" she asked.

"Best panel beater in town." She didn't reply, so he added, "You got a dent, I *guarantee* he can pull it," and she was put at ease by his earnest desire to impress her.

Inside, she sat in a vinyl chair and set her wrists on the sticky table. Bringing two glasses of beer from the bar, Clay announced, "Since you're buying, Randall said we could run a tab."

She smiled.

"You're buying, right?"

"I'd be honored," she said, raising her beer. When he drank, his lip piercing clinked on his glass. She'd barely had a drink once she got pregnant, and only a few sips of wine since Sammy was born. She took three long swallows. Heavenly.

"I thought you'd bring Sammy," he said.

"To a bar?"

"There's no smoking or anything."

"Or anything?"

He didn't know how to answer that. "Well, another time, maybe." She saw that his mind had gone off, and she wondered where his own baby was, how long he'd known the mother, and all at once she had the wavery sensation in her eyes and nose from eating french fries doused in white vinegar with Clair at the hot-dog joint a block from the body shop.

"What's he weigh now?" he asked.

"Twelve pounds, three ounces, a week ago."

"He must be a good eater."

She nodded, her eyes on him. His head twitched, and now she felt exposed, brushing up against the topic of breastfeeding in a bar—where she hadn't told her husband she was coming—with an *anarchist.* Neither spoke for a time, and she wondered if this wasn't a mistake.

But if she was honest, it was this possibility that brought her here. The potential for risk. From the time she let Scanlon rescue her all those years ago, she'd been playing it safe. Anosmia had whacked her. She'd lost her self-confidence. But her nose was back now; she could smell life. She'd never been to a dive bar with an anarchist, and Clay lifted her spirits. She would return to Sammy enlivened.

He went to the bar and returned with two more beers. "Do you play darts?" he asked.

"Not professionally."

He led her to the back. She was lightheaded as she started her second beer, and he put four darts in her hand and pointed at the target: a devilish caricature of Bill Clinton with a thought bubble reading *I'm a gun grabber. Support the NRA.* For all the years that had passed, there weren't many holes in it.

"Who comes here?" she asked.

"Nobody."

She pierced Clinton's left knee.

"That whole area," he told her, "between here and the highway—"

"The Home Depot?"

He fired a dart into Clinton's throat. "It used to be the mill. Crazy Eights was the mill bar. People could get their rigs serviced during their shift." He stuck Clinton in the forehead, then dropped his black jacket over a stool.

When he launched a dart, his wing bone protruded and receded through his T-shirt, the tight muscles in his arm and shoulder flexed and extended like springs. The scent of his body was crushed dried tomato seeds. Sharply boyish. Naomi's dart hit a light switch and fell to the floor.

"Excuse me," she said, and went through the door marked *Ladies ONLY.* She peed, and as she pulled out her cell, her eyes filled with tears—she missed Sammy. "How is he?" she said when Scanlon picked up.

"Excellent. Are you coming home?"

Again her eyes rushed with tears, and her milk ducts were suddenly brimming. "So he settled down?"

"Sleeping. He drank two bottles of what you pumped last night."

"That's good," she said. "There's one more in the freezer."

"You'll be home before he wakes up, won't you?"

"Randall has gingivitis."

"What?"

"That's what it says here. Graffiti in the stall."

"You're on the toilet?"

How did she get here? She studied at Givaudan-Roure. She'd shown promise at Dior and Shiseido. She'd fallen in love and married a wonderful man. And now, from a toilet stall with an empty roll of paper at the end of a gravel road, she was lying to him. "Like a café," she said. "I won't be much longer." She hung up and switched the phone to silent.

The beer was magic: she stood at the sink and, with only the slightest prick of discomfort, expressed enough milk into the drain to take the pressure off.

She was forever in the restroom. He drummed his thumb on his boot, then the door slapped open and he watched her weave between empty tables.

"Oh, I think I've had enough," she said when she spotted the full glass of beer waiting for her.

"Sorry," he said. "Do you need to leave?"

She sat down, shaking her head.

"We can go if you need to," he said. "It must be hard to be away from Sammy."

She didn't say anything—just a gaze that reminded him of the photograph. He preferred to think of her pregnant.

"I miss Ruby Christine every minute," he said.

"At least you could get in a car and see her," she said. "Why don't you?" She sipped her beer.

He wasn't sure what he expected from her. He wished she'd brought the baby.

"So how did you end up being an anarchist?"

"I always was."

"Come on." She drank again, and he noticed the wrinkles at her eyes. "What's your history? You weren't born with tattoos and a pierced eyebrow. When did *that* start? All the anarchist adornments?"

He didn't like this part of her, thinking she's a step ahead of him, not so different from her husband. This was not the pregnant woman in the photo. He gripped one hand tight around his glass, becoming aware of his tic, and with the other he held his neck, covering the *Billy* tattoo, and he looked at her as hard as steel.

The color left her face. He'd scared her. It was that easy.

He expected her to get up and leave, but she didn't. She downed a gulp and held the edge of the table. He'd only ever told Daria, and it wasn't until he did that he realized he wasn't sure how much of the story he'd made up. At night as he lay in bed ready to embrace sleep, if sleep happened to slip under the door and beneath his blanket, the story worked in and out of him. He remembered, he imagined, he re-imagined. The story was his.

Naomi didn't back off. She met him across the table like a challenge, like the government therapist he'd been forced to talk to nine years ago.

"Billy was the smart one," he began. "My brother. Everybody said it." Though Clay was two years older, he told Naomi, he'd grown up in Billy's shadow. As far back as he could remember, Billy was the dominant one. Physically, Clay took after his mom, a slender, timid woman always apologizing and fidgeting with her hair. But she'd been a beauty back in the day, as he knew from photos and from what people in Yaquina said. The high-school prom queen, escorted by his dad, a varsity slugger who lived up to his given name, King. Clay knew lots from talk over in Yaquina—the notion of coastal townsfolk being tight-lipped and never minding other people's business was just another myth. Over fish gutting and net mending, tree felling and road blasting, in the cafés and bars, the gossip went around like at a knitting circle.

This is what he'd heard: King Knudson and Roslyn Stroup had always seemed destined for each other. Both their fathers—Clay's grandfathers—were crabbers, hauling lines through the years for Yaquina Crab, Pressman, and Central Coast, sometimes working side by side, sometimes for competitors. Neither man ever owned his own boat, content to draw a percentage of the catch and to paint houses or grind hulls for the drydock when boats were in port. The two men owned houses on Onsland Spit, at the southern edge of the harbor, where twenty or thirty rickety bungalows were owned by fishermen, loggers, cannery workers, a school teacher, a truck driver, a foreman at the pulp mill. They were family men who worked hard when they worked and spent time off on sunny summer days grilling and drinking beer in backyards high on rocky bluffs overlooking the sea that guarded so fiercely the fruit of their livelihoods. On foggy and cold days, they sat with their wives and children in their small living rooms, a window cracked to let out some of the heat pouring from the woodstove. They fished and crabbed and raised their families without the government banging on the door and peeking in the windows all day and night.

King and Roslyn, born a month apart, were the youngest of each brood. They grew up like brother and sister, sharing a playpen and the bath, exchanging hand-me-down rain boots, candy, and stomach bugs. Digging canals in the rain on the beach, crabbing off the docks with homemade rings, searching for starfish in the tide pools around the harbor, the two were inseparable for the first six or seven years of their lives. In elementary school, King got stockier and gravitated toward sports and boyish things while Roslyn became willowy, a solid if not brilliant student, a reader and precise drawer of kittens, sunsets, fishing boats, and flowers. At school they didn't see much of each other, but in their backyards and front rooms and in the shallows at low tide it was as if nothing had changed: they had developed like one mind, one will, one desire. If Roslyn wanted a Dr. Pepper, so did King. She sat in the bleachers through rain and cold fog at his Little League games; he hung her drawings on the wall above his bed. When he told her he'd been frightened of the ocean the one time he was out on a crabbing boat, she told him that she had too. When she lost a tooth, he knew it was time to yank one of his.

In ninth grade, at the Spring Informal, they had their first real kiss, but each in opposite corners of the high-school gym. Roslyn's date was the second-chair trumpet player in the band, whose lips, even during the break between sets, were red and inflamed in the circle of his embrouchure. When he puckered, his embrouchure tightened up and spasmed, like instead of kissing Roslyn he was blowing a high C. His lips smelled like valve oil and brass and the dry pellets of spittle that collected in the corners of his mouth when he played.

In his corner, King's head was pressed against the wall as Sandra Simmons probed the depths of his mouth with her serpentine tongue until he couldn't breathe and finally pushed her back, taking two deep gasps of air. They both found themselves thinking back to an earlier kiss, in third grade, when they were playing house in Roslyn's bedroom, pretending they had their own house on Onsland Spit, and she said, "Okay, now I'm in the kitchen making dinner and you come in from the docks and kiss me." He walked out the door and came back in, and as she wiped her hands on her apron, he touched her cheek and they pressed their lips together. She wasn't surprised that his lips, always chapped from fishing and playing baseball, were rough. He wasn't surprised by the pleasant oniony smell of her breath. Pretending to be their parents, they also felt like their grandparents. That kiss must have felt like the one that Roslyn's father put on her forehead when she was two hours old, and the one Clay gave Daria minutes after Ruby Christine was born.

In 1968, age eighteen, King told Roslyn that patriotic duty and a debt to his father and hers, who'd both served, had made him decide to enlist in the army. She tried desperately to change his mind, and they argued for the first time ever until he finally relented, agreeing to join the National Guard instead. Then, halfway through boot camp, his company got orders for Vietnam. King was given a month of ordnance training; Roslyn wept for weeks. She'd never had such a foreboding feeling, she told her mother, as if he'd already been killed. Five Yaquina boys who'd gone to Vietnam had not come home.

Days before they were set to deploy, the governor of Maryland made a request to the governor of Oregon for one company of guardsmen, and instead of Vietnam, King went straight to Baltimore, where he wasn't permitted to leave the high-school gymnasium that served as their barracks during the riots that they never helped to quell. By the third week he was stir crazy. He'd caught a glimpse of the Atlantic from the military bus coming in, and when the wind blew from the east he could smell the harbor from an open window, but along with a hundred fellow soldiers he was forced to live on a cot, do PT in shifts at the empty end of the gym, listen to news of the riots on the radio, watch John Wayne and army-issue stag films at night.

So he slipped out a fire escape one evening in search of oysters and the famous soft-shelled crab he'd never tasted. It was dark, and the streets were empty. He headed toward the salt air but got turned around in hilly streets that curved and dead-ended and lost him all his bearings. Slums. King knew poor. On the Oregon coast he knew all about kids without warm clothes or enough food. But what he was seeing here was hopeless: vacant buildings, windows and doors busted in, empty lots of rubble, cars stripped and burned, then a pocket of men at the end of an alley—and a pop and a sting in his eye. But before his hand could wipe it away, the pain inside his skull exploded. He never felt his tooth break on the sidewalk. Mercifully, he was unconscious.

King Knudson was never the same. The government returned him home without his right eye or much control of his judgment and mood. He'd been gone from Yaquina less than twelve weeks. Standing on the bluff one night, King's father demanded of the sea, "Why do we let the government take our children?"

Despite his dangerous unpredictability, Roslyn married King six months later, and the Oregon Department of Transportation hired him for the expertise that the army had given him. He spent the next twelve years blasting through the road from Yaquina to Douglas. For solace he drank, and Roslyn contemplated the boy she'd known like a brother, the teenager she'd fallen in love with, and the man she'd lost forever at eighteen.

"There's no coming back from something like that," Clay said. "She tried kids fifteen years later, Billy and me. Every day she reminded my father who he used to be. She thought she could fix him."

He saw Naomi's head bob. "What's wrong?" he asked.

"I'm sorry." Her eyes were red. "I want to hear the rest, but . . . do you think they have coffee?"

While he was at the bar, she went into the restroom. He pushed the beer glasses aside and set the Styrofoam cup on the table.

But she didn't even try it. Just a sniff, and she shook her head. "I shouldn't have drunk that last beer."

While she paid, he chugged the coffee. It tasted fine.

Stepping around puddles and ruts in the gravel road, she resisted the temptation to take his arm, and at the sidewalk she found her centerline. Half a beer too much. So long without a drink, she'd lost her tolerance.

"We can cut over here," Clay said, not really pointing but raising an arm then letting it fall. "Over to Washington."

"You don't need to walk me home," she said.

"I'll take you as far as Lewis and Clark."

They walked a block in silence, passing a condemned old church that looked half torn down. The bungalows on the right backed up to an old railroad yard. Most had beautiful front yard gardens. She was amazed by how good the gardens still looked in November. And how was it that particular aesthetics grouped themselves around town? This whole street tended toward heaped-up wildflower gardens, bamboo chimes, Buddhas and Polynesian masks, Japanese arbors.

"Do you want to finish telling me?" she asked him.

"Another time," he said. "I should get down to the courthouse. Trial's heating up."

"I could use that coffee."

She thought he was thinking about where they could grab a cup to go, but then his arms went out wide when a little voice called his name from down the block. A girl, maybe four years old, dropped her mother's hand and came running. Clay squatted down, arms still spread, saying, "Hi, Bumblebee," as she hurtled into his embrace.

She rubbed her nose against Clay's chest. "We have a chicken party!"

"Oh, that's great," he said, a rush of enthusiasm in his voice. His face came alive, as it had on the night of her labor and for moments when he talked about his parents. She saw past the tattoos, piercings, and shaved head to his tiny-toothed smile and watery eyes.

"Can you come?" the girl asked. "Please." And then, when her mother caught up, "Mommy, can Clay come to the chicken party?"

"Hey," he said to the mother, who was carrying a battered aluminum stockpot on her hip.

"Hey," she said, eyeing Naomi.

Clay introduced them.

"Come to the party," said Royce, the mother, tipping her hip. "I made lentils."

Bumblebee was hugging Clay's leg. "Please," she pleaded.

"Where's it at?" he asked Royce.

"Right here," Bumblebee said.

Clay looked at the house, shaking his head. "I don't know who they are."

"No worries," Royce said. "She's cool with anybody coming."

"And Naomi's gotta get some coffee," he said.

"You go ahead," Naomi told him, and took a step toward home.

Royce put a hand on her arm. "Good coffee right here."

Bumblebee hung all her weight on Clay's arm, pulling him toward the house like a fisherman dragging a skiff onto the beach. "Pretty please," she said.

At that the decision was made, and they all went inside.

Clay obviously knew some of the women in the living room—no shortage of twenty-year-old moms in Douglas. Preschoolers ran screaming around the tiny bungalow, so far as she could tell just three little rooms with tall windows and dark woodwork and doors. A comfy old couch and loveseat, an oak table piled with papers and a computer. On the wall beside it there was a poster reading *Girls Say Yes to Boys Who Say No.* Then she noticed—what the hell?—a flier headed *The Oregon Experiment.* Naomi could smell the sharp tang of violation releasing from her pores. What had Scanlon *done*?

Royce led her by the elbow into the kitchen. "She's probably got some nice teas, too."

And then Naomi saw her standing there on the black and white tiled floor at a wooden table painted robin's-egg blue, her long back and full hips, her straight blond hair with the tips dipped in brown.

"Hey," Royce said, and she turned.

What a smile. What a mouth. "Hi, Sequoia," Naomi said.

"You know each other?" Royce asked, as Sequoia tried to place Naomi.

"Scanlon's wife," Naomi prompted.

"Wow! Naomi." Sequoia hugged her. "Thanks for coming."

The smell of her was heady, woody overall: cinnamon, sandalwood, baking, lactation, sharp underarms, and the sweet sappy oils in her scalp.

"Is Scanlon here? Did you bring Sammy?"

Naomi was surprised her baby's name rolled so easily off this woman's tongue. "Neither," she said.

"I guess Sammy's a little young," Sequoia said as two boys chased each other into the kitchen, under the table, and out the back door. Then she turned to Royce and said, "Her husband's the director of the movement."

"No way," Royce said. "The professor?"

"He's given us a whole new life," Sequoia said.

"A godsend," Naomi added, pretty sure given the moonbeams shining from the two women's faces that they missed her facetiousness. "Anyway, I can't really stay. I've got to get home to the boys."

"Coffee," Royce suddenly remembered. "Naomi needs a quick score."

"Not a problem," Sequoia said, and in a flash she was pressing a warm mug into Naomi's hands, then a warm kiss to her cheek. Although she used inexpensive and simple solid fragrances, her smell was all her own. It was much too rough for a wide market, but maybe its general personality and attitude could be a guide. Sequoia was genuine and confident. She was, without deceit or illusion, mysterious, with a sense that her mystery was surprising and glorious, full of curiosity. She was fresh without being innocent or girlish. Sequoia was new territory, a new landscape.

Applause roared up from the living room. "The guest of honor's here!" someone shouted. Kids ran in from the backyard and the bedroom, swarming to the front door. Naomi expected a clown or a gorilla, but when she looked back over her shoulder she only saw a mom and, somewhere within the gang of ecstatic kids, her child.

Sequoia pulled two boxes from the freezer and waded into the frenzy of children, calling out, "I've got the popsicles."

Naomi leaned in the kitchen doorway, exchanging a glance across the living room with Clay. He was sitting on a stool in the corner between a guitar and a didjuridu, surrounded by maracas, a tambourine, bells, and oatmeal-box drums. They held the glance for several seconds. He'd laid his life bare. Or he'd begun to. He'd revealed himself, exposed himself. She remembered her labor. The smell of gasoline. His oily boots and tiny red ears. Like Naomi, he had a child who was lost to him. But *he* hadn't sat in a lawyer's office on a cool Thursday afternoon—too close to a paralegal with raw onions and Dijon mustard on her breath, grapefruit-scented carpet cleaner rising from the floor—and signed his baby away. Clay was not culpable. As she surveyed the room, she could believe all of these girls were single moms. The horrible truth was that she could've managed just fine with Joshua.

She gulped her coffee, right back where she'd started, condemning herself for surrendering her baby and resolving further to devote every shred of herself to Sammy.

The kids were trading popsicles, licking each other's, a few at a time. Unnecessarily, Naomi thought, the moms and the three conspicuous dads were encouraging it.

A blond girl squatting by Naomi's feet and sharing a popsicle with her friend said, "I have just one mommy."

"I *know,*" the friend replied. "But if you had *two* mommies, you'd be adopted and your hair would be black."

Sequoia backed up next to Naomi saying, "This is our third party. And not a single infection. But this time I'm hopeful—we've definitely got a live one."

And then Naomi realized the passing of popsicles was actually methodical. One particular child sucked on all the popsicles in turn, then passed them on to the others. And as the crowd of preschoolers spread out, she saw that the lucky child's face—a little girl with pigtails—was completely covered in chicken pox.

"Holy shit," she said aloud, dropping her coffee on the counter and holding her breath until she'd escaped onto the back deck.

Sequoia was right behind her. "Are you okay?"

She wanted to wash her hands. And her face. She wanted a shower. "I just didn't . . ." She stepped out of the rain, under the canopy of a giant redwood tree.

"You didn't have chicken pox as a kid?"

"I don't know. Probably."

"That's the way to do it." Sequoia shook her head. "Now all these parents are letting their kids get shot up with vaccine—it's barbaric."

The deck was fitted around the two-foot trunk of the redwood. A bench led to a hot tub, and a few stairs dropped down to the fenced-in garden, which Naomi scanned for a gate, an exit.

"That one's Trinity's tree," Sequoia said. "A weeping pussy willow. Planted the day she was born."

"Heavy work after giving birth," Naomi joked.

"My friends were here. And the midwife. But I got down on my knees and laid in Trinity's placenta."

The kitchen door opened, and Clay stepped out on the deck. He and Sequoia stared at each other for a long moment until he finally said, "From the park. You got hit in the mouth with the swing."

"Right," she said. That smile.

Clay touched his upper lip. "You got a scar."

She shook her head. "I had that already."

Naomi jumped in and introduced them.

"Anyway, I should motor," Clay said.

Sequoia hugged him. "I'm glad to have you in my home."

When she released him, he and Naomi looked at each other awkwardly, then she stepped toward him with her arms outspread.

"That was fun, Clay," she said, her breasts tender as they hugged, her nose at his ear. They separated, and he looked down at his boots, then abruptly turned and left through the house.

Sequoia had stepped down into the garden, where she was pulling baby carrots from a raised bed under a canopy of milky clear plastic, then swishing them in a bucket of water.

They came out so orange Naomi thought she could smell them. "Winter carrots?" she asked.

"Year-round. I stagger them. Lettuce, too." She pointed to more covered beds. "Broccoli, kale, radishes. If you're serious about being a locavore. . . ."

As she spoke, Naomi examined the three clawfoot bathtubs situated at different levels beside the deck, connected by pipes. They made her think of a stagecoach stop in the Old West, run by a single woman with baby carrots hammocked in her apron, where a man might get a room and his back scrubbed in the bath and maybe something more.

"That's my gray water system," Sequoia said. "The sinks and shower drain through the pebbles and charcoal in the tubs, and I can use it to water the garden all summer."

Naomi looked back to the hot tub. She walked over to it, squatted down, and sniffed with a start. That was what she'd smelled on Scanlon last week. He and Sequoia had been hot tubbing.

She stood by the kitchen door, looking through the glass at the kids chasing and rolling around with each other like a litter of puppies, their young mothers hopeful they'd catch these good chicken pox.

She glanced at the wall clock. God, it was nearly five. She had to get home. She missed Sammy with an ache in her breasts, as if she hadn't seen him in days. "I should go too," she said.

"How's the nose, if you don't mind my asking? And your infections?"

"Nose is great," she said. "Thanks for all the referrals. Nursing's still a pain, though."

She let herself be guided onto a bench beside the hot tub, where Sequoia squatted down in front of her, took off her shoes, and squeezed her feet. Pure pleasure. Slowly, on her left foot Sequoia worked her thumbs harder and deeper into a soft spot between two pearl-sized bones, until she was pressing so hard Naomi began to cry, releasing a wave of relief, like the soft brushing of ferns from her pelvis to breasts. Sequoia did the same to her other foot, then kissed them both.

"Oh my God," Naomi said. "I've been ravished."

Sequoia slipped Naomi's feet back in her shoes. "You deserve a good ravishing. It's hard to have a baby in a new environment."

"At least I'm not alone. I mean, were you alone?"

"I was," Sequoia said, gently tying Naomi's laces. "If you mean Trinity's father. But I was much more alone *before* she was born. Having a baby, having girlfriends around, my garden, the café—my passions—I didn't feel alone at all. I felt I'd finally found my place in the world."

Sequoia helped her stand, and Naomi decided she'd call Blaine Maxwell tonight. After eight years without her nose, she'd been denying herself the full celebration of its return in the name of maternal devotion. She couldn't wait to get a whiff of the Pacific leaping frog. She couldn't wait to get back to work.

As they hugged, Sequoia's blond hair draped over Naomi's face: the wonderful, woody, erotic, dirty scent of Sequoia. How could any man resist her?

With one eye, through the veil of Sequoia's hair, Naomi saw the girl with chicken pox come into the kitchen from the living room, and right behind her—long legs and chinos—was Scanlon. With Sammy on his shoulder!

She shot through the door, knocking Sequoia through with her. "Out!" she shouted. "Out!"

"Hey, Scanlon," Sequoia said. "*Namaste.*"

"Don't touch anything," Naomi told him, then turned to Sequoia. "The baby hasn't been vaccinated!"

"Good for you," Sequoia said.

"*Yet!* Not *yet*!"

The infected kid stood at the fridge drinking apple juice from the jug.

"Scanlon! Turn around," she ordered. "Walk to the door and don't even brush up against anything. Your shoes touch the floor. That's it!"

Chapter 6

A week later, Scanlon was laughing in his office with two undergrads when the phone rang. Strong, inspired students, they were preparing an oral report on the importance of music to the civil rights movement—"the most successful mass movement in American history, and it's got a soundtrack!" Scanlon had said—so he considered letting voicemail pick up, but then, thinking it might be Naomi, he grabbed the phone. Instead, it was a Portland TV station looking for a quote about the Panama Harris sentencing, which was news to Scanlon. "When?" he asked.

"This morning. Twenty-three years. No possibility of parole."

Scanlon sat back in his chair. "Jesus," he said, half to himself. "The kid's a political prisoner."

"Can you hold a second?" the reporter asked, then cupped a hand over the mouthpiece.

The trial had been a joke. Clearly the court intended to make an example of him, but twenty-three years was shocking.

"We'd like to get your comments on tape," the reporter said. "Can I send a crew to your office?"

"I have some students with—"

"They could be there in ten minutes, Professor Pratt. They're at the courthouse. This is a breaking story. The public needs your insights."

He knew flattery when he heard it but still said, "Come right over." He *was* flattered. The public *did* need his insights. This wasn't county court, with locally elected judges, but federal court whose judges were sent by Washington to carry out Washington's agenda. The prosecutor would keep stirring up fears of terrorism. The public defender would continue to underwhelm. Scanlon could put it all in context.

The initial charge was Criminal Mischief, but by the time the trial began that had multiplied to thirteen felonies including three counts of Arson One. Harris faced a hundred-years-plus sentence for torching three SUVs that, his supporters pointed out, had been repaired and sold by Timber Ford.

Scanlon apologized to his students, and they were shuffling out with a list of songs for their presentation when none other than America Sanchez came rushing down the hall. Her face, in breathless reports from rising rivers and burning forests, always reminded Scanlon of photos of infants under water—an ecstatic zest for the moment.

"Professor Pratt," she said, extending her slender hand. "It's so great to meet you." As they shook, she was already looking at the wall behind Scanlon's desk, thinking, he was sure, about the camera angles and leading questions that would put her stamp on the interview. "We'll tape it here in the office," she said. "In your chair." Then she gave him an extra squeeze before drawing her hand away. Shameless.

As a soundman pinned a mic to Scanlon's shirt and lights popped on, glaring in his eyes, he regretted agreeing to this, since anything he said would be reduced to a sound bite. But then he saw his students lingering in the hall, and Ron Dexter hitting on America Sanchez, who was ignoring him, texting, looking altogether unzestful at the moment. Fenton came up behind them with two more department colleagues, Gloria Bishop and Kim Phan. The soundman held up his hands—"Stand back!"—and they obeyed, whispering, watching, and Scanlon suddenly felt two sizes larger. The chair's tidy little arms were folded over his compact chest, his head tipped sideways as he whispered to Gloria. For eight years, ever since receiving his doctorate, Scanlon had bounced around in jobs that never made him feel he'd achieved anything. And even here, finally on tenure track, he'd entered under the cloud of the *Domestic Policy* embarrassment and now suffered Fenton's threats.

But as a pricey-looking light meter passed under his chin, more faculty and students peering in from the hall, he felt as if he'd stepped onto a platform and the department now had to live up to him. Being director of the secessionists could be perceived as naive—akin to his past mistakes—but Sequoia was right, the quality of his research would be enhanced. And as director he was suddenly an important voice, valuable currency in a profession full of people who feared that none of their work really mattered. He might not even need the book; this new visibility and the authority that came with it could be his ticket back east.

Sanchez squeezed into the corner in front of his bookcase and spoke to him with a bubbling urgency. Scanlon leaned toward the camera, straightening his glasses, the glowing lights warm on his face as the crowd out in the corridor, packing in tighter, was hushed by the soundman.

The interview lasted ten minutes. As she left Sanchez said, "It's so great to meet you," in the exact same tone she'd greeted him with.

Everyone was gone from the hallway when Fenton strutted into Scanlon's office. "Quite a show," he said. "Quite a razzle-dazzle."

"Thank you, Cebert," Scanlon said, not trusting him for a moment. "It's really nothing."

"You got that right," Fenton said. "How're those articles coming?"

Scanlon could easily grab the little prick and toss him through the window. "Nicely."

Fenton stepped closer, arms crossed over his chest. "These fleeting spectacles might impress for a week or two, but they're meaningless in the end. Publications, Pratt. Publications are forever."

"I've got a draft about ready to go," Scanlon bluffed. "Needs some punching up, some polishing." Ron would no doubt *give* the café building to Sequoia when he saw Fenton lying with a broken spine on the crushed roof of his Porsche.

"What's your argument?"

Scanlon stared him down. "The goals of present-day American anarchists, while apparently no better than hooligans, do in fact have theoretical ties to Max Stirner and Proudhon and Mutualism."

"Send me the draft," Fenton said.

Scanlon looked away. "You're too busy for that."

"This is what colleagues are for, Pratt. I know a lot of editors. Ties to Stirner *and* the Mutualists. Compelling. E-mail it to me, pronto."

And then, with rapid clicks of his loafers on the tiled hallway, he was gone.

The rainy walk to campus had given Naomi a chill, and she was relieved to find the lab so warm.

"The animals just want to burrow if it's too cold," Blaine Maxwell explained, wiping one hand on her lab coat, the front of it dirty with the prints of webbed feet, canine paws, ungulate hooves. "The heat keeps them excited." In her other hand she held up a syringe like a loaded revolver.

Naomi unzipped her raincoat. Sammy was snoozing against her chest, his head and the green cap pulled into the sling like a turtle.

"I hope I'll get a look," Blaine said.

The lab was much as she'd described it. Half a dozen treadmills, no different from those at the gym, were mounted with cameras and strobe lights. A goat tethered to one of them had figured out how to sidestep the moving belt and stand on the stationary frame, seeming to accept that this is what life had become: someone picks you up and sets you on a rubber belt, it begins to move, you step off, you do it again, and soon there will be food. At another treadmill, grad students were varying the belt speed and experimenting by dropping, placing, and tossing a goose onto it. No matter what method they used, the goose shot off the back into someone's waiting arms.

Naomi felt for the goose. The Oregon Experiment—*her* version, not Sequoia's—would have worked: opening her neural pathways and forming associations between Scanlon's smells and the pleasant smells of Willamette mint and sage and the stimulation of their lovemaking. But he'd blown it, and the betrayal had shot her squawking off the belt.

On top of that, the realization that Sammy couldn't provide solace from the loss of Joshua had made her feel foolish. His birth only made her understand how completely, unforgivably selfish she'd been eighteen years ago. All those young single moms she'd met at Sequoia's—they were packing picnics and walking the dog, taking night classes and holding down jobs. They were living. They were happy.

But it got worse: there were brief, shameful moments when Sammy felt like a burden. She'd been relieved to abandon him to meet Clay at the bar. Just this morning she'd thought, If only I could quit nursing, if only my body could be my own, if only I could walk out the door without a care. The guilt and remorse that followed were suffocating. She was a woman who'd given away her first child and now couldn't rise up to meet her second. If only Scanlon hadn't taken her from New York, cutting her off from her old friends and her old life, if only she felt sure she loved him as she once had, if only she could overcome the goddamn breast infections, then maybe she'd find the inner strength to be the woman she wished she was.

She watched the goose run for its life as they dialed up the treadmill speed. *Bam.* The bird missed the grad student and tumbled across the floor.

Blaine led her over to terrariums along the back wall. The frogs were beautiful—the same electric green of the moss that covered trees from Douglas to the coast, amethyst rimming their eyes, tiny beads of maroon and chanterelle yellow dotting their backs. The Pacific leaping frog. Blaine gave her a refresher course on leaping versus hopping and then, with a wide-eyed reverence at odds with her scientific matter-of-factness, she concluded, "A true leaper."

Naomi held one, the size of a small pond frog. She smelled it: frog. It urinated on her hand, which she smelled: ordinary swamp urine.

Blaine held another between her thumb and forefinger and flicked at its dangling legs. "Five grams of muscle," she said, "maximum. Propelling a ninety-gram animal." She placed the frog on the lab bench in front of the camera, and a green strobe light flashed almost imperceptibly. A video monitor showed Blaine's fingertips holding the frog still. A grad student stood by with a butterfly net as Blaine positioned the frog, aiming it toward a mossy area impossibly far away. "The shock is very mild," she said, removing her hands and pressing a button: the frog fired its legs, sailed through the air, and touched down, calm and cool, in the moss, where the net swooped over it.

Naomi's heart was suddenly racing. "You weren't kidding," she said, with her own reverence for this magnificent spectacle. "Those little legs can jump."

"Leap."

The student handed the frog back to Blaine.

"Now," Blaine said, "let's get what you came here for." She put on a pair of lab glasses, dabbed the frog between the legs with a cotton ball, and stuck in her syringe. A minute later she handed over a tiny vial of the little frog's magic, corked and labeled. Naomi squeezed it in her fist.

"Aren't you going to smell it?"

"Not here," she said. The goat, the geese—it smelled like a petting zoo. "Later, if that's okay."

"E-mail me, then. I'm dying to know what you think." Blaine's tone was girlish and conspiratorial, as if they were at the perfume counter spending too much on a scent too dangerously provocative. "And send me a jpeg of your progeny."

Naomi had misjudged her. The two of them could be friends. "Let's meet for coffee," she said. Blaine's intellect wasn't dryly analytical. Sure, she engaged the world in a lab coat, but it was cloaked with a bright curiosity, a thrill of observation and playful discovery. She could be an excellent friend, and Naomi would make it happen. "Let's meet next week. After I've had a chance to work with the frog juice."

"I thought I told you," Blaine said. "I leave Saturday on sabbatical. Lorenz Institute. In Vienna."

"Oh." Naomi squeezed the vial and touched the curve of Sammy's back, feeling that something had been snatched away from her.

"Nine months," Blaine said. "It's always hard to be apart from Roger for so long, but we've managed before. Gets us both very focused on work."

Not very difficult, Naomi thought, for a childless couple. After regretfully saying goodbye, she left the lab and soon was lost in deserted hallways underneath the building. Finally she found a stairwell—not the one she'd taken before—and pushed through the first of two steel doors, pausing in the overheated space between them, hot air blowing down from the ceiling, mildew rising from the wet mats. She reached into the sling at her chest, plucked off Sammy's cap, and pressed her nose to his scalp: Joshua would turn eighteen in less than three months. On February 5th, if he chose to, he could view the file held on him by the State of New York; he could learn the name of his real mother; he could try to find her.

"Her hair didn't have that floating-underwater look," he told Naomi, "like it does on TV." They were curled up with Sammy on the couch for the six-o'clock news. "It was short and choppy. Didn't Liza Minnelli have hair like that?"

Naomi hiked up her shirt and Sammy crashed face-first into her breast. He settled in, with quiet groans of satisfaction.

The lead story was about Panama's sentencing: America Sanchez, live, outside the federal courthouse downtown. The rain had let up, but angry chanting continued around her. She spoke too fast, breathless.

"Maybe it's her mascara," Naomi said. "She looks under water to me."

Sanchez reported on the increased pitch of the afternoon's demonstrations. Behind her, facing off a strict line of police, was a scraggly collection of local protestors, along with those who'd made this pilgrimage from Portland and Seattle. Scanlon's heart ratcheted up a notch.

After the predictable sound bites from the prosecutor and defense attorney, Scanlon's own face filled the screen. "The prosecutor inflamed the public," he said from behind his battered oak desk, the photo of him with Abbie Hoffman partially visible on the back wall, "with terms like 'domestic terrorist' and 'uncontrollable anarchist.' Playing the press, I might add," he said with a nod to Sanchez. There was a cut during which he'd shifted his weight. *Prof. Scanlon Pratt, Director, The Oregon Experiment* appeared below him on the screen. For the sake of credibility he was glad he'd shaved off his beard. "Twenty-three years is completely out of line with typical sentences for like crimes. We can't overlook the politics of the sentence. The prosecutor essentially argued that these were political acts of terrorism that threatened the nation, and the punishment reflects the fact that the judge accepted those arguments. In my view it's completely without merit. When a judicial system allows the emotions of an event like nine-eleven to blur its judgment of a very different sort of case, it fosters, historically, the kind of atmosphere that can trigger radical and even more violent action."

They cut back to Sanchez outside and, as she spoke, a red splatter burst on the gray concrete facade of the courthouse. Red paint, he realized. A paint-filled glass bottle. Then, when a second bottle smashed against the building, the police, who weren't wearing face shields or riot gear, gripped their batons across their chests and took two coordinated steps forward. The cameras remained fixed on the standoff as Sanchez filled airtime, but after a couple of minutes with no further escalation, the broadcast returned to the newscasters in the studio and a piece on Snake River dams that were devastating the sockeye run.

Scanlon muted the TV with the remote. "I like that last line about triggers, don't you?"

"I'm proud of you," Naomi said.

He brushed a finger along Sammy's milk-filled cheek, then along Naomi's breast. "It felt good. Sort of a rush."

She smiled, the smile quickly turning to a yawn, and toted Sammy off, sacked on her shoulder, to the bedroom.

Sirens wailed without a break, mostly coming from downtown, but then one raced by their house. The news cut back to the protests: police handcuffing a kid in black; the courthouse splotched with dozens of red bursts; shattered plate glass at Starbucks.

He was revved, and when Naomi came back to the couch after putting Sammy down, he muted the TV again. "How are you feeling?" he asked, taking hold of her hand.

"Fine." She nodded. "Good."

He tried to kiss her, but she turned her face away. She'd never answered his question about disliking his smell, but the fact was they'd barely kissed since they got to Oregon, never mind anything approaching a sex life. The day she told him her nose was back was the last time they'd truly made love. Twice since then, lying on her side with her back to him in bed, she'd rolled into a ball of guilt and resignation and invited him in from behind.

"What's wrong?" he said.

"What does any of this have to do with getting your book written?"

He explained the currency that visibility had in academic circles, but she didn't hide her skepticism, and of course he didn't mention Fenton's.

"You always said the book's what counts."

"Or articles, or talking-head stuff on TV. It's all good."

"But you're still writing?"

"It's coming along."

"And does your girlfriend know you're just using her movement to get a book out of it?"

He was *not* using the movement for a book. "She knows about my research."

"And she likes the catchy new name?"

His eyes darted to the TV. "I intended to tell you about that."

"America Sanchez knows. I see the fliers at Sequoia's house, and some single mom tells me it was page two in the newspaper."

"If you read the Douglas paper and not just the *New York*—"

"So that's what this is about? What newspaper I read?"

He said nothing.

"That was supposed to be special for us."

"Use it or lose it," he blurted, immediately regretting it.

She started to cry, and he reached his arms around her. Although she turned her face away, she collapsed against his chest, shaking, whimpering. "If I'm going to be the best mother I can be," she began, and he waited for her to finish, holding her as he hadn't in months, her body warm and brimming with emotion, releasing to him, which released in Scanlon the flood of love and affection knotted up in his chest. While Sammy slept, they could reclaim the Oregon Experiment for themselves with leaves of mint, a mandarin, a pot of spicy tea.

"With my nose back, I'm afraid I'll get depressed if I don't jump into my career. I need to feel vital. I need friends. Otherwise, Sammy'll suffer for it."

"I know," he said. "I know." There was an unopened bar of lavender chocolate in the kitchen cupboard.

"I'm thinking I should maybe do the bicoastal thing." She wiped her tears, then stared at her wet fingertip. "Get an apartment in New York. Not to move, just a pied-à-terre so I can work again."

He slowly pulled back from her. She'd lost her mind.

"It's for Sammy."

"You know damn well it's not for Sammy. It's for the other one, the—" he stopped himself before speaking the words he'd only ever thought—"ghost baby. You refuse to allow yourself to feel good. You can't even celebrate our perfect baby and our new life as a family because of a burden from half your life ago. You insist on punishing yourself. That's neurotic. Truly, you're out of your goddamn mind." Until he saw her face—withdrawn but alert—and heard Sammy's cry, he didn't realize he was shouting.

When he started up the Honda, the Norah Jones CD came on with her romantic anticipation of midlife crisis. He turned it louder, set the wipers on Delay, and headed downtown. At the corner, a police car—no blue lights or siren—roared past and Scanlon followed, a little heavy on the accelerator. When he got to Lewis and Clark, he looked up and down the oddly deserted street, the pavement black and wet, mist shining silver in the streetlights. As he turned toward the courthouse and drove along Central Park, a figure shot in front of him. He slammed on the brakes as the hooded man punched down on the front of the car and rolled on one hip up and over the fender, then sprinted off between two houses. Scanlon was just getting his breath back when two cops ran out from the trees and held up on the sidewalk, bent over and huffing. He hit the gas.

Courthouse Square was a mess. Sixty or eighty protesters stood out in the rain, two of them holding up sticks supporting each end of a banner made from a white bedsheet, the black ink so wet and runny that whatever the message had been was now illegible. Cops in full riot gear formed a line across the square, keeping the demonstrators in one corner. The building was covered with red splashes.

He drove past Starbucks where a crew protected by two cops was already installing plywood over the broken windows. He pulled up to the curb across the street, the idling car a little too warm, so he turned off the heat. With the wipers on low and Norah Jones crooning, he powered his window halfway down, the cool mist fresh on his face. The workers slid sheets of plywood off a pickup and screwed them in place. Where did they get it, he wondered? Do Starbucks and the Gap keep a supply on hand in case the anti-globalists attack? And were the carpenters always on call? Eight o'clock at night and they were already on the job.

He'd left the house angry, and now wished he'd controlled himself. Maybe he should have finally admitted he was jealous of the ghost baby—of the power he had over Naomi—and of the boy in Vermont who'd knocked her up. Many times over the years Naomi had mentioned nonchalantly, or so it seemed to him, that she wasn't at all surprised when she got pregnant because she and the old boyfriend had panted helplessly in the grip of a passion that obliterated reason and precaution—doing it in cars and garages, slipping out to the milk room between dinner and dessert and doing it again in the time it took her grandmother to make coffee, leaving hot dogs and baskets of vinegar-soused fries half-eaten to do it on the restroom counter, then returning to their table to savor the greasy food before doing it once more in the great outdoors.

He was jealous, in part, because of the tangled thread leading from Naomi's stupefying lust all those years ago to her unavailability today. Yes, he missed having sex with his wife—was *that* so perverse?—but there was more: he wanted the closeness back, the shared life, as when Naomi would coach him to discern whether the acidity in a certain *chaumes* leaned toward tart or lemon, and he would describe the cream and mustiness, and it would be as if their noses and brains and tongues were entwined. He wanted them to complete each other; he wanted to not feel abandoned by some "bicoastal thing." But he also wished he hadn't used the word "neurotic," or pointed out that in New York State a married couple living apart for six months (or maybe it was a year) could be granted, on grounds of abandonment, an automatic divorce.

At first he thought the cop in front of Starbucks was waving but then realized he was being waved along, so he pulled ahead and turned the corner. Safeway was open, lights blazing out the windows and flooding the parking lot. Shoppers wheeled carts full of groceries to their cars. It seemed like any other night.

Yet small groups of shadowy figures hustled along in the darkness, cutting down alleys and looking over their shoulders, looking like they had someplace to get to. He cruised by the Green & Black coffee shop, one of Douglas's anarchist hangouts, and when he saw the smokers huddled under the awning out front, he parked in the gravel lot. He'd been there only twice and mostly remembered that the owner was skinny as a heroin addict, with blotchy tattoos smeared over thick veins worming his forearms, black jeans, black T-shirt, and gaunt. Keith Richards gaunt.

The rain had gotten heavier, and approaching the smokers crowded under the awning he quickened his pace. He sometimes liked the smell of cigarette smoke, especially out in the rain, sparking good memories of junior high and summer camp. But when they saw him coming, everyone at the door turned away and most conversation trailed off. Still, it didn't occur to Scanlon to be scared. This was Douglas, Jefferson Avenue at nine o'clock on a Wednesday. It wasn't New York or Boston or Philly.

The death metal inside was blaring, and everybody yelling over it. The urgency in the air was electric, amped up with thrashing guitars and the injustice meted out to Panama. Scanlon leaned into the galvanized metal counter, scratched up with street names and anarchy symbols, and asked for a coffee.

From the tall stainless steel urn behind the counter—*This urn is a pipe bomb* crudely stenciled and spray-painted across the front of it—the owner, whose name Scanlon now remembered was 13½, drew out a cup and took his money.

Finding Clay hadn't been what he'd had in mind when he came in, but now it seemed likely. Scanlon stood by a brick pillar scanning the café, thinking he spotted him, but it was someone else. If he'd come in here with a description—thin and pale with black clothes, a shaved head, piercings and tattoos—there were at least twenty of them with minor variations: blue and purple hair, mohawks gelled up into spikes, chains and safety pins stuck in their clothes. Soon enough they were all watching him, and he evaluated his own clothes: Scanlon was, safe to say, the only patron wearing a cream-colored Patagonia Gore-Tex jacket with a red fleece lining, easy-fit Levis, and suede urban hikers with purple laces and a Nike swoosh.

His eyes found Clay's at a corner table but then Clay turned away, his head twitching. Definitely him. Scanlon took a slug of coffee and moved through the crowd, the sour reek of soggy shoes and damp, dirty clothes. And was it his imagination, or did everyone in the Green & Black smell faintly of gasoline? "Hey, Clay," he said when he reached the table, where he sat shoulder to shoulder with five or six others.

"This guy would be perfect," Clay said to his companions. None of them had a coffee, or anything else.

"You *know* this good citizen?" said a stocky guy in a black vest that was open in the front as if to display his strong bare arms and chest.

"You see the bright clothes," Clay said, "the happy face. It would be a little better if he was wearing a red Gap hat, but this dude could walk right through that line of cops tonight, hurl a device through the courthouse window, and nobody would even notice him. He blends into the background. He's wallpaper. He's Muzak."

"Could I have your autograph?" the one in the vest said, then he turned to the others. "Do you have any idea how much we could sell Barry Manilow's autograph for?"

A rare smile spread across Clay's face, exposing the hole where he was missing a tooth.

"Are you a game-show host?" one of the girls said.

"Or a cop?" another asked.

"Nah," Clay said. "He's good people. A professor." His head twitched. "His wife's a friend of mine."

Slapping his bare chest, the stocky one said, "I'm Flak." He pointed around the table. "This is Ohm, Rebecca, and Entropy."

"Is Naomi with you?" Clay asked.

Scanlon shook his head, narrowing his eyes.

"Hey," said Rebecca, no older than fifteen, "you're the professor who was on the news."

Scanlon smiled.

"He was on tonight," she told Flak, "saying we should do some protests about Panama. Do some damage." She turned to Scanlon. "My father said you should be strung up by your balls."

"Wait a minute." Scanlon held up both hands. "Nothing I said could be interpreted as a call to violence. I only said that radical acts are often provoked by clearly unfair political actions, which Panama's sentence certainly is."

"True dat," said Flak.

"True dat," said Entropy, a big girl, tall and overweight. At first Scanlon thought she was in her twenties, but now realized she wasn't more than a year or two older than Rebecca.

"The thing is," Flak said, "this tells us the fucking corporate capitalist system knows it can't survive. A twenty-three-year sentence is the act of a desperate and frightened government. They know they're crashing, and they'll violate their own laws to hold on as long as they can. On the one hand, this is a dark day, and our brother is martyred. On the other hand, it proves the system knows it's evil to the core, that it's in its last days. So we should celebrate."

"Celebrate," Entropy suggested, "by burning some more SUVs."

"Not worth it," Flak said, crossing an ankle over his knee. The sole of his black boot was torn away enough that he could reach in and scratch the bottom of his foot. With his other hand he pointed at the coffee cup. "Could I have a sip of that?"

Scanlon was taken aback, but handed it over.

Flak took a careful sip, smelling, savoring. Then, looking up at Scanlon, his eyebrows raised, he pointed to Clay.

"Sure, sure," Scanlon said.

Flak passed the coffee on. "Anyway," he said, "it's much safer to roll mothballs into the gas tank, which totally cooks an engine. Overheats so bad the pistons melt. Torching those SUVs, it had a big wow factor, but wasn't worth it. Really fucking stupid."

Clay took a slow sip. Giving the cup to Rebecca, he sneaked a glance at Scanlon, and their eyes met.

"Does everyone want a coffee?" Scanlon said.

"You buying?" Flak asked.

Scanlon nodded, rising from his chair.

"You should know," Clay said, backhanding Flak's shoulder, "he's buying you coffee so he can pick your brain for a book about anarchy."

"That's fine," Flak said, then turned to Scanlon. "I want a cut of the proceeds."

"An academic book," Scanlon said, shaking his head. "There's really no money to be made." Even as he said this, he hoped it wouldn't prove true of his own book.

"The coffee's the down payment," Flak said.

"Go ahead," Clay said. "Prostitute yourself."

Flak turned to him like he was going to say something but then punched him hard in the chest. "What's wrong with prostitutes?"

"The most honorable profession," Entropy said.

"The *oldest* profession," Rebecca corrected.

"Victimless," Flak said. "Just leave people alone."

"Nobody's stopping you," Clay said.

"This," Flak pronounced, "demonstrates the difference, girls. Clay's the idealist, and I'm the pragmatist. And don't I seem happier?" He spread his arms wide, then patted his chest. "Black," he said to Scanlon. "A large one." Then the girls chimed in—coffees for all.

When he got back to the table with cups on every finger, Clay was gone. "Where's the idealist?" he asked.

"Gone off to bring down the system," Flak said. "He's an impatient boy. But the cops aren't feeling lenient tonight, and I don't feel like sleeping on a cement floor in a crowded jail."

"I heard the cops are waiting until everybody gets here," Entropy said, "and then they're going to test one of those noise machines. The frequency that makes people sick."

Flak pulled earplugs from the front pocket of his vest. "They won't bring *me* down."

"They used it on the Iraqis," Rebecca said. "They already know it works. This'll be the first time they use it on Americans."

"Bullshit," Flak said. "They used it in Seattle. These big satellite-looking trucks pulled up, and then the ringing in my ears was like the morning after you've heard a band, and then it felt like I had the flu."

"They probably put something in the food," Rebecca said. "They've infiltrated Food Not Bombs just about everywhere."

"I don't believe it," Flak said. "They don't need to waste time poisoning our minestrone soup when they've got brown noise."

"I saw those trucks in Seattle," Scanlon said, "but I didn't have any reactions." He knew the rumors on the street: Frank Zappa had discovered brown noise, the sound frequency that makes people need to shit. The FBI stole it from him and cranked it up so you get a headache and nausea, too.

"They point those things at anarchists," Flak countered. "Not at professors walking arm in arm singing 'Kumbaya.'" He paused so everyone could laugh. "Trust me. Somewhere in Douglas this very minute, those trucks are parked under cover."

"It's very messed up," Entropy said.

Flak rolled his lime-green earplugs between his fingers and poked them in his ears, then pointed at each side of his head and shouted, "Pragmatism. Patience. Ride it out. I don't need to shit. Do you need to shit? Anybody feel the need to shit?"

"Daria thought that kid was in the FBI," Rebecca said. "The one with the socks."

"This kid," Flak said to Scanlon, pulling out the earplugs, "he's dressed like the professional homeless. Okay, fine. There's a lot of them on the street, but he's a little old for it, and one day when he pulls off his boots to shake out some dirt, Daria notices he's got little sailboat flags all over his socks. Little red and white yachting flags. So Daria's like, 'Where'd you get the fucking socks, Rotor?' and he's like he just got 'em out of a clothes box, but then next time she sees him he's got different socks, so after that everybody's real cold to him, and a few days later he's gone. That's over a year ago."

"Daria *knew*," Rebecca said.

"She was *paranoid,*" Flak said. "Maybe Rotor was a Fed, maybe not. He sure bought a lot of beers."

"Daria stopped being paranoid when Clay got her clean," Rebecca insisted.

"She got *more* paranoid *after* she was clean," Flak snapped. "If she hadn't got pregnant, they'd still be hanging out and Clay wouldn't be such a brooding motherfucker." He turned to Scanlon. "Do you think he's a brooding motherfucker?"

"He's not chipper," Scanlon said.

Rebecca, staring into her coffee, looked thoughtful. "He's been happier these last few weeks."

"But nothing like when Daria was pregnant. Especially at the end. He sold out, getting a regular job and whatnot, but he was doing the right thing. Preparing for the next generation. Getting more patient. Then her freaked-out Christian parents swoop down from Idaho, and Clay starts reliving shit. We've all had a tough run of it, but he for sure deserves a little something. I was much wilder until my son was born."

It became clear to Scanlon that the girls had heard Flak's riffs before. They listened closely, knowing the next line, anticipating the turn the story would take. More kids, and some in their twenties, edged closer to the table. One of them asked Flak if brown noise was for real. "Realer than *shit*," Flak answered, then sparred with Scanlon about the whole dubious history.

But Scanlon could tell he was earning an ounce of respect from the anarchists, which wouldn't have happened if Clay hadn't vouched for him in the first place, which was why he'd let Clay's taunts about his friendship with Naomi pass. Clay's m.o. was to poke things with a stick.

"The last day of WTO in Seattle," Flak was saying, "I had to shit real bad from the brown noise, so I'm heading to the toilets in the park. But this cop's coming in my direction, so instead I veer into the woods, down into this big gully they've got all over Seattle, and under a towering Pacific yew I see blue plastic sticking out of the dirt. I jab it with my boot, then dig it up, and inside the plastic bag there's a literal cigar box all taped shut, so I cut it open and, holy shit, the box is packed tight with hundred-dollar bills. I'm looking over my shoulders thinking this is a setup, but nobody's in sight. Just me and the Pacific yew and scrappy eucalyptus trees and sword ferns. I shove the box under my coat and run out of there, no idea which direction, and come up out of the gully in some neighborhood with fancy lawns and curving porches. This is *not* the sort of neighborhood they like anarchists tromping around hiding stuff under their jackets, and by now I gotta shit so bad my molars are aching, and after four blocks, maybe five, I get to a street with little shops and a goddamn Starbucks, so I barge right in.

"And now, sitting on the shitter with the cigar box on my knees, I count one hundred and one Ben Franklins: ten thousand one hundred dollars. And why the extra hundred? But then I know. I put three or four in my pocket, then kick off my boots and stack the rest inside. Then I take the oddball hundred off the edge of the sink, look Mr. In God We Trust Franklin in the eye, and reach back with the hundred-dollar bill and wipe my ass.

"'How's your day going so far?' the dollface at the counter says when I come out. 'Busy,' I say. 'Keeping my workers in line. Counting my profits.' Then I reach in my pocket and slap a crisp hundred on the counter. 'I'm running for public office, and I'd be honored to have your vote.' Then I walk outside, understanding now what people mean about having a little cushion, a little cash in reserve. Soft in the boots, fresh feeling. It makes you taller.

"But I also know I've gotta get out of this city before I get arrested and lose the money. So I abandon my bedroll in the park and hop into a taxi and tell him to take me to the bus depot, and as I'm looking out at the people on the sidewalk, I realize I like how the world looks from inside a taxi. And right then, squishing my toes against all those bills, I know the money's already corrupted me.

"On the Greyhound I climb over this babe who's got *mass murderer* scrawled with a black marker on her face, and she starts telling me a mile a minute that she was at the Gap when the glass came down. She'd pulled a little sneaker off a mannequin at Gap Kids and flung it at a cop, and it binged off his helmet. And in the park a different cop grabbed her tit. And such a nice tit, I'm thinking, but she reads my mind and says, 'My boyfriend's gonna be so pissed. I'm glad he wasn't there. He would've stomped the fucker.'

"In Portland I buy us some pizza and beers, and while we're eating she wraps a slice in a napkin and slips it in her pocket. Outside it's cold and I'm thinking about a coffee, but she says, 'I know a place to crash,' so we walk along the old Willamette Highway till we get to a gas station, and inside there's this fucking kid with his boots up on the counter. I'm squinting from the bright lights, and this guy's head's twitching, very weird. He looks at her, then at me. 'Where the fuck you been, Daria?' he says. 'Seattle,' she says. 'Oh,' he says. 'It was cool,' she says, then points at me. 'That's Flak.' She pulls the pizza slice from her pocket and peels off the napkin, then sits on his lap and holds it in front of his mouth so he can take a bite. Then she looks back at me. 'This is Clay.'

"Our Clay, friends and neighbors. Pumping gas in Portland.

"At eleven-fifteen Daria and I have to hide out because the owner's coming by for the day's profits. So we're sitting out back in the trees when I ask where this crash house is, and she says, 'You're here,' and I'm like, 'Where?' She nods at the station and says, 'In the bathroom.' And I look over my shoulder at the men's-room door and say, 'In there?' She shakes her head. 'The other one. You know,' she says, 'girls don't piss on the floor.'

"The Mobil sign goes dark, then the lot lights. After another ten minutes Clay comes around back. 'It's cold,' he says, and gives Daria a hand and pulls her to her feet. He gets a bedroll and a duffel from inside a plastic drum, then unlocks the women's bathroom and turns on the heater. He throws a T-shirt over the light—it's kind of weird, we're all three just standing there, face-to-face—and he spreads out a sleeping bag and a blanket, then asks me if I have a bedroll. I tell him it got swiped in Seattle, so he offers me the blanket, and I say, 'No, man. No problem. I'll just curl up here by the heater,' but he tosses it to me. He insists. When we all get comfortable he torches up a fat joint, and the heater's cranking it out real good. Then he tosses me a bag of cheese doodles and opens a bag for him and Daria. We enjoy the heat and silence, the tip of the joint all yellow from cheese doodles.

"Every time I wake up in the night to roll over when my hip goes numb, Daria's sleeping with her head on Clay's lap. And he's sitting up against the wall, his head tipped slightly to the side, eyes open, staring at Daria's heap of hair, his hand on her shoulder, then staring at her boots beside the garbage can, then at the wall.

"I wake up to a rush of cold air. Clay steps over me and sits back down beside Daria. He hands me a hot-dog burrito and a Mountain Dew. He's got the same for the two of them. 'Let me give you some cash,' I say, and he says, 'Don't worry.'

"Hot-dog fucking burrito. Daria's chowing hers down, and when I ask Clay what time it is he says it's six-fifteen. I practically drop my Mountain Dew. 'In the fucking morning?' Then he tells me the owner'll be here at six-thirty to open up, that his own shift starts at seven. And he says he works all day every day and they've been doing this for two months, and Daria's getting bored hanging out in the park all day long. He owes money to someone, but when he's got it paid off they'll have a lot more fun. And I tell him, 'Fuck that. What? A lawyer? Whoever you owe it to has way more than you.' But if he doesn't pay it, he says his mother'll need to. I ask him how much, and it's twenty-seven hundred.

"Where will you go when you've paid it off? I ask him. No idea. How long will it take? A lot longer. Does he know any anarchists down in Douglas? A couple. Does he know something he could teach in the Free Skool? It turns out Daria knows quilting, but Clay shakes his head. 'Not really,' he says. 'Everybody knows something that other people don't,' I tell him. He thinks about that, and his head snaps with a little click. 'Explosives,' he says. 'TNT, ammonium nitrate, nitromethane.' I smile big. 'Hard core,' I say, then go out and around the corner to the men's and take a piss. Then I pull off a boot and pick out twenty-seven hundred-dollar bills. When I walk back in, I drop the money in his lap and say, 'Let's go to Douglas.' "

By now a dozen kids were gathered around listening. "Cool," said a boy with green hair.

"I love that story," said Rebecca.

"You delivered him to us," Scanlon said. Whatever he ended up publishing, it would hum with the unassailable bona fides of Clay.

Flak nodded at him. "A thousand bucks if you want to use that story," he said, but then smiled and tapped his chest twice. Respect.

Scanlon was certain he hadn't actually *found* the money, and he hoped he'd learn someday how Flak actually got it.

"He's the guy on TV," he overheard a kid say at the next table. "The anarchy professor."

His old childhood flaw was finally his strength. Again he'd gotten in with the bad apples, but this time, instead of dragging him down, maybe they'd launch him.

"Where's Clay?" Rebecca was scanning the room. "Where the fuck did he go?"

Naomi drank some water, then set the glass in the kitchen sink. She was finally ready. When she got back from the lab this afternoon, she put Sammy in the bouncy seat beneath his hoop of dangling jesters, bumblebees, and squeaky reptiles, then set up shop in the spare room. Her organ table was two-tiered, with collapsible legs and a curve so pleasing that she'd shipped it home with her from France, at nearly the cost of her plane ticket. It held all the basics: three hundred essences and a few of her unusual favorites like zingiber cassumunar and French hay.

Sammy was asleep, Scanlon was at his demonstrations, and she was feeling clearheaded and alert. It was time.

Sitting at the organ, she placed the vial of frog juice beside her base notes and cut open a fresh package of dipsticks. To wake up her receptors, she smelled jasmine, lavender, grapefruit, and, finally, tobacco. She smelled her own skin, deep in the crease inside her elbow. She opened her nostrils wide, massaged her sinuses, took in the air in the room before ignoring it. Then, without ceremony, she fingered the vial of frog juice, eased the rubber cork out, passed the vial under her nose at twelve inches, and replaced the cork.

The clench of the essence was immediate and profound. Sharper than musk, and cleaner, with a more potent thrust. She reopened the vial and took a closer smell. Heady, disorienting, disturbingly powerful. Blaine was right. It was like snorting adrenaline, coiled-up and explosive, tremendously complex with great rancidity. The gland producing this hormone must be what powered that incredible, inexplicable leap. She sniffed and the sensation rippled through her sinuses, stimulating her lips and the roof of her mouth, quivering in her lungs and intestines. She'd rarely worked with ambergris—whale regurgitation that has soaked up sea and sun for years—but she had used lots of civet cat and plenty of musks, and she was already convinced that the Pacific leaping frog gave her a powerful new base note for a whole grouping of new fragrances. If it existed only in this tiny area of the Pacific Northwest, no one in the industry knew anything about the frog. A breakthrough fragrance was waiting for her. A gift.

She got to work. She dipped the frog juice with jasmine and lavender, citrus and sandalwood. Already she was finding even more complexity: molasses, wet soil, fermented greens, sautéing mushrooms. And something harsher—ammonia or kerosene. She dipped it with an oceanic grouping, with seaweed and an ozone blend, then tobacco. Was it possible?—the suggestion of auto-body putty? She tried several mints. She played with citrus and fig.

She jumped up, paced the room, and guzzled another glass of water. Her mind was reeling, like she'd been blasting music through headphones and lost touch with the here and now. She listened for Sammy—nothing—and looked at the clock. *Nine-thirty*? God, how long had it been since she was so deep in the zone?

Her first task was a prototype. A basic but complete fragrance to work from. She added grassy notes—juniper, dill, lemongrass, sage, eucalyptus, cypress, and fir. She tried sharp herbs and astringents. After dozens of attempts, the sticks were fanning out all around her, each one a nudge toward oceanic, or woodsy, or floral.

She waved a stick under her nose, held it away, waved it again—too much frog, too simple in the top note. A prototype would take weeks or months, but already she'd gotten something in the range of the irresistible smell of Sequoia.

A rap at the kitchen door startled her. She pulled her robe tight and knotted the belt, moving through the living room, pushing through a creative cloud like she hadn't known in years. Putting her hand to the knob, she paused to smell each of the two dipsticks pinched between her thumb and forefinger, then opened the door a crack: Clay stood tight to the house to keep out of the rain, his hands thrust down in the front pockets of his jeans.

"It's late," she said.

His head twitched. "I was wondering if maybe Scanlon was home."

"He's downtown." She put one of the dipsticks to her nose again—still too much frog, like celery rot in a wet bag at the back of the fridge. "Shouldn't *you* be down there?" It might need sage, something to clean up the rot.

Clay was asking about work—whether they needed anything done this week. If sage was too dusty, maybe rosemary, but only a hint. It could get too sweet. He asked about Sammy. And then a breeze came up behind Clay, and she moved the sticks away from her nose. His wet, feral smell had another quality tonight: she could smell the street on him. Worlds away from lavender or jasmine or a hint of rosemary. "Do you want a beer?" she said.

Still holding the dipsticks, she opened a bottle of IPA and set it in front of him on the kitchen table, then refilled her water glass and sat down.

He wiped beer from his lips with the heel of his hand. "None for you?"

She shook her head, reaching across the table with a stick and holding it under his nose. "I'm working." It felt good to say it.

His head jerked back. "Rank!"

"Powerful stuff."

"Who'd want to smell that shit?"

She put the stick to her nose again. "What does it smell like to you?"

"Like shit."

"It smells nothing like shit," she told him. "Urine, maybe, but not really that, either." As he warmed up in the kitchen, the smell of the street grew stronger—creosote and dirty motor oil, exhaust, hot steel and rubber. But she was missing something essential, something that evoked nighttime alleyways, flickering streetlights, a dark car moving too fast.

He sucked down the beer in minutes, and as she opened him another she decided to try an exercise. "Would you like to see how it works?"

She had him carry a straight chair into the room they called the nursery—baby-blue and sunny-yellow paint swatches taped to the white walls, an unassembled crib in its carton, boxes still unpacked, with her organ set up in the middle of the floor. "Quiet," she said, pointing to their bedroom, where Sammy was sleeping in the bassinet.

She pulled his chair close so she could smell his clothes and the back of his neck while she dipped sticks and held them under their noses. "Think of a perfume like a tree," she said. "The fruit is at the top—grapefruit, orange, lemon, the most volatile smells. The flowers are in the middle, the heart notes. And the roots and mosses, like patchouli, are the base—the most lasting." She told him about the hypothalamus and how smells traveled to the brain quicker than sights or sounds. She held out dipsticks, their faces nearly touching, and together they smelled mints, tobaccos, and herbs, and she thought about Scanlon giving the Oregon Experiment to Sequoia, how it felt like he'd shared with her the most intimate, sensual details of their lives.

She impressed Clay with a few party tricks, quickly approximating Mountain Dew on a dipstick, then a corn dog, an orange creamsicle, beer. As he smelled the sticks, she smelled his unnerving watchfulness, his animal wariness, and finally what she was after: the street.

But his beery breath was overpowering. She pushed up the sleeve of his sweatshirt and said, "Smell your arm." Then she gripped his arm and smelled it herself. She added cedar to the frog juice, then fir. She tried laurel, knowing it was wrong.

Street, she kept thinking. She could see the ad for the fragrance already—a gritty black-and-white nighttime photo on the cobblestone of the Meatpacking District, steam rising from manholes, a woman's wrist gripped by a stranger. Passion or threat?

She held another stick under his nose. "Revolting," he said, still not getting it, and she wished Blaine wasn't going to Vienna. She could challenge Naomi in ways that Clay never would; he didn't have it in him. She also wished Scanlon understood that without friends or her career she couldn't be the stable mother Sammy deserved, nor, for that matter, the lover Scanlon desired. And with a hollow guilt she conceded that he was right about one thing: she wanted to be in New York, to be close by, when Joshua turned eighteen.

As she reached over the organ for essences, she caught Clay looking where her robe had fallen partway open. It was the second time she'd seen that he desired her. And his desire was a relief because she felt no obligation to respond. She could let it be something uncomplicated between them, like good music or a shared piece of pie. With Scanlon, if she submitted to *his* desire, he expected something in return, in body and spirit, despite her explanation that after nurturing their baby and her own health she had nothing left to give.

"This is supposed to be perfume?" Clay said. "Nobody would want to smell like that."

She tried another tack, opening essences and lining up the tiny bottles on the organ—the frog juice on the left with some other base notes, middle notes next, then top notes on the right. She opened aqueous essences—seaweed and an ozone blend—and astringent grassy notes of juniper, lemongrass, and dill. "Like this," she said, and stood up and leaned over the table, taking a long breath as she moved from left to right—her nose six inches above the bottles—then back the other way, from top notes to base.

As he stood and passed his nose over the lineup of fifteen bottles, she smelled the back of his neck, and the damp collar of his jacket, trying to get the missing piece. He turned and shook his head.

"You edit it down now," she said. "Pull out the bottles that don't seem right. Think about fabrics. Do you want cotton—light and airy? Or velvet—heavy and smooth? Or thick and scratchy wool?"

His head snapped back. "You're asking me what I *want*?" he said, and she clutched her robe at her throat.

"Wool," she said, taking a step back. "Scratchy and thick."

"What I *really* want?" he said, moving closer.

"You edit it down," she told him and retreated to the kitchen, where she stood at the sink gulping a glass of water, looking out the window hoping to see the Honda pull in. And then, needing to pee, she went in the bathroom, thinking Sammy would wake up any minute for a feeding, and just as she sat down on the toilet, he let out a cry.

She would tell Clay he had to leave.

Then she heard his bootsteps on the floor. "Clay," she called, but he didn't reply. The bedroom door rattled—"Clay, what are you doing?"—and, yanking at the toilet-paper roll, she no longer heard Sammy's cry. "Clay!" She jumped up and raced down the hall, pulling her robe closed. The bedroom was dark but Clay's smell filled up the room—explosive and volatile, the spoiled sulfur of gunpowder—and Sammy's scent was gone! He'd taken her baby!

She slapped on the light to see Clay sitting on her side of the bed over the bassinet, rocking the burbling boy in his arms.

She took Sammy from him, and when he saw his mother he remembered his hunger and wailed, nuzzling and pawing at her chest. "You need to go," she told Clay over the cries.

His bitten-down fingernails scratched at the edge of the bassinet. His head twitched. "You got some odd jobs soon? Should I come back tomorrow?"

"Ask Scanlon," she said, wondering if he was waiting for her to open her robe to nurse. "Go now. Please."

As he brushed by her, she sensed the element she'd been missing in his smell tonight. His black boots stomped across the living room and the kitchen door shut behind him, and she yanked her robe open and scooped Sammy—wailing hysterically—to her breast. Clay's smell hung in the air: danger.

When he left the Green & Black, there were three missed calls on his cell—all from Sequoia. The fact was, he didn't want to go home: Naomi's nightly rejection had become quietly humiliating. He'd go home when he knew she was asleep.

He stood on Sequoia's porch for a minute before tapping on the door.

She threw the door open and flung out her arms. "You were amazing!" she said, giddy, ecstatic, pressing a finger to her lips and lowering her voice. "Trinity's sleeping." She pulled him inside and hugged him. "You got us on the news." She kissed his cheeks and forehead, then said in a mock reporter voice, "The director of the Oregon Experiment."

"You make me feel like the *king* of the experiment." He couldn't stop smiling.

"You should. You *are* the king. You're *my* king. I've gotten over a hundred e-mails since the newscast, and the website had a thousand hits. A few people think we're anti-American and should move to Iran, but ninety-nine percent are from new members. They want to join! You're doing it, Scanlon. You're making it happen." She hugged him again. "I'm so grateful."

"There's still a long way to go," he said.

"Did you talk to America Sanchez about covering a meeting?"

"It all happened so fast," he admitted.

"All in good time," she said, then a ding sounded from the kitchen. She took him by the hand and led him there, apron strings and her long hair bouncing behind her. "I'm trying out some new scones," she said. "A few are complete disasters. But doesn't buttermilk-ginger-cashew sound tasty?"

"Yum," he said.

"Like a sneaker. A terrible combo. And the cashews go soft." She bent over and slid two cookie sheets out of the hot oven, then used a steel spatula to move the scones to cooling racks on the table, and back-kicked the oven door closed with her heel. She wore an airy skirt under the apron; her legs and feet were bare. "I hope your wife wasn't too freaked out by the chicken pox party."

"She was fine. Sammy just hasn't had all his vaccines yet."

"I wish you wouldn't," she said, "but that's your business. Still, I could show you an article—"

"We're pretty set on having him vaccinated."

She slapped him on the chest with the spatula. "In our new country, or at least in my province, there'll be no injecting innocent babies with toxins."

He smirked. "Then my first lady might insist on visas before you can visit my province."

"We can negotiate that."

"And no car alarms," he said.

"Or leaf blowers," she added.

"No 'W' bumper stickers allowed over the border from America."

"Let's remove 'W' from the alphabet."

"Replace it with a Circle-A," he suggested.

She touched a scone—still too hot. "By the way," she said, "did you talk to Ron Dexter?"

He nodded. A little coy. "Gimme some time. I'm working on him."

She reached past him to turn off the oven. "I believe the universe sends people where they're needed, and I'm grateful that you were sent here. You've done more for the movement in a few months than we've done in four years."

She broke off the end of a scone, blew on the steaming piece, then held it in front of him until he opened his mouth. "Buckwheat-banana-raspberry," she told him, laying it on his tongue.

"Good," he said, although it tasted like old layer cake.

She took a bite. "You liar," she said, then walked around the table to the fridge and reached inside for a bottle of milk. She poured a glass and looked him straight in the eyes. "Don't you lie to me," she said. "Just never lie to me." She leaned back against the stove and dipped a hunk of scone in the milk and pushed it in his mouth. "Sourdough-craisin-dried-apricot," she said. "I always test them on their own first, then dipped in milk, then with butter, then dunked in coffee."

"That's good," he said, still chewing, this time really meaning it. "The sourdough and the milk balance out the sweetness." He swallowed. "Really good."

"There's more where that came from." She fed him another hunk and dipped some for herself. "Uh-huh," she grunted, nodding, her mouth full.

Without giving him a chance to swallow, she swiped butter on new kinds of scones and shoved them in his mouth and her own, scones dripping with milk, flavored with butterscotch, caramel, lavender. He edged closer, her body heat indistinguishable from the oven's, smells of baking in her hair, the lavender stirring up visions of Naomi, asleep by now, rejuvenating her precious nose. If he took her at her word, she needed a break because Sammy drained her so completely. That was part of it, he was sure. But when she turned her face away every time he tried to kiss her, he felt a deeper rejection that he didn't understand. Through the years she'd often told him how much she loved the urgency of his desires, but what did she think would happen if she stepped out of the picture? Could she fairly expect to bask in his desire whenever she wanted to, and expect him to shut it down when she didn't?

Sequoia wiped milk from his chin with her thumb. At the fair, the honey-dripping tofu pancakes had been about her, about all that was available to him. She planted her palms on the warm stove and raised her hips up over the edge. He moved closer as she pushed milk-soaked cinnamon scone into his mouth. Her knees touched his hips. Her breasts rose as she pulled the length of her hair over her shoulder and brushed the dyed brown ends on his cheek and nose, his chin and throat. Unbuttoning the top of his shirt, then brushing his chest. Lifting the front of her apron.

Scanlon drove slowly through the newly developed hills of Douglas, streets with names like Deer Run, Pinot Place, and Burgundy Hill. He went left on Laurel Lane and turned into the cul-de-sac of Marionberry Drive. Massive new houses with three-car garages, stonework, and expansive decks, out of his price range by a factor of five or six. It was nearly midnight and most of the windows were dark, except for dim lights in upstairs bedrooms where couples were reading, sharing a lively passage from a mystery, watching TV, or making love. Couples ending the day together.

He drove out to the university's research forest, where a family of raccoons sneered into his headlights before hauling themselves up a trellis on the Forestry Department's log cabin and squeezing through a hole under the eaves. He drove halfway to the coast before nodding off on a dark curve near Burnt Woods; idling in the gravel lot of a closed-up café, he knew that eventually he had to turn back toward home.

And now, as he rounded the corner onto their block, his headlights flashed on a huge RV with *Horse With No Name* painted on the side above an airbrushed collage of an Indian riding bareback, a Mississippi riverboat, Half Dome, the Statue of Liberty.

Scanlon parked in the driveway and peeked through the living-room window between the curtains. Naomi had left the three-way lamp on low; the fleece blanket was folded over an arm of the sofa; the magazines and remotes were neatly laid out on the coffee table. As peaceful as a crypt.

At the curb, a plastic stool stood in front of the RV door, and above the door an airbrushed green street sign with reflector letters spelled out *Ventura Highway.* Twenty years ago, Geoffrey Pratt had used a piece of his Beirut Blast commission to buy the RV at a bankruptcy auction, its former owners an America cover band busted up by bad blood and worse debts.

Scanlon knocked and pulled open the door. The air was greasy with warm butter; Vivaldi's *Four Seasons* played over the stereo.

"Come aboard!" his father shouted, then laughed and gave him a bear hug. "I've passed through Oregon any number of times. Always on the coast, though. Beautiful state." The microwave dinged, and he pinched the steaming bag by the corners, spilling popcorn into a stainless steel bowl. "Can I fix you something?" he asked, by which he meant a drink, by which he meant rum and Coke, by which he meant rum and Diet Pepsi.

"A small one, sure."

Geoff poured three fat fingers of Bacardi into a tumbler, plunked in a few ice cubes, then emptied out a can of Diet Pepsi. "Congratulations," he said, chinking his glass against Scanlon's. "Sammy's a champ."

"So you've seen them?"

"Naomi looked pretty frazzled. Figured I'd best leave her be for the night."

His father had nailed it: Naomi wanted to be left alone. But that's not a marriage.

Scanlon took a big swallow of the icy sweet drink. "You said you couldn't come till Christmas."

"I had to see the grandson, so I tended to certain matters in a more timely manner." He then packed his mouth with popcorn, and as Scanlon noted the resemblance between his father and himself—cheeks and nose crowding his eyes when he stretched open his mouth for another handful—he wondered if an observer would've called the feeding frenzy with Sequoia and the scones erotic or just gluttonous.

When Geoff finally swallowed, he said, "What a town you've got here," and Scanlon knew there were reasons other than his grandson that he'd shown up a month early. "As I came over the river downtown, a bunch of kids dressed in black were giving me the finger, and one of them threw a stone at my rig."

"It's not usually like that," Scanlon said. "Did you hear about the Seattle kid on trial?"

He shook his head, mouth stuffed.

"He got sentenced today. Some of the local anarchists are making a fuss." He paused. "It's a wonderful town." Despite Geoff's sustained midlife crisis—twenty years and going strong—and the fact that since his parents' divorce he hadn't looked up to his father as he hoped his own son always would, Scanlon was conscious of his desire to impress the old man. He still sought his father's approval.

When Scanlon was growing up, Geoff had been a robust lawyer with a hard-edged, nicked leather briefcase, always dressed in conservative suits, a mid-career, middle-aged man who didn't necessarily seem happy with his wife but didn't seem to be looking for happiness or expecting it. He did his job and projected the trappings of a moderately successful career. They had some sort of a family life, Scanlon supposed. He remembered his father making waffles on Sunday mornings and hosting birthday parties at the bowling alley—sitting at the scorer's table with a Styrofoam coffee cup in one hand and a stubby pencil in the other. He took Joey out to dinner for their anniversary, said grace at Christmas. Scanlon had never seen him drunk, rarely seen him laugh. At each meal he ate one plateful of food with a glass of water, no ice.

While the divorce was in the courts, Geoff called Scanlon at his college dorm, inviting him out for a steak. Walking into the restaurant Scanlon saw a stranger with an unkempt beard getting up from his table, wearing a Camp Pine Buff T-shirt, sweatpants, and canvas sneakers. His father gave him a hug, the first one he could remember since the second or third grade. His teeth looked less white, even less straight, and hair sprouted from his ears and nostrils. He'd added twenty pounds to his gut and smelled like rum and onion rings.

Once they'd ordered, he showed Scanlon photos of the nudist camp in the Berkshires where he'd spent the summer and fall: rustic cabins from the thirties, old nudists playing badminton, young nudists paddling canoes, boy nudists playing chess, girl nudists reading in the shade, nudist families with hefty moms and dads and bony, bloodless, knock-kneed children. To Scanlon, it all looked vaguely socialist.

"I know what you're thinking," Geoff said, "but I assure you it has nothing to do with sex or tits or cunts or any of that." Scanlon had never once heard his father swear. "In a week you forget you're naked, and you forget that everyone else is. But more importantly you forget about all the clothing we wear in life. And I *am* speaking metaphorically." He allowed a preacher's pause. "What's a power tie? What's an elegant suit? What's appropriate attire? It's all contrived bullshit. For twenty-five years I've been putting up fronts, which requires enormous amounts of energy. When you're left with just your core self, when you're interacting with no mediation or societal uniforms or signals and codes, all that energy's freed up." He yanked at his T-shirt collar. "You shed everything."

At the time Scanlon had thought, *Your core self and a million dollars. That'd free up anybody.* This man across the table from him sounded like the vegan airheads living in the co-op house at Scanlon's college. He was a textbook midlife crisis and nothing more. But while the airheads had gone on to corporate training programs at Goldman Sachs, Geoff was still a nudist, still a dropout.

Despite the cold Oregon rain pelting the aluminum shell of the RV, the temperature inside had to be over eighty. Geoff wore nothing but an old pair of gym shorts and a T-shirt—a conciliatory gesture to the non-nudist general public. Scanlon pulled off his jacket and took a couple big swallows of his drink. "So how's Parc Elite?"

"Superlative," Geoff said. For the last fifteen years, he'd lived in a nudist RV park outside Vegas. "I moved to a new site. More shade, and I put some distance between myself and Kitty. Everybody wins."

"Admiral Kitty?" Scanlon said. She was a retired naval officer who'd settled in the park a decade ago and hooked up with him.

"Captain," he corrected. "Not her, though. Kitty the mortgage broker. Bitch Kitty." Geoff fingered the last kernels of popcorn from the bottom of the steel bowl, then topped off both their drinks. "She made a fortune in the refinancing boom, and now she thinks she's queen of the park."

Scanlon swigged. It was getting even hotter. He peeled off his sweater. Through buttery popcorn and rum, Sequoia's smell rose off his body.

"She thinks she owns people," Geoff said. "Very controlling. Wants to tell people how to spend their time."

A photo of both bands—America and Horse With No Name—still hung above Geoff's chair; four huge stereo speakers were mounted in the corners, upholstered with red shag carpet; the bar was made from smoky mirrors, a bear pelt covered the bed. All of it had the orgiastic reek of the era of guiltless free love.

The CD had ended, and Geoff told him to pick something out. "I should go on inside," Scanlon said. "Naomi will be wondering."

"She'll figure it out," Geoff said. "Put on some music. Anyway, by the looks of her an hour ago, she's deep asleep."

It was late, but he didn't teach until ten o'clock tomorrow. When he stood up, his face flushed with rum and he had to reach out to grab hold of a cabinet to steady himself. "Can't you turn the heat down?"

"Hey," Geoff said, "*mi casa, mi casa.*" He spun the cap off the rum bottle and cracked a fresh can of Diet Pepsi.

Scanlon pressed the CD they'd been listening to back in its case and put on *America's Greatest Hits.* Sweat trickled down the inside of his thigh, still sticky with Sequoia. He tinked the ice cubes around in the glass his father handed him and took a long, cool drink.

"So anyway," Geoff said, "Bitch Kitty is telling everybody I'm not Parc Elite material. Turns out there's a morals clause in the association charter. I'm charged with licentiousness and moral turpitude."

"I thought she was your . . . whatever you call them. Lady friend."

"She was. But with this gold mine she's made on refinancings, she's become a tyrant, and meanwhile this very fine woman, Kitty Wright—"

"Captain Kitty," Scanlon said.

"No, this is someone else. Just moved into the park a few months ago."

"There's *three* Kittys?"

Geoff pursed his lips, nodding. "This new Kitty, what a gal. She retired early—a schoolteacher—and slipped into the park in a little class-C Breezeline and set up housekeeping. She's a soft-spoken little mouse of a thing. Cute as a mouse. First time I met her, she invites me into her Breezeline, and there's a real honest-to-God gold harp standing in the middle of the floor, and she sits on a velvet-covered stool and plays it for me, moving her hands over the strings like conjuring angels. You wouldn't be surprised if she sprouted wings."

Geoff said this last bit like a self-conscious drunk veering from loose toward sauced. But he was also putting on a show, another act in a twenty-year performance meant to prove that he, not his son, was the wild one, the free spirit.

He twirled the ice in his glass. "I'm so glad I met her nude for the first time. That's how I saw who she really was—the brainy harpist on the verge of spreading her wings. When she's dressed in her straight brown khakis and square-cut shirts, and with her chopped-off hair and blunt features, she looks like a clothespin.

"But nude, her eyes brighten and her nose sharpens. Her collarbones and shoulder blades are as fine as bone china. Her feet curl over the harp pedals, and her lips quiver. When she tips her head to direct her ear at the heart of the sound, her mousy hair falls across her cheek. And those pointy little tits of hers. Little mouse tits that I—"

"Dude," Scanlon interrupted. "Stop."

Geoff froze in a drunken grin. "My point is . . . Take your mother."

"No," Scanlon said. "Let's not, thank you."

His father breathed a sigh of resignation that filled the silence. "One for the road? It's early yet." When Scanlon nodded, Geoff stepped precariously to the stereo to push Play for another spin of America, then to the fridge for ice. "Your mother was always a skinny little broad."

"I don't need to hear this," Scanlon told him.

"My point is . . ." He furrowed his brow, comically trying to coax his point from memory. "Clothes gave your mother some shape. Lent her figure some character. But stripped naked she was a rusty nail."

"Really, Dad," Scanlon said. "Can it."

"It's just I've become an explorer with an eye for variety. Captain Kitty? A hard-body. A quarter would bounce off her gut. The only nudist I ever heard of who puts clothes *on* for sex. Says my chest gets too sweaty.

Says if she doesn't wear a shirt she has to pick my body hair out of her skin. Before sex she rolls on antiperspirant. Very regimented, sexually. Recognize your objective, tuck your chin, lead with your shoulder, get the job done. Left, right, left. Afterward, break camp and police the area."

They'd both slipped farther down in their chairs, and Scanlon was nursing his drink. He'd had enough. Too much. He had to take a shower—a long, soapy shower—before sneaking into bed with his wife. He had to give Sammy a kiss. God, what had he done?

"Now Bitch Kitty," Geoff said. "Talk about *with* clothes versus with*out*. When the clothes come off—" he shook his head "—it's like a landslide. Everything that was pointing up now's pointing down. Not unsexy, mind you. Just takes a moment to adjust to the current switching directions. In her more serene moods it's like riding a barge. But usually . . ." He shook his head again. "You're familiar with sumo?"

"It's to your credit you survived," Scanlon said.

"To survivors!" Geoff shouted, raising his glass.

Pressing his own icy glass to his forehead, Scanlon thought of how he'd always believed—taken for granted, really—that he'd be better than his parents. But tonight he'd cheated on his wife while she nursed their baby and rocked him to sleep. He'd fucked Sequoia, and he'd loved it. He'd loved how much she wanted him. She'd looked deep into his eyes, her face beaming with desire, and she'd gripped his hips and pulled him to her. To be desired. A woman whimpering, wet, and moaning at his hand. It was a lifetime ago that his wife had responded to his touch like that. Climaxing, Sequoia swatted the spice rack to the floor. And through all of it, from the oven rocking and banging, to the taste of sweat on her lips, to the particular undulating, hot-syrup tug of her sex, he was no better than his father.

"About before," Geoff said. "You know, your mother. Don't get me wrong. She had a bit of kick to her. Sexually, I mean. But what's strange is that we were married twenty-five years—and this is related to being a nudist and getting to know someone from their core on out. I mean, I lived with your mother day after day, but if she'd phone me in the office or just came to mind for some reason—" he looked into his empty glass like a crystal ball "—I could never place her face."

She was awakened by the hard beat of a stereo—a car pounding by, she thought. But then, through the closed windows, over Sammy's heavy breathing and the light patter of rain, she heard the raucous singing of her husband and father-in-law: ". . . Ventura Highway in the sunshine, where the days are longer, the nights are stronger thaaan mooooonshine . . ." Two houses down, the dog heard it too and joined in howling. The stereo bumped up even louder. Sammy lifted his head, looked at her bleary-eyed in the darkness, spit up on her shoulder, and dropped back to sleep. It was two a.m.

Like torture, she lugged herself from bed, laid Sammy in his bassinet, and parted the blinds on the front window. Light blazed from the RV. The dog barked. With each beat from the stereo, the storm window rattled in its aluminum frame.

She was tired, and had been for three months. She allowed herself to admit this without guilt. Sammy was an intense baby with intense immediate needs. He was never a little hungry, a little bored with his exersaucer, a little chilled. He never had a touch of a cold or a little gas. He was sixteen pounds of desire and sensation, and he knew his mother was his source of satisfaction. She loved that about him, but he exhausted her. She'd hoped to maintain the creative zone through the night and pick up again in the morning with the frog juice, but now at two o'clock, it was clear that tomorrow was shot.

Zipping her raincoat, she slipped her bare feet into Scanlon's boots and stepped out into a cold mist. They'd already turned the volume down and were no longer singing. Even the dog had gone quiet. Still, she trudged down the driveway and stepped off the curb onto a plastic stool. The RV smelled like aluminum and like the highway—diesel fumes, dusty tar, and grease splatters. "Vo*lump*tuous," she heard Geoff say. Grasping the door handle—"I've never found Naomi sexier"—she stopped. It wasn't Geoff, but Scanlon—his voice gravelly and slurred. "Vo*lump*tuous and soft and womanly."

She yanked open the floppy door and stepped inside. The air was too warm. Syrupy. As she climbed the steps, she saw Geoff in profile, tipping back his head with a glass balanced on his nose. Scanlon was slouched in a chair, his eyes sagging and his face slightly rearranged, vaguely Cubist, like it always got when he was drunk.

"What are you doing up?" he said. His shirt was unbuttoned down his chest.

"Have a seat," Geoff said. "Fix her a drink, son."

Scanlon looked up at her, smiling, a sweating glass resting on the point of his hip bone. His mouth seemed to migrate up his cheek and his eyes seesawed, as if *she* were the drunk one. She desperately needed to sleep. Sammy would be awake in two hours, famished. And she didn't want her husband coming inside between now and then and waking her up. She'd never felt so exhausted, so emptied out.

It wasn't until she saw a bead of sweat running down Scanlon's face that she realized how hot it was in the RV. Sweltering. Beneath her pajamas and the raincoat her skin felt wormy. She could hardly get a breath. "Sister Golden Hair" came on the stereo, and a memory that she hadn't thought of in years appeared in her mind with astounding clarity: twenty years old, alone in a little beach cottage on Long Island that belonged to the parents of her roommate, who was supposed to meet her there but got sick and called to say she couldn't come. At first Naomi was disappointed, but then she ate spaghetti, left the dishes in the sink, stacked some old albums on the record changer, and sat in the dark on the tiny deck looking out at the stars in the black sky over the ocean. And what she remembered, standing here exhausted between these two drunk men, was that other than her friend in bed with a fever in New Rochelle, no one in the world knew where she was. She remembered "Sister Golden Hair," the sound of the surf, the vast sky, and the feeling of being completely, luxuriously alone.

Now she was standing in the ocean, the water weirdly, soupy hot, and a wave pushed against her legs and almost knocked her over. She caught herself, only to be tugged by an undertow she couldn't resist, and her feet were swept from beneath her, and she was buckling, falling toward Scanlon, and he lurched up from the chair, his arms beneath her . . .

And there on the floor, her head in Scanlon's lap, she was awake, or could have been, but she didn't want to be. She fell back to the cottage on Long Island, sinking low in a chaise longue on the ramshackle deck, cocooned in darkness. And then she slipped further back—weak from labor, her skin slick, a tiny pink hand reaching out of the blanket, Joshua crying for his mother. But instead of receiving her baby into her arms she touched her vagina and brought her hand to her nose, holding the smell of his birth. Half-conscious now, she sensed that bodily pool of comfort, then sank beneath its surface.

Chilly water pinpricked her face and she turned her head to the side, curling deeper into the cocoon, trying to forestall her return to the present. But the icy water drew her back—now a spray she couldn't ignore—and she smelled the rain and the wet driveway. She was being carried, hooked under her knees and shoulders. She opened her eyes. Her father-in-law held her legs, lurching side to side as he back-stepped up the driveway, carrying her back to the house, her baby, this life.

She shot awake. In bed. Four a.m. The fragrance of rosemary shampoo: Scanlon had showered. Remembering that she'd fainted, her head cradled in Scanlon's lap, she now lifted the covers to a warm whoosh of smells: before showering he'd tried to rinse it off in the hot tub, but her erotic earthiness had clung to him, and he'd brought her into their bed. Sequoia had been wearing jasmine. Her smell was tangy. Citrus. Her period might have just ended, her hair unwashed. They'd both perspired. No trace of latex. She'd been baking.

Chapter 7

At ten-thirty in the morning, when Scanlon rushed into the kitchen and clattered the kettle on the stove, she didn't turn from the window. "I've gotta bolt to my class," he said, "then I'm meeting my father for lunch and showing him around town."

Naomi sighed. "Not very well," she said, staring through the drizzly gray where Horse With No Name listed toward the curb. "I got woken up in the middle of the night by a couple of drunks. But thanks for asking."

"I'm really sorry," he said. "I had no idea we were being so loud."

She looked at him: a towel hung low on his hips, the dark hair on his stomach was wet, obscene. He carried with him the smell of oatmeal soap and his shampoo, but she had no doubt that even after a hot tub and two showers, if she got close enough, down on her knees, she'd detect the citrus markings of Sequoia.

"What's he doing here?" she said.

"On the run from a woman."

Was there filial pride in his tone? Swagger? "Well, I'm too tired to deal with him. You two can go out for dinner."

"Don't worry, I'll take care of him. You just take care of yourself." He pressed a filter into the cone and measured out the coffee. He still hadn't met her eye. "You fainted again. Have you asked the doctor about it yet?"

She turned over a page of the *New York Times,* the Arts section, spread on the table in front of her. His coffee trickled from the cone into the mug—a black and fuchsia mug with a loopy whorled handle that had appeared one day in their cupboard. "I need sleep," she said. "Sammy, too, if he's going to get over this cold."

"Sammy's got a cold?"

"For two days. While you've been occupied. With research."

He squatted beside the bouncy seat, then reached for a napkin on the table and wiped Sammy's nose. The baby snorted, then coughed. With a hand on Sammy's leg—all wrapped up in fleece—Scanlon lowered his voice: "Sorry about waking you up. Try to get some rest today. I'm kind of worried about you fainting all the time." He stood up, dropped the cone in the sink, splashed milk in his coffee.

"Where'd that mug come from?" she asked.

He took a sip—"Isn't it beautiful?"—then held the mug out for her admiration. "The shape and the balance, the fit of the handle in your hand, the perfect lip." He thrust the mug at her. "Want to try?"

"Where'd you get it?"

His hesitation reeked of guilt. "Sequoia."

"She made it herself?"

"Not sure."

And the lies begin, she thought, the small lies that build the levee, a fistful at a time, around the big lie. She looked down at the newspaper and read a review of a movie that would never come to Douglas, then read it again, over and over, until he came back through the kitchen cradling the mug. She searched his face for remorse but could see only exultance.

"Is it raining?" he said, tying his shoes. Perky, chatty.

"Do I look like a cloud?"

And then he was gone, out of the house, and she put her face in her hands and cried.

But Sammy was sucking on his toes and needed a bath, so after a time she blew her nose, cranked up the oven, and opened its door to take the chill out of the kitchen. Then she scrubbed the sink and filled it with warm water. Sammy loved a bath, never fussed, and seemed, if it was possible at three months, to anticipate it with an eager desire.

She dragged his bouncy seat closer to the oven and unsnapped his onesie, tugging out his stubby arms, and the whole time he grinned, staring into her face with eyes full of love and trust. She sealed up his diaper, dropped it in the garbage, and lifted him by the torso, his delicious fat rolling over her fingers like she was holding up a mound of pizza dough. When she dangled his toes in the water, he shrieked with delight. Intending to kick his feet, he flailed his arms. She lowered him into the sink, splashing, drooling, cackling, his eyes still pinned on hers.

The hundreds of times she'd smelled baby shampoo, it always brought her to a specific place: her first weeks back from France, before she'd found an apartment, spending a night with absurdly rich friends in their co-op on East 73rd, showering in the children's bathroom, using the baby shampoo from the windowsill in the shower, the window open a few inches and letting in the smell—comfort and complacency—of the Upper East Side.

She sloshed the washcloth around Sammy's neck, behind his ears, and under his arms. She bent him forward over her hand and scrubbed his back. He giggled as she washed between each of his toes. She could imagine a life in New York with Sammy. Just the two of them.

The kitchen was getting hot. Splattered chicken fat burned on the oven racks, and finally she no longer smelled Scanlon.

She patted him dry on the counter, then used the blow-dryer, Sammy trying to grab the flow of warm air. She dressed him in a clean onesie and carried him into the couch for the cruel irony she'd come to dread: nursing him was the deepest connection she'd ever felt with another soul, and the worst pain she'd ever known.

He nuzzled through her flannel pajamas, and already she felt the sharp pinch. He latched on and the pain clawed her breast and raked through every hollow and corner of her body, tears spilling down her cheeks and falling onto Sammy's golden face. He gazed up at her, and the pain eased off. Her husband had forfeited all claims on her body.

He'd received a dozen calls in his office from newspapers around the state. Everyone had seen him last night on TV. He'd given short phone interviews and felt a rush of success.

But just before lunch Fenton followed him into the men's room and took the urinal beside him: "I didn't get that article yet."

"Busy morning," Scanlon said. "Statewide interest—"

"Don't yank my chain, Pratt. I mentioned to the dean yesterday that you were sending me a draft. Do you want me to tell him that being director of a bunch of wingnuts has, as he already fears, compromised your productivity as a scholar?" He zipped up and punched the flush.

"It's on my home computer. I'll have to e-mail it from there."

Slowly washing his hands under cold water with the powdered Boraxo, Scanlon thought Dexter was wrong. You don't get used to it. You get the hell out. But he'd never get another job without something to show for his time in Oregon.

The phone was ringing as he opened his office door: a reporter from Bend, asking all the wrong questions, entirely missing the significance of Panama's sentence, lacking even a basic understanding of radical action and mass movements.

He hung up and gazed out the window toward the pool, the patio chairs stacked under a tarp for the winter. He'd write the goddamn piece himself. It was *his* story, *his* ideas. He Googled the *Oregonian* features editor, then called and left a message. In the state's biggest newspaper, he would have a proper venue. It wasn't the scholarly article Fenton wanted, but it should keep the dean at bay.

Then he called his father and told him how to get to campus. They'd go to lunch, but first they'd swing by the demonstrations. He left his office with a notebook and a pen.

His father was waiting by the gates to the old quad, a spot where photos were taken for the website and brochures, the campus's equivalent of a pretty receptionist. A neat elongated quadrangle with classical brick buildings, it was every bit as attractive as anything at Harvard, Mount Holyoke, or UVA. Scanlon had seen pictures of the old quad even before he came for his interview. He'd imagined a beautiful office tucked under the eaves of one of these buildings, with a leaded French dormer window and a fireplace with a drafty flue. But this was the administration's province—the president, the provost, deans, associate deans, alumni relations, public relations, the university master planners. He almost never set foot here.

From campus, they walked downtown. The rain began to fall and they both pulled up their hoods. They passed the public library, then walked along a paved path through the park. Food Not Bombs had taken over the gazebo, and standing in the wet grass outside it were dozens of anarchists, rain pelting their paper plates and their hunched shoulders. Stark and deathly, like a scene from a German movie.

"There's not usually so many," Scanlon said. "They're here to protest that guy's sentencing."

"They don't look like they have any protest in them," Geoff said. "How do you people live up here?"

"It's not so bad. It's usually more of a *misting* rain." It was pouring down at the moment. "There's more annual rainfall in Houston—accumulation, that is—than in Douglas." He was repeating the meaningless things people had told him that had nothing to do with the fact that the rain was oppressive.

A block from the courthouse they heard drums and chanting, and as they got closer the scene on the square was impressive—easily three or four times yesterday's crowd. Rain-streaked banners held up on poles denounced Panama's harsh sentence. Effigies—the judge? prosecutor? governor?—were tossed around a mosh pit pushing up against the metal barriers and the line of police. Dreadlocked hippie kids in dirty tie-dye and harem pants beat on bongos. Anarchists with buzz cuts and any sort of hair sculpture—blue and green and jet-black mohawks, Circle-A's shaved or tattooed onto their skulls. Like yesterday, there was a festival mood, but it felt different—more impassioned chanting by the neo-hippies, and a more unsettling quiet among the anarchists.

"This feels explosive," Scanlon told his father. The volatility in the air was the sort of thing a dog might smell.

"Is this some kind of freak-fest?"

"This is the Pacific Northwest," Scanlon said. "This is what goes on. It's what I study."

For years Geoff hadn't allowed himself to be surprised by anything. He knew it all. But now he looked stunned, like a witness to the apocalypse. "You should move down to Vegas," he said. "It's a pleasant life."

"But this is why I'm here."

"There's nothing wrong with a nice downtown. Ample parking. A good steakhouse."

Why the hell did Scanlon want to impress his father? With his stature in his field, or for that matter the parks, the coast, the mountains? With the hippie and anarchy scene? Why had he shown him the old quad, that small deception? There were times he thought he'd completely written off his parents, but if that were the case, if he'd lost all respect for them, he wouldn't give a damn what they thought.

Then, simultaneously, a smoke bomb and tear-gas container were flying in opposite directions. A ribbon of smoke twisted up behind the police line, a cloud of tear gas engulfed the demonstration. The mayhem was immediate and complete. Protesters were running every which way—out of the square and toward it. Faces disappeared behind bandannas and gas masks. The tear-gas canister was lobbed back at the police, and a second kachunked into the air and clattered amid the crowd, spewing noxious smoke.

Although he and his father were standing half a block away with the wind at their backs, traces of tear gas reminded Scanlon of the thrill of Seattle. He pulled his shirt up over his nose and gestured to Geoff to do it too, but at the same time he flared his nostrils for another taste. Rocks flew and batons swung. An anarchist was down, pounced on and handcuffed. Another picked up a fuming canister and as he hurled it, he was flattened from behind by two men dressed in the same garb, but cuffs came out from under their torn black sweatshirts, a knee driving between shoulder blades. The protesters didn't have a chance. A couple hundred of them against fifty battle cops. In Seattle the numbers had been a surprise, the first arrests had juiced up the anger, fires of protest flared up all over the city with law enforcement spread too thin.

Scanlon's heart was racing. He looked over at his father, who was holding the sleeve of his raincoat ineffectually to his face, tears streaming from his red eyes. He was huddling closer to the bus shelter, his head sinking deeper into his hood. "Check it out," Scanlon said, more to himself than to Geoff, as a bottle of red paint exploded on the face of the courthouse. While his father cowered beside him, paralyzed with fear, he felt wildly alive.

The authorities were corrupt, even the best of them. The power they held was often by default. Isn't that what these clashes proved? They had as much power as we gave them, and when we wanted to take some back we could. Yes, they might jail us in the end, but only because we held ourselves back. Fear and respect flowed in our blood, and despite all the rage and disgust, we were afraid of what might happen if the system collapsed. Even

Flak had said as much. We'll need the water and power and sewers. When push came to shove, we deferred to our fathers. These flare-ups—nothing more than tantrums in the big picture—were our noble and confused expressions of independence.

Suddenly Scanlon was knocked down to the sidewalk. A protester, sprinting away from the cops, spun around and kept going. "Clear the area!" came over a bullhorn, the sirens now wailing, a busload of battle cops appearing from nowhere.

His father was crouching in the corner of the bus shelter. "Good God, son." His face was white. "Get us out of here!"

Scanlon stepped in beside him, shielded by the Plexiglas etched with a historic photograph of downtown, spray-painted over with a Circle-A. "There's nothing to worry about."

"Don't be an idiot!"

"I'm telling you we're fine. The cops aren't going to bother with us, and the protesters need us on their side. Demonstrations are a great coming-together. It's very simple."

Geoff looked completely terrified, and when Scanlon looked away for a moment—the new contingent of battle cops hut-hutting in formation to clear the square—Geoff lowered his head and ran. Scanlon watched him go, his short clumsy legs moving as fast as they could. Sort of a lard-ass, he couldn't help thinking. All dignity cast aside as he ran for his life.

The gas was thicker now and Scanlon pulled his shirt up over his nose again. Anarchists were spread thin, taunting the police, running away and sneaking back. Five or six had been arrested. A small group with a drum was chanting, "Panama," a news camera moving in on them. And then he saw the big white Channel 9 satellite truck inching down the street, America Sanchez sitting in the cab. She looked frightened but determined when the truck stopped near the chanters and she jumped out. At this distance Scanlon couldn't hear her, but she turned her back valiantly on the chaos and talked into her microphone for the camera, steeling her shoulders and wiping her eyes.

He watched the ballet from inside the bus shelter. A tight line of cops swept across the square and into the street, two motorcycles cut off protesters sprinting around the end, police cruisers inched up the alleys. An anarchist in a sloppy red do-rag rushed the cops, then backed off with a quick twirl—a butterfly flitting before the barrier of black truncheons, Kevlar vests, military helmets, and faces barely visible behind plastic shields, a butterfly up against a swarm of dragonflies. The cops steamrolled closer to Scanlon now, and through the plastic shields he thought eyes might have focused on him, but he held his ground, thinking, I'm an ordinary citizen. No crimes. Public property, although it occurred to him that somebody might recognize him as the professor who'd incited violence on the news.

America Sanchez was running up the street with the cameraman, lugging his equipment, struggling to keep up. She was nearly at the curb before Scanlon realized she was coming for him. Whether or not any of the cops recognized him, she had, and now flung herself inside the bus shelter, tears streaming from her eyes, pulling a white handkerchief with blue and yellow lace away from her mouth just long enough to say into her microphone, "Professor Pratt, is this the reaction you were advocating?" then thrusting the mic in his face.

He wasn't taking the bait. "I never advocated violence." She was shaking. Even through the tear gas and the rain, he could smell her fear. This sexy little firecracker who had faced down gale-force winds reporting from the coast and uncontained wildfires in the Siskiyou was tethered this side of complete panic by ambition alone. She needed these demonstrations, these out-of-town anarchists and cops, this *drama,* because news that happened on her turf belonged to her, and because the more events she owned, the further she could go. Her pushy style, her skill at sticking to the narrative and raising the easily graspable questions, at finding the conflict that piques the broadest possible viewership, her skinny legs, her sharp pretty face that would be icy if not for her café-au-lait skin, her hard tits riding high on her chest under a silk blouse—all this would propel her to a bigger stage. America Sanchez needed conflict. She needed events. She needed anxiety in the public, and fear was even better.

"I want to talk to you," Scanlon told her as the Plexiglas bus shelter filled with tear gas, because she needed him. What she didn't know was that he was no longer her source; he was her competition.

Rain snapping on her plastic poncho, Sequoia pedaled a wide loop around the demonstrations. Trinity, riding behind her, said, "But I'm also in charge of the Brown Bar-ba-loots who played in the shade in their Bar-ba-loot suits and happily lived, eating Truffula Fruits." Trinity couldn't read yet, but she'd memorized *The Lorax* word for word, front to back. She'd turn the page and look at the picture and recite verbatim what was written there.

Sequoia slowed for the tracks, then took a left, swinging around a satellite news truck blocking the bike lane. "I am the Lorax. I speak for the trees," Trinity said from under the poncho, buckled into her seat. The poncho draped back from Sequoia's shoulders, tenting her daughter, and was hooked to the gas can Jim Furdy had welded to the rear fender.

Over the swish of her tires on the wet pavement, she could hear drumming from downtown, deep chants, bullhorns, sirens. This was not the revolution she dreamed of. Hers didn't involve tear gas and shattered windows, even at a Starbucks. Her revolution involved consensus and the power of collective will, the inevitability of moral justice. Its symbol would not be a fist but an embrace.

"So I quickly invented my Super-Axe-Hacker which whacked off four Truffula Trees at one smacker."

She coasted along Franklin Park. It pained her to look at the church. By now it should be warm from kids learning to tap-dance as a kiln fired the clay dinosaurs and turtles massaged to life by children's tiny fingers. A signboard out front should be announcing tonight's poetry reading, tomorrow's quilting class, this weekend's talks on Vipassana meditation and peace in the Middle East.

But when she got closer to the church she could see that the wind had again blown one of the tarps out of place and rain was running inside. She pedaled up on the sidewalk and got off her bike, then lifted Trinity—warm and dry—out of her seat.

"What now?" Trinity said.

"Quick stop," Sequoia told her, pointing up at the sagging tarp.

"Not again," she said.

Sequoia ducked under the yellow caution tape. The building inspector had stapled another warning to the old shiplap clapboards declaring it unlawful to enter, occupy, or perform any work including structural, cosmetic, plumbing, electrical, installation of security systems, greenhouses, watering systems, telephone, cable, or satellite dishes.

"Oh, Mommy," she heard, far off, and when she looked back, Trinity was squatting in the middle of the street.

"Out of the street!" she shouted, looking for cars and sprinting toward her. "I've told you—" but then she saw what Trinity had found. "Oh no," she said. A dead squirrel. Blood had trickled out its ears and snout, but it was still bushy and plump. Unflattened. Almost as if it had fallen from a tree.

"Did a car drive over it?" Trinity asked.

Sequoia looked overhead. "Probably that's what happened."

"Why did somebody do that?"

"They didn't do it on purpose," Sequoia reassured her. "They didn't see him."

"But why weren't they watching?"

"It was an accident. A tragic accident." She tugged on Trinity's shoulder, but she didn't budge; there was no traffic in sight, so she crouched beside her daughter. "Nobody would do this on purpose," she said. "Somebody was driving, and the squirrel ran out where he shouldn't have gone. He made a poor choice."

They stared at the stiff corpse on its side, legs sticking out mid-sprint. Finally Trinity said, "He's his own squirrel."

Suppressing a smile, Sequoia said, "That's exactly right, sweetheart." She stood up. "Let's fix the tarp, then we'll go home for the shovel and bury him in the backyard."

Trinity stood now, nodding, and took her mother's hand. Sequoia lifted her into the church and hopped up behind her. Under the sagging tarp, the floorboards were soaked. She set up the rickety wooden ladder that Jim had been using and climbed up to where the roof should have been. Popping her head out, she could see a train creeping past the church's old foundation in the railroad yard and, in the other direction, roof after roof. Then she looked down into Ron's backyard and her own, at the hot tub where she'd led Scanlon after making love in her kitchen last night and where he'd taken her a second time.

She would make it up to Naomi somehow—help with her nursing trouble seemed to be what she needed most. She liked her. A good vibe on the deck during the chicken pox party. And maybe Naomi's love reached beyond her husband. The anarchist kid surely had a thing for her. Sequoia got a vibe from him, too. She felt a connection there, as she always did with damaged people. She felt drawn to heal him.

She climbed up another rung to maneuver a shoulder under the heavy sag of water. Her legs were shaking as she clutched the ladder, taking a breath, then another. The boy had been only nine years old, and Sequoia knew he'd seen her crawling back inside the third-story window of his house. She would sneak out there to smoke pot when she babysat the boy, where a nook in the roof was hidden from the neighbors. She *knew* he'd seen her. With the TV on downstairs, watching tennis, not very stoned, just enough, she heard the rain gutter tear loose, and a quick, muffled thud on the driveway.

She pushed on the belly of the tarp, and rainwater poured out as if through a flume, and when she looked down over the edge Trinity was standing outside, her arms outstretched, under the falling water. "Get back!" she screamed.

"Awesome!" Trinity shouted.

She raced down the ladder, leapt from the church, and ran around the side. "Are you nuts?" she snapped, but when she saw Trinity's face, soaked and half-delirious, she knew she had a fever. She scooped her up and laid a hand on her forehead—hot as a griddle.

"The broken boy," Trinity said. "Under the Truffula Tree."

"No!" But then she modulated her voice. "No, he's not."

"He is, Mommy. He *is.*"

And Sequoia bundled her arms around Trinity—chicken pox, finally—and rushed her home.

Except for the tear gas burning in his nose and the back of his throat, two blocks from downtown it seemed like any other rainy day in Douglas. He heard a siren, and another, but then it was quiet again. The streets were wet and black, the lawns lushly green, the gardens of rosemary, flax, and Japanese blood grass thriving alongside cedar fences. He was working through some ideas: the futility of demonstrations, their lack of connection to anarchist theory (exactly the opposite of what he'd floated to Fenton), what the primal motivations might be.

Cutting through a park he veered toward the café. He wanted to see her. This morning before class he'd gone in for coffee. Behind the counter, she was reaching into a bushel-sized stainless steel bowl pressed to her belly, kneading an elastic orb of risen dough. Her arms were dusted white with flour. Scanlon caught her eye, and her face lit up. "Hey," he said, and she set the bowl aside and reached her arms deliberately around him—a powerful whoosh of soft flesh thinly veiled with smooth cotton. She'd been working with forty-pound bags of flour and the big mixer, and heat from inside her shimmered at the surface of her skin. Gripping his waist, she leaned back, their hips pressing together. No words came to him, and after a minute or two he went off to class.

If he saw her now, most likely he still wouldn't know what to say, so he set a course for home. In the gentle rain the houses he walked past seemed especially quiet and peaceful. During the Seattle demonstrations he'd never gotten away from the hot spots downtown, so Flak's description of the tranquil neighborhood where he'd escaped with the money had surprised him—like in a movie when the gunshots and chase are interrupted by an elevator ride and Muzak. And that was the Douglas soundtrack today in the blocks leading back to his house—"Penny Lane" lightly arranged for strings and piccolos.

The Seattle he'd seen those few days was all about fighting back. Like Clay's old girlfriend, Scanlon had been there when the glass came down in front of the Gap. The thrill that ran through the crowd was electric. They all felt guilty, that violence wasn't the answer and in fact played into the establishment's hands, but they also felt a surge of power when the glass dropped and the rocks and bricks kept flying into the store, knocking over mannequins, tearing posters of smiling Gap-happy lives. Smacking down the man. And he could convince himself he'd seen Daria stripping the child mannequin as soldiers do their dead enemy. He'd been thinking about those little mannequins getting trampled ever since he heard Flak's story. At the time they'd been corporate camouflage for goods produced under exploitative conditions. But now, as he turned the corner onto his block and saw the little boy—Cory or Casey—riding a tricycle in circles on his driveway, those blond-haired, blue-eyed mannequins with their faces ground into the broken glass represented something more personal than sweatshops and multinational greed.

He went into the kitchen and Geoff turned from the window, where he was sitting with Sammy on his shoulder.

"Where's Naomi?" Scanlon whispered.

"Sleeping." Geoff pouted sympathetically. "She was wiped out."

Scanlon bent down to Sammy's sleeping face, touched his tiny head, and kissed his soft baby hair. The gesture felt odd in such close proximity to his father—exposing himself like that—and as he pulled back he tasted the tear gas in his throat, the burn in his eyes, and felt the thrum of dissent in his chest.

When Sammy picked up his head and sneezed, Scanlon took him from

Geoff, cooing and burbling and laying him over his shoulder. Sammy sneezed again and nuzzled Scanlon's neck with a wet nose. "You missed the action," Scanlon told his father.

"Police can be dangerously unpredictable," Geoff said. "Never mind those delinquents. Avoiding conflict's always the best course."

"I've been thrusting myself into it my entire career," Scanlon retorted. "That's my job, my expertise. You've got no idea, man."

Sammy fussed and Scanlon got a look at his face. His eyes were swollen and red, so watery that tears rolled down his cheeks. He coughed, then sneezed, and started to cry. "He's sicker than he was this morning," Scanlon said. "Do you know if Naomi took him to the doctor?"

"Not sure. He didn't seem so bad when she went to bed." Geoff shook his head. "Probably nothing. They sometimes get a little stuffed up while they're sleeping."

What did he know about babies? Scanlon probably did more fathering in these three months than his father ever did in three years.

"It's okay, Mr. Jiggles," Scanlon cooed, putting him back on his shoulder, but Sammy's face reared up, snot running thick from both nostrils, and he let out a wail. "He's hungry," Scanlon said. "And he's sick. The poor guy's getting worse by the minute."

When Scanlon got to the bedroom Naomi, having heard the cries, was already hauling herself out of bed. "I've got him here," he said, and she flopped back under the covers and leaned up against the wall where a headboard would be if they had more than a mattress and box spring on the floor. He sat on the edge of the mattress, reaching to her with the baby, who did a face-plant into her boobs. Scanlon smelled her skin and milk, the warm, sweet sleep rising up from under the blankets and from inside her shirt. As if to rub it in, Sammy sucked and slurped and smacked his lips. But his nose was gurgling and he let out a frustrated cry. Naomi stretched her hand around her plump breast, cocking her nipple toward his mouth as she guided him back to her, a thin white stream spraying Scanlon's arm and hand and Sammy's forehead before finding his mouth. Sammy swallowed greedily, milk dripping down his cheek, but the snot got sucked up his nose and he gasped and let out a scream.

"Did you take him to the doctor?" Scanlon said.

"What's that smell?" Naomi asked over the wails blaring between them. She was stuffed up too, and breathed hard through blocked nostrils to get a sniff. "Something harsh."

A smile escaped his lips, and he said, "Tear gas," lifting his arm and taking a hearty whiff of his coat. "Radical action seeks me out."

"Christ, Scanlon. That's what's doing this to Sammy!"

He backed off the bed, smelling his shoulder where he'd laid Sammy's head, a tickle in his nose.

Naomi tried to soothe the baby, but his screams grew more insistent as he sneezed and coughed, rubbing his eyes against her shoulder. "Get out of here!" she barked. "Get those clothes out of the house!"

He skulked out of their bedroom, arms tight to his sides, trying to draw his fumes with him. Damn. Chlorobenzylidenemalononitrile penetrated mucus membranes—eyes, nose, mouth, lungs—then set about irritating them. Human-rights groups had called for a tear-gas ban, documenting countless instances of fatality. And he'd blasted the toxin right into his baby's tiny pink membranes.

They'd changed so much of their lives for Sammy. They gave up the 1988 convertible Cabriolet for a new Honda Civic with airbags, and they drove more slowly, stopped fully at Stop signs, gave an extra look before changing lanes; they never went out together at night, of course; they whispered and tiptoed and ate nutritious food so Naomi's milk, the smell of her skin, and the air of their home wouldn't be polluted with hamburger fat or tequila, growth hormones or pesticides.

God, what was he doing? He was so fucking lucky, with a dream baby, a *family,* and a beautiful woman who possessed a peculiar genius, a woman he loved. And in the last twenty-four hours he'd cheated on her and swaddled his baby in chemicals listed in Amnesty International's crimes against humanity. Infidelity had been so easy: Sequoia was available, and he took what was offered. He'd betrayed Naomi, risking his marriage, and now he'd been reckless with Sammy.

"Shit, Dad," he said in the kitchen. "We've got to get these clothes off. Sammy's reacting to the tear gas."

Geoff was filling two goblets nearly to the rim with red wine, then he set the bottle on the orange teardrop table. "Cheers," he said, handing him a glass.

Scanlon took a gulp before stripping off his rain shell and yanking out his shirttails. "C'mon," he said, watching his father make a show of tasting the wine. "I'll dump our clothes straight in the washer."

Geoff brought his arm to his nose, inhaled, then said, "No flies on me."

"Fuck! Just do it, okay?"

"I'm telling you. I got out of there before the smoke even drifted our way."

"Just take your goddamn clothes off!" Scanlon shouted. "Sammy's health is more important than debating this. Jesus!" He stripped down to his underwear, picked up the pile of clothes, stepped into the laundry room, and dropped it all in the washing machine. From the kitchen, his father tossed him his shirt and pants, then pulled off his socks and started on his underpants.

"That's okay," Scanlon said. "It wouldn't penetrate that far."

"No, no," Geoff insisted, flinging his white jockeys at him. "Not even a wisp of impurity shall offend thy baby." He twirled his wineglass and took a sip, then reached to the counter for Scanlon's glass and handed it to him. "Take it easy," he said.

"I don't *want* to take it easy! When you're in this house, Sammy's got seniority, not you. Got it?" Scanlon gulped his wine as the washer chugged on the other side of the door. He was wound up, breathing hard. He gulped again, and the wine spread through his chest, calming the thud of his heart.

Geoff cradled his goblet in the palm of his hand—the stem dropping between two fingers—twirling, sniffing, sipping, swishing. "These Oregon pinots are highly regarded," he said serenely, then stood up and opened the kitchen door.

"This isn't a nudist camp, Dad. Let me get dressed, then I'll grab you some clothes from the RV."

Geoff waved him off. "We're all nudists," he declared, "in varying stages of denial."

Her boobs were on fire. How could something so natural be so impossible? The sperm penetrates the egg, the fetus grows, the child's born—okay, it's excruciating, but you get over it—and he's a good sucker and your tits produce milk. It should be simple. Did cows get blocked ducts? Did kangaroos get mastitis? Did antelope have trouble with bacteria in the teats? Somehow she doubted it, because otherwise they'd send their offspring away to fend for themselves. Surely the instinct for motherhood in lesser mammals wasn't more powerful than the avoidance of extreme, self-inflicted pain. Instead of the sacred bonding promised by the soft-focus baby-card photos of nursing mothers, Naomi yelped when Sammy latched on and winced through the feeding. Her nipples and pajamas were stained purple from the hokey and useless "remedy." Sammy had the face of a fat cartoon character caught stealing blueberry pies. As a rule, she had no patience for Erma Bombeck feminism, but sometimes it hit the mark: if testicles became excruciatingly engorged from blocked sperm ducts, there'd be entire institutes devoted to discovering a relief.

Still, when the feeding was over and he fell away from her nipple, milk-drunk or sound asleep, and she burped him while swaying in the glider or standing, as she was now, at the bedroom window looking out at the rain, she did feel the profound communion those ghastly cards advertised.

She wondered if she'd felt it for her own mother, and if her mother had felt it for her. Her mother hadn't nursed—it hadn't been the fashion, and her doctor deemed her breasts too small. But she'd fed, burped, and bathed her, napped with her sleeping on her chest. Naomi loved her, and respected her dedication as a nurse. Childhood had been happy in virtually every respect. But she didn't feel the profound bond she'd developed with Sammy. Could it be that he wouldn't feel it either? Maybe not. And suddenly Naomi was shaking, shaking with the fear of losing Sammy, of his growing up and leaving.

He lifted his head from her shoulder, let out a long belch, and snuggled down again. Was it merely a mother's projection that her baby loved her? A calf stayed close to the cow for protection and warmth, one eye on the dangling teats. But was it love? Did Joshua long for her as she longed for him?

She watched the little boy at the corner riding his tricycle up and down the sidewalk in the rain, and then saw Geoff, strolling toward his RV, a glass brimming with red wine in his hand. He bent down to snap off and sniff a pinch of rosemary. Except for her own yellow rubber clogs, he was naked.

After Sammy fell asleep, she laid him in his bassinet, slipped into jeans and a fleece, and clicked the bedroom door closed. She was so angry she didn't even glance at Scanlon. "Did you wash everything? And Geoff's clothes too?" She drank a glass of water. "Geoff needs to shower before he goes near the baby." Finally she looked at him: he'd showered and was wearing his robe. "There's milk in the freezer. Feed him at six if I'm not back." Out of the house at last, she gasped for air as if she'd lunged from a collapsing coal mine.

Tiny drops dampened the shoulders and hood of her raincoat, but by the time she got to the corner the rain had stopped. She walked past the high school, a park full of Canada geese, and a street she'd never noticed lined with maples, their wet leafless branches the color of the Pacific leaping frog's belly.

Soon she was on Sequoia's street. As she approached her house, the bamboo chimes caught a breeze and chunked, froglike. She wondered what she'd been baking, whether they'd fed each other. She didn't doubt that Sequoia was a more energetic lover than she was. Had Sequoia been aroused by his smell? Had he noticed hers? It wasn't until Naomi lived in France that she came to appreciate the smell of lusty sheets and bodies, of unwashed hair. Although less sophisticated, Sequoia had olfactory lineage in a Parisian woman's sensuality. *Much* less sophisticated, practically a hillbilly. Naomi could hardly believe she'd taken her advice—boiled cabbage leaves on her breasts?—or thought she might be a friend. Of all the betrayals, one sat like a stone in her chest: in Geoff's RV, her head in Scanlon's lap, those first semiconscious whiffs had summoned Joshua, and it wasn't until later that she realized the smell wasn't of his birth but of her husband's infidelity.

Her true friends were in New York; she had to move back as soon as possible. For now she'd take trips east with Sammy, and they could stay with Liz. They'd be women in the museum with strollers. She'd order takeout and rent movies with Maria and Peter, show off the baby, eat lunch at Tartine, window-shop in SoHo. Sammy would learn to crawl in the park. She'd splurge on cabs and get a good table to hear Jimmy Scott one more time before he, too, was taken away.

Four blocks from the courthouse—she was surprised and relieved that the demonstrations were contained to the square, leaving the rest of downtown life untroubled—a bus lumbered up to the curb, and she spotted the shabby doorway in the alley beside the Greyhound station. Four buzzers. She pressed the one without a name, then rang again for a good twenty seconds.

But he wasn't home. She stepped back onto the sidewalk and watched the bus unloading passengers, an assortment of anarchists among them, half of them resembling Clay. Two cops pointed them down Jefferson Avenue to where barricades surrounded the courthouse.

Then Clay walked out the front door of the station, taking a bite of a burrito and almost bumping into her. They stared at each other for a moment, then he offered the burrito, holding it out to her like a joint.

She was trying to make sense of the hot dog sticking out from a nest of lettuce, tomato, beans, and sour cream wrapped in a white tortilla when a cop strode up to them. "Proceed to the demonstration area," he ordered, pointing to the courthouse with his nightstick.

"Nice afternoon for it," Clay said, "but I've got other plans today."

The cop's helmet was cocked back roguishly, and his fleshy chin was red from the dangling strap, all protocol abandoned in battle. "Move it," he said, and prodded him between the shoulder blades with his stick.

Clay's head twitched. His back tensed, then he took a bite of his burrito in a forced display of cool. But the cop wasn't budging and Clay's anger expanded—his head snapping, his ears going red.

"He lives here," Naomi blurted. "Right here." She pointed. "I was coming to visit him. We were just going up."

The cop didn't like it—he knew her type—but he backed off, watching until Clay produced a key and the two of them stepped inside, the heavy glass door springing shut.

"Never do that," Clay muttered. They were standing on wet Domino's fliers and color photos of pot roast and Huggies on special at Fred Meyer. "Never give in to them."

She followed him up the stairs. "I just thought it might defuse—"

"Never concede their authority. Just—" He turned at his apartment door, glaring down at her from two steps above. His head twitched. "Don't."

It was a single room. Gold carpet, decades old, a bare mattress on the floor, a sink and counter, a hotplate and a small fridge, three cardboard boxes half-full of clothes. Clay sat cross-legged on the corner of the mattress and ate his burrito without pleasure, or even interest. Naomi stood at the tall window. She could see the bridge into town, the Bank of America, and the signboard in front of the Church of the Savior: *In all you do His blood's for you.* A bus pulled out from under her feet, a black cloud shooting from the tailpipe. Diesel fumes seeped around the loose window sashes.

Over the auto-body shop belonging to Clair's parents there'd been a studio apartment—usually vacant, since few tenants could endure the smell of body putty for long—and from the window she could look out at the heating-oil depot across the street, two blue-black tanks propped up on timber trestles. As grease and spices from Clay's burrito mixed with diesel exhaust, she remembered parting the curtains (a kitcheny pattern of garlic heads, oregano, chili peppers, and thyme, each identified in loopy script by its Latin name) and seeing the oil tanks in the bright sun as Clair, behind her, zipped into his coveralls only minutes after Joshua was conceived.

He felt funny with her standing two feet from the bathroom door, but he had to piss, pretty bad. Daria was the last woman in here, the only woman. Every hour, all night, when she was pregnant, her surge and tinkle would fill the night's empty silence.

The light through his window haloed Naomi's hair. You didn't see much kinky hair like that in Oregon. After a long time she turned from the window, her hand on her belly, saying, "How was the burrito?"

He shook his head. He had no patience for meaningless talk or the garbage that filled the airwaves. His struggle was keeping it from worming into him, like brown noise. "We're better than that," he said. And then he asked, "Why didn't you bring Sammy?"

She looked away for a moment, then back. "He must remind you of Ruby Christine."

His daughter was fitting triangular blocks through triangular holes. She was finger-painting and eating peeled grapes. She took naps curled up next to Daria. "I like babies," he said.

"And single moms." She smiled.

"I do," he said. "It's what my mom pretty much was. Three reckless boys, my father worst of all." He envied single moms because they were released from meaninglessness.

And in the way it was with Naomi, he now felt at ease, and after a while, he picked up with the story from Crazy Eights about his father, how King's *instability,* the doctor called it, turned more frightening, more violent, as Billy and Clay became teenagers. He swiped explosives off the highway job and blew craters in the backyard with his boys, teaching them how to make their own electronic detonators.

In the blue suit that Clay's mother had bought King for his father's funeral, he got drunk and punched out his brother-in-law, who'd moved with King's sister to Walla Walla for a factory job where he had to wear a hairnet and a paper gown. They could only spare an afternoon back in Yaquina. When they said their goodbyes fifteen minutes into the reception, wolfing down smoked salmon on the way out the door, King hit him. Most of Clay's parents' large families had moved away as fishing, crabbing, and timber dried up.

When Clay was in high school, his father drove him and Billy along the newly constructed highway to Siuslaw Butte, which he and the ODOT crew had spent the last month blasting away in order to straighten the road through Burnt Woods. King pulled the El Camino off the shoulder and drove through the tall, dry weeds around the backside of the security lamps that bathed light on the giant dump trucks and graders, engineering trailer, and steel lockers. He parked the car in a dark level patch along the river and displayed in his palm a padlock key, his grin devious, dangerous. King told the boys to wait, then set off in the shadows. Billy threw rocks into the river. Clay imagined his father hiding in the shadows of the high school in Baltimore the night he sneaked out. He thought of his parents at Yaquina High, the same age he was now, kissing in the shadows behind the bleachers after King Knudson slugged the varsity team to another victory.

Half an hour passed before he returned with a heavy red box in each hand. "No more sneaking home firecrackers in my Playmate, boys. You need to see what your powder-monkey dad can really shoot. Now, sit tight."

This was before the period when Clay would not have sat tight. In the next couple of years he began to intervene in these misadventures. But on this night, he was still the child, full of bad feelings and doubts about his father's judgment but, despite everything, living under the comforting, self-sustaining illusion that King would ultimately know what was best and do the right thing. It was as childish as believing the Easter Bunny hides eggs in your yard even when you see your mother close the shades during breakfast and slip out the back door with a paper bag, but belief was sometimes its own reward, like an Easter basket puffed with colorful nesting and rich with foil-wrapped chocolate eggs.

Until. Until his father scrambled back, dragging a det box and cord, and called Billy up from the riverbank. Before Clay had even gotten out of the El Camino, four booming explosions flashed up in quick succession: a grader, the engineers' trailer, a utility locker—

Clay cut off the story there, then told Naomi that his father had been fired the previous afternoon, which wasn't true. King didn't seem to have a reason for doing it. Nothing beyond *instability.*

By dawn the state police had surrounded the house, and King was hurling pots and pans at them from a second-story window. Hammers and wrenches and aerosol cans. When they took him, he was shirtless, handcuffed, and bleeding from his left shoulder.

Clay told Naomi none of this. He didn't tell her that the fourth explosion blew up a unit of six Porta-Potties. He didn't tell her the VA hospital was as worthless in the next three years as it'd been in the previous fourteen. King was medicated, strapped to chairs in windowless rooms with locked and reinforced doors. He was released and repeatedly jailed for disorderly conduct that was provoked by the drugs the VA mandated he take as a condition of his release. Nearly every time he was arrested he put up a fight before they tackled him to the ground and cuffed him.

He didn't tell Naomi that his father tried to hang himself three times in a jail cell, twice with bedsheets, once with the elastic waistband of county-issue underpants. And he didn't tell her that finally, at the start of Clay's junior year in high school, King bought his wife a bouquet of flowers, then walked the seven miles to where he and Roslyn had grown up neighbors on Onsland Point, cutting across parking lots of high-priced condos unimaginable a decade earlier, and when he got to the bluff where they used to watch fishing boats come in, now the fifteenth green of Hadley Point Golf Club, he stood at the edge, where the country ended and the Pacific Ocean began, and he jumped for his life.

Naomi had drifted from the window and was sitting opposite him, cross-legged on a corner of the mattress. He thought she looked maternal and middle-aged, with her arms crossed over her belly and her shiny blue raincoat still zipped. Was it cold in here? It had exhausted him to put this history into words, these memories a dense and formless weight at the back of his neck that he couldn't move out from under, couldn't buck off. But the way she leaned toward him to listen made him want to try.

He couldn't stand it any longer, so he went into the toilet and pissed a wicked stream. The relief was tremendous.

And when he came out she was stretched diagonally across his mattress, reaching for the photo of herself eight months pregnant, sunbronzed shoulders, covering her breasts. She darted a look at him—her face flushed with confusion, fear, then anger—and he stopped in the bathroom doorway as a police car howled past. His head wouldn't stop twitching, so fiercely that he stumbled against the doorjamb. And Naomi came to him. She laid her hand on his neck and guided him back. He fell on his side and curled up in a ball, his head convulsing against the mattress. She sat beside him, her warm hand between his shoulder blades, and gently coached his breathing, leading him through the spasms until his head lay still.

Chapter 8

That night, they ate like the war-weary, staring into Styrofoam trays of burritos, pinto beans, and brown rice, the whole time listening to sirens in the distance. Scanlon had worked all afternoon on his piece for the *Oregonian,* but goddamnit, he couldn't find an angle. Neither anarchy theorists nor Proudhon and the Mutualists were suitable for a newspaper feature. He needed on-the-ground research, primary sources, the street-level perspective that colleagues sitting in their offices at Princeton would never have. The kind of details that would impress even Sam Belknap.

When they finished dinner, Geoff took Sammy on his shoulder to the RV to watch Baby Mozart anime on satellite from Japan. Naomi was too exhausted to even put up a fight. She flipped past several channels of live news from downtown Douglas before settling for a rerun of *Friends.* During a commercial, Scanlon snatched the remote from her lap and switched to the demonstrations: two girls with scraggly wet hair and black sweatshirts were being cuffed with plastic zip strips.

"I talked to Rachel," Naomi said.

The cops gripped the girls' arms, loading them into a paddy wagon. Scanlon chomped on corn chips from the oily takeout bag.

"A sublet opened up in her building. A studio. It's cheap."

Scanlon kept his eyes on the TV, slowly allowing what Naomi was saying to sink in.

"I could freelance, so I wouldn't be tied to New York. Either that or part-time."

On the TV he saw a clip of himself in the bus shelter this afternoon, the air milky with tear gas, America Sanchez holding the microphone to his face. His mouth was moving, but a reporter was talking over his voice.

"I need to get back to my career," Naomi said. "I figure Sammy and I could be back here for two weeks or more every month."

He turned away from the TV and looked squarely at her. He ate a chip. "But you're incapable of taking care of yourself," he said. "You always have been."

"That's your fantasy. What you want to believe so—"

"Be patient, please. I swear I'll get us back to New York. I promise."

"But *when*?"

"We said a few years. It's only been five months."

"But I didn't have my nose then. I e-mailed Blaine Maxwell. She said I could have all the frog juice I want. This could be so big."

"So work on it here. You've got your organ set up, the house to yourself all day."

"I . . ." She shook her head. "There's nothing for me here."

"How about your fucking husband?"

"My fucking husband," she said calmly, "is tied up with his research and his various movements."

"I'm trying to make a family," he shouted. "I've been working my ass off on an article all day. I'm doing this for you and Sammy. Tapping all the sources I can so I can write—"

"You're tapping your sources for me and Sammy? My *fucking husband* is tapping Sequoia for us. I bet she's an amazing resource."

Scanlon's heart thumped. Goddamnit, she knew. "You don't have to leave. I don't want you to."

"I've got my life and Sammy's to think about."

"If you go," he said, staring at the chip in his fingers, feeling his face darken, "Sammy stays here with me."

Her breath caught. She shook her head. Her shoulders hunched up and her eyes narrowed. She squeezed his elbow and guided his hand with the chip toward her. When she opened her mouth, the chip at her lips, a moan, more like a growl, sounded in her throat. She stared into his eyes, the growl deepening.

Then she pounced, biting with the force of a wild animal. He screamed and jumped back, blood spurting from his thumb and finger, blood and Naomi's saliva edging her clenched teeth.

The police stopped him at a barricade across Lewis and Clark Boulevard, and when they turned him back, he pulled into the lot behind the city library and cut the engine. On a side street, idling in the darkness, was a canvas-backed truck: Oregon National Guard.

He locked the car, pulled up his rain jacket hood, and set off toward the courthouse. Passing by the truck, he studied the various high-tech-looking orbs and cones surrounding a small satellite dish, and heard a smooth, deep hum occasionally interrupted by an electronic bleep or scratch of static. Heat radiated from behind the canvas tarp, green lights flashing dimly, and the whole rig smelled like dust burning on top of a light bulb, like the hot tubes of his father's old stereo.

"Stand back." A soldier suddenly appeared at the rear of the truck, cupping a cigarette in his hand against the rain, his face completely shadowed.

Scanlon's gut dropped.

"And move along."

"Right." And as he walked quickly away, Scanlon was sure he felt his bowels loosen. Could it really be true?

There were, of course, plenty of other explanations: stress, pinto beans, Naomi's attack. She'd gotten up from the couch and gone into the bathroom, returning with a wet washcloth and Band-Aids. She'd cleaned and dressed his wounds, the whole time sucking at the blood in her teeth. Then, without a word, she'd gone into the bedroom and closed the door.

A cop on a Harley roared past. Scanlon sneaked along Fifth Street, crossed the railroad tracks, and came out by city hall. The Starbucks was closed, still boarded up with plywood, and when he rounded the corner, he saw cops and kids lit up with floodlights in front of the courthouse. From this distance—three or four blocks—it looked like a raucous street fair, as if a Ferris wheel might rise up from the chaos.

But as he got closer the tone changed—no cotton candy or corn dogs here. Three battle cops picked off a protester from the edge of the crowd, their batons thudding across his back until his face slapped the sidewalk, a knee in the spine pinned him down, his wrists were bound, and he was flung into a paddy wagon.

Scanlon stepped back into a doorway, thinking twice about thrusting himself into the mayhem. In Seattle there'd been safety in the masses of marchers who weren't there to make trouble, a buffer between him and the cops and the anarchists. But this looked like a Revolutionary War battle—the spiffily outfitted cops and the ragtag militia meeting head to head.

So he hung back in the doorway of the Toy Maker. In the window a kid-sized school chair was brightly painted with coyotes, geckos, and snakes. Sirens were howling everywhere, and the glow of at least two fires reflected off low clouds in the starless sky.

He decided to go down past the Rainy Day Café and the bookstore to the Green & Black. The streets were eerily deserted, shiny black with the rain. He heard a motor roar and looked back over his shoulder: a police car screamed by him at highway speed, lights flashing but no siren, going the wrong direction on the one-way street. He continued past the music store—trumpets, violins, and guitars propped up in the window—and when he glanced down an alley, he was blindsided—knocked down on the sidewalk with someone on top of him.

"You fuck!" the guy spat, getting up and rubbing his elbow, trying to limp off a pain in his hip. All in black, he made two fists—blotchy tattoos on the backs of his hands and forearms. A second guy caught up with him, sprinting out of the dark alley. Thick black eyebrows, a scar on his face, a scowl.

"Sorry about that." Scanlon touched the blood at his nose, worked his sore jaw, then pushed up on his hands and knees. "I didn't—"

Blue lights twirled at the far end of the alley, and the two anarchists ran off.

A patrol car idled in front of the Green & Black. He pulled back his shoulders to stand upright and wove through the subdued crowd. In the same spot where he'd seen them last night, Clay and Flak were huddled in tight, elbows on the table, heads hanging between their shoulders. Clay nodded when he saw him. Then Flak looked up and smiled. "Citizen," he said, "you're bleeding."

Scanlon shrugged. The worst of it was that Naomi's bite had reopened when he hit the sidewalk, blood seeping out from under the Band-Aids and trickling down his wrist.

Clay flung him a paper napkin.

"Are you okay?" It was Entropy, leaning over from the next table.

Scanlon wiped his nose, then wrapped up his finger. He nodded.

"Some bad-ass motherfuckers have come to town," Flak said, kicking a chair out for Scanlon. "On both sides of the law."

"Crazy shit," Entropy said.

Flak nodded solemnly. "I just hope they don't burn down the town. These guys are looking for a fight. They give anarchy a bad name."

"A kid from Boise I was talking to," Clay said, his head twitching, "said they're *getting* themselves arrested. To bust Panama out from the inside."

"They'll move him," Flak said. "Probably already have. The Feds maintain holding tanks all over the place."

As they talked, Scanlon listened. They trusted him now, at least enough to ignore him. They discussed conspiracies, infiltrators, getting free refills on pop at Subway with someone else's cup, pouring gravel into bulldozer manifolds. They told stories of past protests and corrupt cops. Flak wondered aloud about selling rain ponchos, and Clay asked about Sammy's jaundice. And as Scanlon spit on the napkin and wiped dried blood from his nose, he felt himself sinking into the sort of dark hole he'd watched Naomi spiral down into over the years. She knew about Sequoia; she might leave him. And all he had up his sleeve for holding on to her was sitting around this table: his research. But he began to doubt they were the real thing. Flak cared too much about money and his godlike status with the kids, who were naive and uncommitted. To his credit, Clay had torched the SUVs, but ultimately he just wanted to set up housekeeping with wife and child. Scanlon felt so desperate that he wished the PVC pipe he'd bought for Clay really was for pipe bombs.

"Shit," Rebecca said, holding up her ringing cell phone. "I gotta go. My dad thinks I'm at the bowling alley." She turned away from the others and said brightly, "Hi, Daddy."

These were his sources? Hopeless. His finger throbbed.

"They'll bust Panama out," Entropy said, "and trounce the cops."

"Not gonna happen," Flak said. "That's a fight the cops want, because they know we can't win it. They have camps where they're *trained* to beat the crap out of anarchists. That's their job. Helmets, shields, tear gas, sticks. And if those don't work they'll just bring out the guns. You can't beat 'em in the street. You just get your ribs cracked. Yes, we must end the last, worst empire, but don't think that throwing a rock at those fuckers is gonna do that."

Armchair anarchists, Scanlon thought. This was the best he'd done.

Rebecca was standing beside the table, waiting for Flak to finish his speech. "I told him I was working on two strikes in the third frame, but he's picking me up at Starlite Lanes in half an hour."

"Oh my God," Entropy said. "You better run. You'll never make it in time."

"He's gonna kick my ass," Rebecca said.

Scanlon took a slow breath and dabbed at his nose; the bleeding had stopped. "Do you want a ride?" he asked.

"Thank you!" The relief of a high-school girl.

They all left together, Flak and Clay a few paces ahead, Scanlon following with the girls. At the corner they stopped, looking down the five or six blocks to the bedlam at the courthouse. That was where Scanlon needed to be—street level.

"What do you think?" he said to no one in particular. "Get a closer look?"

"Bad-ass motherfuckers," Flak repeated. "No doubt."

"I gotta kinda hurry up to the bowling alley," Rebecca said.

"I'm parked at the library," Scanlon told her. "It's on the way."

"He bought you the coffee," Clay said. "You owe him. That's how it works. Professor wants to see his lab animals in their native habitat."

They all stared at Clay, then he shot ahead, striding down Jefferson toward the courthouse, and the rest of them followed.

At the edge of the square, somebody bumped into Scanlon, and he realized he'd hurt his elbow in that collision. His thumb and finger throbbed. Bottles and rhetoric and strategies flew through the air. He and the girls stood on the periphery as Flak and Clay talked with a couple protesters. The word was that the cops weren't arresting anybody else—the jail was full, and so were the paddy wagons—but the Feds had infiltrated the crowd, choppers of U.S. Marines were hovering downriver with shoot-to-kill orders, Douglas was sealed off, and the only possible retreat was on the logging roads through the coastal range. There was pointing, down alleys and up at rooftops, where claims were made about snipers. They waded in a little deeper, where rumors about meth and Ecstasy rattled through the crowd, and that violence had flared up in Portland, Seattle, and Sacramento, and that somebody had torched the house belonging to Panama's judge.

Scanlon got looks. He thought he saw the punk who'd run into him. Flak was right about bad motherfuckers. Narrow eyes and slanted mouths. Four-day stubble on shaved skulls. Scarred, oversized hands and huge, misshapen knuckles. He was as close to the real thing as he'd ever been.

His mind sharpened and dialed in on the energy of rebellion, the beat in the air. Wet pavement, sirens near and far, shattering glass, the double blast of fire-truck horns, protesters' outraged screams, the stern monotone commands issued through a bullhorn. Debris was flying overhead—plastic bottles filled with dirt from street planters, an orange traffic cone, the head of a parking meter and, suddenly, hundreds of DVDs in Blockbuster cases.

A white news van was parked at the end of Third Street, a camera poked out the half-open passenger window. The driver had both hands on the wheel, ready to bolt. If Sanchez was still on the scene, she was tucked safely in back.

"Choke holds," Flak said. "A guy just told me. The cops are getting rough."

"A girl in Portland showed me how to break a choke hold," Rebecca said, her eyes electric. "They'd never get me."

Flak looked at her dubiously. "We should get out of here."

But then a roar went up, as if for a breakaway run in a football game, and the crowd suddenly rushed in every direction at once. Scanlon was spun around, flipped by a crashing wave, sucked under, then hit by the next breaker, and he lost sight of the others as every face was suddenly covered by a bandanna. He jumped up on a bench and saw two cruisers roar up a basement ramp under the jail. The protesters pushed at the police line as the first car screeched around the corner. The second car flew off the ramp too hard and bottomed out, and under the floodlights Scanlon could see Panama's face in the backseat. The newsman hopped from the van and up on the running board with his shoulder cam for a better shot. A line of batons drummed on the surge of protesters as the cruiser accelerated into the turn, the rear tires slipping on the wet pavement, and a uniformed, helmeted cop bounced off the hood with a gut-wrenching thump, spun through the air like a rodeo clown, and landed on the roof, where he was snagged by the blue lights until the car fishtailed around the corner and he shot over the trunk and tumbled to the street.

For a moment there was total silence, while rules changed and power shifted, so quiet that Scanlon could hear the scratch of police radios. The protesters took a step back, and the police ranks grew. He looked for Rebecca, for any of them, but then tear-gas canisters hit the pavement and spewed all around him. A black bus with cages on the windows lurched out from behind the jail and battle cops charged out the doors.

Protesters scattered, running, sprinting, stumbling. Scanlon held his ground on the bench, but as he watched the cops—the precision, efficiency, and indiscriminate violence of their attack—he knew Flak was right and joined the stampede, racing for the river. But after two strides he was tripped up and hit the pavement. When he scrambled to his feet, a kid in black shoved him down again and shouted, "Cop!"

"I'm not!" he yelled back. Standing over him, the kid pulled a leg back to kick him, so Scanlon stayed down, backing into an ATM niche in the wall of a bank as chaos engulfed them. The kid lunged forward—jittery and sweating, a poster boy for meth—and Scanlon cocked his fist, but suddenly someone grabbed the kid from behind and threw him aside. It was Clay. The kid swung at him wildly, but Clay ducked and head-butted him, cracking the kid's nose with his forehead. The kid went down, blood gushing over his face, and two cops were closing in as Scanlon sprinted away with Clay on his heels.

He covered four blocks and got to the river before looking back, but Clay wasn't there. Clusters of three or four were catching their breath and regrouping in the park, pointing back at the courthouse and talking about another charge. But the cops were methodically marching toward them, and it was clear this moment was over, so they disappeared down steep trails through the brush along the riverbank.

Scanlon collapsed on a park bench beside a bronzed, larger-than-life beaver, wetness seeping through the seat of his jeans. At least the rain had stopped. Four blocks down, by the courthouse, he could see the red flashing lights of a fire truck. No doubt Hank Trueblood was on the scene, helping the paramedics tend to the police. Things had turned bad here tonight. The poor cop who'd flipped up and over the cruiser—a father, a husband—probably had some broken bones, maybe wouldn't walk right again. A total disaster.

A loose line of cops reached the river walk. "Clear the area," one ordered through a bullhorn. Scanlon looked up and down the park. He was the only person here. Most of the police fanned out along the river, but three others approached him, shining a flashlight in his face. They stopped directly in front of him, and when he tried to shade his eyes, they shined the beam around his hand in what became an absurd little game.

"Where do you live?" one of them asked.

"Douglas," Scanlon said, then felt compelled to lie. "Born and raised."

"What's your address?"

He recited it.

"Go home, sir."

He rocked to his feet. "I was supposed to give someone a ride."

"That way." The cop pointed upriver with his flashlight. "And don't return to the area of the courthouse."

Scanlon strutted off, aware that he'd fallen into the snarl and wise-ass posture of a juvenile delinquent, refusing to snap to or surrender.

Down Washington Avenue he could see a paramedic van hit the siren and speed off. Another ambulance raced up the street, then a third. Scanlon walked two blocks to Jefferson and headed west, making a wide loop back to his car. Cops shined their lights on him and kept going. He was frankly a little resentful that he so obviously posed no threat. They were indiscriminately beating anyone who crossed them, yet they called him "sir" and sent him home in his cream-colored Gore-Tex jacket and his "dry as a duck" Bass shoes. Even with one of their comrades fallen, they couldn't work up a little brutality when it came to him.

He passed by the boarded-up Starbucks, crossed the tracks, and skirted the park. The rain blew back in, and he tugged up his hood against it, muting the distant sound of sirens. The clock in the courthouse tower struck eleven. He had papers to grade for tomorrow—John Locke and the Fourth Amendment. He'd go home, make an espresso, take up his green felt-tip, and try to get halfway through the stack. As he crossed Lewis and Clark, the cops at the corner were dragging their barricade to the curb. It was over.

Naomi and Sammy would be asleep. Geoff would be sipping a drink and watching television in his RV. Scanlon would drive the mile home, and the events of the night—frightening, heart-stirring—would slip into the past, having accomplished absolutely nothing. The ache spread from his elbow to his shoulder to his neck. Worse, he'd learned nothing of any interest to the *Oregonian.* He needed that article, at the very least. He also, and more importantly, needed to beg Naomi's forgiveness, and for her to grant it. And of course he needed to get her back to New York. He'd never in his life felt more desperate.

A block from the library he cut across the corner of the park, but shadows moved in the dark bandstand and he veered back toward the sidewalk.

"Yo," someone called.

He stopped, saying nothing.

"Yo," came again, and an anarchist stood up on the stage.

"I'm in a rush," Scanlon said.

"We need a few dollars."

Scanlon rubbed his elbow. It was stiffening up. "I'm fresh out," he said, and started to walk away.

"C'mon, brother. We gotta get back to Seattle."

He stopped again and, when he turned, saw a cell phone light up in the bandstand. The show was leaving town, and he'd gotten nothing. Forget the academic article, the book chapter; he didn't even have thirty-six hundred words for a newspaper.

He pulled out his wallet. "I've got twenty-nine bucks," he said, walking up. "But first I want to ask you a couple questions. Don't worry, I'm not a cop." There were two of them, almost indistinguishable from the hundreds of others. One put his cell phone in his pocket and sat down, and Scanlon held out the cash in his hand.

"Sure, bro," the standing one said when Scanlon came up to the steps. "What's on your mind?" His bandanna dangled around his neck.

"In your own words, not some bullshit somebody told you once, why do you think anarchy's the answer?"

"You should ask him," the guy said, nodding at his partner sitting on the edge of the stage—and the kick, for a split second, seemed nothing more than a brush against Scanlon's coat, but the boot hurtled into his ribs like a cinder block dropped from a second-story ledge. His spine caught fire and he was blown flat on his back, his eyes bleary, his molars loose. He was suddenly in a hot sweat and up on his feet in a karate pose, his mind sharp and racing on adrenaline. But the two punks were already halfway across the park, stomping off without even a backward gaze. He sprawled across the stage and gasped for breath, the pain spreading down to his stomach and groin then up into his armpits, and he puked over the rail.

Maybe ten minutes later, he shuffled around the side of the library. At first he thought his car was gone, which put him on the verge of tears. He just wanted to get home. But then he realized that an SUV had parked beside him, dwarfing his Honda and blocking the view. He stood behind both vehicles. The SUV's fat rear end had nearly clipped his car. Twenty empty spaces for the asshole to choose from, but he parked a rear wheel and a thousand pounds of fender in Scanlon's spot. A Nissan Armada. It was huge, but evidently the American family needed an entire fucking fleet to ship the kids to soccer. Plus an American flag bumper sticker, a Christian fish, and California vanity plates reading BUY-BUY.

He unlocked his car with the remote and walked around to peer into the Armada's windows, looking over both shoulders and scanning the light poles for cameras.

Then, rubbing his thumb along the edges of his keys, he selected his office key—chunky and institutional, with sharp pronounced teeth—and gripped it like a switchblade, leaning in with his hip, pressing it through a dozen layers of hard white paint from front fender to back with a dry, satisfying scrape.

Chapter 9

Hammers tapped slender nails into the back of Naomi's skull. Every time Scanlon moved in bed, he groaned. She laid ice packs on his ribs. He couldn't sit up on his own, so she hauled him off the mattress every hour to shift his position, until finally at three-thirty she wrapped ice around him with an Ace bandage, gave him a double dose of NyQuil, and he slept. She didn't. Sammy, whose stuffed-up nose kept him from filling his belly, woke up often and hungry, and she now had throbbing infections in both breasts.

As the sky lightened, she held Sammy sitting upright on the kitchen table, trying to get him to take a bottle. Famished, he snapped at the rubber nipple like a wolf, sucking out what he could before his breath caught in his nose and he snorted down snot, choked and spit out the milk, and wailed. If only he could eat enough, they'd sleep anywhere, even on the floor, and then maybe something other than misery and the wan hope of survival could come of the day.

All the years she'd believed that one day she no longer would feel tormented by the loss of Joshua, she had imagined a future in which she'd magically matured into a newly formed woman. She'd gotten glimpses of that woman—in the weeks when it looked like Marc Jacobs was going to produce her fragrance, or the two short months in the sunny sublet with a courtyard on Bank Street, or the year she deeply loved an Indian painter named Sameer. She would simply step into this woman, inhabit her, and everything that came before would dissolve. It wouldn't matter that she'd stupidly convinced herself in the first months of her pregnancy that Clair would call, and she'd explain, and she wouldn't have to decide about an abortion alone. It wouldn't matter that she could have told Clair in a letter, or that denial and apprehension, maybe fear, subdued all reason until she scheduled the appointment knowing what they'd say: she was too late. It wouldn't matter that she never told Scanlon that the news her father delivered before rear-ending the taxi was that Clair's wife had given birth to twins; she hadn't told him, or anyone, to evade the silent accusation that her anosmia might have been more about the news than the accident.

But she now knew it all mattered and always would, and she no longer carried the bright certainty that her *real* life was ahead of her. Then she looked at Sammy and hated herself—loathed herself—for feeling this way.

One of her rich New York friends, Louise, had a husband, James, who was a struggling writer. Waiting on line for movie tickets one day, she'd made Naomi laugh. "New York was too distracting for James," Louise said, "so we moved out to the suburbs. 'I can't write in Connecticut,' he says after six months. '*No one* can write in Connecticut.' So I buy the townhouse on West 11th, but he can't write there because of the kids and the nanny. So I rent him a studio." She grinned. "*Where he can't write.*"

But she stuck by James, and Naomi understood his struggle. Yes, she'd been inspired by Oregon, but to develop a fragrance, to immerse herself in a creative zone, she needed to be surrounded by other noses, by the industry itself. She needed to be in New York.

Then there was her marriage. She supposed they'd talk. But talking required language and analysis, systems of logic much more evolved than her instinctual olfactory sinews where the smells of Scanlon and Sequoia fucking were firmly lodged. Our most primitive sense, smell was the first to come and the last to go. Babies, born essentially blind, followed their noses to survival; except for humans, mammals born without the sense of smell faced certain death. And for now, her reaction to their fucking was holed up in a primitive lair.

With enough milk in his belly that he was sick of the effort, Sammy clamped his lips closed and twisted away. She opened the shade and bounced him by the window. Seven-thirty and the fog was so thick that the streetlights were still glowing. Sammy burped, and she opened the kitchen door for the newspapers. The rain was enlivening, and she took a deep breath before stepping back inside. Scanlon would wake up, bleary from NyQuil, and he'd need her. She had to get out.

She would let Sammy fall asleep, then put him in the stroller and escape for a latte. She moved Scanlon's keys and briefcase off the table, resolving not to be his nurse today. Geoff could do it. She spread out the Douglas paper and, as she read the front page, a slow bubble rose in her heart, her hands forming fists. "Oh my God," she said aloud. "Clay."

"It's a certainty of physics," Flak had once told him, "that the day after tomorrow could be yesterday."

On the mattress Clay curled to his side. Streetlight barely illuminated the quarter moon curve of Naomi's belly in the photo inches from his face. For him, time funneled into two points: Billy's death and the birth of Ruby Christine. Although he couldn't shake the assumption that time was moving forward—proof, Flak would say, that he'd been brainwashed by the system—he sensed that everything in his life was moving backward to those two moments, time reversing so he could return to the hospital and hold tight on to Daria and their baby, refusing to let them go.

Last spring he'd spent a week busting up driveways for a contractor. He'd start jack-hammering near the edge until a crack opened up, then pound away with the chisel until the slab lost its hold on itself and crumbled. This was how he followed the cracks back to the places where wrong things had solidified and hardened in his life, demolishing the hold they had on him.

He'd been backing up the car. Late at night, sleepless on his mattress, he thought with deceptive clarity of how easy it should be to return to the moment and make the car go forward, and if it's going forward then they're pulling into the driveway rather than backing onto the road. Through the long night, such thoughts took the place of sleep.

"Fuck it," Billy had said. "I'm not going."

"We *have* to," Clay told him. "It's for Mom."

"It's for *them,*" Billy said. "The army. The government. So they can say they did the right thing."

Clay had been wearing his father's blue suit. Yards too big for him, it would fit Billy if he were alive today, stocky and barrel-chested. The suit their father had gotten for his own father's funeral.

He unknotted the tie—his fourth or fifth attempt at getting the ends to come out right. At seventeen, he'd worn a tie no more than a few times in his life. Billy, fifteen, was lying on his unmade bed doing PlayStation on the old TV. He was wearing his good pants—already too tight—and nothing else. His smooth chest and muscular arms, his defiance.

"Now!" Clay commanded. "You're gonna make us late."

"Then go!" His eyes pinned to the TV, his thumbs flicking buttons. "You and Mom can show them how proud we are."

Clay pounced on his brother, straddling him and punching his chest and ribs as hard as he could.

"Offa me!" Billy covered up but didn't fight back. "Offa me, you insane fuck!"

But Clay kept pummeling him until Billy finally kicked him off, swatting him in the mouth and splitting open his lip. "Okay!"

Clay licked at the blood. "Get your clothes on, get in the car, and tell Mom she looks nice." He touched his lip with the back of his hand. "Two minutes. We're already late."

From the driver's seat—his mother sitting behind him in the back—he watched Billy walking stiffly, tight in the ribs, from the kitchen door to the car. Fat raindrops blanketed the car and the wipers slapped on high speed. Waiting for Billy they'd fogged up inside, and Clay flipped the defroster on full blast, but like most things in the old Toyota it didn't work and they steamed up worse. Billy slumped in the passenger seat, slammed his door, and belted in. When Clay gave him a look, he glanced over his shoulder and said, "You look nice, Ma."

Clay peered at her in the rearview mirror. Even that was steamed up, so he wiped it clear with a finger. She *did* look nice. With quiet and resigned grace, she was dealing with the day—a Veterans Day celebration honoring her husband and another local vet who'd died that year. He knew she hated it as much as Billy did. The fierce bitterness that gripped her in 1968 had never let go.

Still, her perfume sweetened the dank smell of sodden floormats, and her hair was swept up beautifully. She adjusted her bright floral scarf and straightened the collar of her pink raincoat. "Thanks, dear," she said. "You boys look nice, too."

The routine for backing out onto Highway 101 was ingrained in all of them. Never violated. Even King, whose judgment was compromised by the bullet in his brain, would say, "When you boys drive, don't ever forget how we do this. Never cheat it."

You backed out through the row of cypress, a tall and thick barrier from headlights and the rumble of trucks, and swung your rear end onto the wide shoulder of packed dirt where the mailman pulled over to reach their box. It had to be a tight, precise turn to stay off the highway but avoid swiping the mailbox. After a hundred times, it became second nature.

The rain had been heavy for twenty-seven days straight—not a record, but extremely wet—and the pullout was muddy, the edge sliding into the drainage ditch. In the last few days, to avoid it, Clay had been swinging out farther from the mailbox and closer to the highway—a matter of half a foot—rolling the driver's-side tires up on the pavement for traction.

Billy punched on the radio—the Prodigy's "Firestarter"—and twisted it loud. Shifting into reverse, Clay glanced at the mirror and saw his mother's closed eyelids quiver, her crow's feet radiating like cracks through glass, her patience and understanding for her husband and now her boys slowly shattering her from the inside.

Gunning the Toyota backward—they were late—and looking over his shoulder, he turned down the music, but Billy dialed it back up. His mother pressed her temples, and Clay reached forward and switched the radio off, still rolling, seeing only a fogged-up rear window. Normally he would've asked her to wipe the glass clear with the rag, but her hands were on her face, her eyes still closed, and Billy blared the radio again. "Goddamnit!" Clay yelled, punching him hard on the shoulder. "Turn it off!" He brushed his sleeve against the window to try to see the side-view mirror, but Billy was shouting over the music: "You're not the father now!" Backing through the cypress row, he looked past his brother for the mailbox, old galvanized steel the color of fog, and, inching the steering wheel to the right, beginning a blind swing, he was about to tell him to roll down his window when Billy yelled, "You act like my father, like you've got authority, but you don't!"

"Fuck you!" Clay shouted, thrusting his face at him as the rear tire rolled onto the pavement and he swung the wheel, already wishing for his mother's sake that he'd held his tongue.

The headlights out Billy's side window were a faint white illumination, like the Yaquina Head lighthouse seeping through curtains of fog, so distant and faint that his first thought—no, his *last* thought—was to keep rolling and back all the way into the far lane.

But in an instant the lights filled the windows on both sides of Billy's face, the headlights widening, the grille of a Cadillac Escalade framing his shoulders and head. Clay thrust his hand out, reaching to Billy's window to hold off the SUV, his fingers spread across the glass, his cheek touching his brother's. He remembered the cold moisture on his palm and the first nudge of impact. He pushed against it, his face butting Billy's, their cheeks grazing, Billy's nose poking against his ear. The grille pushed against the car, and Clay pushed back. He'd stopped it. The Cadillac had rocked the car sideways on its springs, but when the grille tapped against the window Clay stopped the vehicle cold and saved his brother, who flung his arms around him and kissed his cheek, his breath smelling of milk and Cheerios. Clay turned to see his mother, arms open wide, exuberant joy in her face, hurling herself toward her boys, thrilled that they'd reconciled and proud that Clay had protected them. He'd stepped into the man's shoes, holding the family—the three of them—together.

The music had stopped, silence except for the buzz of a short circuit under the dash. Billy's toothy kiss bit into Clay's cheek. The noise grew louder, insistent . . .

Light. It had been dark and now it was light. He'd slept. It was the buzzer downstairs, which could only be bad. Cops or worse. He'd seen Flak get taken down, but the sound was what he remembered. The club glancing off his own elbow had been a pop. The clubs on Flak had crunched.

The buzzer didn't quit. He got up, holding his sore arm, and peered out the window. No cop cars, no crew, just the front wheels of a baby stroller.

Down the stairs he let himself imagine—still sloshing in the dip into sleep—that he'd find Daria and Ruby Christine waiting in the alley. But when he saw Naomi's relief that his skull wasn't wrapped in a cast, that he wasn't in jail, the fact that she cared that much made him glad to see her standing there. Her baby was screaming, powerfully.

"Sammy can't nurse," she said, then kachunked the stroller a step at a time up to Clay's room. "He's too stuffed up."

Clay coaxed Sammy from his mother, lay back on his mattress, and held him up on a straight arm, his good arm, airplane style, the baby's tummy on his palm. Sammy choked and screamed in protest, but quickly calmed down. Clay rotated his face toward his mother, and his red eyes brightened.

"It's something about compressing their diaphragm," Clay said. "I don't know. Or that they tighten their backs."

"A miracle." She eyed the photo of herself.

"When it works."

She took Sammy back in her arms, and he stayed quiet. "Did you see the paper?"

He rolled his eyes. The *paper*. Don't get him started about mind control.

"You were there last night," she said. "You're hurt."

"Not bad," he said, touching his elbow hidden under his sleeve. He hadn't looked at it this morning, and he didn't look now.

"Your friend, the one you talk about. Flak."

Flak's name on Naomi's lips made him smile.

"I'm sorry, Clay. He's unconscious. Maybe a coma."

Time. His last eight hours were now different from what they'd been. Last night he'd run cold water over his elbow, eaten aspirin, looked at Naomi's photo, dropped into sleep, woken to her and Sammy. But now that time had changed into the hours after Flak's skull got smashed by the cops.

He went to the window. Government workers in DayGlo vests and polished white hard hats rose up the side of the courthouse on boom trucks, power-washing the splatters of red paint, while below them street cleaners, yellow lights twirling from their tops, were scrubbing the square. He'd dreamed about the accident again last night, as doctors picked skull fragments from Flak's uncommon brain.

Flak had Billy's same build but was older than Clay; it was a relief to be the young one. He leaned into the fridge and flipped open a can of beer. He should swallow some more aspirin, he thought, back at the window, guzzling from the can.

"Can I do anything?" she asked, and when he didn't respond, she said, "I'm relieved you're okay."

He wasn't okay. If you lived a true life—no, back up. (That's what Flak liked to say before amending an argument.) If you strive to minimize your own hypocrisy, some government somewhere will eventually kill you for it. Clay didn't believe that a North Korean furniture mover, an Iranian fisherman, a Sunni whose little brother died, or a Shiite separated from his baby were any different from him.

Out the window, a dark wall of fog had tumbled over the coast range from Yaquina and was bearing down on them a mile a minute.

The apartment smelled of blood. Reckless, Naomi thought, bringing Sammy here. They should leave, but despite his gaspy, snotty breaths the baby was finally sleeping, and the beer was helping Clay relax. He stretched his arms wide across the window, looking west. "Brother Flak," he muttered. "Brother Billy." Then he thrust his fist at the windowpane and held his palm to the glass.

After a moment he turned and sat on the windowsill, the sky darkening behind him. Naomi saw surrender in the slump of his shoulders and back. He held one arm close to his side as he tipped back his beer, sucking at the rim of the can. Fog pushed against the cracked panes as if the room were submerging.

"I was backing out the driveway," he said, "and I put out my hand to stop it, to protect him. The impact snapped my wrist and Billy flew into me, knocking out his teeth on my cheek." He touched the half-smile scar beneath his eye that she knew but couldn't see on his shadowed face. "And when everything was quiet, the shouting over, the radio and engines dead, the glass done shattering and metal done groaning, our tires plowed sideways so hard that the rubber was stripped from the rims"—he paused, as if remembering this for the first time—"Billy was lying in my arms. I didn't feel my broken wrist or contusions or cuts. My mother was unconscious for a minute or two, and except for a bloody mouth and two missing teeth up front, Billy was resting peacefully in my arms. I'd saved him, but I couldn't move. He was pressed on top of me, and hanging over his head, just a foot or so from my face, there was a license plate bolted to a bumper, an oil pan, and the underside of an engine. The radiator was dripping on Billy's pants, and I remember thinking he'd have to go back inside and change before the ceremony. 'Clay?' It was my mother. 'We're fine, Mom,' I said. 'Billy?' 'He's good, Mom. Resting.' And I talked Billy through the hour it took for the firemen to rip the car open. 'I'm sorry I yelled,' I told him. 'I know I'm not the father. You're too smart for me to father anyway. I just want us to be a family. Like Mom and Dad used to dream of, before he went away. And it's up to you and me to take care of—Mom? Are you still back there?' 'Yes, dear,' she said, her voice soft and close. We felt the closest we ever had. 'Remember all Dad's business scams for the three of us?' I said to Billy. 'Restoring muscle cars of the sixties, buying an old diesel locomotive and some track and charging people to drive it, building fancy tree houses for rich newcomers. You and I can still do any of it. It'd be in Dad's honor . . . Are you cold, Billy? It won't be long now. Hold on to me tight, and I'll keep you warm. Mom?' 'Yeah.' 'Won't be long.' I'd never, in my entire life, felt more at peace."

Sammy choked on his phlegm and woke up, but magically he didn't start bawling. He focused his dark watery eyes on his mother and grinned, then remembered he was hungry and gave a tiny, plaintive cry. She draped a fleece baby blanket over her shoulder and, still sitting cross-legged on the mattress, unbuttoned the top of her shirt and lifted Sammy up.

She winced against the merciless pinch inside her breast, and he cried when she pulled him off. She took a deep breath and brought him to her again, grinding her teeth against the pain, then Clay was standing over her, tapping a cold can against her shoulder. She shook her head, Sammy lost his hold, screaming in protest, and Clay said, "I've seen this before."

Good God. She took the beer. Keystone. She'd never heard of it. Sammy wailed and she chugged. Whether it would help with the mastitis or not, the beer tasted damn good. She drank more, then stood up and bounced Sammy, though his crying didn't let up. She had a bottle in the diaper bag, but her breasts were bulging full—beyond capacity—and she needed relief.

Clay cracked open a second beer for himself and waggled another at her. She shook her head, and he set it on the edge of the sink. For the first time she noticed a toy soldier beside his hotplate, not much bigger than her thumb, and posed like a javelin thrower, one hand tossed back, clutching a grenade, the other pointing toward the enemy line. Clay lowered himself onto the mattress, his face twisting in pain, and bit the cap off an aspirin bottle. He shook a few pills straight into his mouth. She finished off her beer, set down the can, and picked up the soldier, surprised by its weight in her palm.

"Billy and my father spent hours and hours casting lead soldiers," Clay said. "Filing the seams, painting them, then they'd melt 'em down and recast. We must've had twenty molds. A full home-foundry kit. It'd been my dad's. Maybe *his* dad's." He stared out the window, as if he could see through the fog to the coast. "All that stuff's gone now."

Sammy reached for the soldier—anything to please him—but then she realized it was lead—*Jesus!*—and yanked it away. He shot her an accusing look, insulted by this new level of incompetence and disregard, and cranked his howls to the top.

But she felt a letting go in her breasts—again, Clay was right—and grabbed the full beer from the counter and settled back onto the mattress. She held Sammy to her and felt a muted discomfort as he began sucking with abandon.

"I'd forgotten all about the lead soldiers, for years before my dad died, but for some reason, or for *no* reason, that soldier there, after the accident, was deep in Billy's pants pocket. World War Two commando raider, chucking a grenade."

After a time, when Sammy had pulled away and was nodding off, she flicked her nipple over his lips to try to rouse him. But it was no use. He was zonked, even more exhausted than she was. He'd drunk the top off one breast and hadn't touched the other. The beers—she'd now finished two—had eased the tightness and pain, and filled her bladder.

She rose from the mattress—very tipsy, off balance. Clay grinned, which made her laugh. "Shit," she said. "Two beers before breakfast." Then she laid Sammy, sound asleep, in his stroller.

"Daria used to call it the triple-B: beers before breakfast. It took some discipline to wean her off those when she got pregnant."

Naomi squeezed her legs together and stopped outside the bathroom door. "I wish you'd try again with her," she said. "Find a compromise that won't freak out her parents. Anything to be with her and the baby. I know how much you want it."

Clay leaned away, shaking his head.

"Get out of Douglas. Find a new place. A new life together. The three of you."

He laughed, harshly. "You gotta have money for the little house on the prairie, then you need furniture, and then—"

"Maybe her parents could give you a loan, just to get you started. My parents gave us money for the down payment on our house."

"They'd get me arrested for asking."

"It's in their interest. They don't want Ruby Christine to grow up without her father. Or for Daria to be a single mom."

"You don't get it," he said.

"I do—" she began, but Clay turned his back on her.

When she closed the bathroom door, the smell of blood was thick, the wastebasket heaped up with blood-soaked toilet paper. He was injured worse than she'd imagined. She should examine it. For all his stoicism and his bevy of single moms, he was an orphan with no one to look after him.

She peed a flood, grateful for the beer that had lightened her spirits and pain, but it had also shaken loose her emotions. She pressed her eyes closed against the tears, smelling Clay's blood and her own body; she'd soon resume her period and the monthly visitations from Joshua.

She dried her hands on her pants and opened the door. "Let me see where you're hurt," she insisted, and after token resistance Clay let her ease his arm out of his shirt.

"Holy shit!" she gasped. His elbow was swollen to the size of his knee, blue and purple and a sickly yellow. "You've got to get to the emergency room."

He shook his head.

"I've got the car. Seriously, Clay. It's bad."

He smiled. "There's gonna be cops, and if they get in my shit right now and I start thinking about Flak . . ." His face went dark.

"Who did this to you?"

"I requested his badge number but—"

"This is brutality," she said. "It should be reported."

"Silly lady," he said.

But she was digging in the diaper bag for the camera. "I want pictures of this," she said. "Scanlon will know what to do. He'll know the proper authorities."

"The authorities are the problem," Clay said. "*Authority* is the problem."

But instead of listening she was snapping pictures. "Hold up your elbow," she told him. "Take off your shirt." He let her shoot a dozen or more pictures before he sat down on his mattress and curled onto his side, just as he'd done yesterday, staring at the photo of her propped against a soda bottle a foot from his nose.

She folded Sammy's blanket and held it on her lap. She considered leaving, but to do what? Hang out in a café? Go home to Geoff and Scanlon? How do you nurse a husband who smells of another woman?

"What happened with Billy," she asked, "when the paramedics arrived?"

Clay rolled over and looked at her, confounded, like he wondered if she'd been listening at all. "He was dead. Instantly. His spine sliced in two. Don't you get it? I killed him. It was all my fault. And now—I can't do this again with Flak. Maybe I should bust into the ER and let the cops put *me* in a coma. Isn't that like sleep?" He rolled back to the photo, holding his smashed-up elbow.

She glanced at Sammy, still snoozing in the stroller, and when she turned back Clay's shoulders were quivering, his knees squeezed closer to his chest, and he was choking back tears. She thought he might be embarrassed, thought she should leave, but instead she put her hand on his calf and held it there, and through the black jeans, his skin and muscle seemed to rise to her. "You should eat if you can," she said. "I'll get you one of those burritos you like."

He rolled over to face her. He touched his forehead to her knee and stretched his arm around her side. She stiffened. One breath later, he slid his hand down her thigh. "No!" she snapped, and darted a look at Sammy, still asleep.

Clay was shivering, so she spread the yellow fleece baby blanket over his shoulder. After a time her head dropped, jolting her awake. She was painfully tired. Fog pressed as thick as gray curtains at the window, and she imagined it blanketing the building, the whole town as she watched Sammy sleep, her own exhaustion growing heavier, and then she wiggled away from Clay, curled up on her side in a ball, and drifted off.

And then, dreaming the recurring dream, she's reaching for Joshua as beads of sweat from her labor worm down her face, her weak arms clutching empty air to her chest until she's tugged back to consciousness by her milk letting down, Clay's scalp bristling her chin, his face nuzzling her chest. Deep within her, warmth trickled and then cascaded as he released one button at a time on her shirt and closed his scratchy lips on her breast. She touched the back of his head, like teaching a baby, and guided her nipple to his mouth.

Naomi's milk ran hot in his throat, instantly warming him right down to his toes. He was visited by Daria's lips and her grizzled laugh, by Ruby Christine's nuzzle and cry, and wide-mouthed yawn. And then he was with them. He followed the crack back through time to pulverize the moment she took their baby to Idaho, and then he was an infant again with his mother, with his father's brain put straight, and they lived together in the old house on Onsland Point, where he and Billy played horseshoes overlooking the sea. And after a time, when Naomi pushed his cheek to switch him to her other breast, he was sitting in their kitchen in Yaquina during his middle-school years, when every single morning his mother made oatmeal for breakfast. Not the one-minute kind. She paid extra for slow-cooking Irish oats. From the table he watched her standing over the stove, stirring in a dash of cinnamon with a wooden spoon, then slicing in a banana and tossing in a handful of toasted walnuts. She prepared the oatmeal like a meditation, like something that might save them.

After spooning it into bowls, she added honey and milk. Lots of milk, so when Clay finished up there was always a gray puddle at the bottom. Every morning with both hands he'd pick up the bowl and tip it to his lips—the white porcelain filling his face—and eye his mother over the rim as he drank those last swallows. Creamy and warm, a husky grain flavor of oats and nuts, a hint of cooked banana, sweetened with honey: the taste of Naomi's milk.

PART FOUR

Chapter 10

Two weeks after the protests, waiting for a phone call, Scanlon stood at the window eating organic chicken salad from the tub and watching Clay, suspended in a harness thirty feet up the tree in their backyard, prune branches with his good arm. The moving company didn't want him back until his elbow healed, so Scanlon was giving him extra hours. A branch dropped to the ground and Clay belayed lower, a wave rippling through the rope that hung between his legs.

Naomi was lying back with her eyes closed on the couch, Sammy asleep on her chest, his little body wrapped in the yellow fleece blanket. She hadn't mentioned New York since the bite, but relations had been tense. He was still squirting Neosporin on his thumb and wrapping it in a Band-Aid; she still eyed him warily. It didn't help that Joey had been visiting for a week.

The call came in, and Scanlon took the phone into the nursery. "It's fine," the *Oregonian* editor said, "but shift the focus. I want it more personal, more up close. Focus on the anarchist who saved you that night, the injured one. What's his name?"

"I didn't want to use names," Scanlon said.

"So we'll run it with pseudonyms. At any rate, your analysis of the whole thing is great—really smart stuff—but I want to be inside that anarchist's head."

Scanlon closed the door, told the editor he'd have it done in a few days, and hung up, a slow panic clutching him. He held his ribs—not broken, it turned out, just bruised. Clay passed by the window, rope coiled over his shoulder, and saw him but didn't meet his eye. Shit. He'd never let Scanlon inside his head.

But Scanlon would make something work, as he'd made so much work in the last two weeks. News reports of the police violence produced tremendous antipathy for the government and a surge of local support for the Oregon Experiment. When Baxter Hazelton tried to exploit the "riot" to pump life into his languishing SWAT team bond measure—defeated twice since he first introduced it after 9-11—a backlash resulted in even more support for secession as checks, pledges, and inquiries poured in. Sequoia was gushing with appreciation, though he was careful to stay away from her house in the evening.

Flak was still in a coma, and surprisingly the media had portrayed him sympathetically. He was by all accounts a loving father to his four-year-old son, Ryan. He worked odd jobs, or for Labor Ready, or not at all, and he'd founded Free Skool to teach self-sufficient, low-impact living.

Panama, too, had his sympathizers. Although no one publicly condoned the violence and vandalism that surrounded the protests, many agreed that his sentence was unjustly harsh. Panama had been a senior-citizen organizer, a Sierra Club canvasser, a tree planter, and he'd built wheelchair ramps for a volunteer group, but he finally decided the system was so entrenched that only radical action could effect real change. He also contended that his first priority when torching the SUVs was that no one be injured. The contrast between that and the police brutality was obvious to everyone.

Three days after Flak was put in a coma, when the news cycle had played out, Scanlon saw his opening. First, he wrote a short piece—a treatise, really—on micro-secession for the region. The empire had gotten too big, he began, and as the last days demonstrated, it had lost its moral compass. Only with a return to life on a more human scale could past injustices be righted. He argued that secession would allow economic and environmental sustainability, and that it should begin with the sacred land of the university longhouse downtown and radiate out from there. He e-mailed the article to the *Douglas Union-Gazette,* and they ran it the next morning.

Second, he called America Sanchez at the station and invited her to cover a meeting of the Oregon Experiment. When she declined, he invited her to go online and read the hundreds of letters to the editor sent to the *Union-Gazette.* Those in support of Scanlon's argument were predictable, but the vitriol and fury of those in opposition were combustible enough to attract her interest. He also promised her an injured anarchist at the meeting, someone from Flak's crew.

Sanchez arrived with lights, camera, and sound. But as hard as Scanlon begged, Clay told him, "I don't do movements," and he didn't show. Still, Channel Nine aired a ten-second clip, most of it a close-up shot of a stoner in dreadlocks, somebody Scanlon had never seen before, eating a cookie. No matter: the movement was suddenly on everyone's radar across the state. And Clay seemed to genuinely feel bad about his refusal to attend and promised to help out with something else. One way or another, Scanlon was making things happen.

He was still sitting in the nursery, paint swatches still taped to the walls, surrounded by unpacked boxes and Naomi's organ, clutching the phone and listening to his mother in the living room—her voice lubricated with mudslides—give Naomi advice about Sammy's first Christmas. He dialed Sam Belknap's number, and while it rang he looked at the notes he'd jotted down. "We'll keep most of what's here," the editor had told him. "But let's double the length and devote the rest to the kid who saved your ass that night. *He's* the story." It rang a dozen times before an unrecognizable voice answered.

"Is Sam there?"

"Scanlon. Good to hear from you."

"What's wrong, Sam?"

"Nothing's wrong."

"You don't sound like yourself. What's going on with the hip?"

"A touch of a chest cold," he said. "Rotten weather in New York." He held the phone away as he coughed. "But you? How's the book coming?"

Scanlon told him a little of what was going on—there'd been a backlash to the backlash, and cars all over town had American flags flapping from their roofs. But mostly he was worried about Sam. "I could make a quick trip during break," he offered. "Stay with you for a few days."

"You've got a wife and a baby. Priorities, man."

Scanlon loved how Sam's "man" sounded like Kerouac reading his poems in the Village.

"Take care of my namesake, and don't worry so much about me."

"I'd be happy to come if it would help." The line was silent for a moment; through the window Scanlon watched the mailman come up their walk and put a bundle of envelopes and fliers in their box. "You still there, Sam?"

"None of this makes up for your real work. You know that, right?" He coughed again. "I know the thrill of shattering glass, Scanlon. I've been there. The power of an impassioned mob. But your real job—" he broke off into a coughing fit, and Scanlon heard his phone rattle down on a table, then he coughed into the kitchen and back again. Scanlon felt helpless. "We'll talk," Sam choked out. "Later." And the line went dead.

Damn. Scanlon held the phone to his heart. He'd done what he never wanted to do: he'd disappointed Sam. And what would Sam say about his fucking Sequoia? In the last two weeks he'd edged toward asking for Naomi's forgiveness, but each time he held back. It seemed to him that forgiveness for cheating could be requested only once in a marriage; the second time around it was a toss-off line stripped of all credibility.

He was keeping away from Sequoia, but Naomi had pulled further back into a burrow of the baby and her organ of essences. Sammy no longer spent time in his bouncy seat or bassinet; he hung from her body in the sling, even as she spent every night mixing and sniffing at her organ. She'd started bathing with him and sleeping with him on her chest. Last Saturday morning she declined Scanlon's offer of French toast, and when he reached toward her cheek to brush back her hair, she growled, and he yanked his hand away, a moment so suddenly tense that Sammy reared back, a string of milk and saliva stretching from his lips to her nipple. Scanlon couldn't ask for forgiveness because he wasn't sure he wouldn't go to Sequoia again.

He held the phone under one arm as he reached out the front door for the mail. The letter on top, addressed to him, was from the U.S. Department of Justice, District of Oregon. He tore it open and, reading the first paragraph, backed into the nursery and closed the door. His guts and legs felt watery, and he dropped into a chair and read the four-page letter three times, each time more slowly: seventeen bulleted and bold-faced "apparent" violations of federal statutes, "cease and desist" repeated over and over, Sequoia Green, a.k.a. Marcia Beckmann, and Clay Knudson, named co-conspirators in the "apparent" unlawful enterprise: the Oregon Experiment.

. . .

Clay avoided the circles of swampy light dropping from lampposts, his duffel bag tucked under his arm, the strap cutting down his chest. The paved path wound between a stand of firs—an uprooted stump from the big windstorm last winter—and a dense thicket of rhododendrons, their leaves so shiny with rain they reflected lamplight.

The rain suddenly fell heavier, which was good. It kept people inside and washed out any noise. He glanced at the clock on top of the student union—eight-thirty—then over his shoulder—no one in sight—before ducking into the rhododendrons and crouching low beside a rushing copper downspout at the corner of the old brick building.

The windows were dark, and so were the rest of the buildings nearby, mostly full of classrooms that shut down at five. He'd come out earlier in the week to study the tree in daylight—a red alder with a low-hanging dead branch and a thick healthy branch stretching out ten feet above it. Too easy.

He strapped on the cleats, cinched his duffel tight to his back, and darted out from the bushes, keeping low in the shadows of the trees. At the alder he started climbing, tough going at first, but he worked his fingers into a crevice in the trunk and, after a few false starts, got hold of a branch stump, bit into the wet bark with his cleats, and scurried up, still favoring his left arm. The chip in the bone would float, they told him. Nothing to worry about. And the inflammation would slowly settle down. He'd fully recover. But if he put a big load on it, his mind took over and made him believe the bone was about to snap.

He stood in the first crotch of the tree on a bed of moss at the base of the dead branch. Mushrooms and shoots of sword fern grew from the rot. He grabbed a branch overhead, the thickness of his wrist, and took a few steps out on the dead one, then bounced. Not rotten enough, it didn't even creak.

So he slowly and carefully scanned the area. Except for the gym and pool, all the buildings within sight were dark. A figure was hurrying up the sidewalk at the end of the parking lot, shoulders hunched, head pulled back deep inside a pink rain hood. In the streetlight, heavy raindrops bounced off the pavement.

He climbed up to the next branch. He picked off surface moss with a finger and stomped into the wood with his cleats. Very solid. Then he quickly unzipped his duffel and slipped into the harness, fed his line through the carabiner, tied a Munter hitch, tightened his duffel to his back, and shimmied along the branch. Six feet out, it nosed down with his weight—not as stout as he'd thought. But no worries. He wrapped his line, yanked it tight, and flipped a leg off the branch and into the air.

With some of the money he'd found in Seattle, Flak had bought this gear for Suzy Creamcheese, who was treesitting in the Siskiyou with a bunch of girls from Ashland. What Clay first knew of Flak was the big spender: money to pay off Clay's mother's back taxes so she could sell her house, money for beers, for vet bills and baby strollers, money for his ex-wife to have a wart removed from her cheek, plus dentures for a kid who'd lost most of his teeth in a car accident, and all this gear for Suzy Creamcheese. He'd spent the money fast and well and told Clay he felt much better, much relieved, when it was gone. "Money *is* the measure of the man," he said. "The virtuous have none."

Daria and Clay had gone down to the Siskiyou with him to demonstrate against the Eden Creek sale: 4,100 acres of old growth to Coastal Timber. There was no time to build platforms for the treesitters. The Bureau of Land Management had rushed through the sale on a Saturday and cutting was to begin on Monday morning. BLM goons and armed Coastal Timber guards manned the gates. But the Ashland girls—nearly fifty of them—clambered up foot trails at dawn, and when the first loggers rolled up the dirt road, the girls were hanging from branches like ornaments high up in the canopy.

When the three of them showed up, a lot of pissed-off loggers were leaning on their equipment, smoking and spitting chaw and yammering with the entire Jackson County Sheriff's Department. News reporters napped in their cars, hoping the standoff would escalate.

It was Clay's first time in the Siskiyou, and he was dazzled by the enormous thousand-year-old trees. Standing at the base and looking up, the canopy seemed as endless as a night sky, the girls as distant as stars. Nearly overcome by the sense of infinity, he put a hand on Daria's belly—round with their baby—and felt limitless possibility. Then he envisioned this forest clear-cut to supply redwood decks for the McMansions defiling Wakonda Hill, their Oregon trees cut up and loaded on trains for Hilton Head, Orlando, Kennebunkport, and the other blights on the earth.

At noon, a judge accepted the Sierra Club's petition and ruled that logging couldn't begin until the Eden Creek sale was reviewed. The girls belayed back to earth, triumphant. Reporters photographed the freakiest ones—dreads, mohawks, piercings, tats. Loggers and cops spun their tires and raced off throwing up stones and dust.

At five o'clock that evening, on a favorite bicycling road east of Ashland, a computer programmer on a three-thousand-dollar road bike, wearing a fluorescent-yellow Gore-Tex jacket and a lime-green helmet, was cycling with four friends who later testified that the fully loaded logging truck had intentionally crowded him on a curve, forcing him onto the sandy shoulder, where he lost control and was crushed beneath the truck's wheels. He was dead on the spot. An investigation by the Jackson County Sheriff's Department discovered no wrongdoing. Another shot in class warfare.

And now Clay let out line, descending until his cleats bit into the dead branch. He pulled out some slack and started to bounce, looking straight down at the vintage Porsche. He'd told Scanlon to go fuck himself at first, but when he found out the car belonged to Fenton . . . Shit. They all knew Cebert Fenton. In the late 1970s, he and some business-school professors bought most of Wakonda Hill, agreeing to keep the top half as open space if they could develop the bottom. But when a property-rights ballot measure threw out nearly all restrictions on land use, Fenton informed the city of Douglas that they could either let him carpet the hill with houses or compensate him with fifty-four million dollars. Day by day, Wakonda Hill was getting infested with massive houses, three-car garages, non-native plants, macadam, water features, and steroid-injected sod.

Making the destruction look like an accident wasn't Clay's first choice, since nothing sends a message like a molotov cocktail. But he figured he owed Scanlon one for sucking on his wife's tits. In a few minutes they'd be even.

But the branch wasn't breaking so easily. He had a good bounce going now, the branch surprisingly springy for all the rot. He let out more line and held on with both hands, bouncing harder until a sudden crack at the base vibrated through the wood and up into his legs.

Except when he lay on his mattress staring at her picture, he tried not to let himself think about Naomi, the fire that morning in her breasts, her nipples swelling to his tongue, the rush of her milk at the gentlest tug of his lips, the warm milk soothing his throat scorched by tear gas and his empty stomach churning up with the pain in his elbow and the loss of Flak. Naomi had nurtured him, sustained him. He had slept afterward, deeply and soundly for two or three hours. And when they both woke up, when she couldn't meet his eyes as she jerked Sammy's stroller out of the apartment, she made it clear that it would never happen again, but also, maybe, that she didn't regret that it had.

Maybe the damn branch wasn't going to snap. He rode it hard, the dead twigs at the end nearly tapping the hood of the Porsche, then springing up so high he could touch the branch above where his rope was tied. Up and down, pushing and rising, his muscles tiring. And when he stared at her photo in the night, he desperately wanted her again. Wanted more. Wanted to have her. He wasn't the same man he'd been before that morning. He loved her.

And he would not give up on the branch. He pounded it down and got another crack, a quiver. He pounded again, breathing hard, the muscles in his legs and back nearly spent, sweating despite the rain slapping his face and trickling down his neck.

He would have her. He had to have—

Two deep cracks, a release, a split between his feet, a sudden drop. He gasped as the branch twisted away beneath him, free-falling until the harness jerked at his groin and butt. Then he rested his head on the rope in the gently falling rain, swinging from side to side, weightless, his feet dangling, his heart still throbbing with desire.

The next day Naomi sat by the picture window watching the rain turn to hail, BBs of ice pelting the glass and collecting on the sill. She shifted Sammy to her other breast, and by the time he had his fill the dark clouds had given way to a deep blue sky and a blindingly bright yellow sun.

"This place makes me dizzy," Joey said over the top of *Gourmet* magazine.

When Naomi didn't respond, Joey asked, "What're your Christmas dinner faves?" She dog-eared a page.

"But you'll be gone by then," Naomi said. Joey had gotten a deal on a Christmas Caribbean cruise.

"That's why we're having *our* Christmas a couple weeks early." She turned a page and gasped. "Divine."

Christmas. Naomi had a problem with Christian holidays, reeking, as they did, of sanctimony, self-sacrifice, and virgins. A week after that last time she and Clair made love—she didn't yet know she was pregnant—

Clair told her without tears or apology or ambivalence that he was leaving UVM for Catholic University and becoming a priest. She was shocked silent as he blathered platitudes about his "profound calling" and "spiritual yearning." Then he was gone. When she wrote the many letters pleading with him to at least talk on the phone—they *had* to talk, she insisted—he wrote back saying he couldn't "tempt temptation." That idiotic redundancy, in the end, softened the blow of losing him.

"Ham," Joey declared, answering her own question. "The Pratts *always* have Christmas ham. Thanksgiving is Turkey. Easter's leg of lamb. And Christmas is ham."

"We don't really eat ham," Scanlon called in from the nursery.

"Nonsense," Joey told him.

If Naomi's own parents were here for the holidays, her father's smell would soothe her: crushed dry leaves, apple cider, and sweet cigars. She hadn't smelled him in nine years. She wished they could see her with her baby. In those weeks and months after Joshua was born, her father took her to the Catskills and quiet restaurants, and curled up with her under an afghan on the couch to watch movies on TV. His was the scent of solace and recovery.

"Don't you have a raincoat?" Joey said.

The kitchen door stood open, and his smell was blowing in on the wet air.

With Sammy on her shoulder, Naomi went to the door as Clay stepped inside.

"I didn't know if maybe you need some help with something in the yard or whatnot."

"You're soaked," Naomi said. "You must be freezing."

His face softened. "I'm good."

"Could you get a towel?" Naomi asked Joey. "There's some clean ones in the nursery."

Sammy made a floundering grab for Clay's nose, and Clay replied by twirling his finger in front of the baby's face, producing a delighted shriek. That morning two weeks ago at Clay's apartment, Sammy had been deeply asleep, she was certain, but as we know things from sounds and smells not consciously registered, was it possible, she wondered, that her son understood what he and Clay shared?

"Drop everything straight in the washer," she said. "I'll pass some of Scanlon's sweats to you."

His socks squished across the floor, wet prints leading to the laundry room. She hiked Sammy high on her shoulder, then squatted down to loosen Clay's laces and draw out the tongues before setting the boots upside-down on the floor vent.

"Odiferous, oh my God," Joey said, rushing back into the kitchen. "What in heaven's name?" She sniffed her wrists, one after the other, and when Naomi stood up, she knew that Joey had gotten into her work at the organ. She was wearing the latest frog-juice prototype.

"I'm still developing it," Naomi said. "It's a long way off."

"It's heavenly. Don't change a thing."

Although pleased by her reaction, Naomi said, "Give it half an hour. It crashes." She hadn't been able to subdue the base note through the finish. The spearmint and fig were lovely for a start, and the frog juice gave the fragrance a tremendously frank authority, so honest and raw it drew you closer with the promise of revelation. But as the top notes dried down, the base became corrupted—a urine smell at the throat and the sides of the tongue, like eating kidneys improperly rinsed.

She got clothes for Clay, and he came back into the kitchen in fleece pants bunched up around his ankles; the rag socks, outdoorsy on Scanlon, looked preppy on him. The NYU sweatshirt hung off his shoulders. To be fair, it was even a little big on Scanlon. There were no pockets in the pants and Clay didn't know what to do with his hands—resting them on his hips, touching the counter, then leaning on the stove.

"Smell me," Joey said, thrusting her wrist under her son's nose as he came into the kitchen. "Your wife is Aphrodite herself."

"It's very nice," he said, leaning toward her tentatively.

"Ugh," she groaned. "It's irresistible." She feigned a swoon in the doorway as only a toothpick-thin senior citizen in tight black jeans and spike heels can. "Ravage me," she said to Scanlon, disturbingly.

"Would you like some tea?" Naomi asked Clay. "Anyone else? Joey?"

"Mountain Dew," Clay said.

The four of them sat at the kitchen table—Scanlon and Naomi with mint tea, Joey with a white Russian, Clay with tap water—as the washer chugged on the other side of the door.

"I heard you talking to that newspaper editor," Joey said to Scanlon. "Big to-dos with the anarchists?"

Clay shot a look across the table at Scanlon.

"No, no," Scanlon said, rubbing his chin on his shoulder like he always did when he was stalling for time in which to formulate a lie. "I was thinking about an article on the secessionists. But I'm backing away from them now."

This was the first Naomi had heard of that. Although she'd kept her distance from Scanlon, she passed close enough every day to check for Sequoia's scent. He'd seen her but hadn't fucked her again.

"I'm just not sure there's anything there for me." Beneath the table, Scanlon laid his stockinged foot on top of Naomi's. He smiled at her, but there was darkness behind it—desperation or fear. They might never cross the void that had opened up between them. "I should probably focus more on theory. More scholarly work."

He rubbed her ankle with the instep of his foot, and she didn't pull away.

"Is your family local," Joey asked Clay, "or on the other side of the world like mine?"

"My mom moved down to Crescent City."

"California border," Scanlon told his mother.

"You're going down for Christmas, I hope," Joey said.

"Supposed to. But my ride fell through."

"Unacceptable," Joey said. "You should be with family. Isn't there a bus?"

"No, I'm . . ." He shook his head.

"We could give you money for bus fare," Naomi offered.

"Thanks, but—"

"A loan," Naomi clarified. "An advance on yard work."

"She lives with her sister's family down there. Them and I don't get on." He finished his water.

"Then join us," Scanlon said. "We're having a pre-Christmas dinner. Tons of ham, right, Mom?"

Naomi curled her big toe into the bottom of Scanlon's foot.

"Always plenty of ham," Joey said. "And Naomi? Add coffee cake to the list. You know how Scanlon loves Entenmann's on Christmas morning."

She'd never once seen Scanlon eat coffee cake.

Suddenly, filling their view out the front window, a pink motor home the size of a yacht eased to the curb and glided to a stop. Geoff was sitting in the passenger seat, and as the driver swiveled her captain's chair and stood, Scanlon uttered, "Bitch Kitty."

He rose from the table as Joey sniffed her wrist, horrified, and Naomi could smell it too: the frog-urine aftertaste. Joey jumped up and scoured her skin at the kitchen sink, and Scanlon was striding down the driveway toward the RV before Naomi realized with a thud in her heart that the stockinged foot under the table was still caressing her.

That night, Trinity answered the door naked. Her dreads were gathered in an elastic band at the top of her head, like a pineapple, and with one hand draped over the doorknob, she had the mellow ease of her mother.

Sequoia peeked around from the kitchen and, when she saw it was Scanlon, came running and threw her arms around him. "Thank you, thank you, thank you!" she sang out, kissing him up and down his face and squeezing him tight. She was wearing a cotton Japanese robe and as she held the embrace, the warm pillows of her breasts pushed into his chest, emptying out his lungs.

"What's so exciting, Mom?" Trinity said.

She released him. "The church," she said. "It's Scanlon who got Ron to lay off." She squeezed his hand, the look in her eyes loving and grateful, sparkling with tears. It was one he hadn't gotten from Naomi in months. From his mother, yes—creepily. But not his wife. "And there's more," she said. "He's selling me the Skcubrats building."

Scanlon grinned. "No," he said, though he already knew. He'd driven a hard bargain with Ron.

"Yes!" And again she threw her body against his.

"We're having smoothies," Trinity said.

Sequoia looked at him directly. "For you?" Her lips held the "you."

Scanlon nodded, Trinity swung the door shut, and they followed her to the kitchen, where she lifted the blender with both hands and poured the last few swallows into a clean glass.

Sequoia took her own glass, still half full, and poured it into Scanlon's. "You deserve all of it," she said. With a pink mustache, Trinity sat up in a chair, her little hands wrapped around her glass, and watched the adults like they were a puppet show.

"How did you ever?" Sequoia asked.

He'd anticipated this moment: "If I told you I'd have to kill you."

Trinity gasped.

"A joke," Sequoia reassured her. "Something people say."

Trinity smiled knowingly. "An expression."

"Tell me," Sequoia persisted.

He ducked again. "I gave him a little something in return. Department related. Small to me, big to him."

"You're really not going to tell me?"

He shook his head.

Trinity was licking out the inside of her glass. "Can we still have a soak?" she asked.

"Let's do it," Sequoia said, and Trinity was already yanking a beach towel from the pegs by the back door. "You?" she asked Scanlon.

He swallowed hard as Trinity's bare butt shot out to the deck.

"It'll be a quick one," Sequoia said, "in case you have to get back. Trinity's up too late again, and I'm exhausted from all the meetings." Her face brightened. "It's looking good with the oystermen, though."

As she tugged at the belt of her robe, Scanlon stood frozen in place, stabbed in the heart by the painful irony that he'd made his deal with Ron for exactly this reason: to please Sequoia and see her smile, to keep her from sleeping with that prick, and to get inside her robe.

But he clenched his teeth, reminding himself of his love for his wife and baby, and said, "The reason I came over. I got a letter from the Feds today." And he told her every detail.

"That's great!" she said when he'd finished, her robe flapping open as she hugged him again.

"You don't get it." Scanlon pulled away. "This is the first step toward prosecution. For these crimes, Sequoia, they can put you away forever."

She was having none of it. "They've noticed us. The movement's a genuine threat. And all because of you."

He couldn't bring himself to say they'd always be a *movement,* that secession itself was completely implausible. "It's not worth going to prison for. Think about Trinity."

"There's too many of us to put in prison. Since you were on TV, we've recruited over two thousand members. We're doing this, Scanlon."

No. No, they weren't. But when she dropped her robe to the floor and reached for his hand, he followed her onto the deck, where lanterns alight with votives ringed the trunk of the redwood. Trinity was submerged to her chin. Stars were out, silhouetting the sage and laurels, the expansive succulents, the trellis-topped fence. Sequoia sank into the dark water. He stood there with his toes curling down over the edge of the tub. "What if elves could toot?" Trinity said.

"Then their toots would smell like candy canes," Sequoia replied. "What if turtles had no shells?"

"They'd wear helmets and elbow pads," Trinity said.

Scanlon set his glasses on the bench and got in.

"What if boobs could fly?" Trinity asked.

Sequoia took a deep breath. "Then milk would spill from the clouds."

Trinity looked up at the stars, as content as any human being Scanlon had ever seen, then rested her head on her mother's shoulder.

"You're tired, aren't you, chicken?" Sequoia said.

"No," Trinity chirped.

Sequoia smiled at him across the water, across the length of her naked body and his. "Thank you," she told him again, maybe only mouthing the words. He wasn't sure. "I'm so grateful."

Trinity pawed at her breasts. "Mommy milk," she said. Baby talk.

"Why don't we have some in bed. Do you want to say goodnight to Scanlon?" But the child didn't budge.

"Are your chicken pox all gone?" Scanlon asked her.

"Like six months ago," Trinity told him. Ancient history.

"A week ago," Sequoia said gently.

"I have a scar," Trinity bragged, and held out her lip. "Right here. Just like Mommy's scar. We're scar partners."

Although he couldn't see either scar through the dark steam, he knew Sequoia's well: the pink pencil line curving down her upper lip, a feline and sexy asymmetry. "What's that one from?" he asked.

"I've had it a long time."

"You should never hit another person," Trinity said.

Sequoia touched her lip. "Once, another life ago, I made a monstrous mistake, and when I tried to make amends, this is what I got." She put her arms around Trinity, hugging her tight. "There's always a price, Scanlon, for doing the right thing." She kissed the top of Trinity's head. "Bedtime," she whispered. Then, to Scanlon: "Can you wait twenty minutes?"

He nodded, a zing of ambivalence, guilt, arousal.

As she rose from the tub and wrapped a towel around Trinity, then took up her own, he closed his eyes, pretending not to be imagining, movement by movement, Sequoia toweling her soft shoulders and broad back, her throat and chest, raising her arms to reveal sparse puffs of blond hair, lifting her breasts, reaching inside her thighs. If he looked, he'd touch. He wasn't strong enough not to.

The slow boil of panic and desperation was heating up inside him—too big now to know where to focus. He needed to keep the Oregon Experiment alive long enough to become a case study for his research, but it was insane to risk inciting the Feds. Panama's sentence had proved that.

And Fenton's threats were just as real: Scanlon had e-mailed him the piece on the protests, and he'd marched into his office saying, "Something you dashed off for the campus paper, or your idea of scholarship?" When Scanlon explained it was for the *Oregonian,* Fenton said, "This article better be dropped by the paperboy at my doorstep within the month, and then you better start doing some real work." His threats produced genuine fear in Scanlon, and hearing the echo of Sam Belknap's voice produced only shame.

He wanted a family. He wanted to make Naomi feel fulfilled, to provide Sammy with the carefree childhood he'd never had, which meant getting them back to New York before Naomi went there on her own. Which brought him back to the secessionists, and to Sequoia. She was the only person offering him support and comfort, and he wished that could continue without turning into infidelity. He didn't want to disappoint her, but what if she realized he was more interested in a book about the movement's failure than its success? What if she knew he'd got Fenton's Porsche destroyed in exchange for Ron's cooperation? She was highly principled, and principled people could behave inconveniently.

He rose from the water and sat on the deck, steam pouring off his skin. Would she even listen to his explanation? Scanlon never would have sicced Clay on the Porsche if Fenton hadn't had it coming.

Two nights ago, a visiting speaker had come up from Pomona—"Consensus Building in the Eisenhower Cabinet," as dreadful a topic as Scanlon could imagine—and Scanlon had arrived early to get a parking spot in the lot behind their building, not far from Fenton's car. At the reception afterward, with a wink and a nod, he told Ron, who always walked to campus, that because of the rain he'd drive him home tonight. So the two of them walked with Fenton and the visiting speaker back across campus to Blodgett Hall. The rain was coming down hard and, even better, a good wind had stirred up. Under umbrellas, after they'd thoroughly probed every conceivable aspect of Eisenhower and consensus, Fenton told the Pomona guy, "Now, this could be the highlight of your visit." And, when he was met with silence: "Fifty-seven Porsche Speedster. One of twelve. Original flat-four engine. Far and above what an academic deserves, but I've made some nifty real estate investments. You two—" he turned to Scanlon and Ron "—should get smart in that area. This isn't Pomona, salary-wise."

As they rounded the corner into the parking lot, he strode a few steps ahead, excited about showing off his car and sealing his chumminess with the visitor. Then he stopped dead, with a horrible groan, and Scanlon was instantly flooded with remorse, once again a ten-year-old boy shoving a firecracker down a frog's throat and then recoiling from the blood and tattered flesh.

Fenton ran to the car, his umbrella nose-diving to the pavement. The branch was twice the length of the Porsche and as thick as a phone pole, much bigger than it had looked up in the tree. Fenton grabbed hold of it and tried to pull it off, but there wasn't a chance. The roof, hood, and trunk had been caved in. The running boards sat nearly on the pavement. He strained at the branch with the same futility with which he'd kept swinging his ax, weak and frustrated, at the Mr. Douglas log chop.

Scanlon allowed himself a glance at Ron, who radiated a monkish elation, a serenity he'd never seen. Not particularly happy, not even smiling, he was rubbing his belly, deeply at peace.

Fenton turned to the three men watching him. "It's all your fault!" he spit.

Scanlon bit his lower lip in a sudden panic: Fenton's revenge would be absolute. And as he came at them, his finger pointed like a gun, Scanlon was already forming the words to explain to Naomi that he'd lost his job.

"I didn't even want you for this lecture." Fenton thrust his finger in the visitor's face. "It was boring! I paid you way too fucking much. It—" Fenton was howling, out of his mind. "It was *shit*!"

In the hot tub, Scanlon's heart raced. He wasn't proud of what he'd orchestrated, but what could he say? More good than harm came of it. Maybe Sequoia *would* understand. He knew she believed it was justifiable to break a law to prevent a greater moral violation, that since nuclear weapons violate international law, it was proper to break a nation's laws to prevent their deployment. Sequoia would get her neighborhood center *and* the café. And Ron planned to retire at the end of the semester. He gave Scanlon a long hug in his office this morning and said he no longer had any reason to teach, that everything he'd hoped to accomplish at the university had finally been done. He'd enrolled in a twelve-week course in Reno to run craps tables and had already lined up a job at Five Feathers Casino, west of Eugene. Scanlon would never again return to his own office with a cup of coffee to find Ron splayed in the chair across from his desk, waiting to suck up hours of his day.

The bathroom window went dark. Sitting out here under the redwood tree, Scanlon had lost track of time, but it wouldn't be long until Sequoia stepped naked across the deck and joined him in the hot water. An affair with Sequoia—an affair with strict parameters. He thought of the boost it would give him to do the very things his family needed from him. Compromises would have to be made for the greater good. Everybody wins, as Geoff would say.

Chapter 11

Although she didn't eat it, Naomi found the smell of bacon pleasing. But a sizzling ham was the blubbery-sweet, braised-flesh wafting of cannibalism and semen. Sammy seemed to like it, though, and had been all giggles since Joey'd slung the chunk of pig in the oven. On the couch in the living room Naomi raised Sequoia's hand-thrown coffee mug to her lips and sipped mint tea.

"Merry Christmas," Joey sang, when Scanlon emerged from the bedroom in sweat pants and a T-shirt, his bedhead worse than normal.

"Jesus!" Naomi blurted. "It's not Christmas."

Scanlon and his mother looked at her like she was a stranger.

"Sorry," she muttered. "I thought I was talking to myself."

Scanlon leaned over the couch to kiss the top of Sammy's head, and then went to the kitchen, where she heard him pour a cup of coffee. "Morning, Ma."

Joey clanked down a spoon. "No sign of the love boat," she said.

"Maybe they went out for breakfast."

"That RV's got more kitchen than my condo. Not to mention a waterbed. Seems like they could fry their own eggs."

When Scanlon had come to bed last night, he reeked of her hot tub, but nothing else. He hadn't showered. He'd made advances—a leg over hers, lips at her ear, a hand crowding Sammy on her chest—but finally backed off.

She waited until he fell asleep and investigated more closely—*his* smell alone at his crotch, crushed dandelions and rain vapors rising from a hot sidewalk. On all fours with her head under the covers, she wept at the smell; she wept because he hadn't slept with Sequoia, but also because she'd perceived the faintest trace of almonds. Of Sammy. Of course. Sammy had inherited the almond scent, and she'd just unearthed its source. But now the stink of ham intruded on her reverie, and she shuddered as the olfactory sentiment dissolved.

At the kitchen counter, she refilled Sequoia's mug from the teapot and glanced at Scanlon sitting beside his mother, dunking coffee cake in his coffee and sucking at the drippings. Joey licked glaze from her fingers, leaning into her son and remarking from the corner of her mouth, "Waterbeds." She shook her head knowingly, conspiratorially. "No good for sex."

Naomi returned to the living room with her tea. Sammy awoke, and they gazed into each other's eyes as she took his hot body into her hands and laid wet kisses over every inch of his face—rapid, over-puckered, and popping like champagne corks. *Fish-kisses.* She blew a raspberry on his stomach, lipped the fat on his arms as if she were biting, then brought him to her breast.

In the next few minutes she heard Joey describe to Scanlon the episiotomy she'd had "in honor" of his birth—"they sliced me from the vagina to the rectum," she gloated—and her attempts to self-catheterize after her hysterectomy—"the hardest part's finding the hole!" She'd told him these stories verbatim a dozen times.

As the pain subsided and Naomi and Sammy slipped into the shared bliss of nursing, Scanlon sat down at the other end of the couch with the Douglas paper. He put his feet up, sipped coffee, and flipped pages with a display of domestic pleasure that bordered on gusto, as if he deserved praise for not sleeping with Sequoia last night.

The rustling newspaper was finally too distracting for Sammy, who twisted away from her nipple, snarling. He spit up, and Naomi wiped his chin clean, then fish-kissed him until his mood improved.

"Alert the governor," Joey called from the kitchen. "The *Queen Elizabeth* makes a port of call."

Filling the picture window, Kitty's motor home dropped its stabilizers at the curb and with hydraulic shrugs and jerks leveled itself. Naomi never understood why it took so much longer to get out of RVs than cars, why no one simply pulled up and hopped out. Like the preparations of royalty, involving ante rooms and courtiers, mysterious rituals forestalled disembarkation.

"What's this one called again?" Joey shouted from the kitchen.

"Kitty," Scanlon shouted back.

"Hmm," Joey said. "I'll bet she is."

How could Scanlon bear it? "Doesn't it skeeve you out?" Naomi whispered. "Taking the full blast of your mother's libido?"

He leaned toward her, whispering even softer. "She just feels threatened by Kitty."

"She always acts like that. You're oblivious," Naomi said. "What's it called in porno? A facial?"

"*You're* oblivious to the fact that hers is just a more perverse version of *your* lovemaking with Sammy. Hers is creepy and sad. Yours is truly sick."

"I'm sick? You'll take it wherever you can get it. Even with your mother."

"All your sensuality," he hissed in a stiff-jawed whisper, aware of his mother in the next room, "all your love. He's right there with his face in your boobs. I was your surrogate nose, now he's your surrogate lover."

Yes, she knew he felt praiseworthy, but he also held it against her that he'd denied himself Sequoia. "And last night, what was on your mind when you wanted to mount me?"

"To make love to a consenting adult. Sammy's like an object—"

"Which adult?" she said. "Was it me getting you horny, or visions of Sequoia in her hot tub?"

He took a slow tight breath—as close as she'd get to an admission.

"Why didn't you just fuck her?"

"I didn't want to," he said.

"You wanted to last time. I can't imagine she was disappointing. Or maybe you let her down. I never mentioned that sex with you hasn't lived up."

His face went red. "It was great with her. Amazing. She's got sexual instincts you can't even imagine."

They were faced off like animals, circling with bared teeth. They'd wounded each other and were now calculating how much more they were willing to risk. Then Scanlon fell back to his end of the couch and stared up at the ceiling. "I'm sorry," he said. "I'm sorry I did it with her."

"Get a load of Dolly Parton!" Joey exclaimed from the kitchen.

Through the front window Naomi watched Kitty's red-carpet descent from the RV, her arms wrapped around the belly of a giant stuffed panda. Scanlon had retreated, he'd apologized. Why wasn't victory any sweeter?

When she awoke, two hours had passed. Sammy lay sucking on his toes next to her in bed. She'd been so exhausted and had slept so hard she needed to sort through the last hours, separating dreams from reality. Yes: she and her husband had said those savage things. Yes: she watched Scanlon and his parents lined up at the kitchen table dunking and sucking at coffee cake like mirror images of one another. No: she hadn't watched Kitty take Scanlon's hand and lead him with Sammy on his shoulder up the steps of her pink RV. Yes: when Kitty held the baby, she'd watched Joey's hackles rise, and she smelled her own edginess too. No: Scanlon hadn't filed for divorce. Yes: she'd called Sequoia herself and invited her to Christmas dinner, two weeks early, three o'clock, we insist.

And yes, this was *definitely* not a dream: she'd set out plates and glasses on the table and chose napkins from their mishmash collection in the linen closet: two red damask that she'd bought in France, a few striped from Crate & Barrel, and then a single floral-patterned one that she took into the bathroom, where she peed a torrent, then used to wipe herself before rolling the napkin neatly and slipping it into a silver-plated ring for Sequoia.

In Naomi's driveway, Clay heard a child singing. He glanced over his shoulder as Sequoia and her daughter came pedaling up behind him. *Trinity,* he thought the girl's name was. She stopped singing when she saw him.

Sequoia dropped her kickstand as Naomi came down the steps. Sequoia hugged her, and then Clay. They all discussed the weather. Naomi said how lucky they were for a break in the rain, and asked if the café was busy over the holidays, speaking the bullshit of the sad and stupid world. She was better than that.

In his pocket, in his fist, he squeezed a plastic troll with a plume of blue hair. A present for Sammy.

Then Scanlon's mother called from the kitchen stoop and they went inside, the house too warm with cooking, too filled up with family. Another old broad stood on the hearth looking at photos of Sammy in fancy frames on the mantel, holding a three-foot panda perched on her hip. Clay fingered the troll in his pocket and decided he'd leave it there. Cheeks were kissed. Scanlon's father pawed Sequoia. Everyone was trading pleasantries. Global warming was irreversible; corporations owned the U.S. and enslaved whole peoples; species became extinct at the rate of one per hour; and people still said, "What color is your lipstick?" when it was obviously red.

Naomi told everybody where to sit, pointing Clay toward a chair at a card table, butting up to the dining table and standing an inch lower, spread with a cloth and crowded with dishes. Sequoia made room for a huge wooden bowl that had ridden in the wire basket between her handlebars. Chairs scuffed. As Sequoia scooted in, Scanlon's father angled for a glimpse down her shirt. Scanlon's mom and the panda broad exchanged a glance and rolled their eyes. Naomi and the baby sat beside Clay. Sammy grinned at him, blowing spit bubbles. A tiny hand tugged on his, and when he turned around, Trinity was looking up at him like she knew who he was, and then whispered, "You're here."

Scanlon laid out a platter of ham. The smell was very good. In Yaquina, they used to cobble together three or four tables for holiday meals. Cousins, nephews, grandparents, aunts. He'd lied about going down to Crescent City to spend Christmas with his mom. His uncle would never let him in the door.

Scanlon kept an eye on Naomi. She was drinking from Sequoia's mug. He didn't think she'd make a scene, but inviting Sequoia meant mischief, and he knew Sequoia suspected it, too. "Cheers, everyone," he said, and they raised their glasses. "Welcome."

Geoff piled his plate with slices of ham, then passed the platter across the table to Clay, who took a big helping of meat and heaps of everything else. The ham platter passed without stopping from Naomi to Sequoia and past Trinity to Joey, who tipped it back toward the little girl.

Her eyes widened and she forked a pineapple ring onto her plate. "What's the pink stuff?"

"Ham," Joey said.

"What's ham?"

"A porker," Geoff said. "Oink-oink. It's pig."

Horrified, Trinity watched Geoff stab his fork into a huge hunk, hold it in front of his face, then fold it into his mouth. "Joey," he said, chewing blissfully, "why did I ever leave you?"

Trinity burst into tears, burying her face in her mother's lap.

"Damnit, Dad," Scanlon said.

Sequoia stroked her daughter's hair. "We've talked about this," she said soothingly. "Some people eat animals."

"Is it Buster?" Trinity whimpered.

"No, honey. It's not Buster." Then, to the others, Sequoia explained, "Our neighbor has a Vietnamese pot-bellied pig. A pet."

"Excellent pets, I understand," Geoff said. "Loving, loyal. Cleaner than dogs."

"Buster's a real friend," Sequoia said, patting her daughter's back.

Still sniffling, Trinity lifted her head from Sequoia's lap and unbuttoned her blouse, took a breast in her little hands—the hummingbird breast—and closed her mouth on the rosebud nipple. Beside him, Scanlon could see Geoff's thighs swaying back and forth.

"After dinner," Geoff said, his gaze fixed on Sequoia, "you should come out for a tour of the motor home with Kitty and me. Your daughter can stay in here and play with Sammy and the big panda."

Scanlon felt his face go red. His eyes darted to Naomi. She'd been watching him, and she knew he'd flushed not over the affront to their guests, but from jealousy, possessiveness.

"We'll have a drink," Geoff told Sequoia, reaching his arm around the back of Kitty's chair. "Just the three of us." His thighs went to double time, and Kitty stuck him through his trousers with her crimson nails.

Joey finally caught a whiff of what was going on. "Very classy, Geoff. At Christmas dinner. Again."

"Please, Mom," Scanlon said.

"No. I think the assembled guests might appreciate the historical continuity. It was at Christmas, the year before he left me—"

"No one's interested," Geoff cut in.

"—that he hit it off with a friend of my sister's who'd joined us for dinner. And Geoff proposed . . ." In deference to Trinity, she held up three fingers and mouthed, *a three-way.*

"Okay," Geoff said. "Nice story."

"Really, Mom," Scanlon said. "Enough."

"But I haven't gotten to the punch line. You always cut me off before the punch line." She held up her hands for drama. "Number three was a—" again, for Trinity's sake "—M-A-N."

Kitty's fork clattered on her plate.

"I wonder, Geoff. Did you ever get that area of yourself, shall we say, *explored*?" Joey took a belt of her drink.

"Well?" Kitty asked. "Did you?"

Geoff calmly filled his mouth with creamed onions.

"Made for some awkwardness in the Christmas celebration," Joey continued. "You invite a man over for a honey-glazed ham, he doesn't expect it's a euphemism."

They ate supermarket pie. Naomi had agreed to make some, but the prospect of baking produced visions of her husband collapsing onto Sequoia, spent and sweaty, his mouth at her neck, her cozy bungalow warm with cinnamon, butter, sugar, yeast, and ginger. So they were eating Tillamook French vanilla ice cream on pumpkin pie from Fred Meyer.

"When in the course of human events," Sequoia was saying, "it becomes necessary for one people to dissolve the political bands—"

"I know, I know," Scanlon said, "but those words sound pretty different depending which side of the dissolving you're on. We need to ask ourselves why the United States would let any part of the country go without a fight."

Sequoia had laid the floral-patterned napkin over her lap as soon as she sat down. Twice she used it to wipe her fingers—she and her daughter did most of their eating with their hands—and once to wipe her mouth, and after nursing she wiped a dribble of milk from her breast. She still had no idea how special this napkin was.

"We'll win people over," she argued. "With principles, and with respect for humanity and the earth. Not violence."

Clay's head twitched. Throughout the dinner, as Naomi kept watch on Sequoia, Clay lurked closer: resting his arm over the back of her chair, letting Sammy suck on his pinky. When he put his face down in Sammy's and rubbed noses, she whisked her baby into the kitchen to nurse.

But Clay followed her and sat in the chair beside her, swiveling so his knees touched her thigh. "Come by my place again soon."

She scooched away from him. "Very busy now. The in-laws."

"After they leave."

"I'm getting back to work."

He screwed up his face, revealing the dark hole at his molars. "You mean perfume?"

"All the time I can."

"The photo's good for when you're not there," he said, then tore at his thumbnail with his teeth. "Maybe I could get a few more."

She closed her blouse tighter around Sammy's head, remembering the night of her labor: his breath as he coached her, the potent mixture of gasoline and amniotic fluid, his bristly scalp scraping her face as he lifted her hips and adjusted her pillows.

"If it would help," he said, "while you're working sometimes, I could watch Sammy. Good for him to get to know me."

"Probably not a great idea," she said, and Clay followed her back toward the table as she burped the baby. But then she stopped in the middle of the kitchen and turned to him, looking him in the eyes. "You should focus on your own child and the mother. Truly, I'm rooting for you, but without some changes you'll have a hard time convincing her parents or a judge that you're not an unfit father. It sucks, I know, but it's how the world works." She knew she was crushing him, but also that he needed to hear it. "Throwing bricks through windows doesn't make a better world." She turned away and returned to her seat at the dining table.

"How many secessionist movements are nonviolent?" Sequoia asked Scanlon. "Successful ones, I mean."

"Less than five percent."

"So we'll be one of those."

Scanlon conceded her a smile. "We will," he said. "We'll try."

And Naomi saw Sequoia brighten at his "we." If Sequoia had doubted whether her *sexual instincts* held sway over his commitment, to her ears that single syllable rang out a resounding endorsement. In his wife's presence, no less.

Still chewing her last bite of pie, Sequoia plucked the napkin from her lap, opened her mouth, and made long, slow swipes all around her lips and across her chin and cheeks. And then she froze, surprised and aghast, already recognizing the smell as she touched the napkin to the tip of her nose and took a quick, shallow sniff. To her credit, the shock passed from her face as a series of recognitions and understandings revealed themselves. She folded the napkin carefully and set it beside her plate. She waited three breaths or five before slowly turning her head, and when their eyes met, they both smiled, tightly, and Naomi's nostrils flared: she could smell her mark on Sequoia's face from here.

"Naomi," Joey pleaded. "Back me up on this."

Naomi turned to her.

"Do you want Sammy to grow up in America or some asinine province of vegetarians and anarchists?"

"Not exactly how I'd characterize it," Scanlon said, "but let the question stand."

"In twenty years," Joey persisted, "Sammy's an American college boy or . . . whatever these experiment lunatics want him to be?"

"I suppose," Naomi said, "if his choices are a scholarship to Cornell or tossing molotov cocktails, I hope he takes Cornell."

"Why is it," Sequoia jumped in, "that no one understands *peaceful*? No violence, no destruction, no rocks at police." With her fingertips she was brushing imaginary crumbs from her face.

"When the U.S. recognized Kosovo—" Scanlon began, but he suddenly went silent, staring at the end of the table, and Naomi turned toward a hot metal smell, like raising the hood on an overheated engine, as Clay's head snapped two times, then three, audible cracks sounding from his neck.

Naomi pulled away, clutching Sammy tight.

"Hypocrites!" Clay shouted, dishes jumping when he punched the table. "You're all *no destruction* till you need something busted up. *Make it look like an accident,* you tell me." He was pointing at Scanlon. "Sleazy! You don't even have the conviction for your own fight."

Scanlon stood up, but didn't move from the head of the table.

"And you!" He pointed at Sequoia. "Spewing ignorant crap about anarchists. But for a *business,*" he spit the word, "a profit-making business paying minimum wage and taxes to the *government,* and for a *church* for *yuppies* doing *yoga,* you call in the anarchist to smash up somebody's Porsche."

Naomi didn't dare move from her seat, though she cupped her hand over Sammy's head. Clay's rage smelled like burnt hair.

He held his finger on Sequoia like a gun. "I never trusted you."

Then he aimed his stare at Naomi, his anger displaced by loss, the same loss she'd seen on his face when he talked of Billy's death and his father's, when he'd learned that Flak was in a coma. His head jerked, the crack from his neck snapping louder.

A distant wail rose from Trinity. "It's *him,* Momma."

"Shush," Sequoia told her.

Clay pounded the table. "You're *all* guilty."

"That's enough!" Scanlon shouted.

Trinity was sobbing. "The broken boy."

Sequoia jumped to her feet. "Get out of here, you crazy fuck!"

No one moved or spoke, and Naomi felt his eyes piercing her, even as the kitchen door closed behind him and they listened to the scrape of his boots receding down the driveway.

Later, Scanlon watched Sequoia push her bike down the sidewalk, Trinity walking beside her. He drifted through the laundry room to the picture window in front. Halfway down the block, Sequoia stopped. She squatted down and Trinity said something to her. After a moment, the girl touched her mother's face, then hugged her, and they continued on.

He'd tried to convince Sequoia that Fenton had it coming, listing his various crimes. "If the dean had let him rescind my offer, I would've never even come to Douglas," he'd explained, and both Sequoia and Naomi rolled their eyes like he'd made an argument for the other team. Geoff had thrown in with him, calling the branch the perfect touch. And Joey, her hands still shaking from Clay's outburst, was fixated on whether she'd been driven to a college dance in a '57 Porsche Speedster or a '62 Triumph Spitfire the night after Kennedy was shot.

Sequoia left without a hug, and much remained unresolved. He couldn't blame Naomi for being pleased, although it hadn't yet occurred to her that both of his sources had just evaporated, so now the *Oregonian* piece could not be written, and Fenton still held the strings.

Nor did she realize he and Sequoia weren't the real objects of Clay's rage, that it was her line about Cornell and molotov cocktails. When she said it, Scanlon had seen his neck spasm, his whole body clench, his eyeballs go berserk. She was in his head, all right. She knew Clay far better than she was letting on.

He should wait till dark, but fuck it: precautions could be as stifling as doing nothing at all. Time wasted. He pounded down the strip—a new Starbucks, Domino's, the Dress Barn. He walked straight through the lot of Timber Ford-Lincoln-Mercury, weaving between rows of pickups and SUVs, green and red Christmas lights sparkling on wires overhead, plastic candy canes as big as a man. He cut by the old railroad yard and passed Sequoia's house. He didn't like her. More personal than just that she wanted to replace one system with another. For all her big-titted, self-satisfied generosity, she seemed too sure of herself, like a rich girl with her eye on something she knew she could buy. She seemed reckless. He felt sorry for her daughter.

He reached the tracks and followed them to the river. Rain had come up, and the wind got under his jacket. Beneath the bridge, he slid down the riverbank, holding his elbow tight to his side, and came around the piling slowly, never knowing who might be huddled down there, jumpy transients or kids, drunk or asleep. But there was nobody.

He slipped in the mud and had to scrabble back up the embankment to the little cave where he'd stashed the garbage bag, knotted up tight. Slick with mud he crawled inside, reaching blindly in the dark.

PART FIVE

Chapter 12

Two days later, at airport security, Scanlon hugged his mother, and then watched her walk away between the ropes, as steady as a runway model in her high strappy heels, pegged black jeans, black sweater, and red stringy shawl. She tapped a TSA guard on the elbow and pointed to her bag, and without waiting to see if he'd put it onto the conveyer belt, without removing her shoes or glancing back over her shoulder, she strode through the metal detector to the other side.

Naomi wiped Sammy's nose. Scanlon read the departures monitor: Albuquerque, Anchorage, Atlanta. Geoff and Kitty, in the pink RV, were halfway to Vegas by now. Naomi unzipped the diaper bag, counted the diapers, and zipped it back up. They'd planned a date, but neither of them knew how to go about it. "Let's get a tea here," he said, "before we head downtown."

They were seated at a small square table in a dark corner of the restaurant, Sammy sound asleep in his carrier on the chair beside them. Scanlon smelled bacon, tuna melts, and the bar, and he wondered what Naomi was smelling, what her experience of this moment was. When they were falling in love, they did what all couples did: they recounted past loves, childhood fears, unrealized hopes, secret dreams and vulnerabilities, all in the glow of endless months of making love, of walking in the park as a prelude to making love, of going out to eat after making love. Food tasted better then. Completely spent, they'd fall into the love seat at the back of San Padre's with too many tapas and sangrias and the understanding that they shared not only a nose but all of their senses, even their skin.

The roar of a jet came muffled through the wall—an old photo of barges dredging the Columbia—and the waitress clanked down a lavender teapot for Naomi and a cup of coffee for him. He tipped in some milk, stirred.

And then she started talking. She told him of the profound disconnection she'd felt when they met. She wandered through her days in a world she couldn't perceive. "It wasn't just that I couldn't smell or taste," she said. "I couldn't read people. I'd hear their words, see their expressions, but fail to understand them. God, I couldn't even carry on a conversation with Rachel walking around the reservoir."

Scanlon shook his head; he didn't get it.

"I had to concentrate so hard to look for mud or ice—to *see* it, because I couldn't smell it. And all summer long I couldn't smell that soupy New York humidity so I thought I had a fever.

"And you were so charming and attractive and intelligent." Spontaneously, she smiled. "I could slip under your arm and you'd lead me through dinner parties and weekends with our friends. But I relied too much on you, *deferred* to you, to tell me how to act, even how to feel." She stared into her tea, taking a deep breath. "I've resented you for being a reminder of what a wreck I was. For seeing me so low."

He took her hand in his on the table.

"But I love you," she insisted. "Not just because you saved me. I'm less fragile, less desperate for your love, than I was nine years ago, but everything I fell in love with then, I love now."

Their knees touched under the table, and Scanlon felt the delirious rush he remembered from those early months, transported from the Portland airport to a sidewalk table at Tartine. "I love you," he said.

She sipped her tea. "It was nice last night," she whispered. He'd stayed up late reading, trying to find in scholarly theory what he'd failed to grasp on the ground. Naomi was asleep when he got in bed, but she turned to him and they made love silently in the dark.

On the table she rubbed her fingertip in the dip of the spoon. "I think sometimes the body has to forgive before the heart can."

. . .

They had a late lunch in the Pearl, and afterward, tipsy from pinot gris, bought her a too-expensive lime-green skirt. They went to the museum, nursed Sammy, changed him, made him giggle. They said little more to each other, but with Sammy riding in the Baby Bjorn they walked arm in arm, holding hands. And in the back of a café with lattes and truffles, they kissed on the slumpy couch, as he napped beside them.

They tired quickly and decided not to stay in Portland for dinner so they sped back down I-5 for home. When they crossed the bridge into Douglas and stopped at the light, with Bank of America and Church of the Savior on opposite corners, he laid his hand over hers and nodded at the church signboard: *Prayer is love on your knees.*

The light turned green, and Naomi said, "I thought that was a blow job."

The Oregon Experiment had signed a lease on a little office in the Odd Fellows Hall, but Sequoia was afraid to leave Trinity with a sitter and was working at home. Checks had been coming in since the protests, mostly twenty-five- and fifty-dollar contributions—more than enough for the rent and another computer. Rico was adapting the website to accept credit cards and foreign currency; he suggested they invest in short-term bonds.

From timber companies, environmental groups, and Indian casinos, the promise of money came with strings attached. A splinter group of Mormon polygamists—some of them already living south of Portland, others who'd come from Utah—had pledged thousands, even millions, if their "religious imperative" could be accommodated by the new nation.

Against her better judgment, she agreed to have coffee with a golf developer who drove over from Bend. "We'd build twenty to thirty courses on a dozen resorts," he said, opening a color brochure on the table. "In ten years—"

Golf, she thought. Except for strip mining and genocide, nothing violated their principles more.

"The courses and facilities are inviting to the Japanese and Koreans," he yammered on. "But the real money drops when a billion Chinese can afford a world-class tee time. We'd contract a spokesman, a Tiger Woods or a Michelle Wie." He reminded Sequoia of her father's friends.

Chemical herbicides and fertilizers, forests leveled, whole rivers redirected. Ghastly outfits and polo shirts. She wanted to outlaw golf, not turn their new nation into a preeminent destination resort.

When the developer left the café, she ducked into the pantry and cried. Were these the compromises she'd have to make?

And now, nearly midnight, she shut down her laptop and went out back for a soak. Trinity's fever had been up and down for a week, and she'd been torn from sleep by bad dreams, shaken during the day by hallucinations. Sequoia had stopped taking her to daycare; she'd play at Skcubrats and ride with her on errands. But two days ago Sequoia was closer to phoning her father than she'd ever been. In the café Trinity wouldn't stop screaming about the broken boy, and when Sequoia tried to nurse her—a blazing fever—she hurled a cocoa mug at the pastry case, shattering the huge sheet of glass.

Sequoia had barely spoken with her parents since the fall and its aftermath, four or five times in nine years. She'd dreamed that when she finally did call them, it would be as the admired, idealistic founder of a world-changing revolution—like Václav Havel magnanimously checking in with the folks—because then she wouldn't need them. She toweled off and closed up the tub.

If she called her father for advice . . . No, she'd never do it. Even the thought of letting a child psychiatrist have a go at her daughter turned her stomach sour.

She touched Trinity's forehead. Cool and dry. Getting better already. She crawled behind her in bed, slipped under the comforter, and spooned her little girl back into her body.

The trip back from Portland always felt long, and when Scanlon turned off the engine, she was reminded of the first time they'd pulled into this driveway and he'd carried her over the threshold, Sammy nesting in her belly no bigger than a robin, as her nose sputtered back to life. Now, she craned around to see their chunky baby asleep in the back and gave Scanlon a long kiss, lingering to smell his neck, the almonds more apparent every day.

Scanlon lifted out the car seat, and she carried the bags with diapers and her new skirt into the kitchen, and she smelled them immediately. "Stop!" she yelled. "Don't move." She took two slow steps into the living room and flipped on the light.

"What is it?" Scanlon said, standing in the doorway with a firm grasp on the car seat.

"Someone's been in the house."

"Who?"

She detected perspiration and a coat that needed cleaning, deodorants, aftershave, mousse. Their *bodies.* They'd had burgers and fries for lunch, sat too close to the grill.

"Is it Clay?" Scanlon whispered.

She shook her head. "Call the police."

"And say that my wife smells somebody in the living room? Couldn't it be Joey? Or Geoff?"

"Then go look through the house," she said. "I think they're gone, but be careful." It was a man and a woman—middle aged. "Go!"

He passed her Sammy, still asleep, and opened the front hall closet. Then she heard him in the bedroom and the nursery, doors opening and clicking shut, the scrape of metal rings on the shower rod, and he returned to the kitchen shaking his head.

"Is anything missing?"

"Not that I noticed," he said. "No broken windows. The computer's here." They both looked at the TV. "What else do we have?"

"They were in the house for a while," she said, and walked tentatively across the living room to the couch, bending down to sniff the cushion. "The man sat here." She placed the car seat on the coffee table and put a hand on Sammy's stomach.

"You're sure?" Scanlon locked the kitchen door, then stood by the fireplace.

She was positive, the smell as sharp as if they were all packed into an elevator. "I'm scared, Scanlon. We should go to a hotel. Or back to Portland."

"Someone probably broke in and didn't find any—"

"But they didn't break in. They *came* in."

"Has to be Clay," he said. "And some of his friends."

"Anarchist girls don't wear Obsession."

He leaned on the mantel and rubbed his chin with his shoulder.

There was something he wasn't telling her. "Listen," she said sharply. "After today. After our day today, you need to tell me if there's something you know."

His face flushed, and his eyes filled with tears as he told her about a letter. She demanded to see it, and he dug it out of his sock drawer. She read it slowly, then looked up at him, sitting on the raised hearth with his head in his hands. "So you fucked Sequoia, and you're being investigated for treason by the FBI. Is there anything else you haven't mentioned?"

"It's not the FBI. Just some government lawyer at this point."

"At *this point*? So you're going to keep at it?"

"No, I'm done with the secessionists. Sequoia basically knows that already."

"I'll bet she's crushed."

He didn't respond.

"How many times did you fuck her, anyway?"

"Just once. Twice. But just, you know, one night."

The good feelings from the afternoon evaporated. "Any other secrets you're keeping from me?"

He stuttered and hemmed and hawed, then finally spit out that he believed Fenton's threat to fire him—from the job they'd transplanted themselves for—was very serious. And that the *Oregonian* editor wasn't interested in a piece that didn't lay Clay's consciousness bare. "It's like they want a goddamn *New Yorker* profile. Of an *anarchist*! Well, why not a roundtable discussion? Political wife Laura Bush, actress Angelina Jolie, and anarchist Clay Knudson talk about the importance of social engagement!"

And as he ranted, her eyes drifted over his head to the fireplace, her heart pounding so hard she no longer heard his voice as she moved across the carpet to the photos framed on the mantel, one of her and Scanlon at Devil's Tower, and beside it two brightly colored wooden frames with pictures of Sammy bathing in the kitchen sink and lying in the sunny grass of their backyard. Except both of these frames were empty.

Scanlon got his father on the phone right away, and neither he nor Kitty had snatched the photos. Over and over throughout the night he called his mother. Her cell phone was turned off; she didn't answer at home. He called the airline to confirm that her plane had landed, then called his aunt Jill, who might have picked her up at the airport, but hour after hour he got her voicemail. Deep into the night, hearing his mother's phone ring unanswered in her East Hartford condo, he feared Naomi was right: that Joey hadn't taken the pictures, that it was a shot over the bow by the FBI, viciously cruel, extremely effective, and easy to deny.

So effective that by six the next morning he was pacing the kitchen, counting the minutes until he could go to Sequoia's and then Clay's to warn them. By now he'd realized that since Clay had nothing to do with the secessionists, it could only mean that the Feds had been watching *him*, maybe listening to his phone calls and monitoring his e-mail. They'd stumbled across his connection to Clay and made some wrong assumptions.

At six-fifteen he left Naomi with the phone in her hands, locked up the house, and drove to Sequoia's. He parked in front and dialed his mother again—nothing—then knocked softly on her door.

She didn't greet him with her usual ebullience, but once she saw his distress, her rigid face and shoulders went soft, and she held out her arms.

"That's weird," she said, the two of them still standing in the doorway. "There's not another explanation?"

He shook his head.

"This kind of shit . . ." She scowled, genuinely angry. "This is why people are joining us. I'll post this to the website."

"No!" Scanlon said. "That'll just goad them on. The only thing to do is to shut it all down. Publicly announce that the movement's finished."

"Wait a minute, *please.*" She took his hand and led him to the love seat. "This is when we torque it up. To show we're not intimidated. They won't hurt your baby, but it's a great example of their sleazy—"

"Even if you're right," he said, "I've got to provide for my family. I can't risk getting arrested."

"Nothing would stick. Remember everything you told us? Kosovo and East Timor. America's own separation from Britain. *We're* the ones with moral principle and history on our side."

"Even if I'm not prosecuted, just getting arrested could get me fired. I've got to think about my family. About tenure."

"*Tenure!*" Her hands were in fists. "The director of a viable secessionist movement, and you're worried about *tenure*?"

"It's *not*!" he shouted. "It's never going to happen. It never *was* going to happen. It's just"—he was shaking his head—"an academic, impossible hypothesis. I'm sorry."

"You're wrong," she said. "Please, Scanlon." She put her head on his chest, crying, and reached her arms around him—the warmth of her tears, their dampness, the soft pressure of her body weighing on his own. He held her. She had believed in him.

After a time he slipped out from under her. At the door he said, "I'm stepping down as director. You should quit too." He turned to leave.

"No!"

It was a word he thought he'd never hear her say.

He had to shout up from the street, and when Clay came down to open the door he followed him up the stairs. Pliers stuck out from the back pocket of his jeans, and he wore boots but no shirt; his milky, hairless torso looked raw, like a body under the surface of an icy river.

It was the first time Scanlon had been in here, and it took him a moment to realize that the wires criss-crossing the floor, leading from a clock to mini flashlights, weren't part of the regular décor. Clay dropped to the mattress, cross-legged, and crimped a wire, using the cutters Scanlon had bought him at the hardware store. The lantern batteries, the PVC, cut into one-foot lengths—it was all here.

"What are you going to do, Clay, blow up a post office?"

He didn't respond, except to bite the red sheath of insulation off the end of the wire and spit it on the floor. He seemed to be daring Scanlon to react, maybe to turn him in, like when he popped his elbow through the garage window.

"Blowing up buildings doesn't work, Clay. It doesn't accomplish anything. At least that much I can tell you for sure."

Without once looking up, he kept cutting wire into lengths, stripping the ends, then coiling them up one by one and stowing them in a black duffel.

"The reason I'm here," Scanlon said, "I got a letter from the Department of Justice. It's full of threats about the Oregon Experiment. It's aimed at me, but the letter names you too. You should lie low for a while."

He packed batteries in his duffel with the coils of wire.

"Whatever you're planning, you've got to forget it. It leads to nothing good. What did torching those SUVs accomplish? An old cop with a broken hip, and Flak in a coma. You and Panama are indirectly responsible. And you don't know a thing about anarchy, by the way. You're just . . . it's adolescent foolishness."

He was prepared for an angry outburst, but all Clay did was walk to the window and look out at the clock tower on the courthouse and adjust the time on the travel alarm clock attached to the wires.

"Look," Scanlon said. "If you won't talk to me, then talk to Naomi. This is serious. You don't want to end up in prison. Or worse."

Clay wound the clock with the wire and stowed it in his bag, and straightening up he finally looked Scanlon in the face. "I sucked your wife's titties," he said, then gave a rare smile. "I sucked the pointier one first. And the droopy one was so ripe the spray hit me in the back of the throat as she squeezed it. I was gulping like a madman to swallow it all."

She heard the car while she was rocking Sammy to sleep for his morning nap, but after several minutes she hadn't heard Scanlon come in, so she laid him in the bassinet, clicked the bedroom door shut, and with growing trepidation moved across the house to the kitchen window. It was raining, and Scanlon appeared distorted through the wet windshield, sitting behind the wheel, staring straight ahead.

She had to rap on the passenger-side glass, then again, before he turned, startled, and unlocked the door. She got in out of the rain, thinking he might be listening to NPR, but there was only the plunk of raindrops on the car. "What happened?"

"Thinking it all through," he said.

"What did they say? Did they get any letters?"

"No letters. No concerns. They're very gung-ho."

"Why are you so calm? What's wrong?"

"Thinking it all through," he repeated.

She folded her arms across her chest. "Can you think it through in the house? It's cold out here. And I don't like leaving Sammy alone." Her anger remained on edge; he'd brought this threat into their home.

He gripped the steering wheel and for a long moment was silent, then he said, "I wish Fenton didn't hate me so much, but there's no changing that. If I hadn't spent all my time on the Oregon Experiment this semester, I might have some allies in the department, but there's nothing there either. The only hope I've got—and it's barely a shred—is that I give the *Oregonian* what they want on Clay. It won't be scholarly, it won't amount to much, but it'll buy me some time. And it'll get Clay's story out in the world." He spoke in a monotone, as if she wasn't even there. "I won't kid myself. I hope this article can help me, but if there's something meaningful in how Clay's living his life, in what he believes, then getting that out in the public is the right thing to do. And maybe it'll save my job." For the first time since she got in the car he looked at her. "I gather you and Clay have a special relationship, so I want you to tell me what you know about him, all of it, and I'll use whatever I can."

"I can't betray his confidence."

Scanlon laughed, neither happily or meanly. It was a consuming laugh that possessed him totally, frighteningly.

"Did you get stoned with one of them?" she said.

"This isn't stoned. This is brooding detachment. You should be relieved that *my* reaction's brooding detachment and not animal bloodthirst."

"Reaction to what?" but as soon as she said it, she knew. "Oh."

"Oh," he said, looking at the scabbed-over wound on his thumb.

For the second time in two days, she felt their family crashing down.

"Your honorable concerns about betrayal aside, I want you to tell me everything. The editor already agreed not to use Clay's name, and although they'd love pictures, if they sent a photographer Clay would probably stomp him and throw his camera under a bus. He hates newspapers and so do his friends. He probably won't even know when the article runs."

Nausea rose up in her as she contemplated a betrayal that might save her husband as well as their lives together. "I have pictures," she blurted before she could change her mind.

"Of what?"

"From when he was injured. They're on the camera. I was going to show you—it's police brutality—but then . . ." She didn't know how to finish. "Things got weird."

"'Weird' is sex with men in donkey costumes." He opened his door and said, with one leg already outside, "The word you're looking for is 'perverse.'"

Naomi caught up to him in the laundry room, where he was tearing through the diaper bag. When he got hold of the camera, he switched it on.

She kept her distance, but soon their faces were huddled together over the tiny screen showing pictures of Clay—shirtless, distraught, holding up the yellow and purple grapefruit of his elbow, dark and violent storm clouds looming in the window behind him.

"I'll tell the editor they have to black out his face," he said. "Those black bars over the eyes."

Studying Clay's eyes in the photos, she remembered his vulnerability, the muted groan of his agony; this was the boy, a short time later, she took to her breast. With their elbows leaning on the washing machine, she turned away from the camera to tell Scanlon what she knew.

She talked all through Sammy's nap about the bullet in King's brain and about his blowing up the doghouse and a tricycle and a bulldozer. When Sammy woke up hungry, Scanlon loaded the photos onto his laptop, and with the images filling his screen, she gazed at Clay's face and nursed Sammy on their rumpled bed while Scanlon took down what she recited in a notebook.

She talked about her belief that Billy's rage had been passed on to Clay, and about his carelessness when the SUV plowed into them, and about what she imagined to be Roslyn's persistent dignity. She'd told him about Clay's loneliness, his feral watchfulness, and described as precisely as she could how he filled her with fear. One truth, though, she didn't speak, even if it was plainly visible on Clay's face—obvious to her, maybe to anyone, but not yet, she believed, to her husband. That he loved her.

A boom startled them both—a neighbor dragging his garbage can to the curb—and she was surprised it was already dark outside. For a whole day Clay's story had distracted them from the threat that had gripped them last night. Oddly, he'd provided them with some relief.

Scanlon reheated pesto and brought it back to bed in one big bowl along with two glasses of wine. "You know," he said, twirling spaghetti on his fork. "There's a good reason we haven't heard back from my mother, and it's because she snagged the pictures. It's exactly the sort of thing she'd do. Since we didn't give her copies, she just took them without asking."

"But there were people in our house."

"They came in to poke around, but I think there's a limit to how low they'd go."

He believed it, she could tell, and in the warm bed surrounded by good food and wine, her husband and son, she let herself believe it too. The strength of a family, the sacred bond, was its own protection. Sammy was safe with them. After they'd eaten—nearly six-thirty—he called the editor and caught him at his office. For over an hour, they discussed the article while she sipped her wine and hummed softly to the baby.

During the long afternoon she'd found herself saying the sort of things that Scanlon might say: "The loss of his daughter prevents him from trusting the institution that enables it, compounding his distrust of *all* institutions . . ." They were both aware she was filling a need, not so different from when he was her nose.

She heard herself comparing Clay's contempt for the system to what she assumed was Scanlon's justification for his infidelity: that he was not bound by middle-class values. "Such bullshit," she said, and he wrote it down. She told him she didn't yet understand why she'd done what she did with Clay. "But," she added, "I'm sorry." At that, he stopped writing and looked her in the eyes.

Through Clay—his image on the screen all afternoon—she and her husband had stumbled back together.

He was still on the phone as she tickled Sammy's belly then kissed him under his arms—and there it was again. In the last few days new smells had emerged from his growing body, younger and fresher versions of his father's, poking out like day-old shoots of grass: dried figs, crushed dandelions, pickle brine; first the almonds and now the rest. Her reaction to Scanlon and his body had already shifted.

And a slower transformation was already underway, one she believed had started on the day Joey splashed the frog-juice concoction on her wrists and the aroma had crashed, turning to urine. The fragrance was another in a long, predictable series that led her back to Vermont, to Joshua. When it turned to piss on Joey, just as Clay's toe had risen to her instep beneath the table, she began to pry loose the eighteen-year grip of guilt and regret. Clay and the fragrance were only two of the many dangerous, unnavigable roads that would never take her back to Joshua. This understanding had taken time—like forgiveness, it had to happen in her nose, and olfactory demons are not easily dislodged, olfactory connections not easily rewired.

It wasn't until right now that she realized she was precisely where she wanted to be—in an unmade bed with Scanlon, nursing their baby. She knew she *could've* cared for Joshua on her own, but that if she had, she would've embarked on a life other than the one she was living. Those primal impulses of motherhood, rising so fiercely in her these last months, were focused on *this* life—hers and Scanlon's and Sammy's. She'd kill for her family.

"He loves it," Scanlon said when he finally hung up. "If I can get it to him tomorrow, they might run it this Sunday." He rolled toward her, leaning over Sammy at her breast, but before he could kiss her the phone rang and he grabbed it. "Yes," he said, instead of "Hello," and then his voice dropped. He put the phone down, looking hollowed out. "Joey doesn't have the pictures."

In the thick silence Sammy jerked away from her nipple and turned toward the middle of the room, staring.

Chapter 13

Three days had passed since Scanlon had said he was quitting, and Sequoia was determined to move ahead without him. But the cavernous Eagles Hall in Parsons was nearly empty, even though Rico had promised that interest here was high, and when she wrapped up the presentation and asked for questions, the fifteen people slumping in metal chairs looked at her blankly. Several had already left, and the two who'd come in late, a couple standing in the back, were too spiffy for locals. A question finally came from a white-haired woman wearing a USS *Maryland* cap: "When you say Pacific Rim, sweetheart, are you saying Parsons should join up with the Japanese?"

Sequoia didn't even distribute the questionnaires. She loaded the boxes of fact sheets into her car, then the poster-board charts depicting how the Pacific Northwest's resources were being handed over to the rest of the nation. "Buckle up," she said to Trinity, who was climbing into her booster seat.

The whole day had gone wrong. This morning she'd discovered that despite budgeting the down payment for the café, after closing costs she was coming up short for the hoods, drains, sprinklers, and other upgrades that County Health demanded. (She'd considered, and immediately ruled out, calling her father for the money.) And rafters from a teardown were supposed to be delivered to the community center, but if she understood correctly, a boom truck was stuck on a job in Sweet Home, or a crane needed a flywheel in Brownsville, or maybe both; and the bottom line was that months later, the church was still propped on railroad ties, surrounded by yellow tape and warning signs, more degraded since the move to Franklin Park than in the entire previous century. She slammed down the hatchback.

The ragged firs on the ridge—half of them logged, the other half sick—stood high above the rising steam and smoke pouring from the vast pulp mill that occupied all three sides of the dredged inner reaches of Yaquina Bay. The town rose up from the mill, steep streets intersecting at sharp angles, zigzagging up the hills, with cafés, pawnshops, western and marine suppliers, schools, clinics, churches, and cemeteries. They're born here, they live here, they die here . . .

And then she spotted them. Half a block down the hill, the couple who'd come into the meeting late—*not* a couple, she realized now. The woman was standing behind the open passenger door of a big brown car, and the man was leaning on the hood, arms crossed over his chest. *Watching.* So she offered a tentative wave, and they didn't respond at all.

"What's wrong, Mommy?" Trinity asked when she got in the car.

"Nothing." She turned the key and revved the engine too high before releasing the clutch, lurching away from the curb. Her view out the mirror was partially blocked by the poster boards, but as she wound up and out of town it didn't seem that anyone was following them.

"You're not being truthful," Trinity said.

"You're right. I was disappointed by the meeting," she told her daughter. "It's put me off balance."

They got on the Douglas-Yaquina highway and headed east for home. After a few minutes she heard a whine that was getting louder fast, like she might have a flat tire, but she was afraid of stopping to check and instead looked in the mirror, trying to get a clear line of sight, and the whine became a pounding rumble as she looked overhead for a helicopter, and suddenly light glared through the back window, the noise overtaking them, and then, as she began to panic, three motorcycles raced by doing a hundred miles an hour, their little red taillights disappearing ahead like fireflies. Insane, she thought.

"Crazies," Trinity said.

Those two at the Eagles Hall had set her off. They'd scared her and probably that was their purpose. But they'd come. They'd noticed. Let them monitor, she thought. Let them infiltrate. The group had no secrets, no illegal tactics, nothing to hide.

They banged through a construction zone—patched-together sections of pavement around Siuslaw Butte where a new route was being blasted through the rock—and reached the summit of the coast range at Stillman Pass, then dropped into the thick cover of firs. In a matter of minutes it was dark, fully night. A totally wasted evening.

Twenty miles outside Douglas, a car appeared behind her and drew so close that she had to twist the rearview away to keep from being blinded. She accelerated, but so did the other car, tailgating them, its high beams eerily lighting up her interior. Finally she came to a passing lane and eased off the gas, but the car stayed tight to her bumper, so at a gravel turnout, she pulled over to let it pass. But instead it pulled up right behind her, headlights still glaring.

In her booster seat Trinity strained to look over her shoulder. "Who is it, Mommy?"

"Quiet," Sequoia said, and reached back to lock the doors. If it was police, there'd be blue lights and a loudspeaker. She waited, trying to see something through the glare in her mirrors. Her engine was running, her foot was on the clutch, the car in gear.

"I'm scared," Trinity said.

"I know, sweetheart." There was no movement she could see, nothing but the flood of light.

"Who is it?"

How long had they been stopped? Two minutes. Maybe three. Still nothing. A car sped by in the opposite direction, heading toward the coast.

Fuck this, she decided, and floored it. Her tires spun in the gravel and squealed when she hit the pavement. Picking up speed fast, she eyed the mirrors, but all she saw was black. She shifted to third, looking back over her shoulder. They'd switched off their lights—nothing but darkness. As if they were never there.

For four days, except to dash out for the mail and the papers, he and Naomi didn't leave the house or even unlock the doors. Every voice outside, every light after midnight behind a neighbor's curtains, provoked suspicions. When a bunch of boys rumbled down the street on longboards, Naomi hid in a closet clutching their baby.

By Saturday night, Scanlon's article was supposed to be up on the *Oregonian* website. He'd drafted the whole piece in a day, believing he was getting his mind off the threat, but in the two revisions that followed, he recognized that, far from distracting himself, he'd written his own sudden and acute sense of fear into Clay's life.

In e-mails to his editor, Scanlon repeatedly said he wanted Clay's name changed and his face obscured. But after the final rewrite the editor had called him: "It's no different from *Newsweek* going into villages in Darfur and photographing babies with distended bellies. And don't you think papers should be allowed to run photos of military caskets? Or publish the names of dead marines? How about reporting that it was friendly fire, or that an Afghan orphanage got bombed by mistake? This is no different, my friend. Self-censorship's still censorship. It's the public's right to know, and from the anarchists' point of view, I gotta say it's the most sympathetic goddamn story they're ever gonna get."

Scanlon heard him out, conceding many of his points, but also thinking about Clay in his stocking feet stretched out in their backyard, chewing on a blade of grass, lightly stroking his belly while Naomi folded his laundry and Sammy slept. He remembered the smell of Naomi's amniotic fluid on Clay's hands, the windowpane still busted in their garage. And, as he had a thousand times, he fought *not* to imagine the suckling that conjured itself in his mind whenever he let down his guard. "You're saying I really have no choice," he finally said.

"Basically," the editor told him, which Scanlon knew wasn't true.

When the *Oregonian* site had loaded, he saw his own name and clicked on it: a stark picture of Clay resolved on the screen. It was page one. They'd exaggerated the black-and-white contrast, the raven-black stubble on his skull, the deathly gray skin. He scrolled through the rest of the photos. They'd manipulated the elbow, now so swollen and discolored it looked like it would never heal. They'd amplified the turmoil in the clouds out the window, sharpened the detail and color in the Greyhound sign. And in all seven pictures, Clay's face was traumatized, full of pain and frustrated anger.

But there was more: a hunger, soft and eager, that Scanlon had never noticed. He clicked through the pictures again. He'd never seen that look on Clay's face because his gaze was for the photographer, for Naomi, and it was suddenly obvious that he was in love with her.

On Sunday, sitting in the hospital by Flak's side, Clay remembered his mother's long vigils by his father's bed. Both Flak and his father wards of a government that destroyed their lives but kept their hearts pumping. Flak's eyelids flickered. His nose twitched. Today marked three weeks. Clay almost envied the poor fucker. Sleep.

As he did each time he visited, he palmed a disposable razor, a tiny bottle of baby shampoo, and two paper-wrapped bars of soap from the glass shelf above the sink, slipping them into his pocket and wondering who'd visit *his* bedside should the time come. And then Flak's kid and his ex walked down the row of beds. Their words were meaningless, but the voices breaking the silence were a relief, like the howls of drunkards when the bars closed at two. He hoisted Ryan up to the edge of the bed saying, "Touch him here," laying the boy's hand on his father's broad chest. "Scratch him a little, and he'll know it's you." Scared and confused—like a wounded animal—Ryan scratched. "See that? See his eyelids move?" Clay said. "He's saying, 'Hey, Ryan. Hey, son. Keep up the fight.'"

He mussed Ryan's hair and reached in his pocket. "Here you go," he said, and gave him the baby shampoo and the blue-haired troll, then clasped hands with the ex and left them.

At his apartment he washed. He shaved his face and his head. He put on clean socks and laced new strings in his boots. What he needed was already packed. He didn't believe in talismans or luck, but nevertheless pocketed Billy's lead soldier and the photo of Naomi.

Downstairs, he sat on the curb—hot-dog burrito and Mountain Dew—as men from the Siletz tribe in traditional feathers, beads, and bones spread filleted Chinook on wet cedar planks and laid them over a fire raging in the middle of the parking lot. Kids watched an elder begin to shape a bow, pulling long shavings from a branch squeezed tight in a stump-mounted vise.

Tobacco was scattered over the skin of a drum.

The slow beat began.

. . .

Sundays were busy, and it was mid-afternoon before Sequoia took a break. With an iced tea and a muffin, she sat at the table up front and collected a discarded newspaper from the window seat. She flipped over the front section and gasped at the image: his haunted face, his bruised and broken body, reached inside her chest.

When she turned her gaze from the picture to the article, she was shocked again: it was written by Scanlon. She read about this sad and misguided life, shut out of real opportunity, cheated by institutions. She read it a second time, more closely, taking in the futility of his actions, his failure to cope with loss, his longing for his daughter, for family, for his mother. The article took up most of the front page, then most of another section, with color photos of Clay that made her tremble. "Much of his destructive anger," Scanlon had written, "resides in the blame he places on himself for his brother's death."

"What is it?" Journey asked, her fingertips on Sequoia's arm, and she looked up from the paper.

She was crying, surging with her own guilt over destroying a life, a family. And she was crying for Clay. Trinity had known, had tried to tell her, but instead of listening to her daughter, she'd screamed at him in Scanlon's house when he needed comfort. Clay bore a crippling burden. Everyone did. Ron Dexter, the police chief, the building inspector, Scanlon, Naomi—they were all bearing something, maybe something unspeakable.

"Trinity, come," she called behind the counter. "Get your coat."

"What's wrong, Mommy?"

"On the bike," she said.

If she could release Clay from even a little of his burden, the world would be lighter. And if she could *heal* him, she might free Trinity from the trauma she'd perceived and internalized. Sequoia could no longer deny that she'd passed it on to her daughter.

"You remember Clay?" she asked, pedaling downtown.

Trinity didn't reply.

"Well, he's hurting—"

"I know," she chirped.

"—and I want to try and make him feel better. We'll find him. He lives right over the bus station."

She pedaled through heavy traffic along the main route through downtown, pushed sideways by gusts from passing logging trucks and

RVs, then cut toward the river. The powwow was going on—a teepee erected by the longhouse, a fire blazing in the parking lot.

"There he is!" Trinity announced, and she was right. Clay was sitting on the curb in front of the Greyhound station, eating a burrito. Sequoia welled up with tears. She was shaking.

Across the street from the bus station, she leaned her bike against the rack and Trinity climbed down. She tried to catch Clay's eye through traffic, but two buses pulled out of the station and blocked her view.

She locked up her bike and reached for Trinity's hand to cross the street, but she was gone. Sequoia looked up and down the sidewalk. She scanned the street and the group around the fire. The light had turned green, cars were rolling. The two buses angled into traffic, lurching forward before halting abruptly. An office party spilled from Filbert's, spreading out across the sidewalk. Douglas was a safe town, no need to panic, she told herself, but her pool of anxiety was already brimming. "Trinity!" she called over the traffic noise, the flutes and drums and chants. She looked again in the street, then back toward the music shop, up on her toes trying to see behind parked cars. In an adjoining lot, kids were stringing chokers under a tent, and she quick-stepped, then started to run. In front of the longhouse, dozens of people were watching the dance. "Trinity!" she called. Streetlights had come on with dusk, but it was harder to see by the minute. "Damnit!" she shouted, running toward some kids on skateboards in the alley. "Did you see a girl?" she asked. "A little girl with dreads?" but they gave her blank shrugs. She ran out to the sidewalk and glanced in the music shop, then turned back toward the bus station. She dodged a pickup pulling out of the parking lot, then a pack of college kids, and finally she saw her under the streetlight on the corner, squatting down, talking with a boy. "Trinity!" she called, and her daughter waved. Sequoia was dripping with sweat.

A few steps away, she heard her say, "What's her name?"

The boy was Native American, maybe twelve years old, squatting with a pet rat. "Caramel," he said.

Sequoia laid her hand on top of Trinity's head, and she looked up. "Hi, Mommy."

"They're very sentient creatures," the boy said. "Most people aren't aware."

"Don't do that again," Sequoia said. "You can't run off like that."

"I was right here," she said.

Sequoia looked across the street, but he wasn't on the curb. "We'll have to find Clay's apartment."

"He's gone," Trinity said.

"I know."

"He said he'd speak with you later."

"Who did?"

"Clay."

"You talked to him?"

"Just a minute ago. I said you wanted to help him."

"Where did he go?"

She pointed toward campus, and Sequoia looked but he wasn't there. "He's going on a trip for a few days. He had a big bag." Sequoia looked down the street again. "He gave me this." Trinity opened her hand: an old toy soldier.

"Why did he give it to you?" Sequoia asked.

"What's wrong, Mommy?"

"What did he say?"

"He said, 'See you later.'"

"And what did you say?"

"I said, 'Thank you for the gift.'"

"And then what?"

"I didn't say the thing you don't want me to. I didn't." Trinity was smiling, though tears spilled down her cheeks. "I told him it wasn't safe."

"That what wasn't safe?"

"He said he really had to go, so I told him, 'You're your own squirrel,' and he laughed."

"*What* wasn't safe?"

"I promise I didn't say the thing that makes you mad." The front of her jacket was soaked with her tears. "I just said goodbye."

It was dark when he got to the edge of campus. He kept to the unlighted pathways until he came up through a line of firs behind the oceanography building, the gravel lot where they kept their vehicles. Boats, vans, and three Ford pickups from the early seventies, their Cal-star ignitions almost easier to start with a quarter-inch slotted screwdriver than with the key. The breeze blew up from downtown, and he could hear the muffled beat of drums from the powwow. He cut a blue tarp off a boat and threw it in a pickup, then he ganked the truck and headed into the coast range. The cab smelled like Yaquina—damp salt and sand, fish and fog. He wished he were going that far tonight, but it was too risky—someone he knew might see him.

When he'd driven for half an hour, an orange construction sign flashed in his headlights. He slowed down passing the site, taking stock, then turned off the road. The trailers were lined up same as they'd been ten years ago: one for engineers, another for foremen, and two more for tools. Ammonium nitrate would be stacked up in one, nitromethane in the other.

There'd be no security, he knew. Take a hike on public land near a clear-cut and you're all but attacked by armed timber company guards and vicious dogs, protecting the earth-raping machinery. But the highway department lacked the timber companies' cash, so they relied on floodlights and the accepting nature of Oregonians.

Clay intended to be quick. He pounded the pickup over the rutted dirt road and skidded to a stop behind a grader. He popped the kill switch on the generator that illuminated the trailers and withdrew the hacksaw from his duffel. In the time it took him to break a sweat he'd cut through both padlock shanks. Two minutes more and he'd loaded the truck with three cases each of the two chemicals, completely inert until they were mixed. Without headlights he banged back up to the highway and pulled them on when he hit the pavement, lighting the road back to Douglas.

The sudden knock at the door startled them both. Naomi's heart dropped, and Scanlon clicked off the TV. In stocking feet she ran silently to the bedroom, where Sammy was sound asleep in the bassinet. When she returned to the living room, Scanlon was at the front door. She hung back by the hallway, with one eye on him and the other on the bedroom.

He pulled the door open. From the darkness behind the screen—they'd kept the porch light turned off—a man asked, "Mr. Pratt?" and a woman said, "FBI," and pulled the screen door open, holding up her ID. "May we come in?"

"We're looking for an individual," the man said once they were both inside, wiping their wet shoes on the mat.

"An associate of yours," the woman said. "Clay Knudson."

"Would you call him a friend?"

"It's urgent that we find him," she said.

"We believe he might be a danger to himself and others."

And at that moment a breeze blew in the front door, carrying their smells, and Naomi screamed, "Get out!"

All three gaped at her.

"Get out of our house!" His same sour coat, Right Guard, and cinnamon gum. Her Obsession and drugstore mousse. Their greasy diets and middle age. The stench of too much sitting.

"It's okay," Scanlon said, reaching toward her.

"Mrs. Greenburg?" the woman said.

"Get out!"

The woman took a step forward.

"Stop!" Naomi shrieked. They wouldn't get any closer to her baby.

"Do you know, Mrs. Greenburg, where Clay Knudson is?"

Naomi pointed her finger at the two of them. They acted cool, but she could smell that she'd put them on edge.

"We don't know where he is," Scanlon said.

"When was the last time you saw him?" the man asked.

Scanlon was rubbing his chin on his shoulder, stalling. "About four days ago," he said. "At his apartment. Last-minute fact checking for a newspaper article."

The female looked steadily at Naomi. "How would you describe *your* relationship with Clay?"

Naomi sharpened her stare and clenched her teeth.

"Specifically, Mrs. Greenburg, can you tell us what you were doing at Clay's residence on the morning of November nineteenth?"

Her legs began to shake, so she reached out for the wall.

The man took a slip of paper from his pocket and glanced at it. "Can you confirm, Mr. Pratt, that on October eleventh you bought Clay Knudson wire cutters, batteries, and PVC pipe?"

A mile shy of Burnt Woods, he dropped off the pavement through a curtain of Scotch broom and rocked down a pitched dirt road, narrower than it was back in the day, blackberry thorns scraping the sides of the truck. At the river, on a slow bend where salmon and trout used to pull back below the rocks, Clay stopped the pickup under the white oak and shut her down.

This had been their secret spot—Dad's, Billy's, and his. In a pinch they could roll out of bed at five and wet their lines by five-thirty. When Clay was in grade school they'd pull in a couple steelhead each on a good morning. By the time his father died ten years later, they'd be lucky to hook one keeper a season. These days, no one even bothered. The salmon and trout runs up this river had been decimated by clear-cutting along its banks and by the Silver Point Dam.

Clay dropped the tailgate and set the lantern on top of it, then tore open the boxes. One by one, slowly, patiently, he assembled the kinepaks: kneading together the white ammonium-nitrate powder and the pink nitromethane liquid, carefully massaging the high-explosive Play-Doh and tamping it into PVC tubes. He inserted blasting caps, the size of pencil stubs, twisted on his wires, and fished them through the holes he'd drilled in the end caps. He sealed each kinepak with tape and laid it on the tailgate.

When his dad was moonlighting for the electric company, he'd shoot five power holes at a time. If Clay had gotten the det cord that night at the Green & Black, he could've had simultaneous explosions, too—safest and most effective—but with blasting caps and wire, the short delay between shots couldn't be avoided.

With the kinepaks assembled, he loaded them into the empty boxes—more volatile now than TNT—and pushed them up against the back of the cab, then covered it all with the blue tarp.

He walked down the steep slope to the river, taking in the smells and listening to the gurgle. He washed off his hands and face. Back at the truck, he stretched out on the seat and rested his head on the duffel, staring through the windshield and up through the trees at a few stars struggling through cloud breaks, and soon fell into the sometimes dreamy, sometimes tortured state that took the place of sleep.

Trinity was smiling. Ever since she was a baby she smiled in her dreams. Sequoia pushed the hair off her face, her long eyelashes flickering, then slipped out of bed and pulled the covers up to her daughter's chin. On the bedside table, under the lamp draped with a red scarf, Trinity had stood the toy soldier—all chipped paint and dull lead—next to her shiny *Bleigiessen.* As the soldier heaved a grenade, the bursting rays of the *Bleigiessen* sun transformed into an explosion. They'd look for Clay again in a few days.

She kissed Trinity's forehead, turning down the light, then shut the door and buttoned her shirt. It was late; already past ten—too late for Trinity. As she pulled the curtains over the front windows, her breath caught: the car, the brown car, was parked at the curb. In the weak streetlight she could see two silhouettes in the front seat. "Bastards!" she hissed, snapping the curtains closed. She turned off all the lights, then dropped to her knees and parted the curtain enough to peek out. They were sitting in the car, looking straight ahead. She considered going out to confront them, but then thought of Trinity sound asleep; if anything were to happen, if they were waiting for an excuse to arrest her, what would happen to her daughter?

Lying on the floor, cowering in the dark in her own house, she called Jim Furdy.

"Don't move," he said. "Give me ten minutes."

Sequoia sat cross-legged and breathed deeply, letting her energy rise up and hover over her head, expand and fully occupy the space for a time before settling back down through her body. She believed it. They were all one.

Then she heard voices. She rose to her knees and with a single finger parted the curtains. Jim and his son were coming down the block, and behind them were John and Alice, Kenny and Deana. Oliver glided on a skateboard. She opened the curtain and saw the whole pack of them. Ruth, Ellie, and Hannah. Paul and Susan, Todd and Karen, the other John walking on his stilts. Jenna, Emir, and Renaldo. Daren and Aaron. Mike and Michelle. Phil and both Amys. All of her wonderful neighbors were rolling up the street like a slow, powerful wave.

The two figures in the car looked over their shoulders, squirming, as the wave rolled toward them, half on the sidewalk, half in the street. Her friends encircled the brown car, peering in the windows, surrounding them. Alice waved. Everyone was talking all the while, and Sequoia listened to their voices. Deana had put elephant garlic in her winter beds, more than she could ever use. Ruth's first batch of pinot noir was "young, but very bad." Karen was forging a series of poppies from copper and glass.

Susan's watercolors were showing all month at the Rainy Day Café. Paul offered Robbie his old iMac. Oliver smacked the pavement with his skateboard, still trying to flip it midair.

The brown car's engine started, then its headlights came on. Her neighbors stepped back, and the agents slowly skulked away.

When Sequoia opened the front door, they all turned to her. Alice held up a yogurt tub. She'd brought her some three-bean stew.

Chapter 14

At seven a.m. Clay left the motor running outside the Burnt Woods Café and bought two pieces of Oregon cherry pie and a Mountain Dew to go. By seven-thirty he was glancing down on Douglas from the bypass, then rolling across the valley toward the Cascades and the snowy peaks of Mount Jefferson and the Three Sisters.

At nine he rose up past the reservoir and entered Lincoln, slowing to twenty-five as he passed the chainsaw carving of a logger, his ax raised in welcome. Napa, McDonald's, DQ, a vacant Rexall, the Chat 'n' Chew. In the next block he passed a strip mall where six cars were lined up for drive-thru espresso.

Then there was a sudden flash, and blue light cut through his windshield, a police car speeding in front of him from the side street. He hit the brakes hard and the kinepaks slammed against the back of the cab. The cruiser stopped in the intersection, blocking the street, lights still flashing, and gave one quick wail of the siren. His heart missed a beat; he could feel the sweat on his forehead. The cop glared out his side window as Clay's truck screeched to a stop ten feet back. With more momentum he could've T-boned the cop's car with this solid old pickup. Push it aside and speed out of town.

He jammed it into reverse, but there was a car behind him and two more behind that. The cop played it cool, picking up his radio and calling in. Clay would have to slip away, but where? It was thirty miles to the next town. He didn't have a chance.

Goddamnit, why hadn't he changed clothes this morning? Then at least he could've tried to talk his way out of this.

The cop got out and took two steps toward the pickup. If he was going to run, it had to be now. If he could make it down to Eugene, he knew some anarchists there who could hide him. But on the mountain roads they'd pick him up in five minutes. He'd have to hide out in Lincoln long enough to gank another truck.

The cop looked at him over the hood, and Clay grabbed the door lever. He'd go on three. But then the cop abruptly turned—his gun belt, cuffs, and pouch of latex gloves a foot from the truck's headlight—and crossed his arms over his chest, rocking on his feet. More blue lights came flashing up the side street, and then he heard the National Anthem, a police motorcycle inching into the intersection in front of the Lincoln High marching band. Clay loosened his grip on the door handle, his throat tight and dry. A hearse came next, draped with American flags, then half a dozen National Guard soldiers. Freshly washed cars with their headlights on rolled past for a good ten or fifteen minutes—it must've been the whole town—and Clay slowly relaxed as the cop rested an elbow on the hood of the pickup, its door marked *State of Oregon—For Official Use Only.*

Just past noon, he parked at the Meriwether Lewis Scenic Overlook and walked through the exhaust of idling RVs as the tourists yakked about what an awesome fucking sight this was. Like a mile-wide bulldozer blade, taller than Portland's tallest skyscraper, a million yards of concrete that had buried two men alive, the Silver Point Dam was shouldering back twenty million tons of water. Clay had never seen it in person. He'd never imagined the scale. From above it looked like a prison: lights and fences, squat buildings, a street, and a parking lot. All to make electricity cheap enough to light cities so bright they can be seen from the moon, and so Banana Republic can prop their doors wide open and air-condition the sidewalk. An old man whose sweatshirt boasted that he was spending his kids' inheritance turned to him and said, "You see something that glorious, you understand that man can do anything he sets his mind to."

The geezer hadn't given him a second look. It was that easy. He'd changed into Scanlon's clothes—the white pants and green shirt—and removed his piercings, tied a bandanna around his neck to hide the tattoos, and topped it off with the red Gap hat. And that's all it took for this old fuck to chat him up like he was his uncle.

But the rest wouldn't be so easy. Seeing the dam now, he knew his plan was naive. He drove down the switchbacks for a closer look, and as he emerged from the trees, the dam looked even bigger. He had no reference for its size and remembered what people said about standing at the edge of the Grand Canyon. He rolled slowly by the entrance. Vehicles driving onto the dam were routed through concrete barriers and stopped at a guard booth this side of the concrete runway. Shit. He drove on into town.

He found a café, and from a phone booth in the parking lot dialed the number from the website.

"Silver Point Emergencies," the voice said.

"Wrong number," he said, and hung up.

Inside, he ordered oatmeal with a dish of marionberries, and when he asked the waitress for milk, she pointed to the little steel pitcher on the table. "Duh," she said, flirty. Under the dopey uniform she had a solid body, like the girl from Duluth. Big, pretty lips with piercings—no metal, just the holes. He squeezed in three packets of honey and poured in extra milk. He took his time. When she came back, he ordered a Mountain Dew.

"Could I," she said, clicking a pen and then holding it out, "do you think you could sign this for me?" and she slapped a newspaper down on the table.

He thought he was asleep, that he'd fallen seamlessly into a dream and the clicking was a random noise his dream had fit into its story. But the longer he looked at the front page—the broken image of himself, the professor's name—he realized that even his own twisted demons couldn't have created this.

"If it's a problem . . ." the girl said, a tremble of fear in her voice.

He took the pen and wrote his name across his ghostly bare chest.

"Cool," she said, reaching for the paper.

But he pulled it back. "Lemme just—"

"Yeah," she said, and went back behind the counter.

Looking at the picture made his elbow hurt. It was him but it wasn't him, just like the King Knudson who the government destroyed wasn't the real King Knudson, and Flak was no longer Flak. Clay wasn't as *alone* as the kid in this picture, he wasn't weak or busted up. He wasn't so easily betrayed. But when Naomi took the photos that morning, were they for this? When she offered him her tits? He looked at the injury and the isolation, and didn't see himself at all. He saw her.

Flipping the pages, seeing more pictures, he read that Clay Knudson believed his brother was alive when he held his corpse, pinned in the mangled car; he read that he felt a connection to Daria's father when he recognized Ruby Christine in his meaty face; that he felt shut out of the world, disconnected, as if he lacked one of his senses; that he had an odd, unhealthy obsession with pregnancy and young mothers. None of this was true.

What was true was that when he was with Naomi, the ceaseless shouting inside him quieted and he could believe in something other than destruction. Though they never got below the belt, never did the deed, she knew, as he did, that they'd made love. Despite this betrayal, he still loved her. And whether she'd ever admit it to herself, he knew she loved him back.

He smacked the table when it dawned on him: she'd stolen these pictures for her husband, for ambition, for money, to write off her guilt. And he'd swiped the picture of her to remember Daria and Ruby Christine, believing his daughter would save him if he could just get her back. But we save ourselves. That much was clear.

He tipped the girl big, leaving the cash on top of the autographed paper, cash he'd been given by Scanlon. Outside, he checked the tarp, twisted the screwdriver in the ignition, and rolled back toward the river. As he passed the dam's entrance, two army guards in full gear right up to their camouflaged helmets directed traffic through the suicide-bomber-proof maze of barriers.

Vehicles waiting to enter were lined up on the shoulder. A Pepsi truck, a couple cars, FedEx, an Army Corps of Engineers panel truck, a Baronne Brothers cement mixer, and two State of Oregon pickups loaded with tools for cement work, half-covered with blue tarps. The doors of the construction vehicles hung open, and the crew was huddled together in their rain gear, smoking and drinking from thermos cups. He made a U-turn and parked behind the last pickup. He lowered his window and spit on the ground, fairly certain his head wasn't twitching.

A National Guard Humvee pulled in behind him. Ahead, the driver of the Pepsi truck rolled up his doors. A soldier inspected. Clay had twice the brains and ten times more principles than this kid with the machine gun slung over his shoulder and a cigarette dangling off his lip.

As the soldier approached the cement workers, he said something that made everyone laugh. They opened their doors and lifted their tarps while he pushed his chin to his chest, speaking into a radio attached to his vest. He looked down the row of vehicles at Clay's pickup as the Pepsi and FedEx trucks pulled ahead, carefully navigating the barricades.

Clay opened his door so the kid would see the state markings as he approached. The pickups ahead were a decade newer, and the soldier glanced in their beds at the cement-encrusted wheelbarrows and trowels. Talking again into his radio, he waved them on.

Clay slid off the seat, standing behind the open door, and said, "Hey." The soldier looked at him blankly, and Clay pulled his visor low and adjusted the bandanna around his neck. The soldier reached into the bed to pull back the tarp, but Clay said, "You know what's fucked up?"

The soldier stared at him.

"You swallow your spit a thousand times a day, but if you spit in a cup and look at it, swallowing it just once is revolting." He'd channeled Flak.

The kid's face screwed up—like what the fuck?—and he dropped his ear to the radio to hear the scratches coming through, sneering at Clay, squinting against the cigarette smoke. He'd recognized him from the newspaper, and Clay felt his guts turn to water, the soldier's hand still resting on the tarp. "Frig that!" he barked into the radio. "You tell the lieutenant that me and Pudge is due to be off the guard booth eighteen minutes ago." He glanced back at the Hummer and nodded to the soldiers blaring death metal in the cab, then dropped the corner of the tarp and moved down the line.

Clay jumped in his truck and hit the gas too hard, throwing up gravel, but caught up with the others and stayed tight to them through the barriers, past the second soldier in the guard booth, and out onto the acres of concrete.

When the trucks ahead sped across the dam, he eased off the gas and slipped in beside two maintenance vehicles and shut off the engine. Goddamn. He'd done it.

But now what? It was maybe three o'clock—light for another couple hours. He couldn't sit here in the truck all that time. He got out and tucked in the tarp.

The day felt too warm for December. No surprise that rising river temperatures were killing fish before they could spawn. Anything he would accomplish tonight was too little, too late, but by hitting back hard he'd demonstrate the absurdity of the Feds' position: that since the dams had been on the rivers so long, they'd become part of the landscape and were therefore entitled to environmental protection. That bullshit would collapse along with their dam.

He walked purposefully toward a squat building near the center that looked like the bathrooms on interstates. Battleship gray, windowless. He tried the knobs on two steel doors—both locked—and walked around to the other side, where a garden hose attached to a spigot was snaked through a door, propping it open. He slipped inside onto a catwalk at the top of a stairwell, and below his feet an abyss of steel and concrete descended for what seemed like miles into darkness. He dropped down a flight of stairs to a landing, then another. Thirty or forty feet beneath him a man was power-washing the catwalk. Water dripped on the back of Clay's neck, then the power washer suddenly cut off. He froze. Through the grating between his feet, he could see the guy climbing the stairs toward him.

On the other side of the rail, a steel shelf stretched the width of the dam, one of a hundred, stacked from bottom to top like ribs. The guy was getting closer, his boots ringing the steel grating with each step, so Clay hopped over the rail and crawled along a narrow ledge barely wider than his shoulders until he came to a vertical I-beam. Wrapping his fingers around its lip, he swung to the far side, and curled up to hide as the worker clanged by and rose up above. He heard the hose get disconnected and thrown inside, then the door slam shut.

And now he waited, pressing an ear to the concrete. He didn't know how thick it was, but he could feel the river pressing on the other side. Water that had traveled from glaciers, from springs surging deep within the earth, upwelled through fissures in the bedrock. The water jabbed and shoved and pushed, but most importantly it kept up the pressure to get where it needed to go. He slipped his hand in the space between the concrete and the steel ribs. Just one crack would be enough. The water, rightly, would finish the job.

He took out the photo of Naomi and held it on his knees, inches from his face, squinting to transform her into Daria when she was filled up with Ruby Christine. To him, Naomi had always been pregnant, always the woman who'd covered his arms with the water cascading from her womb;

he hadn't washed until the smell of iron faded, days later. In the article, she'd been right about his mother. He missed her with a pain that cops and their clubs couldn't ever match.

He stared at the picture, waiting, curled up in the belly of the beast.

They must've been watching Clay for some time. Someone who knew about the SUVs might have talked, maybe Panama himself. But now Clay had disappeared, and to find him they'd threatened Scanlon and Naomi with aiding and abetting a terrorist. "Twenty years, maybe thirty," the female agent had said last night, then looked at Naomi. "You'd need to make arrangements for your son."

She screamed and charged the agents, but Scanlon jumped in front of her just in time. Her arms were flailing, and he caught her fingernail under his eye, and when he got her settled down on the couch, she started growling, her eyes pinned on the agents still standing inside the front door, apparently unruffled. A trickle of blood dripped from Scanlon's cheek, dotting his white shirt.

The man was squinting at the blown-up photo of the Yucca Mountain protests. "Is that you in this picture, Mr. Pratt?"

Scanlon considered spilling everything—the SUVs, the wires hooked to the timer, the pipe-bomb comment at the hardware store, even the branch on Fenton's car, for God's sake—but held his tongue. The Feds were clearly making no distinctions between the torched SUVs, the Oregon Experiment, anarchists from Seattle, and Clay's disappearance. It was all the same, and anything he said would heap more trouble on what they already knew about Clay. And with every word he spoke, he saw them working connections back to Sequoia and himself, even to Naomi. How much did they see that morning she was in his apartment?

Scanlon had known. Damnit, he'd known. But there was no chance of talking Clay out of it. His only choice would have been to turn him in.

The agent had waved the copy of the hardware-store receipt.

"Fish tanks," Scanlon repeated.

"You better hope so."

Since last night they'd strategized, considering scenarios and various plans to protect themselves. They hadn't slept or changed clothes or brushed their teeth.

"I could ask my father about a lawyer," he said in the dark kitchen, peering out the blinds. Up and down their block the houses were strung with Christmas lights, but Scanlon hadn't dared go out even for a tree.

"Bad idea." Naomi was searching through the fridge. "Maybe Sam knows someone in New York?"

When he'd determined there were no strange cars on the street, Scanlon switched on the ceiling light. He picked at the bloodstain on his shirt.

At the counter, Naomi sniffed a chicken carcass that had been in the fridge for a week. She got a good grip on the remaining thigh, cracked it back against the bone, and tore it off. She bit into the meat, barbecue sauce running down her chin, and reached out to Scanlon with what was left.

He woke with the sensation of falling, his heart racing. It was time. Shimmying along the steel rib, he felt like he'd already succeeded. He bounded up the catwalk and leaned his hip into the panic bar on the door, surprised there were so few lights outside. At the far end of the dam, under floodlights, the cement workers were skim-coating a parking area. He stuck the hose back through the doorway, walked down to the truck, and put his hand on the kinepaks through the tarp. Then he drove the hundred yards back to the building without headlights, off-loaded the boxes and stacked them along with his duffel inside the stairwell door, pulled in the hose, and looked up into the dim lights. Rain had started to fall. He breathed in the smell before letting the steel door close.

One at a time, Clay shouldered the boxes and descended the three flights. He stuffed a loaded PVC tube in his jeans and stepped off the catwalk onto the steel shelf. If he dropped one, the game was over, so he moved carefully and wedged the tube tightly into the gap between the concrete and the I-beam. He shuttled back and forth like this, one kinepak at a time, then attached the wire clusters as his father had taught him years ago. He wished again he had the Chandler G-99 det cord, but the grim dude from Portland did not give second chances. He took a lantern battery and a roll of wire from his duffel. Clenching the wire in his teeth, he shimmied out to the third I-beam and twisted the connections.

Just a crack, he reminded himself. Concrete—preferred by governments for their prisons and barriers, for plazas and monoliths to celebrate their power—crumbles when pressure is exerted on a weak point. When he fell into dreams, he sometimes saw his forearms and hands gripping a jackhammer, following a crack that was opening faster and wider, and then the river rushing through. He'd already dreamed his success tonight. The crack would take him back in time—to Billy, to the river restored. Everything returned to its natural state.

Sequoia awoke suddenly, thinking she'd heard a tap on the glass. Her body ached. She walked straight to the front window and peered through the curtain.

The brown car was back.

Then, with the first panicked thud of her heart, her daughter let out a piercing, primal cry and she rushed to the bedroom. Trinity was sitting up, her naked back heaving. She took her into her arms. "Just a dream," she said. "Did it scare you?" Trinity shook her head, gasping for air between sobs. She was burning up with fever. Sequoia lifted her shirt, but Trinity refused to nurse, wailing inconsolably into her mother's chest, pushing her fists into her cheeks, one of them closed white-knuckle-tight around Clay's lead soldier.

It was midnight, but she dialed the number anyway, holding her sobbing child to her chest. After five rings she heard her father's groggy voice: "Dr. Beckmann speaking."

"It's me."

"Marcia?"

"I need help."

The detonators were on a three-hour timer. He would get off the dam and make the phone call immediately, giving them plenty of time to evacuate. As he finished the wiring, a drop of water landed on his wrist. Then another on his shoulder. His detonating system was foolproof except, he realized, for the exposed twists of wire. If he'd had the Chandler G-99s, water wouldn't be a concern, but with what he'd devised, as soon as he hooked up the battery a drop of water could short-circuit the whole thing—and it would blow. First rule: no one gets hurt. Never cheat it, his father had always warned.

The water was dripping from puddles overhead left by the power washer. He'd packed three concentrations of explosives behind three I-beams, with three connections. He checked the first set. Dry. He covered them with the Gap hat, then shimmied out to the next I-beam. Dry again, and he unknotted his bandanna, folded it in quarters, and laid it over the wires. Arriving at the farthest load, he looked himself up and down, but he had nothing left. It would draw too much attention to drive off the dam without a shirt—how many people *hadn't* seen his face in the paper? Too dangerous on this narrow shelf so high above the abyss to take off a boot and get a sock. So he took the photo of Naomi from his pocket, creased it down the middle, and placed it like a little roof over the wires.

On the catwalk he zipped his duffel and hung it over his shoulder, then made the final connections. First the clock. Toggles dangled from the alarm—two quick twists of wire and it was hooked up. Finally the battery—hot, then neutral, and the system was live. He'd done it.

He took a moment to admire his work: the kinepaks neatly situated at twenty-foot intervals. Three explosions, a quarter-second apart. He took a final look over the rail of the catwalk, where concrete and steel faded to infinite blackness in a shaft to hell. But the updraft from the turbines carried the wild, fresh smell of the river he was about to set free. He leaned farther over the rail, looking down, and a birdlike fluttering caught his eye—it was the picture of Naomi, pushed up on the rising air, then fluttering down, then pushed up again in the vast empty space at the heart of the dam.

As he watched the photo's flight, a drop of water splashed on his cheek, and he jerked his head to the far connection as a dim spark flickered across the wires, and if not for the turbines he would've heard an electrical buzz before the first load blew, launching him backward. He heard the railing groan as it bent, then the snap of his spine. He saw the second explosion flash silently just ahead of the smoke from the first, silent because his eardrums were in tatters. Instinct told him to brace for the third, but when he tried to grip the steel grating, his fingers and hands weren't there. Two explosions so far—one more to come, the closest one—but he wouldn't see it because his eyes were on fire and couldn't distinguish darkness from light. He tasted scorched gunpowder and cinders, and then those tastes were overpowered by a bloody surge up his throat, the taste of his stomach, his bowels. And the *smell*! Sulfur, singed hair, burnt flesh, the tissues of his spleen, heart, and lungs—and, yes, the acrid, dry, concrete dust. He'd done it. Just two explosions had busted open the dam. He smelled the river. The final charge blew, and its force lifted Clay up, lifted him on a warm, buffeting wind, then set him down peacefully, at last. Sleep.

Epilogue

She blew on the scrambled eggs until they were cool, then tipped them from the plate onto the high-chair tray. Sammy swatted at the eggs and smacked fistfuls into his mouth. Scanlon bit into a piece of toast, leaning over the kitchen sink and holding his tie carefully to his stomach. He was wearing his new suit.

Naomi had planned to set up her organ this morning—it would be good to unpack her essences in the stale-smelling nook off their bedroom—but now she thought she'd lie down with Sammy for his nap instead. There was no hurry on the organ anyway. Blaine Maxwell had promised her all the frog juice she wanted. She'd get back to work when she started sleeping better.

"I'll drop the car at the shop," Scanlon said, "and they'll drive me to the train, but can you pick me up at the station? Probably the 6:51 or the 7:19. I'll call you from the city." He pecked Sammy's forehead, then hers. She wished him luck, and while Sammy finished eating, she listened to him scraping ice off the car.

He had a meeting with a publisher today, "to see if there's a book in it." There were issues of rights—the *Oregonian* was making claims to the story and so was the *Washington Post.* Lawyers were involved. Still, Scanlon was pretty confident there *was* a book in it.

She'd had some meetings of her own in the last month. She didn't mention the frog juice, but she told them her nose was back and she might be on to something. She needed a good prototype before she said more; she'd have to start over again. The fragrance that was so compelling in Douglas, Oregon, didn't seem right in Helman, New Jersey. Too much Clay in it.

She'd betrayed Clay to rediscover her love for her husband. She'd betrayed him for Scanlon's career, and her own, to get them back east where they belonged. She'd betrayed him for her family. This was something he never would've done. Although she recognized the bitter selfishness of the sentiment, she missed him. He'd been in love with her. And that one morning she'd loved him as only a woman can, and that love had nurtured her as well, even helped to expel demons that had been gnawing at her for eighteen years. Which wasn't to suggest he didn't smell like danger. He did. But he also smelled like life—life when she'd felt dead.

She hoped he never saw the article, never knew the brunt of her betrayal. "We're better than that," Scanlon had quoted Clay as saying. She hoped he died still believing it of her.

Scanlon also wrote that Clay had developed a psychosomatic tic out of guilt and loss over his brother and Ruby Christine. Although he stopped short of referencing a "ghost baby," she knew he was really thinking about her nose.

While she wasn't sure if he was right about that—or if it mattered—she did know he understood her, believed in her, as no one else ever had. She loved him: his mind, his heart, his instincts as a father and husband, his smell. Their infidelities and rage now seemed as distant as her walks around Douglas, bending down to smell rain-misted rosemary and woolly apple mint, the Pacific breeze lifting salt air and cedar and the sap of young firs over the coastal range and down into the valley.

She picked spilled eggs out of Sammy's lap and took off his bib. She wiped his hands and face, then put the washcloth to her nose and recoiled: mildew. She parted the curtain and examined each car parked out front. She submerged the washcloth in a glass of water and poured in an ounce of bleach.

. . .

On the train into New York, Scanlon opened his leather satchel and took out the notebook in which a month ago he'd recorded everything that Naomi had told him about Clay. He started reading from the beginning, but his thoughts quickly turned to the call he'd received from the *Oregonian* editor two days after publication. "Highest bidder," he'd said. "Bizarre timing. Sometimes you get lucky." They'd just sold Scanlon's article to the *Washington Post,* who wanted him to add another thousand words on the dam, and they'd run the rest in their Sunday magazine as is. The editor spoke in a flurry, and Scanlon didn't ask him to explain the parts he wasn't grasping—*bizarre timing, tremendous explosion, more than a coda to the story*— because he knew, in the way Naomi knew things with her nose, that something very bad was linked to his own good luck.

But by the end of the conversation he understood exactly what had happened, and in tears, holding Naomi, he said, "He was just a kid." She was crying so hard she couldn't get a breath, and that night he woke to the sounds of her sobbing in her sleep.

For days they prowled the house like animals, waiting for the FBI to pound down their door. Despite the fact that no one came, no one called, they were still, always, waiting.

After talking to an editor at the *Post,* he'd phoned Sam Belknap, and an hour later got a call from the poli sci chair at Rutgers. "This is more detail than you need," the chair said, "but our new hire was banging a freshman in his office during exam week when the department secretary walked in on them. Very sordid. Budget cuts as they are these days, I don't want to lose this line, so we're doing an accelerated search. We'll want to wait for the article in the *Post* and see whatever else you're working on, but could you fly in just after the new year? How's Sam, by the way? He's a dear friend."

It wasn't until the committee lobbed him a softball to open the interview—"How did you get inside that anarchist's head?"—that he felt the depth of his dishonesty. He obviously couldn't tell them why the portrait was so revealing, so naked. He didn't lie, but neither did he divulge that the most compelling research wasn't his at all.

It was a no-brainer that he'd take the Rutgers job when the offer came two days later; they wanted him to begin immediately. He and Naomi didn't even discuss it. They sold the Douglas house in a week and found a rental with a six-month lease in New Jersey. Naomi and Sammy flew back and he made the drive alone; by the time he arrived, she'd already done most of the unpacking.

Neither one of them had yet mentioned that they'd finally gotten what they wanted.

As the train passed the meadowlands, he bit into the pear he'd taken from the bowl on the kitchen counter and almost gagged. Although it was firm and unblemished on the skin, the inside had gone mealy and brown. He spit it out into his hand and wrapped the whole mess in a napkin, then threw it away. He hadn't had a good piece of fruit since they left Oregon. Although Naomi was being a good sport, their apartment was a problem—busy street, no parks or even a peaceful place to walk Sammy in the stroller, noise from a loading dock around the corner, and nowhere to buy decent food.

After glancing up at the skyline, he pulled out his laptop and skimmed through the article as it had appeared in the *Post,* clicking on Naomi's photos as the train entered the tunnel beneath the Hudson. With a jerk that slammed his laptop against the back of the seat in front, the train slowed and then stopped. When he clicked on another photo, the train went dark and the heaters quit blowing. Peering through the glass, he could see the tunnel walls and the murky water and muck seeping in from the river bottom.

When he shifted his eyes, his heart thumped at the reflection of his computer screen—Clay's ghostly face—looming in the train's greasy window.

The morning was quiet. Just below the clouds, the sun sat like an egg yolk on the ridge of the Cascades. She rose from the hot tub, toweled off her body, slipped into her robe, and sat on her zafu, breathing. When she opened her eyes half an hour later—the rumble of an engine, the voice of a child—the world had come alive. After she coaxed Trinity awake, they had smoothies and walked down the block to Franklin Park.

A head and arms were working inside the engine of the crane. Then, emerging with a ratchet and an engine part, Jim Furdy saw her and raised a hand. Yesterday they'd removed the tarps and unloaded the old barn rafters from a borrowed flatbed. Standing on the crane's fender, Jim clipped the engine cover down.

"Mommy!" Trinity called, through a hole in the wall where a window would soon be, and Sequoia waved.

The Feds had refused to release Clay's body for a month, so the funeral was held up until last week. She'd considered taking Trinity along—when she gently broke the news, Trinity had blurted, "I know"—but in the end she'd left her at Chezzi's house. Thank God, because after the service at Church of the Sea in Yaquina, the two FBI agents detained her, grilling her about Clay, about other dams and other "targets," about Scanlon and the movement. But they finally let her go, acting like she'd been as eager to chat as they were. And when she got back to Douglas, their office in the Odd Fellows Hall had been emptied out—files, computers, phone, lamp, even a box of granola bars.

Her laptop and the new computer were FedExed back to her just yesterday, their memories wiped clean. In response to her calls, a credit-union lawyer said he was prevented by law from telling her why the Oregon Experiment bank account no longer existed.

Pete helped her drag a picnic table under a tree in case they got some showers, then she called the café and asked Journey to bring an urn of coffee down to the park first chance she got. Pete helped his father monkey with the hook and pulleys on the end of the crane's long arm, and Trinity ran to her mother across the damp grass, her lips purple from a berry scone.

At the funeral, Sequoia had recognized some young moms from town, and she'd shaken Roslyn Knudson's hand. "I'm so sorry for your loss. If there's anything I can do, anything to help—"

"Thank you, dear," she said, a far-off cast clouding her eyes.

After the casket was carried out, she sat for a time at the back of the church, unable to let go of the details of the explosion; the news reports were fixated on the fact that it cost more to clean up the splatter of his body than it did to repair the "superficial damage" to the dam. She finally left the church, and at the bottom of the steps, the two Feds were waiting.

Sequoia hugged her daughter, then they stacked scones and muffins on platters. She heard a squeak and looked up to see Paul rolling his compressor into the park in his wheelbarrow. Not far behind him came others, wearing tool belts and ratty old nail pouches, carrying hammers, pry bars, and ladders, tubes of caulk, gallons of paint. They dragged sawhorses and drop cloths. They rolled insulation and felt paper. They brought salads and salsa, bread and juice. Hank and Chezzi brought hula hoops for the kids. There was no limit to the goodwill of her neighbors.

Acknowledgments

I'm deeply grateful to Gary Fisketjon, Joe Regal, Michael Strong, Emily Milder, Jennifer Richter, Jason Brown, Kirstin Valdez Quade, Robert Nye, Tracy Daugherty, Yosh Han, Nancy Wogan, Chrissa Kioussi, Brian Bay, Mark Leid, Mark Zabriskie, Shannon Bedford, Tom Barbash, Leila Giovannoni, David Robinson, and the Oregon State University Center for the Humanities.

A NOTE ABOUT THE AUTHOR

Keith Scribner is the author of two previous novels, *Miracle Girl* and *The GoodLife*, a *New York Times* Notable Book and a Barnes & Noble Discover Great New Writers selection. He is a recipient of Stanford University's Wallace Stegner and John L'Heureux fellowships, and is currently a professor at Oregon State University in Corvallis, where he lives with his wife, the poet Jennifer Richter, and their children.

A NOTE ON THE TYPE

This book was set in Minion, a typeface produced by the Adobe Corporation specifically for the Macintosh personal computer, and released in 1990. Designed by Robert Slimbach, Minion combines the classic characteristics of old-style faces with the full complement of weights required for modern typesetting.

Composed by Creative Graphics,
Allentown, Pennsylvania

Printed and bound by Berryville Graphics,
Berryville, Virginia

Designed by Soonyoung Kwon